EXISTED PRIOR TO SERVICE

EXISTED PRIOR TO SERVICE

MARIA AUER SALMON

ONWARDPRESS.ORG
LOS ANGELES, CALIFORNIA

Published in the United States by
Onward Press, an imprint of
United States Veterans Artists Alliance, a 501-c-3 educational non-profit organization.

www.onwardpress.org
www.usvaa.org

Edited by Timothy Wurtz
Cover design and Formatting by Teddi Black

Existed Prior to Service

ISBN Paperback: 978-1-954988-16-3
ISBN Hard Cover: 978-1-954988-15-6
ISBN E book: 978-1-954988-17-0

for Lili and Zinnia
and my husband, Nick. For my dad, mom, sister and brothers.
For my family.

Dedicated to those women and men who suffer military sexual trauma and are forced to endure. Do not suffer in silence.

PROLOGUE

Camp Buehring, Kuwait

CAMP BUEHRING, KUWAIT, was the kind of US Army post that sucked the will to live right outta soldiers. Ninety kilometers south of the Iraqi border, it was the worst. The wet bulb hit 129 degrees most summer days, so exposed metal burned hands. Scorched dog tags charred chests. Worse, it wasn't dry heat. Warriors practically swam through the humidity. Whole place smelled like swamp ass.

It was hot as hell, but Camp Buehring was the main staging post for troops headed north into Operation Iraqi Freedom. Warrior transitional post, for most. Those who remained behind here were POGS—*people other than grunts.* Losers not allowed into the real fight. The support staff left behind battled broken A/C units, while the heroes drove north to save the world.

Specialist Tony hated Camp Buehring. Every day there was the worst day of his life. He wished he were infantry, instead of a lame network technician. Day after day, him and Sarge sat in the small, ground cockpit and roasted in their own juices. Their responsibility was to watch what the surveillance balloons picked up and report unusual activity outside the wire. He spent hours listening to the low hum of radio chatter, with nothing to report. Tethered high above the base, the high-flying spy kites only worked about half the time. It didn't bother the higher-ups. Attacks on Camp Buehring were practically non-existent. Hot. Dusty. But Safe. Soldiers feared getting sandblasted while smoking a cigarette, not incoming enemy fire.

Specialist Tony scanned two large monitors while Sarge ate his second lunch of the day. His many meals could make the cockpit smell like corn chips and cheese dip. Specialist Tony liked these days. It was a nice change from the days that Sarge basically oiled his 9 millimeter in Hatchet aftershave. Smelly cologne made him want to punt a hamster.

Day after day, it was always the same. This day started normal. Afternoon time, though, that changed. As Specialist Tony stroked the splotchy, blonde peach fuzz he called a mustache, something beyond unusual showed up on the grim screen.

"Holy shit, that looks like Special Forces," he practically shouted in shock.

"And I'm the fucking tooth fairy," Sarge answered, chomping with his mouth open.

Sarge didn't even look over, the idea was too strange. A compact, New York Italian E-5 buck sergeant, he looked like an olive-toned warfighter but acted exactly the opposite—uninterested in everything except chow.

"Those vehicles… that's SF…" Specialist Tony's voice trailed off, confused. Special Forces never came to Camp Buehring. Not for nothing.

Sarge grunted as he smacked his lips against his teeth, dislodging crumb sludge as he said, "Green Beret ain't never been here, both my deployments."

Specialist Tony shook his head. What he saw wasn't no missing one-hump camel or lost officers driving SUV's looking for the front gate. He knew he was right and sat up straight. Until that exact moment, life had been dull. Things were about to change; he could feel it.

Specialist Tony pointed with confidence at his grimy screen. "Look, Special Forces, Sarge, guaranteed. Come on, man. Look at my screen."

Sarge wiped his mouth as he stepped towards the monitors. Specialist Tony's joystick followed the convoy all the way to the front gate. Poles on swivels blocked the entrance near the clearing barrels, so the vehicles stopped. Two of the three guards stood under the shade of the tiny gate shack's roof. The lead vehicle cut its engine. Per regulation, soldiers dismounted at that point to clear their weapons, even though there was no reason to chamber a round in Kuwait. No matter. Those were the rules.

Nobody moved to or from the vehicles. Seemed as if the Kuwaiti sun melted the three gate guards in place. Slowly, the smallest guard with a tightly slicked back bun peeking out from under her Kevlar reluctantly moved to the souped-up Humvee's door, no doubt to ask for their papers and ID. She was sluggish and slow, as if she moved through quicksand.

They waited. Only noise in the cockpit was Sarge crumpling up his foil bag as they watched. And then.

Seconds later, the female guard took a half step back as her knees buckled. It looked as if she would fall. Either by instinct or training, she regained her footing. Fast as hell she gripped her M16A2, turned the selector level from Safe to Semi and squeezed the trigger. Shot at the Humvee, point blank. She recoiled hard. Sarge and Specialist Tony gasped in unison.

"Zoom in!" Sarge ordered as he chucked the bag into the trash.

The Specialist did as he was told. "Sarge? Is she like... *Taliban*?"

Sarge cuffed him on the back of his head, "This ain't no Afghanistan, bro."

Both were frozen for a hot second. Then Sarge squinted and pressed his face to the screen for a better look. Kuwaiti sun burned bright like a nuclear blast. He put on his high-speed Eyepro and said with confidence, "Shit… it's that cunt... the one that charges ten bucks a blow job. She shot at *SF*… Jesus…what lame trash."

Specialist Tony glistened with sweat, "Why she shoot 'em?"

"Don't matter why, Jackass," Sarge shouted at him, the screen steamed by his breath, "She's a sack of shit. Shooting at an armored vehicle, whatta dumbass."

Two male guards left the shade and tackled her from behind. Slammed her to the ground, her Kevlar bouncing hard off the ground. As they did, a dozen men, each with the body type of Arnold Schwarzenegger and the beard of Grizzly Adams, emptied their vehicles, and charged her. The female shooter thrashed harder the closer they came. The men were Special Forces operatives, all wearing different versions of uniforms under ballistic vests, except for their boots. The men wore identical performance-enhanced, high-top, steel-toed tactical combat boots.

Two operators reached the shooter and flipped her onto her stomach. Full of fight, she kicked and thrashed. The guards yanked her arms behind her back and hog-tied her up tight with 550 cords, while an SF kneeled on her face and held it down in the powdery silt of the desert. A third SF operative strode over, reeled his leg back like he was ready to kick a football and smashed her crotch. The others cheered, sweaty arms raised as if to announce a goal. The kicker grinned as the girl's rigid body went flat.

Specialist Tony leaned back from his monitor, his eyes big and wet.

Sarge bounced between monitors and laughed. "Damn, he kicked her in the muff *hard*."

Specialist Tony shuddered. Wiped sweat from his brow. That female gate guard shot at the armored door of a Special Forces vehicle, but without good aim. It was basically suicide.

Sarge nudged him. "Good, bro?"

Specialist Tony nodded, but that was a lie. He felt like crap. The worst thing about Camp Buehring *should* be the weather. Gunshots were as rare as paved roads. More locked and loaded people strolled around the mall near his house in Texas than this miserable post.

"Immagonna call the MP's," Sarge said, hustling towards the DSN line. "Print them images. I'll give 'em to the MPs. Write a statement. That bitch's last good day was yesterday."

Disturbed, Specialist Tony zoomed the monitor out until he could only see their silhouettes. It's a crime, he thought, that he'd never know why she took the shot. Or why SF continued to kick her, even when they had her tied up. Specialist Tony pressed print and looked away. Some things weren't worth knowing. Some things were better left ignored.

PART 1

Prior

CHAPTER 1

Years Before

"AMANDA. GUESS WHAT?" my sister yelled as she ran into the kitchen. Breathless and jumping, she held the Sunday edition of the *Post Circular News* high over her shiny blonde hair like a trophy. Her pale face was flushed and her smile was wide, almost bursting with excitement at whatever was in the paper. I leaned back, taking her in. She was too beautiful to wear the manure splattered faded t-shirt and ripped jeans she had on.

Half-asleep, I set down my coffee mug and reached for the paper.

"Not so fast!" She hit the paper over my head and pulled back, out of my reach, "I said to *guess* what."

"God, stop, Jo," I said. It was more like a groan. "Just tell me."

She laughed. "That's no fun."

It was 5:30 a.m. I uncurled myself from my kitchen stool, annoyed. I was not a morning girl. As I did a slow, deliberate spin away from the counter, I heard the door to our old farmhouse slam shut. Connor's barn boots pounded on the bottom of the mudroom stairs as he grunted and pulled them off. Both my brother and my sister had something on me, besides being irritating morning people.

He skidded over the linoleum floor in socks. "Diddashowher, Jo?"

"Not yet." Paper held high, Jo's blue eyes sparkled.

"Show me what? Just tell me, goddammit."

"Wouldn't you like to know." Jo clutched the paper to her chest, eyes narrowed with a smile. She always acted as if she knew something I didn't.

"We told you Sarah Sucher was garbage, now we got proof," Connor said with a hint of sarcasm. He still wore his rubber barn gloves and stood with hands on his husky hips.

Sarah. I'd forgotten about her. I flinched. Connor snatched the paper from Jo and pretended to read it. Middle child, he's short but full of muscle and strength. She let him have it without a fight. *What was this?* No argument. Not even a small protest. I had to know.

"What about Sarah?" I jumped up, tightened the belt to my robe and lunged for the paper. Connor hopped back and like a dumbass, I fell forward, howling all the way down to the hard floor. He crouched next to me, half laughing, half concerned.

"You okay?"

I grabbed him by the elbow and wrestled the paper away.

He gave way, then held out a hand to yank me up. I rolled onto my side, away from him.

"You trying to kill me?" Touching rubber was my personal kryptonite.

"Sorry. I Forgot." He slid the gloves off and put them on the far end of the table. I scrambled to my feet and moved away from him. He could be a big dope, an airhead.

I teased him, "You forgot your favorite sister is allergic to rubber?"

"Second favorite." Jo said.

I walked back to my stool. Both followed, nipping at my heels. Jo's been doing that since she could walk; I couldn't even pee without her. Connor, not so much. Something about Sarah was going to be good.

"Page seven!" they said in unison, as if in Kindergarten again. I stared at both of them, then couldn't wait another second. I yanked the paper open.

"Just let me read," I said. They leaned on the table, eager for me to figure it out.

Sarah Sucher. A small, grainy mugshot of her stared out from the page. Her dyed blonde hair and bold, fiercely lined lips were the same as always, but her eyes were shrunk into slits.

Jo pointed at the photo, "She always looked like a starved barn cat."

Sarah had lost weight since I'd seen her, and not in a good way. Her face was bony and harsh. Her hair was stringy. She looked like what I imagined a criminal to look like. My skin prickled. I'd look like her, too, if I were with her in a Milwaukee prison, and I could've been.

❧

IT'S BEEN MONTHS since I saw her. We both graduated just over a year ago and we'd hung out at the Pit that first summer. I never went to the Pit while in high school—people said that it was the stoner's turf. I was in three high school sports plus band and choir. I had barn chores every night. Plus, I was President of my 4-H club, a Catholic church server, a good girl with no time to do nothing. Not only that, Mom threatened to lock me in the basement if I ever got caught at a party and I wouldn't put it past her.

Only when I couldn't figure a way out of New Manchester, like the lucky jocks with scholarships, brainiacs, and rich kids, I did what Dad always said, *if you can't beat 'em, join 'em*. Along with the other graduates and drop-outs who never left town, I met up with Sarah at the Pit, rode in the back of beat-up pickups, and shone deer as we drove through bumpy hay fields. Me and Sarah drank the warmish Old Milwaukee beer from the can like everyone else. I left the Pabst in the cooler; I had some standards.

We called it the Pit, even though there's no pit of nothing, really. It's a field near an old quarry littered with dip spit-filled Gatorade bottles. Every weekend we met up late at night, wearing worn-out jackets and work boots, and piled wooden pallets in the middle for a bonfire. There was hooking up, talking, and stories about those who left, one way or another.

I hadn't been to the Pit since Sarah left, so I was blindsided by the news about her.

Article said Sarah's junkie boyfriend broke into a fancy lake house and stole a professor's laptops and widescreen TVs. Trashed the place and set it on fire. Sarah didn't go in but drove the getaway car. Cops caught them red-handed trying to pawn it. Girl's responsible, even if she just drove, prosecutor said. Sarah Sucher could be locked up for years if she gets the maximum sentence. That's beyond shitty.

I looked up from the paper. Connor and Jo had gone already, back to the barn. It was 6 a.m. and I was late getting out there. Mom would yell. Well, tough. I had to think.

Sarah was obviously in a much worse place than me, but honestly, I was no better than Sarah. I lived at home. I worked the farm. Put up a damn front every day, acted like having no plans for myself was hunky-dory when really, deep-down, I felt lost. Felt like my life was passing me by, as if counting crop seasons is a way for a teenager to think of time. It's not.

I read the article over and over until I couldn't take it anymore.

I crumpled up the paper in my fist and looked out the kitchen window above the sink. I had a clear view of green pastures and blue sky. Dad owned 300 acres, 220 cattle, a hundred milking cows, twenty pigs, a dozen barn cats, five goats, four sheep, and one dog. I was the oldest of three kids, his three farmhands, along with our hired man, Elias. I spent my day fixing fences, feeding animals, scooping shit, washing the pipeline, and overall, general upkeep. No real kind of life at all. I wasn't behind bars, but I wasn't free.

Sarah had almost talked me into going with her. It was my last memory of her.

"You can do anything in Milwaukee, you can be anyone," she said as she held my hair back when I hurled up crystal-clear Zima. She said it like Mi-waukee. Like we all did.

"Who am I gonna be?" I asked her after wiping off my mouth with Dad's kerchief. She gave me a blank look, as if I was pulling her chain. I wasn't. I really wanted to know.

"Come with me and see for yourself." She looked dead serious.

"Yeah right," I said in a jokey voice, in case she wasn't serious at all. I had never been to Milwaukee. She must've felt snubbed by my response 'cause her dreamy smile vanished.

"Fine. Stay here where people crap their pants over Drive Your Tractor to School Day."

I should've taken her serious. Drive Your Tractor to School Day *was* the most exciting day in New Manchester, and my least favorite one of the year.

I swiveled the stool, jumped down, and I flipped on the lights. Back at the long kitchen island, I smoothed the paper out. I opened the junk drawer and grabbed the scissors. I sat back down and opened it up again, ready to cut out the story. I thought of keeping it.

I opened it up to the wrong section. This was the World News Section—*Your trusted source for breaking news*, it promised. A giant, blocky headline announced, "U.N. asserts authority in Kosovo" above a black and white photo of a tank. Off to the side, a picture of a U.S. soldier taking a weapon from a scuzzy-looking dirtball demanded my attention.

The American soldier wasn't looking at his prisoner as he worked. He stared directly out of the page and into my eyes. That soldier could've been my cousin or my brother. Had the same tough look of a kid that had a million other worse days than pulling a weapon from a civilian gunslinger.

His eyes spoke louder than Sarah's did. Even in black and white, I heard them loud and clear saying—*You're not the only person in this country who needed a way out.*

That soldier could be *me.*

I wasn't rural trash. I wasn't a no-been or never was. I had to a chance to become someone else, far away from here.

I was gonna be all that I can be. In the Army.

CHAPTER 2

Lost and Found

THAT DAY IN the kitchen wasn't the first time I considered joining the service. Midway through my junior year, I told my English teacher, Mr. Peet, that I wanted to be a soldier after we read *Catch-22* in class. Mr. Peet responded, "The book should have the opposite effect."

I stood near his desk, embarrassed. He sighed, stood up, and clapped his hand on my shoulder, "Amanda, don't waste your potential." He sounded mad. I hated it when teachers got mad. I promised I wouldn't.

Except that I had. College talk increased throughout senior year, everyone kept asking what school I was going to, but I didn't know. Once I realized I had to fork out tons of cash to send out ACT scores and to send in applications, with no guarantee I'd even get aid to afford it, I got discouraged and gave up. I'd been stuck since.

But a year was enough. That picture of the soldier unstuck me and I was going to get gone from this place. That next morning after chores, I drove forty-five minutes to the Army recruiter and signed up. I spent a day at the Military Entrance Processing station and finally had orders for basic training at Fort Jackson. Nobody could stop me.

I had liked being at MEPS. If I had just tested a little lower on the ASVAB, I could've been an officer, the recruiter told me with a laugh. I liked his laugh—it was loose and happy. I felt giddy in Milwaukee, in the same town that Sarah was in jail. After my medical and mental screenings, a female sergeant called me over. Large coffee in hand, she told me that my choices for my MOS were Signal, Intelligence, or Chemical; but in the end I got Supply based on the needs of the Army. She asked if I was cool with maintaining weapons and ammo. I knew how to use grandpa's 12-gauge pump action shot gun, so I figured I could. *No sweat,* I said.

Only problem was that I didn't want to tell my family. Half of me wanted to crawl out the window and make a run for it. I knew there'd be a shit-storm about my decision. What I didn't know was how strong.

Every night we ate dinner at five o'clock sharp. At five thirty exactly, Dad went into the barn, put feed down, let the cows in and turned on the milk pump. Three hours, and a lot of work later, we finished chores. I decided to tell them at dinner. I knew my family wouldn't kill me, since then they'd have to do my share of the work if I were deceased. I waited until only three days before my flight out to spill the beans.

Like the farmhouse, the dining room was built in 1896 by my Irish great-grandpa and hadn't changed much. In the corner of that room was a thick-glassed hutch filled with the good dishes we never used and, on the wall next to it, a poster-sized framed copy of Jesus' Last Supper. The rest of the walls held up crucifixes and a family picture taken in church when I was seven years old. The dinner table was a long wooden solid piece, hand-carved by the Amish.

On my right sat my sister, Jo. She turned sixteen over the summer. Everyone loved nice-little-sweet Jo. When she wasn't feeding orphaned baby kittens, she was a Marie May cosmetics model for our Aunt Ellie. She wore iridescent lip gloss when bottle feeding calves.

To my left was my brother, Connor, the seventeen-year-old cowboy jock, headed into his Senior Year. He had tousled, curly hair and the family deep dimples like Jo. Wore his letterman jacket year-round. Very high school jock, but smart. Head of the school's investing club. His one weakness was dumb chicks. He dated airheads who stuck to him like cling wrap.

My parents sat across from us, chewing in silence. Dad sat directly in front of me. He spent all summer on a tractor and his farmer's tan was so deep that his lower arms were as leathery as mom's handbag. His blaringly white forehead was only visible when he took his hat off at mealtimes for manners. At forty-three, he was still a good-looking guy. He had striking, deep-blue eyes that were flecked with coppery-gold nuggets and thick black eyelashes. I was damn lucky to inherit them, everyone told me that. He could've probably had any girl when he was my age, but he chose Mom.

Mom was third generation German. She was originally from Missouri where there's this big community of Deutschers. She met dad at a Future Farmers of America Nationals Meeting when they were both juniors. Even though she grew up on a crop farm, she *just* barely tolerated being a dairy farmer's wife. Petite and thin, she had corn-colored thick curls that turned blonder as the summer went on. Blonde didn't mean weak or dumb. Mom could lift a calf clear over her head; I'd seen her do it more than once.

Dinner was getting cold on my plate. Mom noticed. Her face turned into a mixture of annoyance and irritation. Nerves stopped me from eating. I had to tell them—now.

"For cripes sake! Now you don't like hot dish," mom said the question, not asked.

I shrugged. "I like it."

"Then eat it," she ordered, her lips forming a frown.

I swallowed then said, "I joined the Army." Blurted it out.

Dad stopped shoveling dinner. Ground beef sat trapped on his spoon, mere inches from his face. Mom almost choked on her water, pounded her chest, shook her head and coughed.

"No way in hell," Mom said, her cat-like green eyes focused on me, "No way they'd take you with all your allergies."

I swallowed down the lump in my throat. "Yes, way."

She refocused her eyes on her plate and pushed her food. "You'll have to get out of it otherwise you'll be dead in a minute."

I nervously snorted. "I can't get out of it, mom."

She mixed her mashed potatoes into the meat. "You didn't sign anything did you?"

I nodded as I chewed a corner of my lip. "I signed all the paperwork. Don't care that I'm allergic to rubber. So what."

She stabbed at her plate. Growled. "So *what*? I'll tell you *so what*. I spent years saving you. How many times I take you to the hospital, huh? Now you're trying to get yourself killed? That's the *so what*. You go back there and *un*-sign it, missy."

Mom had a short fuse. Being stubborn made it worse, for both of us.

"Jeez, Mom, I can't. Recruiter said—" I was stopped by her look.

Mom's pretty face twisted into an ugly scowl. Her eyes narrowed into the same slits as Sarah Sucher's. Bad sign.

She slammed her fists onto each side of her plate and snapped. "You're not going!"

My heart palpitated and my throat went dry.

I said louder than I should have, "Yes. I. Am."

Tension mounted quick. Mom's face turned as red as a cherry, and she stared at me like I sprouted horns and a tail. She picked up her plate, piled high with uneaten hot dish, and whipped it across the room at the wall behind me. I turned to watch as bits of mashed potato stuck to the wallpaper. Ground beef and corn slid to the floor. The mess hit millimeters from the worshipped Last Supper picture. I turned to face her, my heart in my throat. Unbelievable, even for Mom. Dad's eyes darted between us, his mouth hung open, catching flies. Everyone waited.

I knew better, but I spoke. "I report to Fort Jackson for Basic Training."

Dad took a deep breath and set his spoon down, ready to talk it out. She clutched his arm; cast him a look, then fixed her eyes directly on me.

"Get me the number of the recruiter." Mom said.

I held my voice steady. "I leave in three days. I got the flight ticket and everything."

"Three days?" Her hot temper boiled her words to a high pitch, "Three *days*?"

"I turn twenty in two months. I think it's now or never."

"*Fergodsake*," her lips tightened, "You don't know nothing about life. You don't always get to do what you want to do—that's how it goes…"

Resentment flooded me. I had to cut her off before I got a lecture on her favorite topic—what she gave up for us, or her second favorite topic, honoring thy father and thy mother. Mom thought she always knew best. I was so sick of it. Something broke inside. I yelled back at her for the first time in my life.

I shouted. "I'm going whether or not *you* like it."

She snarled. "Amanda Anna Ashe. You always thought you were better than me."

I kept her gaze. "It's not hard."

Dad gulped disapprovingly and shifted in his seat. Jo skidded her chair back over the linoleum, away from the table. Connor leaned back in his chair at a 45-degree angle. Something was going to happen, but nobody saw it coming.

Mom stood and slapped me hard across the face. My head flapped to the side. I recovered and looked at her, stunned. She ignored me.

I was too shocked to speak or move. I saw her chair fall to the floor and heard her stomp down the stairs. She slammed the mudroom door on her way out.

My eyes burned with tears. Nobody had ever hit me on the face before. I wanted to flee, but I was stuck in place. What just occurred? It happened in less than six seconds, but everything changed.

Jo broke the silence, "I'll write to you."

I somehow managed to mumble a thanks. My face burned, and I felt a welt forming on my cheek. Dad saw it and told Connor to bring me a bag of frozen peas.

"I don't think I'm better than anyone," I said to all of them, still astonished.

Dad waved me off with his hand, and tried to explain away Mom's behavior, like he had done millions of times. "Midwest had low draft numbers in Vietnam. Your mother knows some people who never made it back. She doesn't want you to get hurt."

I almost laughed at that crock of shit explanation. Mom hit me across the face because she didn't want me to get hurt. Bullshit. She wanted to control me. Well, she couldn't stop me from living my own life. I sucked up the pool of snot pooling inside my nose and swallowed.

Connor tried to lighten the mood as he raided to freezer, "If you want to find a husband so bad, I know that Travis is into you."

"Shut up, Connor," Jo said as we made eye contact.

I took the frozen peas from my brother and said, "There's no war right now. I'm not going to get hurt."

I felt my voice waver, so I coughed hard and smashed the frozen peas against my cheek. Dad pushed his plate back so he could clasp his hands together on the table.

"Soldiers and farmers got a lot in common. We both work hard, day in and day out. Only reason I didn't go was because of the farm. With grandpa dead, and me being the oldest, well, couldn't do it. Never even got drafted. I was the man of the house at sixteen."

We all knew why dad didn't go to Vietnam, while Uncle Jack, his younger brother, the one we never met, did. Dad thought the farm had saved him from certain death. For me, life was the opposite. Living here felt like I was drowning in the manure pit.

I closed my eyes and exhaled. When I opened them again, I saw all eyes on me. I wanted to reassure them, so I repeated what I heard the day before.

"The recruiter said I'll miss my chance at Kosovo or Bosnia and be stuck on a base for my entire enlistment."

"How long is the enlistment?" my sister asked in her soft voice.

"Four years."

"I'll be twenty. I hope you come back sooner than that," Jo said with a sigh then reached over and touched my arm. I put my hand over hers, her touch calmed me down.

Connor had other concerns. "Who's doing her chores," he asked dad, alarm spread all over his angular face. I was the real worker of us three, the others were my support staff.

Dad shrugged, "I'll give Elias more hours."

Connor frowned as he continued to talk, "Mom said you can't trust beaners—"

"Four years," Dad repeated, talking over him. "Get yourself that GI Bill. Murray's kid came back from the Navy and went to college on Uncle Sam's dime, all paid for."

Four years was my plan. Be a supply clerk, stay out of trouble, save every paycheck, then check out with GI Bill in hand and live my life somewhere nearby. Shawano or Clintonville. Close. That's what I thought I'd do. That was the plan.

Until Mom slapped me across the face.

❧

BASIC TRAINING WAS easy. I was used to getting up in the dark, and hard physical labor was second nature. Mom prepared me to deal with the Drill Sergeants and Dad taught me every farmer fix he knew, so making do when we went to the field was simple. Basic Training Graduation came and went, but I knew my family wouldn't come with it being football and crop season. There's lots of moving parts that go along with harvest, and everyone has to pitch in.

I graduated from Advanced Individual Training eight weeks later as the top 92Y in my class. We learned procedures for stock control and accounting measures, but I mostly learned how to sleep with my eyes open. Never been so bored in my life. Some guys weren't so happy when I aced the exams, being one of the few females in the class, but they couldn't argue with percentages. This time, it was winter, so Dad and Jo drove all the way down to graduation.

Dad whistled loud and Jo stood when my name was called. I lost all military bearing and smiled as I stood at attention. I was proud of myself and glad they could see me in uniform.

"Is Mom still mad at me?" I asked Dad after the ceremony.

"She'll come around," he said, but appeared as if he doubted his own words.

I thought she'd probably be happy if I got KIA, so she could be right. She'd rather be right than anything else. I kept those dark thoughts to myself; that night was fun, and I wouldn't let mom ruin it from hundreds of miles away. I wanted to celebrate.

"Let's go to dinner," I said and took them to Olive Oil Place. Told Jo to order the meatballs, her favorite, and Dad had a steak. I paid for it, and knew they'd tell Mom.

❧

GRADUATING AT THE top of my AIT class didn't help me much. I was still assigned to one of the worst army posts in America. Literally in the middle of Bumfuck Nowhere, America. The base was large, almost the size of my hometown when you included the training grounds. It had its own gym, housing area, barracks, post office, PX, Shopette, Burger Joint, bowling alley, medical and dental clinics, commissary, and a much-visited Class Six—what they call the military liquor store. Needed to, 'cause base was near nothing. Army bought swamp land to build the fort. The mosquito was the state bird.

Best part of Fort Shithole was the other soldiers. I met my best friend—Shelly Weisengard—at in-processing. She's the same age as me, but taller and with red hair and light freckles. According to her, she failed out of Michigan State because she didn't like to study. I felt jealous at first, then she started to tell me dirty jokes, which made me laugh so hard I snorted. Found out later that her family is totally loaded—living in a suburb outside of Detroit called Grosse Point with three garages packed full of boats and cars. Their neighbors were related to Henry Ford. I knew she had money because of her perfectly straight, white teeth. And her big, perfectly round melon boobs that feel like softballs under her skin when I hugged her. From my calculations, her body updates cost more than a plow.

Our backgrounds were different, but the uniform and rank were the same. I was grateful to find such a friend, especially during that first week when everything was new. I also got to give her credit for what came next.

Me and her didn't miss meals. We both thought that Army grub was pretty good. Military chow halls have huge salad bars, selection of drinks, tons of main meals options and lots of desserts; the fried chicken days were my favorite. At 11:30 sharp every day, we headed to the dining facility—DFAC—for chow. The entire base seemed to arrive at the same time for Taco Day. It was a cold and rainy day in January. We hadn't been issued our winter BDU's yet and were freezing to death. Swampland got cold. Weisengard's hands turned blue, so she stuck them inside her pockets. Didn't know better since no one told us at Basic we couldn't' do that. Basic was 100% atom-vibrating heat, so pockets were used only for storage.

A Staff Sergeant who was half turned in front of us glanced our way and stepped out of line. He walked directly towards us. We knew something was wrong. Nobody leaves their place in a chow line.

"New here, soldiers?" He had a hint of an accent, just like Elias.

We snapped our hands behind our backs to Parade Rest, ready for a stern talking-to.

"Yes, sergeant," we said together.

"From AIT?"

We both nodded. "Yes, sergeant."

"Privates First Class already? Impressive."

We said nothing; unsure if this was a question or not since our rank was on our collars.

I watched Weisengard's pale cheeks burn bright. I was intrigued by the shade of red, but my eyes were drawn to the Staff Sergeant. He was a muscular '80's heartthrob Benjamin Bratt look-alike with a trimmed black mustache. He could cite me regulations any day.

"Met your new chain of command yet?" he said.

Butterflies spun in my stomach as he spoke. NYPD Detective Rey Curtis seemed super nice in real life, and better looking. On his crisp, ironed uniform, his nametape said "Martinez."

Weisengard didn't answer, so I jumped in, "Not yet, sergeant. Still in-processing."

He smiled a little at my response. I'd given the correct answer, or so I thought.

The sergeant said, "Okay, so listen up. While in uniform, personnel will not place their hands in their pockets, except momentarily to place or retrieve objects," he glanced between us then continued, "Army Regulation 670-1. You'll have a lot of regs to learn. Any questions?"

Weisengard shook her head, but I was puzzled. What a dumb rule. My lips formed the word *why* but I felt her boot hit the side of mine, so I kept my trap shut.

I was curious about this reg, and so many other regs, which was worse than being a troublemaker. In the Army, curious soldiers step on landmines. He said something else that I barely heard, then left us and joined his buddies. I shook my arms down to my side and saw him give me a long look when he got back in line. I winked, he smiled.

"Rules should make sense," I told Weisengard who looked a bit green. "No pockets even when it's cold out? What next? No trash in the trashcans?"

❧

MY ORDERS TO Fort Shithole assigned me to a unit that didn't exist no more, so those first few days I ran back and forth between Finance, S1, and Personnel units until it was straightened out. I was the last to finish in-processing the second week at 17:45 on a Friday, which was too late to make it to chow before the DFAC closed at 18:00. I left the reception hall and began the mile walk towards the barracks. I wondered how to get food with no car and no more bus shuttle for the day. I was tired and hungry. My legs got heavier with each step. The only things in my room were a new roommate named Marge, a self-proclaimed video-game addict, and a double pack of mint gum. Weisengard was with her dad, who drove over from Houston after a big business meeting.

I was walking slow and feeling sorry for myself as I heard a shout, "Hey, PFC. Private First Class."

I turned towards the familiar voice and saw hot-guy Sergeant Make-the-Correction Rey Curtis named Martinez driving a red Mustang. Still in uniform. Looked pleased to see me.

"You need a ride to the barracks?" he said, his right arm slung over the wheel.

I shook my head, never one to take favors. "No, sergeant, it's not far."

He made a face. "That's over a mile, and it's freezing."

I smiled and held up my freezing hands, "Can't use my pockets, either."

He laughed out loud then smoothed down his little mustache. "No, you sure can't."

I felt awkward as I shifted and crossed my arms. I was cold and hungry, which was my real emergency. I didn't do well without food.

"Sergeant, is the Commissary close enough to walk to?"

He shook his head. "That's farther. Close to three miles across base. You hungry?"

"Starving."

He seemed to consider the situation. He looked at me, my rank and frowned.

"Listen, I'm all about taking care of soldiers. But I'm not…unfortunately… not in your chain of command, so it's…and you're a female…" He searched for words.

I'd be lying if I didn't say it hurt that he seemed to care more about what others said about him, than about me. Just like mom, I double-clutched and jumped to pissed off. By-passed annoyed, irritated, and several other stops on the mad train. And I was still hungry and cold.

I shook my head. Frowned and said, "Never mind. Just forget it."

My face blushed with embarrassment at my words. *Way to go, Amanda, screw things up before they start,* I remember thinking. *I'm the anti-poster child of easy, breezy, beautiful.*

"I'm sorry," I heard myself say before he could respond. "Sorry, sergeant. I'm just hungry."

He regarded me silently for a minute. "You said you were starving. Low blood sugar. I guess it's my duty to get you some chow. Don't need new soldiers fainting from starvation."

He was letting me off the hook, but I felt bad for being rude, and for showing my temper. In fact, *I wanted a ride from him.* We both knew it. I uncrossed my arms and gave a lame smile.

He reached over, unlocked the passenger door and pushed it open. "Go ahead and get in."

I walked to the door and slid into the seat. I grinned at him as I snapped my seatbelt.

"You know; the Army'll probably give you a medal. It'll be all over the Stars and Stripes. Local hero saves new soldier from certain death." I air quote the mock headline.

"MSM then, at least," he grinned, "Hopefully not a purple heart."

I smiled wider. Put up my palms and said innocently, "I'm harmless."

"Ashe," he said as he put the car in gear, "You are definitely not harmless."

❧

LATER, I'D UNDERSTAND that it was a serious reputational risk to drive me around, for me more than him. Dropping me off at the barracks was one thing, riding around base was another. That night, I bought a takeout burger and fries from the bowling alley and he drove me to my room, joking around the whole time.

It was easy to laugh with him. For weeks, all we did was make jokes. His full name was Staff Sergeant Manuel Martin del Campo Martinez, but everyone called him Manolo. He'd broken up with some civilian girlfriend months ago. We kind of conveniently ran into each other all over base, which is not easy using a bus schedule. I guessed he noticed because he gave me his number in case of emergencies, but when I called to ask a question I already knew the answer, we ended up talking for hours about everything besides the Army.

I was the one who asked him out, as a thank you for the rides he gave me and Weisengard to the commissary, the laundromat, and the PX when I lost my running belt. To my relief, whenever I needed a lift, he said yes immediately. On a Saturday night, he met me at the deserted base library and drove as I gave him the directions. I'd found out about an Italian place miles and miles from base, so nobody could see us and give him crap. I acted like it wasn't a date, and went so far as to put money in an envelope for gas, which he didn't accept. Dinner was nice. We laughed and talked like we knew each other our whole lives. When the check came, he grabbed it. I was not surprised, but still protested.

"Look," he said as he squeezed my hand, "I'm old-fashioned. Please."

Back in the car, I leaned over and pecked him on the cheek.

"Thanks for dinner," I whispered into his ear.

"*Con gusto*," he said then faced me.

I could feel my heart beating as he pulled me closer and placed his lips on mine. My whole body felt this kiss—top to bottom. He ran his fingers through my hair as he slid his tongue to meet mine. His kiss grew deeper and more intense.

My body trembled. My head was dizzy with excitement. I spread one hand out on his well-defined chest and the other into his hair. He kept his hands near my face, completely PG. He didn't try for my bra or up my skirt. We kissed until his mustache rubbed my upper lip raw.

I leaned back, out of breath. I had never been kissed like that. Never. He saw my lips and gently ran his thumb over them. "You need some recovery time."

He kissed my hand and started the car.

We both held our breath as we reentered base through the rear gate. Luckily, the guards were so haphazard that they just waved us on. When we pulled into the barracks' parking lot, he reached for my hand and stroked my fingers. I didn't want time to continue. I didn't want to leave. I wanted to stay in his Mustang forever.

Finally, he spoke, "Amanda, you're a PFC."

My heart sank into my stomach. "I know," I said, not ready for disappointment.

Us dating wasn't against the rules, but people got massive hang-ups about sergeants going out with soldiers below the E-5 rank, with good reason. Sometimes creepy older guys pressured the younger, new females. Worse, they gave them undeserved reputations. But I was twenty years old, not seventeen. If guys accused me of sleeping around to get over, I'd ignore it. Still. Females can't be too careful; I was starting to realize.

He squeezed my knee and kissed my cheek. "We'll need to be very careful."

I breathed a huge sigh of relief. Keeping my mouth shut was easy, staying away from him would be much more difficult.

We kept our secret for months. I trusted Weisengard. Marge turned out to be a solid roommate and we got along super-well. Me, her and Weisengard took turns picking out movies from the base rental place every Thursday night and shared take-out most weekends. Weisengard spent 80% of her free time in our room since her roommate kept her pee in 24-ounce pop bottles under her bed. The smell could've killed you.

Me and Manolo spent a few nights a week together, but we still had our own sets of friends and separate lives. My problem was that most dudes in the barracks thought I was looking for dick, especially *theirs.* I had trouble with an Infantry private who kept cornering me. After I told him no a few times, he spread the rumor that I was a lesbian. I wanted to give him a swift kick to the bugle, but I should've thanked him. Kept most guys away.

I fell hard for Manolo. It was easy to. He was funny, gorgeous, and smart.

I wasn't the only one who was in love with him.

Sergeant Yarely Gonzalez had a thing for Manolo. Manipulative-as-hell-passive-aggressive-crazy Gonzalez. Dressed like a slutty Grim Reaper

Gonzalez. Only twenty-six, she had four ex-husbands and two civilian arrests. I was scared of her. We all were.

Eventually, someone saw us making out in his car. I never knew who let the cat out of the bag, but I found that out the hard way when it happened. Late one Saturday night, me and Marge were together in our tiny barrack's living room, hanging out. We lived on the third floor, far away from the noise. Nobody usually bothered us at night, so when I heard a sweet, soft knock I should've been suspicious. *Should've.*

From outside we heard, "Hey ladies, anybody in there?"

I wasn't sure who it was. Marge sat closest to the door on her beanbag chair, playing video games. She heard the voice and blasted the volume. I thought she was being unsocial, so I walked past her to open the door. She put her arm up to stop me.

"Don't," she said.

"You know who it is?" I asked. The voice was both unfamiliar and familiar.

"Don't," she repeated.

"Why? You have to tell me why." Marge didn't like people, so this was a valid question on my part. When off-duty, she avoided humans. Her motto: People Suck.

She shook her head, unwilling to explain. Instead, she picked up her Big Gulp from the floor, found the straw with her tongue, and sucked hard. We heard the knock again.

I opened the door, thinking it could be the duty officer. Mistake *numero uno.*

Gonzalez pushed right past me into the barracks room. Her breath reeked of cigarettes and cheap, bottom-shelf whiskey. Marge jumped up and away from us, Big Gulp in hand.

"You leave Martinez the fuck alone," Gonzalez said. Her words were slurred. She socked me hard on the shoulder, and grazed my face as she pitched forward.

I got nervous. She was at least five inches taller than me and twenty pounds heavier. I backed up further into the room, my hands up, wanting peace.

I tried an overly friendly voice, "What's going on, sergeant?"

She regained her footing and got into my face. Her breath stank.

She grabbed my shoulders, shook me and snarled, "Fuckin' White Trash Barracks Rat. Leave the Latinos alone. You ain't got enough ass for them."

Her eyes were wild, completely unfocused. I was a dead woman. It was me or her. I pushed her as hard as I could in the chest. She stumbled back and fell on her ass in the doorway, but not far enough into the hallway to close the door. Mistake *numero dos*.

I didn't know what to do. I looked behind me for *something*, but I wasn't sure what. Marge stood by. She was tense. Clutched her Big Gulp with both hands. She sucked on the straw and made an irritating gurgling noise. Empty.

I was distracted by the noise and didn't see Gonzalez regain her footing. She pounced, grabbed my hair and pulled with nuclear force.

"Stop." I said. Hell, I screamed it.

I tried to push her out of the room, but she was a million times stronger than me. I continued to yell for *anyone* who could help. Her left fist hit me hard, right between my eyes and I went down in pain. She stomped me, then pinned me like a Professional WWE wrestler.

"Help me." I screamed to Marge as I wriggled on the floor, avoiding fists and shoes.

"You stay out of this." Gonzalez yelled as she pulled my hair.

"Call the cops," I pleaded. Marge didn't move a muscle.

Gonzales yelled, "Shut your trap, cunt," and slapped my mouth.

I bucked and yelled loud enough for a person on top of a silo to hear. "Marge—call now or I'm breaking your Xbox!"

By this time, soldiers in other barracks rooms heard the commotion and crammed themselves in the doorway for a peek. Clowns wanted a catfight and loudly chanted *fight, fight, fight*. I was in shock and didn't know what the hell was happening. Lucky for me, a broad-shouldered male soldier wrestled his way in and tried to hold Gonzalez back, but in less than twenty seconds, she slipped away like a greased pig. During the pause, I jumped up from on the hard floor and backed up as far from her as possible, my head pounding.

"Gonzalez, stop," I pleaded but it was like she didn't even hear me.

Marge snapped out of her frozen coma at some point because the Military Police came. I never heard their arrival over her taunts and threats of what she was gonna do to me if I didn't stop seeing Manolo. I didn't hear or see the MPs, unfortunately. As soon as they busted in, Gonzalez looked over and I got in one decent swing. That's all the cops saw.

As my fist connected to her jaw, the duty officer ordered, "Soldier, stop."

I lurched and held on to the wall as I yelled, "She started this."

"Not a chance," Gonzalez said as she pointed at me, "Self-defense from that whore."

"No way." I was too weak to be heard over the commotion.

The shorter, rounder of the two MP's whispered something to the other. The Duty Officer whipped out his pencil and took some notes. The taller, skinnier Military Police soldier ordered my roommate to take me for a walk outside so Gonzalez could be interviewed.

Marge walked me outside in the cold air and offered to let me use her phone.

"I wouldn't break your stuff," I told her as I bent over to get my breath, "I just said that."

"I know," she said then added a minute later, "I told you not to open the door."

I rubbed my jaw. "You were right."

"Yeah," she said. "People suck."

Gonzalez sucked. I couldn't argue with that.

I called Manolo to tell him what happened, but he was already on his way. Someone had alerted him when they heard his name mentioned. He told me to pack *pronto*. He said he'd be there in fifteen minutes. Marge went inside and threw my gear in the duffle I stored under the bed, so I could avoid seeing that evil bitch Gonzalez. Marge said everyone had cleared out when she returned with my stuff, but I didn't dare go in.

A few minutes later, Manolo pulled up outside of the barracks in his Mustang, popped the trunk, and threw my duffel in the trunk without so much as a backward glance.

"Should I talk to the MPs first," I asked, holding in tears.

"Do you want to?"

No, I did not. I got in. We drove in silence to his place. He parked and brought my gear inside while keeping a hand on my back. He steered me through his vanilla-scented hallway and into his well-lit double sink bathroom. In the mirror I couldn't believe it was me. I looked weak and beaten. Powerless.

My face was on fire, my head throbbed, and my whole body ached. I took off my dirty top and jeans. I sat in my sports bra and panties on the pristine toilet as he cleaned my wounds with a white washcloth. It was always warm in his place, so the cool water felt nice on my skin. Watery blood stained his clean towel, but he didn't notice it. He was restless but quiet, methodically rinsing off every inch of me. When he reached the back of my head, he stopped.

"What?" I said.

"Nothing." I always knew when he lied.

"Tell me."

He sighed. "A patch of your hair is gone. It's ball."

"Ball?"

"Ball. No hair."

"You mean bal-*d*." I over-pronounced the "d", so he heard the difference.

I looked up to see him standing over me, inspecting my ball-bald spot. I laughed, which made my stomach hurt so I stopped, but couldn't stop the grin that spread across my face.

"I'm ball," I said, which made him laugh.

"Easier in Spanish. *Calvo.*"

As he spoke, I reached back and felt the spot where my hair used to be. It was bumpy and raw. I didn't mean to do it, but I cried as I touched it.

"It's okay, baby," he said, alarmed. I tried to stop, but I cried harder.

"*Dios mio*, she crazy," he said. "So sorry she did this, baby. We'll go the MPs tomorrow, make sure they get your statement."

I nodded. I didn't want to go to the MP's tomorrow but knew it was the right thing to do. Gonzalez might do this again to someone if she got jealous again.

I was exhausted and dizzy. I tried to stand but sat back down. Manolo picked me up to a standing position and slid one of his arms under me. He bent down and placed his other arm behind my knees, lifted me up and soldier carried me to his bedroom. I sniffled as he laid me down over the top of his silky, cream-colored duvet. He handed me a Kleenex and I wiped my nose as he pulled off his shirt and pants.

"It's the second time I got hit in the face," I said as I looked up at him.

He bent down and kissed me softly on the lips. He tasted like a cold beer and lime. "Nobody will hit you again."

As he said it, I believed him. I stopped sniffling. I was reassured. Nobody would ever hit me again. He spread a thin sheet over me then laid down next to me on the soft bed and reached for my hand. We interlaced our fingers, and he kissed the inside of my palm.

"You must be tired," he said as he reached over me and turned off the light. It was after two in the morning. I was so sleepy and thought I should at least brush my teeth, but my eyes closed, and I didn't want to open them again.

I asked without opening my eyes, "Babe, do I have enough ass for you?"

"You're more than enough of everything, baby," he answered with a little laugh.

He kissed me on the lips, then forehead. "*Buenas noches,* baby."

Manolo lifted my torso until my head laid on his upper arm and his arms were wrapped around me. I trailed my free hand along his biceps. I was exhausted.

My body was so, so tired, but my mind kept me awake. Mom's angry face and hand slapped me again and again. I saw Gonzalez's foot stomp me while she called me a slut. My eyes popped open. I saw nothing in the dark room, but I heard his soft, almost shallow, breathing. This was not how I would let the night end.

I reached behind and slid a hand under the waistband of Manolo's boxer briefs. Slid my fingers lower and lower. I fought for him. I deserved him.

"Baby, you need to rest…" he said as I stroked him.

"Please," I said, and didn't stop.

Up and down. I felt him become hard. I turned to face him, and pushed myself up to straddle him. I kissed him. His lips felt so good. Tears came to my eyes. With great tenderness and care, he rolled me under him and kissed away every tear. I watched him leave a trail of kisses down my stomach. He slipped off my panties, and soon licked right where he knew he should. I came quickly. My whole-body shuddered. *More,* I moaned. I was dying of pleasure, but I wanted him inside of me. He was mine, dammit, and nobody else's. I crawled on top of him, rocked hard on his hips until he came. I laid down on top of him, both of us damp with sweat and hearts pounding. He slid out of me but kept me in his arms as he fell asleep.

I listened to his breathing and said his full name out loud. Manuel Martin del Campo Martinez. "*Te quiero,*" I whispered, the only words I ever learned in high school Spanish class. I wasn't clear on what this relationship was beyond "dating." That's all I said we were doing when Marge asked. What I felt was a whole lot more than that. I'd wait until he realized it, too.

CHAPTER 3

De Oppresso Liber

WHAT I REALIZED the next day is that MPs can hush up anything they want. The duty officer decided to write my statement for me and sign it with an X. Nothing about Gonzalez jumping me in my own room. But nothing about me, either, or the little punch I got in at the end. Report said we had an argument in a common room. I told the MP on duty that this wasn't what happened, so he said, *the duty officer told me he saw you hit her, so you really wanna open this up?* I felt so icky inside and couldn't get out of there fast enough. Whenever I was dealing with MP's, I always got the feeling they were projecting childhood power fantasies over me.

In the car, I asked Manolo why MPs were pricks. He shrugged.

"They're the only MOS that's given the job of fucking over other soldiers."

I felt antsy and ready to get the hell away from the station, but still angry about everything. It hurt. All of it. I pouted. "Gonzalez gets away with kicking my ass."

He said nothing for a minute.

I pulled down the passenger side visor, flipped open the mirror and stared into my own eyes. They were bloodshot and tired; even the gold flecks seemed tarnished. I looked at Manolo. He was beat, but I saw in his eyes that he was worried.

"What?" I said. "It's not fair."

"I know, baby," he paused for a beat, his voice tender. "Watching people with lots of power do the wrong thing is eye-opening. Makes a lot of soldiers cynical and bitter, but don't go down that path. It's bad what happened to you, I know, *okay?* I know. And it's my fault for not telling people you're my girlfriend. But I can't let you get pessimistic about the Army. We got so many jaded soldiers as it is, sucking the life out of everyone."

He said some more stuff, but I didn't hear it all. I was stuck on something he said, which kept whirling around in my head. *His girlfriend.* My lips curled into a smile. My anger was replaced with pure joy. Nervous, he stopped talking then licked his lips. It was his turn to ask me, "What?"

I repeated it in case I misheard. "I'm your girlfriend?"

He didn't even blink. "Of course."

"You're my boyfriend."

He looked confused. "You have another somewhere?"

I couldn't stop myself from bursting out with a laugh. My hands flew up to my face to shut my trap, but I couldn't cover the huge grin.

I giggled, overjoyed to hear Manolo admit it out loud. "You called me your girlfriend." He raised his eyebrows. He had a look on his face.

"You're living with me now, baby, remember?"

My grin made my face ache. "I'm going to tell everyone."

He smiled and said, "Go ahead."

I rolled down the window and shouted, "Manolo Martinez is my boyfriend."

The base was empty at 11:00 on a cold Sunday morning in early April, so nobody heard me, but I didn't care. I yelled it again. I felt like a huge weight was lifted off my chest. For months, we'd cared what people thought, but that was behind us. We were authorized by ourselves to tell anyone.

I was warm all over my body and said, "Let's go back and make it official."

❧

WE DIDN'T GO immediately. We stopped by the barracks, and I let myself into the room. It was dark and stuffy but everything was in its place. Marge slept like nobody's business, so I didn't' wake her. I saw Weisengard asleep in my bed. I sat next to her and gently shook her shoulders. She opened her eyes, realized it was me, kicked off the sheets, and sat up.

"Oh my God, are you okay?" She reached over and hugged me. I squeezed her back.

"I'm fine. You can stay here all the time now if you want."

"Gonzalez is such a bitch," she said and released me. "You're staying at his place now?"

"Yeah." Couldn't stop or hide my smile. "And get this. He called me his girlfriend."

She rubbed her eyes. "What in the hell did you think you were?"

"I…I guess I thought…"

She smirked at me. "For being smart, you're so dumb sometimes, Mandy."

My smile shrunk. "You sound like my mom."

She hesitated. "Oh, right. She called an hour ago. Supposed to call her back."

A giant pang hit my heart. Mom never called me, not once. Something must be wrong with Grandma. Or Grandpa. Dad. God forbid, something with Jo or Connor.

I sprang up off the bed. "Did she say anything else?"

"Take it easy, I'm sure it's fine. She didn't sound like anything bad happened." Weisengard fluffed the pillow and laid back down.

"Yeah, but that's how Mom is," I said as I made my way to the mini living room and grabbed the phone, silently praying that everything was okay...

In just a few rings, she answered. Something must be wrong…she never does…oh, God.

"Mom. What's wrong?" I said.

She ignored the question. "Where were you so early in the morning?" Mom used her normal huffy tone. No how are you. No normal chitchat.

"Is everything okay?" I asked, confused.

"What do you mean?"

"Is it Grandpa?" He wasn't old, but he did have that accident a few years ago…

"What on earth are you mumbling about?"

I searched for words that wouldn't tick her off. "It's Sunday morning…I guess, I mean, I don't know. You usually don't call that much. Is Dad okay?"

"Your dad's always fine, everyone's just fine." She took a deep breath. "I'm checking in, is all. I suppose you weren't at church this morning."

"I was…out getting breakfast," I said. I've never been a great liar.

"With who? Your roommate answered."

I knew I should come clean. Even hundreds of miles away, she knew when I lied.

I fibbed anyway. "You don't know them, mom, just some new friends."

"Is that right? Well, I overheard Jo talking with you last week. And the week before that. Don't be so shy, Amanda. I know you're not a kid anymore. So what's his name?"

"Well…ummm…yeah, I…" I paused for a second too long.

"Don't tell me it's Carlos," Mom moaned, "Or Juan."

My pulse quickened and my headed pounded. I didn't let Gonzalez ruin it for me and Mom sure as hell wouldn't, either.

I said, "His name is Manuel, but I call him Manolo."

Pause. I held my breath.

"You better get that outta your system real quick," she said.

"I'm living with him," I felt brave and scared all at once.

Her voice was low. "How can you do this to your own mother?"

I was ready to defend us. I was ready to fight and to tell her all the feelings I've wanted to share for weeks, months, and years. What I wasn't ready for was what she did.

She hung up.

❧

I CRADLED THE phone in a daze, grabbed another duffle, said bye to Weisengard and fled the room as quickly as I could.

Back in the Mustang, I told Manolo everything was fine, and I was tired. I didn't mention mom and what she said. But I was quiet, and I've never been a quiet person. He reached over and squeezed my hand as he shifted gears.

As we drove away from the barracks, the shock wore off and I chimed in here and there as he brought up making rank. He was practically an expert on promotion boards. "You're smart and good at your job. You'll be a Specialist in fourteen months. If you're high speed, below the zone, you could become a Sergeant eighteen months later."

His words brought me back into the present. I owed it to myself to make rank as fast as I could. To do well, be the best and get promoted. It was clear I wasn't going back home. I said with confidence, "I'll be below the zone. For sure."

He smiled. "If there's another war, you could advance quicker."

"Nobody wants to fight us," I smiled, over-confident.

As we turned towards the base exit, a shiny black pick-up sped up and passed us in a 25 mph zone. The driver then gunned it way over the speed limit, right in front of a parked MP car by the gate. On the back window a bumper sticker stated, "*De Oppresso Liber*" next to another sticker of three lightning bolts and a fighting knife against a background of a blue arrowhead. An airborne tab sticker was placed atop the patch. I expected the truck to get pulled over in a heartbeat, but the MP car didn't bother to flash its lights.

"What the hell?" I said in disbelief.

"Special Forces," Manolo answered with a shrug.

"What do they do?"

He matter-of-factly told me. "Counterinsurgency. Covert missions. Counter terrorism. Kill the bad guys and make it look like an accident kind of stuff."

I was impressed. "Sounds high speed."

"They're the elites."

I wondered how I had not noticed this group before, especially if they drove crazy. That made me a little mad. Kids were on the base.

"That MP didn't even bother to stop him. He's going way over."

"SF guys even outrank the MP's."

"Good," I said at that time, which I felt. But I didn't feel like that later. Much later, I regretted I said that at all.

CHAPTER 4

32 Months Later

LESS THAN THREE years later, America didn't just have one war, but two. My division wasn't lucky enough to be sent to Afghanistan after 9/11, but by 2003, our entire base geared up for Iraq. Fort Shithole was busy everywhere—gym, motor pool, shooting ranges, and especially the Class Six. A few days before we were slated to go, there was a big deployment ceremony for the families at which the Commanding Officer gave us a speech about the importance of our deployment and how we were making the country a safer place. Our task was to stop terrorism.

As a new E-5, a three-stripe buck sergeant, I wasn't a squad leader yet, but I oversaw other supply soldiers and had real responsibilities. We stood stone-faced in formation; one thousand percent ready to go. Sure, I had some pre-deployment jitters, but I was proud to wear the uniform. The Army gave me my friends, my boyfriend, a purpose, and money for college that I would cash-in on when we got back. The least I could do was go to the sandbox for six months. *Join the Army, see the world*, Dad reminded me when I called and told him.

The ceremony didn't last long. Afterwards, we got the afternoon off to spend with friends and family. Manolo and I spent time squaring away our place, donating food, and giving away the plants. We bought last minute crap—wet wipes, batteries. Washed the Mustang.

That night nearly the whole base was going to party off base—one last time. Me and Manolo pulled into the far corner of the secluded gravely parking lot of La Casa. Tons of cars were already there. La Casa was the unofficial NCO club. From the outside it's an ancient artifact with a falling-down balcony. Inside it was all sticky floors, jukebox and cheap beer.

We had been here a few weeks ago when I made rank. Everyone congratulated me on my below the zone promotion and Greta, the chubby bartender from Honduras, gave me beers on the house to celebrate. Not bragging, but I deserved the promotion. While other PFCs and Specialists were busy partying in the barracks, I read books from the Commander's reading list and studied the maximum effective range of every weapon in the U.S. arsenal. Manolo quizzed me on knowledge and showed me how to shave a beret. I was squared away.

He parked far away from the other cars. Cut the engine. I reached for the handle to get out. Our friends waited for us inside. He reached across, stopped me.

I looked back, puzzled. "You don't want to go in?"

He let out a big breath, as if he was holding it for hours.

"It's gonna be hot, then it's gonna be cold. Soldier's will bitch and complain the whole time, but you can't get complacent even when we've been there for months. Don't drop discipline. Set the standards and keep them. Check body armor. There's a reason it's issued—"

I squeezed his hand. The past few days were nothing but last-minute NCO wisdom sessions from him. He made rank and was an E-7 – Sergeant First Class. That made him a tank platoon sergeant. He had real responsibilities compared to me. That night we were supposed to party and forget about it.

I shook my head to stop him. "Manolo. I'll be fine."

He rubbed a hand over his face. "Baby, I'm serious. You can't control a lot of things over there, but you can control yourself. Your soldiers will live up to your standards."

I couldn't help it, but I busted out laughing. He frowned, looking disappointed. I reached over to him and touched the back of his neck.

"I'm sorry, I didn't mean to laugh. But come on. You've been so serious since we got orders. You promised you'd be *normal* tonight. Please stop worrying about me."

The tense lines on his face deepened. "We're deploying to a warzone, baby. It's going to be more dangerous than you think. Snipers. Suicide bombers. We don't know what else."

I rolled my eyes. "You already told me a thousand times. Maybe we should've gotten married so you can collect the big bucks when I get blown up."

He looked like he might cry. My smile faded.

He said quietly, "Don't say that. Baby, please, never say that."

We stared at each other in the darkness of the car. Six months of separation coming up. That was no joke, but we'd make it through.

"I have something for you," he said as he reached into his front pocket and pulled out a silver necklace. He held it up in front of my face, the circular silver pendant dangled in front of me. My heart skipped a beat.

"It's beautiful," I said as I cupped it in my hand. A flower head was delicately etched into it. The chain fine and feminine.

I felt him looking at me as he asked, "You know what it is?"

I shrugged, unsure. "A...flower?" Duh, Amanda. But I didn't know what kind.

He laughed. "Violet. It's the Wisconsin state flower."

"I didn't even know that," I said, flushed. He took it from me and put it around my neck, clasping it on. I held the pendant in my right hand.

"Thank you, babe," I said, meaning it. So thoughtful.

He held my face in his hands for a few seconds. "You have to be careful, even when you go to the latrine, bring a battle buddy."

After such a beautiful moment, not this again. I leaned over and kissed him. "I'll carry a weapon. And ammo."

He shook his head. "Everyone will have a weapon."

I held up my hand to the necklace. "Nothing is going to happen."

He sighed heavily. "Anything could happen."

I looked out the clear front window and saw a sky full of stars. It was quiet out here, in the middle of nowhere. Almost like we were on the farm in Wisconsin. Crisp air, a clear night, and a half moon. I would miss him like I'd miss an arm. I felt my heart start to break. I had to lighten the mood, or I'd die thinking about being away from him.

"Anything could happen right now," I said, "If you stop being so damn serious."

I quickly unbuttoned my blouse and flashed him my lace bra.

He smiled and laughed. "Baby, you're crazy."

"Crazy for you," I said as I hitched up my black jean skirt, pulled off my panties and crawled over the middle console into his lap. He let out a little laugh in surprise. I pushed his seat back using the side button until he was almost in a supine position. He kissed me then held my shoulders back slightly. His eyes looked worried.

"Promise me you'll be careful."

I held myself over him. "I promise, okay? I promise. I promise. I promise. I promise. But I want to have fun tonight and if I have to screw you in the middle of Greta's parking lot to make you relax so we can go in, then I'll do it."

"*Dios mio*, what will I do without you?" He laughed as he unsnapped my bra.

"You'll be bored for sure," I said, "But six months is nothing."

"Seis meses, then we'll talk about a ring."

My heart galloped in my chest and my arms collapsed. He held me up.

"Seriously?" I choked, straightened my arms and looked him square in the eyes.

He nodded and pushed a stray hair behind my ear, "The necklace is only a promise. I wanted to ask, but…too soon?"

"Not too soon!" I was almost panting. "We've been together *three years*."

He searched my face. "But I don't know your family."

Something I avoided talking about at all costs. I was damn near out of excuses why we couldn't visit. I touched my new necklace and tears welled up. Manolo was so good to me. Anyone—even good old Mom—would see that. And isn't that what parents want for their kids? Happiness? I smiled down at him. We could make it work.

"You're right. We'll go to the farm when we get back."

It had the desired effect. He broke into a grin. I kissed him. I could not help myself and continued to kiss him as he laid back in the seat. It was perfect. His hands in my hair, my hands on his high and tight, the soft buzz of his mustache on my lips. His hands followed my curves down until they moved up and down my thighs.

"I should've have asked sooner," he said.

I laughed. "Amanda Martinez," I said my future name out loud.

"Beautiful name." He slipped his hands between my legs.

As I kissed him that night, I didn't know then that six months was a suggestion for a deployment, and that Uncle Sam and his Department of Defense could extend it. Six months could be twelve, and then eighteen. I'm glad I didn't know. Somethings are better left ignored.

PART 2

Now

CHAPTER 5

Amanda, Three Years Later

BEFORE THIS DEPLOYMENT, the chain of command said that Kuwait was all dry heat and wouldn't be hotter than our last deployment to Iraq. I'll add that to the list of lies I've been told since I enlisted. Kuwaiti heat sucks some serious ass.

Worse, I gotta pee something fierce. That's what happens when it's a million degrees outside and we've been ordered to drink about six canteens of water during the past few hours while we've waited on the tarmac. Military gear is made for men, so it squashes my lady parts straight down into my lap as I sit. Metal plates push directly onto my sore crotch. There's no Girlie May edition body armor, though I wish there were. Shitbags kicked me hard yesterday.

Inside this C-130 it's stifling. A stale diesel odor fills the un-air-conditioned cow of a plane. About forty of us face inwards towards each other, trapped and strapped into the bright red jump seats that line both sides of the greasy walls. We've been sitting on the runway for hours now and my butt is numb from the tattered, tough nylon seat. It's hot and loud, like sitting inside a live firing range.

Most soldiers are racked out. For a Medical Evacuation flight, nobody up front with me looks sick. That's good news. A C-130 is far from a smooth ride and once a soldier pukes, it's a chain reaction and we'll all vomit.

Barf is not my concern—yet. Good Lord, I'm about to pee myself. I thought I could wait but I can't. I'm a grown woman but I gotta ask to use the latrine. I raise my hand to get the attention of an Air Force crew member. A small group of guys are roaming free near the cockpit with their clipboards and walkie-talkies. To me, they're from a different stratosphere with hands stuck in their pockets; their too-long-for-regs-shaggy hair falling over their foreheads, and all of them wearing aviators inside the plane, like Top Gun extras.

After a minute or two, a short, 5 foot-nothing airman sees me wave then steps away from the cool kids. Not much taller than me. I pull my hand down fast. He's the last airman I want to ask. When we loaded, he looked me over head to toe, each long look creepier than the last.

He wades towards me through the sea of soldier's extra rucks that cram the narrow aisle. I'm jammed next to the only other female on the flight. My new battle buddy sleeps next to me. Her head slumps over her chest plate, snoring. Her curly hair is bunched up under her Kevlar helmet that rises and falls with each loud breath. Shorty Airman stops a few feet away. My hands sweat and stomach knots. I keep eye contact. He looks away.

"Drink up," he yells and turns towards the rest of the cabin, holding up a half-empty clear plastic liter of water over his head. In the other hand he carries the Almighty Clipboard with the printed flight manifest that flaps as he moves. No doubt he's the Loadmaster.

Across from me, soldiers wake up and unscrew their canteen caps. They gulp long slugs as he lords over them. Not me. I'm motionless, with my Resting Bitch Face plastered on, as it is nearly all days now. It lets soldiers assume I'm unapproachable, which is fine by me. I don't need any of them.

Shorty Airman walks straight towards me, his jaw clenched. From the expression on his face, he's not used to being challenged.

He hovers and hollers, "It's hot as balls in here and you will pass out. Drink. Now."

Imaginary spiders crawl up my back. I slowly pull out my empty canteen, unscrew the top and turn it over. A droplet of water plops on to the greasy floor.

"Need to use the latrine," I shout over the noise.

He rolls his eyes and his jaw clenches.

"Females," is all the prick says, like I'm a disease.

"It's an emergency."

"No can do. We're about to take off."

"We've been "about to" take off for hours," I shout back.

Our discussion wakes up my battle buddy next to me. She looks around, shakes her legs, unbuckles, and stands up.

She's a tall, lean and perfectly postured Black woman. She might be in her late-20's, but has a rank of Specialist, so maybe younger. She's a good six inches taller than Shorty. I like how she owns her height, and looks strong as she stands in the middle of this plane. I see her name tape. Grey. It gives me pleasure to see Shorty crane his neck to look up at her.

"How far are we?" she says over the engine noise.

Shorty frowns. "Haven't left yet. Sit."

"Damn," she says and wiggles into her tiny seat. She's no fat dumpling, not by a long shot, but real estate is rare in here. Anybody would have trouble cramming in between me and Big Blob two seats over. Big Blob's so overweight his body armor can't close, and his tree trunk legs fill the aisle. Recruiters enlisted him to make monthly quotas, most likely. Since 9/11, it's been like this. No matter the level of *hoo-hah* at enlistment, still too fat for service.

My battle buddy squeezes into her seat and glances at me.

Her eyes cause my blood pressure to shoot up. She wears super-fakey purple lenses, like she's advertising some discount contact's company. They look more like Easter pastel grape skittles popping out of her face than seeing devices. Army's supposed to have uniform standards. I look at my lap and squeeze my eyes shut for a second. Why do I care what she wears for contacts? Why should I care about Army regs? Didn't do me no good. I'm irritated at myself, not her. She's a pretty girl and so what if she likes purple eyes?

I grit my teeth to stay calm and shift my eyes to Shorty, who studies his clipboard.

"You're Ashe, right?"

My gaze doesn't waver as I nod.

I repeat, "I need to pee. Your choice if I do it here or in the latrine."

He's not listening. His sneery grin is a mile wide. I know he's heard about me. My so-called reputation precedes me, even in the Air Force. I'm straight-out dry humped by his look.

"We got us a little Desert Queen on board," the tiny jackass says loud enough for me and anyone else nearby to hear. I glare but before I can react, he turns and books it to the front.

I feel as if my pee reaches my brain and my thoughts swim around. I know this guy without knowing him just by that sleazy remark. Of all the dudes in the military, 90% are decent. But that other 10% is full of douche bags, big-headed bastards who get away with being assholes because nobody says nothing. Shorty probably thinks he's God's gift and that any female would be happy to suck his shrimp dick. Jerks like him made my last couple of years miserable and I know for a fact that the rest of those Top Gun extras won't say nothing to him.

Skittles pushes into my side to get my attention and I turn with a scowl.

"Want it?" the beautiful Specialist Grey holds out a pack of gum.

I shake my head but force a half-smile. "No, thanks," I'm irritated but no reason to take my anger out on her. She blinks and I realize I'm staring into those fake eyes.

"I need them for medical reasons. Right?"

As if I asked. I shrug, "Okay."

"Purple is a really comfortable color," she says, which makes no type of sense, but I say nothing and just nod.

She holds her gum out again. "Come on, take the whole pack. I got plenty. Right?"

"Okay." I slide the tip of my tongue over my dirty gums, and feel grit the size of pebbles. She's being really kind to me for no reason. I soften at her smile. I take the pack, pull out a piece and stash the rest in my cargo pocket. The gum tastes like winter.

"Thanks, thanks a lot. Racking out now." Not that she can hear me above the engine noise. She nods and mouths "right" before she wiggles herself into a more comfortable position.

Soldiers understand rack-time. It's an across-the-ranks accepted military rule—if you can get some sleep, do it. My tongue tucks the gum in the space between my bottom molars and cheek. I adjust my body armor and cover up the spot between my legs that could show a wet spot if I leak. I'm used to holding it in like a camel—females can't whip out their lizards like the men—but if I piss myself, the fewer people notice, the better.

❧

I CAN'T KEEP my eyes shut for long. I've been hyper vigilant for months. I scan my small perimeter. All our duffels and overfilled backpacks are palleted down in the center; a year's worth of uniforms, PT gear, socks, boots, sleeping bags, and the rest of the packing list stuffed inside. My chain of command seized my weapon, so I don't need to worry about that; but I feel for it. Carrying an M16A2 for months will do that to you. Gives you a phantom limb.

It's my first time on a Medical Evacuation, or Medevac, flight. The mood-stabilizers they pumped me with in the TMC after confronting that dipshit Special Forces Captain Butler have worn off. At first, they knocked me out cold. Then the nurse on duty woke me up from that drug-induced sleep so I could be added to the manifest out of here. She shook me hard, called my name, prepared me for headcount, hoping to clear a bed for a new nutcase.

"Sergeant Ashe, Amanda Ashe, Last Four 1234! Wake UP!"

That's me, although she got my rank wrong. The last thing my chain of command did was demote me back into a Private, just like my first day of boot camp. My new Commander visited me in the tent, a frustrated look on his face. He was too new to understand the history of what happened, so I let him be disappointed.

He carefully chewed on the tip of his pen as he spoke. "You've been on a downward spiral since I took command. Today you hit rock bottom, Ashe. You'll have to be held accountable for your actions and I'll have to send you back to face the music."

That's how the Commander talked—in metaphors. Rock Bottom. Face the Music. I think he was an English major, but I knew him for weeks, not months. He relied on what others told him instead of learning about me on his own.

I was there with him, but the drugs were so strong, it was like watching some version of my life I wasn't part of. Blinking took effort. I heard him but had zero ability to respond.

The air force loaded us at 0-Dark-Thirty. The weather was throwing a tantrum with a sandstorm coming in from Iraq, so they said we had to get on the plane quick. The winds never came, but even without a sandstorm blasting outside, we were delayed. *Hurry up and wait* is the military's unwritten motto. But our destination is Landstuhl, the biggest American military hospital in Europe, and to hell with anyone who doesn't think we should have left right on time because it is, after all, a Medevac flight. I don't care about *me*, but time is ticking for the injured. Over the roar of the plane, I hear them moaning.

A few feet from me hangs an olive-green curtain that leads to the back. Earlier, I saw medics carrying a soldier whose forehead looked like raw beef shank. Another one was missing an arm, but I didn't get a good look before a nurse pulled the curtain shut. Kuwait isn't Iraq, where the real war's going on, but training accidents can happen. Practice can be deadly. Exercises can mess soldiers up.

❧

I FINALLY CLOSE my eyes, but I focus on the insult instead of sleep. *Desert Queen*. It's a worse insult than whore. Not that I deserve that name, either, but it's less offensive since it's so overused. Female soldiers are called whores all the time. If they turn a guy down, or if they accept a date. If they wear make-up, or if they don't. Civilians on base are whores for talking to anyone who isn't their husband. Not hard when the entire Army base is 92% men. Whores are everywhere on base, in and out of uniform. We're all whores to the guys.

But Desert Queen is reserved for those female soldiers who take advantage of being a female in a male dominated job. Gals who normally register a one or two on the looks scale are suddenly a nine or ten in the sandbox, fawned over like some goddess by sex-starved men. Desert Queens bat their Bonne Bell coated eyelashes and a dumbass opens his wallet, looking for some bunker love. Dipshits go to the DFAC like it's date night. They're the real whores.

I keep my eyes pressed shut and sit straight up, chin to body armored chest. It's hard to sleep like this, but it'll do. In this position, I don't need to rely on the soldiers to my left or right. I bury the insult as I keep my eyes closed. My thoughts fade to black.

❧

A SHARP PAIN shoots through my side followed by a tug on my arm. My head rolls towards the hurt and I rip open my eyes. My body and feet are quaking slightly. Good. A shaking floor means we departed. I hear a faint sound of shaking metal and a bang under the constant engine roar. Purple-eyed Skittles nudges me again.

Disgust drips from her highly glossed, sparkly lips. It's the same lip gloss that Jo uses on the farm—iridescent but with a purple tint. It brings out Skittles' eyes, I can see why she uses it.

"You're drooling," she mouths simply while wiping her own mouth. Her breath smells of tootsie pops and my stomach churns with hunger, which I swallow hard to ignore.

I wipe my mouth and thank her with a nod. Then I realize that I *must* go—ASAP.

"You pee yet?" I shout so she can hear.

She shakes her head. "We're four hours in. Maybe you can hold it, right?"

No way. I can't hold it for two minutes, let alone two hours. I look around and the crew is nowhere in sight. I take off my sweaty Kevlar and moist body armor and set them on my seat. It's cooler in here now, so my skin is clammy. I pat down my cargo pockets. Kleenexes and hand sanitizer—check. The plane shifts and Skittles reaches up to steady me. I give her a quick nod of thanks but I'm okay, even with my bladder in my throat.

Latrines are always in the back, in this case, probably by the physically injured. I make my way over to the olive curtain and grab ahold of it, ready to sneak through. Out of nowhere, a hand reaches from behind and clutches my hand. I shrivel back, as if bitten.

Through gritted teeth I demand, "Let go of me."

"You're not authorized to go back there," Shorty Airman says in my ear. I yank my hand loose. Turning around, I see he's taller than I thought. I feel tiny and stand up straighter.

"Emergency," I say, impatient.

"Jesus Christ, you females. I'll get a bucket."

"You're kidding me." My voice cracks.

"I heard you weren't so picky, Jelly," he says that damned nickname and smiles. I freeze. Jelly is worse than Desert Queen; Jelly is the shit pit of names. I clench my fists. My cheeks burn. Every thought is knocked out of me except for: *Die, asshole.*

Raising my hand, I shriek, "Fuck you!"

He quickly catches my small fist in his. Gives a nasty yank and I stumble into him.

"Do not disrespect me, Private." He says "Private" like an accusation as he glances to the side to make sure no one has seen us. He drops my hand and fakes a smile.

Inching closer, he says, "Getting excited, huh? Damn, Jelly. I like the frisky type."

Gross. I feel disgustingly sick, but more than anything, I need to pee. To get away from him. We stand face-to-face, and his eyes linger on my lips. He snaps his teeth in a fake bite. I flinch. He laughs at me and I suppress the desire to strangle. I turn away and reach again for the curtain to get away from him.

"Wait," he says in a direct command and is about to grab me again, but I step back before he can lay a hand on me. He rips open the curtain, steps through, and pulls it shut.

"Don't move." I hear him through the curtain.

Can I hate him any more? Not possible. But, I wait. I have no other choice.I stand with my dick in my hands, as the guys say. I keep my legs zippered together. He comes back a minute later, motions his head for me to follow. I open Unauthorized Curtain and catch a whiff of a vinegary smell, a mix of sweat and stank. I cover my nose with the back of my hand as I scoot through a narrow passage. On all sides are soldiers in bandages, all in various degrees of pain. On my right, a writhing soldier lies on a cot, twitching this way and that, eyes closed and moaning for his mom. A skinny white nurse who looks like she could still be in high school sits next to him, but doesn't look up. She clutches a bag of clear medicine that drips as she scans *Women of Today.*

I stop in my tracks. A catheter runs up his leg, straight into his privates, his dirty boxers barely cover his nuts. Wet marks darken the green cot. His thrashing unnerves me; he looks disrespected. I glance around for a blanket to put on him, something, *anything* to cover him.

"Keep moving."

I ignore the order and grab a balled-up, crumbled sheet from the bottom of the cot and smooth it over the soldier. A split second later the nurse glances at me with red rimmed, tired eyes, but says nothing. The soldier relaxes under the covers.

I continue to walk through the narrow aisle and keep my eyes focused ahead. There isn't a whole lot I can do to help these guys. Shorty waits, his boot tapping, as if he is totally unaware that we share the plane with wounded warriors.

I follow him another few feet until he grabs a tarp that hangs from the wall. A triumphant look covers his face. I peer beyond him to see a makeshift latrine–a bucket, a small toilet seat obtained from God-knows-where, a plastic bag and the tarp that he's holding for privacy. A bungee cord connects the tarp to the wall of the plane, the rest of it's in his hand.

At the sight of this, I almost forgive him for being a jerk. My bladder expands and I begin to unbutton my camouflage pants.

"Not so insubordinate now, are you?" he says. I shrug. I want the toilet.

"Privacy, please?"

"I'll hold the tarp, Jelly," he says in an over-friendly voice, like he's all of a sudden some officer and gentleman.

My body coils up tight at the insult, but I keep my trap shut. I step behind the tarp, unbuckle my belt and sit on the seat. I let loose a stream as hot and loud as a heifer in heat. A strong pee shiver tingles up and down my body. I keep my thighs pressed together to keep from spraying my uniform bottoms. As the last of the piddle drips out, I think of the hurt soldier. Thank God above I don't need no catheter. I read male patients with pee bags can get horrible infections, so bad their privates resemble a kielbasa sausage, even if they got nurses on standby.

I stay on the seat as I clean up with the tissues from my pocket, then stand, pull up my pants and place the plastic bag over the top of the toilet seat and bucket to keep it from spilling.

"Taking a deuce?" he shouts through the curtain. So annoying.

"Gimme a second, will ya?"

As I rush to buckle my belt, he slithers around to my side, tarp in his hand, held up over his head so no one can see us. My pulse jumps and I back up a few steps away from him.

"Uh, thanks," I say and mean it.

He scans over my shoulder, looks to correct, but it's all in place. I squeeze out sanitizer and rub my hands. I look at him, his face hardens and then relaxes into a happy, shit-eating grin.

"Excuse *me*," I say as I try to step around him and his tarp holding hand. In one motion, he firmly grabs onto my wrist and bends it back.

Pain shoots through my arm and my body twists away. My heel hits the bucket.

"Stop!" I feel my wrist crack. I swing my free arm but it's useless and pathetic.

He pulls my hand back harder and whispers, "*Sssssshhhhhhhhhh.....*"

"I got fifty bucks," he says in a low hiss, "I'm hard. I'll hold the tarp… just suck…"

"Fuck you," I spit out through clenched teeth. My entire body shakes.

"Fine, fifty-five." His violent grip tightens, and I feel pinned in place. Acidic puke creeps up my throat. I feel the bones inside my hand rearrange.

"It's a bunch of lies, none of it's true," I choke out. My chest constricts and I can barely breath through the mixture of pain and panic pulsing through me.

"I know about you," he hisses, "Get more dumped in you than a clearing barrel."

His venom spit lands on my cheek as he speaks. His breath is hot and steams my cheek. Twists my wrist again. Pain is deep and it feels like it might break. My arms are so awkwardly arranged I can't push him away. Struggling is worthless.

"Stop..." I'm pleading. Fresh tears spring up in the corner of my eyes.

"Do it and I'll let you sit in the front with the crew afterwards..."

My head pounds and grey spots take over my vision. I'm doomed. A few shit-bag military men have prepared me for this moment. If I scream, he'll break my wrist, or even worse...and get away with it. He's the Loadmaster and knows it. My options are limited—*think, Amanda, think.*

"Okay...okay, okay," I say. His grip loosens a smidge. He laughs.

"I *knew* it."

I continue, "Seventy?" My voice is high with a fake level of interest. I'm stalling.

He sneers his upper lip. "Sixty."

I shake my head.

"Fine, I got money. It's in my pocket. Fifty and a twenty."

Ha. I know he probably doesn't. "Let me see it first."

He releases my wrist, but stomps on my foot. Fuck. One pain for the other. I rub my hand. It's beyond sore. I half expect him to admit he lied, but no. He keeps the tarp up with one hand, reaches into his chest pocket, pulls out a dirty, partly ripped fifty and crumbled twenty. That's what he thinks of me—ho' looking for torn cash.

"It's yours, *afterwards*," he says. He emphasizes the word as he stashes it in his pocket and pushes on the Velcro pouch to keep it in place. His free hand reaches up to unzip his flight suit zipper as he presses on my foot—harder—so I can't move.

"Start slow, we got four hours." Fucker cups his balls from the outside of his uniform.

I stare up at him, so nervous my hands shake. This jerk heard a false rumor and decided to believe that I'm willing to gobble his cock for money. I can't think of a thing to say, or how to get myself out of here. I want to disappear.

I gently sweep my unhurt hand towards him. His too-erect hard-on pushes against his jumpsuit and he fumbles to push his undergarments out of the way. I get a big whiff of days-old sweaty balls. Gag.

He mutters sternly, "On your knees."

"No," I croak.

He stomps my foot and kicks at my knee. "Now, Jelly. Stupid bitch."

Jelly.

A jolt of white-hot hate pulses through me. As if on automatic, I grab his waist with both hands and knee him as hard as I can in the gonads. I spit my gum in his face.

"Bitch!" he shrieks and backs up. Doubles over as his hands cover his crotch.

I see no way around him. I can't escape how I came in, but I need to get out of here. A diversion. I bend down behind me and fling the plastic wrap off the bucket. With one heave, I slosh my reeking pee all over his open coveralls. He freezes. Surprise, surprise.

"Whore!"

He lunges at me; the bucket falls with a thud. Quick, quicker than I thought, he grapples me down with his big hands and I writhe in my own urine. I try to lift my head but one of his paws pins my neck down on the oily, metal floor while the other has full control of my wrists. I buck and twist with him laid out on top of me. His hard-on jams into my spine and it grows each time I thrash, trying to get away.

"You're a sick bastard," I say as I suck down the blood filling my mouth.

"Bad move, Jelly. I was a semi-finalist State wrestler," he says low into my ear. I feel his stiff penis on my back. My ribs feel as if they are cracking against the floor. He fumbles, pulls something from a cargo pocket and I hear the unmistakable sound of tearing duct tape. He wraps it around my hands, which feel brittle and ready to break. I panic. He will do what he wants when I'm tied up.

"And now for your fat mouth..."

My heart pounds. I scream out as loud as I can, "HELP!"

I keep shouting. "Help ME!"

I'm frantic. I kick with all my strength. My foot connects with the toilet seat, and it echoes as it clanks to the ground. Clank…clank…clank…I hear it roll.

He presses my face down. "Shut the fuck up!"

Too late. Together we hear loud footsteps rushing towards us.

He slaps the duct tape over my mouth. The skinny nurse sees us both on the floor, him sitting top of me. I turn myself as best as I can towards her.

She scans the scene then says, "What are you doing to the *patient?*"

Her voice is shaky, like she doesn't want an answer. I'd not once been more grateful for anyone in my life. Sure, I judged her five minutes before, but that's how it goes in the Army. Things change fast. I plead with my eyes and she glances away.

Shorty Airman jumps up and shoos her from me; they talk for a while as he tries to save face. Tiny drops of water spring from my eyes but I press my eyes shut. Slowly my heart rate decreases as I shut down. *Hold it in, Amanda, nothing happened.* I count my breaths to 100.

It seems like forever before he saunters away from us without a backwards glance. Nurse crouches down and rips the duct tape off my mouth, which hurts worse than pre-waxed strips. She rolls me over and helps me on to my rear. I lean forward, desperate, but not sure for what.

"You alright?" she says to me with round eyes. *What a question.* I don't know where to look—even my eyes are sore. I manage a small nod as I scoot closer to her.

"Can you undo my wrists?" My voice is raspy. I lean forward with hope.

She mutely shakes her head, then adds, "I told him I wouldn't."

Neither of us speak for a second. My heart hammers as I ask, "But…why?"

"It's what we agreed on," she says, shrugs, and retreats away from me.

Before she turns away, she says, "Scream if he comes near you. I'll come back."

I don't understand why she won't help me, but I want to say thanks. She rescued me from that sadistic pervert. I look at her but can't get the words out. I watch her leave. I sit on my ass with my head between my knees. I slide up and I maneuver my numb hands to my front and bite down. Duct tape tastes like paint, but I need to be free, just in case. My eyes water and my nose drips as I gnaw through it and pull it from my skin.

I'm in pain, but not hurt. Slow breathing calms me down. Controlling breath is a lesson I learned on the shooting range. Inhale, hold and exhale. I am in control again.

Except I'm not. My winter gum is in a tiny ball on the floor, inches away.

I can't help it. I cry. Big tears roll down my cheeks. The worst part is this—even though Shorty's gone, who's next? I sit, shaking and worrying for hours, up until our boots hit the ground in Germany. It seems so unfair. Germany is Mom's ancestors' home and all I can do is focus on the small things. Inhale. Hold. Exhale. Sit up. Don't get raped. The nurse comes again and I feel a sharp needle enter my right arm. Breath. Live.

CHAPTER 6

Amanda, Hospital Nummer Eins

I'M SPRAWLED OUT in a small, plain room when I wake up. My eyes open because of the damned bright fluorescent lights. I feel like a shined deer. I cover my face with the crook of my arm until my eyes adjust.

I remember when we arrived at Ramstein Air Base, the nurse knocked me out with a shot. I let her. I was groggy but aware when the Military Police came on the plane, pulled me up, dragged me off and drove me a few klicks to the hospital. I was still awake when they dumped me in this isolation room. It's a few hours later now, I think. Maybe days, I don't know.

I pull myself to sitting. I'm still squinting. It takes a bit, but when my eyes focus I see a small camera mounted above the door with a flimsy sign next to it that reads: YOU ARE RESPONSIBLE FOR YOUR OWN ACTIONS.

The small laugh that escapes me hurts my ribs. What a joke. Responsible, my ass.

I try to stand but my legs shake so I sit again. Drugs make me woozy. I look down at myself. My BDU blouse is off, my belt gone, and I don't have my boots. My Army-issued thick socks stick to my sweaty toes. The room is full of dark, curly crotch hair scattered over red, foam wrestling mats that line the walls and floor. Cramped cell is contaminated with old sweat and my pee. We both need a good cleaning.

What I wouldn't give to get a shower right now. Or to have a window and figure out where I am exactly. *Join the Army to see the world.* Instead, I'm seeing pubic hair tumbleweeds tinged by green-fluorescent light in the far-off land of wiener schnitzel and beer.

I wipe the crusty drool off my chin with my tee-shirt. Reaching into my pocket, I take out a piece of mint gum and chew and chew. Wasn't it funny that I had refused this gum from Skittles? Now I'm so grateful for it. Chew, chew, swallow, repeat.

I rub my crunched wrists but then stick my arms into my t-shirt to stay warm. Air is ice-cold, very different from Kuwait where 90 degrees was hoodie weather.

The minty gum revives me and I glance around the room, but my eyes are pulled up again to that fricking sign, which bugs the shit out of me. Who the fuck is responsible for what these days? I drag myself to my feet. Next, I fold a mat and stand on it. On my tippy-toes I unstick that damn sign from the wall. I pull the wad of gum from my mouth and hang the paper over the camera. *Watch that, motherfuckers.* I sit cross-legged, satisfied nobody can see me.

Some minutes later, a scowling male nurse throws open the door. This punk looks like he works at the Dairy King, all dolled up in a white nurse top and spandex-waist pants, paired with stained knock-off Keds. He wears latex gloves over his gorilla hands. Only thing missing is an ice cream scoop. A grayish buzz cut tops off his pinkish-whitish pockmarked face and his skinny legs hold up a big gut. A few too many pieces of Black Forest cake for that chubby bastard. He struts in and stands with his hands on his hips.

"You cover up that camera, Ashe?"

I shrug as he glowers down on me. I focus on the deep lines between his eyebrows. I don't want to look him in the eye.

He speaks again, "I asked you a question."

My heart rate picks up so I pick a frayed seam on my bottoms and stare hard at it. I can tell he's the German word for *asshole.*

"Heard you got a bad attitude from the C-130 loadmaster," he says, "A *real* bad one."

I grit my teeth. Dude hovers over me but I don't respond because I bet that fifty or twenty, when Shorty the Airman complained about me, he didn't mention his hard-on.

He continues. "Messing with government property is a federal offense."

He grunts as he tries to jump up and grab the sign. I smile inward as the gum holds and he loses the battle with the air.

"I'm government property," I mumble as I flick a pube hair away from me.

I meet his eyes and see his face reddening. "You're a Desert Queen."

Argh. Bile rises in my throat. That dumbass name. I open my mouth, then stop. Instead, I watch as he soars three inches off the ground, and rips the sign down.

"I need a shower, Sergeant."

Balling up the paper he says, "You need to in-process. Get up and shut up."

❧

IN CONTRAST TO the dank isolation room, the rest of the floor sparkles. A cleaning crew must've just left as there are several "Do not slip" signs up and down the wide hallway, which gleams and smells strongly of lemon-scented disinfectant. Sunlight pours in from windows that reach as high up as the ceiling. I hang back a few steps as I follow Black Forest Cake past the nurse's station. Two nurses, one in BDUs, the other in green scrubs, sit on swivel chairs behind a large oak desk. They smile as I walk by but don't look up.

In the opposite direction is the exit. It's locked. I know from my arrival that nurses buzz soldiers and staff in and out. Double doors, double locks. No escape.

We enter a bare reception area with three closed doors to my front. Black Forest Cake stops and points to a row of wheat-colored chairs. Army bases have these chairs, waxy and hard.

"Wait here to in-process at Reception. No horsing around. You gotta complete an intake. We got cameras watching you, got that?"

I sit. "Shower?"

He ignores the question. "If I catch you moving, you're back in Isolation."

I stay silent at the threat and feel him search my face for a reaction. I give away nothing.

"If you want," he continues with a wink, "We can cover up the camera again."

I keep my eyes anywhere but on him as my face flushes. My heart pounds and my arm hair prickles. He's cut from the same cloth as Shorty—the type that does what's right only if there are witnesses. He doesn't have to bully me. He could just leave me alone.

Fucker stands for a split second, chuckles, and says, "Not so tough anymore, are ya?"

I glare hard as the oxygen thief walks away. The hallway T-bones to another corridor and he turns right, out of sight. I suck in my breath and let it out slowly, relieved.

I glance around. A large dry erase board stands floor to ceiling at the hallway intersection. It announces the "DAILY SCHEDULE," which is written in slanted cursive. I'm curious but my vision is blurry. I'm tired. A common side effect of being in a rage repeatedly is being drained. My operational readiness is zero.

Reception door opens, and a red-eyed Skittles walks out, clutching a tiny bundle of blue clothes, looking a little smaller and a lot sadder. A skinny Black staff nurse with salt-and-pepper braids carries a shoe box sized pinkish-coral plastic bin and follows her out, but the nurse is speed marching and passes her. Sniffling, Skittles watches the floor as she walks, ten feet behind the skinny nurse as she turns into a room.

I wonder what these nurses will ask me. Do I tell her I ache all over, inside and outside? I know I can't say nothing about loser Black Forest Cake. Or Shorty.

Nurse hurries back. Her bright pink crocs squeak as she rolls up her sleeves. Flashes me a quick smile of Rimmel Red and shows off straight, gleaming teeth. Her eyebrows are almost non-existent, but her eyelashes curl all the way up to her lids.

"Follow me, honey," she says. My mouth twitches but I stay silent. A female civilian calling me honey is okay, but I'm about as sweet as hot sauce these days.

I step inside the reception conference room. It smells peachy. Every Army office I've been to uses that same air freshener to beat bad odors, to cover up the funk. Fluorescent lights above us turn the room into a Lite Bright. The nurse sits at the long wooden table and motions for me to do the same. I pull out a chair opposite her and she fishes for a sheet of carbon copy paper. Her brown eyes are as dark as Cuban coffee, but soft. I know I'm a rumpled mess and she must smell me, but she doesn't react. It's like she smells piss for breakfast.

"I'm Mrs. Gowan, Sergeant Ashe. I'm here to do your inventory and explain some things. Please make yourself comfortable."

I move from butt cheek to butt cheek, not comfortable.

I admit to her, "I'm a Private."

"We don't need to discuss any of your history yet, that's not my job."

"Just telling you." I'm ashamed as I say it. I worked hard to make rank and lost it all.

"We can sort that out." She frowns and continues, "But first things first. We need you to lay out the items from your duffel so I can take inventory. No contraband, no electronics, no phones, no extras go inside the ward. You get one box of Sharps and undergarments."

"Sharps?" I'm confused.

"Toothbrush, toothpaste, shoes without laces, combs."

"How the fuck are shoes sharp?"

"No cussing," she says as her thin eyebrows rise.

"Sorry. First time in a psych ward."

"You smoke?"

"No."

"Good." A softer tone. "Contraband – which means anything not allowed– are things like razors, phones, cameras, and belts. We lock those up, but you get them back as soon as you're discharged. Sharps are controlled items that we keep for you in a closet, and you can use them 15 minutes after meds in the morning and 15 minutes before bed. Shoes, toothbrush, shampoo, a comb and toothpaste. They aren't contraband." She emphasizes the words like I'm special. My temper flares. I'm not stupid.

"I know what *contraband* means," I say too quickly then look away.

Goddamn. I'm no dummy but I am completely drained. A numbness overcomes me, from my brain down to my socks. My head is a rock and pain shoots through my neck. My eyelids blink longer than I intend.

"You okay?" Her nice eyes soften with concern, "You eat yet today?"

"I'm fine, Ma'am."

"You don't look fine. I'll get you something. Chocolate bar okay?"

"Don't bother." My stomach growls and I pretend I don't hear it.

"Oh come on," she insists.

"I'm kinda weird about food." My stomach twists as I speak. That's an odd way to describe it. I have myself a list of safe foods, but when I'm forced to eat anything else, I vomit. Been two years since I ate like a regular human being. She seems so nice, but I'm kinda mad she's doing this. Making me tell her things I don't want to for no reason, since, *it's not her job.*

She looks straight into my eyes. "Everyone else had a meal when you were in Isolation."

"I'm fine." My stomach betrays me and growls louder. "But I need a shower."

She smiles a half smile. "Sure, later. Let me get you something."

She pushes her chair back from the table, winks, and leaves the room. I lay my head on my folded arms and close my eyes. *Let me get you something…* as if I had a choice in the matter. I admire her for caring, but she doesn't know what I need. I close my eyes and see the sign—YOU ARE RESPONSIBLE FOR YOUR OWN ACTIONS.

How come that's not true for everyone?

Sarah Sucher just got out of jail, according to Jo when I called home a few days ago. Five years in jail, she got out early on good behavior. She spent more time in jail than her lame goon of a boyfriend who stole the crap. She was more responsible because she had a worse lawyer. She was responsible for both their actions.

And if that sign was true in the Army, I wouldn't be here. I'm no angel, but I'm the only one held accountable for what happened. Some soldiers can get away with rape, stealing, assault, or murder and still get a paycheck every two weeks. Some can't get away with reporting it.

❧

IN LESS THAN a few minutes, Mrs. Gowan returns, and I sit up. On the table she places two granola bars and a juice. I want to hug her for her kindness, but I won't take it. The less I eat, the less hungry I am, the less I need something from somebody.

I try to smile. "Thank you, Ma'am, but I'm not hungry. I can pay you back."

"Don't worry about money. You've been through a lot today."

The granola bars sit on the table. I feel guilty she wasted her time and money.

She scrunches up her lips. "You're thin. Don't have to worry about your weight."

I close my eyes and memories flash through my mind. I'm not thinking about weight. I'm thinking about Shorty trying to make me drink water. I'm seeing Butler forcing himself on me, and I'm seeing Vincent and his sidekick. I'm thinking about all those times I didn't get to have a choice. I'm not thinking about calories or fat. I'm thinking about control. Food is my sharps, and

I get to say what goes in and out. If pain is weakness leaving the body, then food is weakness going in. I open my eyes to see the concern on her face.

But Mrs. Gowan doesn't know that about me. She's just being nice.

"You should eat," she says. I'm embarrassed she thinks she needs to tell me this.

"I know," I say, "But I'm not feeling good. I don't eat…much."

"Ah," Mrs. Gowan says, "I'm guessing that's something you'll need to work on."

I take the juice and set it on the floor. As I do, I swallow the saliva that pools in my mouth. Disguise my appetite with a cough.

I sigh, thinking about this place. "How long am I here?"

"That's up to the team assigned to you. Average is ten to fourteen days, then you either go to Walter Reed or back to your unit. I'm guessing that in your case, it will be Walter Reed."

My mouth falls open. I can't be here for another minute with the threat of that Black Forest Cake hanging over me. What if he really does make me go back into the Isolation room with him… I pinch my lips with my fingernails. I'll find a way out sooner than that.

She clicks her pen open. "Put the sharps inside of the pink basket."

It's the same shoebox basket that I saw her carry for Skittles.

I'm careful not to squash the granola bars as I heave my Kuwait moon-dust-covered, Army issue duffel onto the table. I feel her eyes follow my movements and I push the bars to her side of the table. I open the bag, sending up puffs of dust from the inside.

Mrs. Gowan's eyes drop to her notepad. "Let's start, then I'll take you to your room."

I say, unable to hide my hope, "And shower?"

She nods and smiles, "Absolutely."

I take a deep breath. Her promise gives me a small hope that I'll feel less-gross again. I reach inside to pull out my gear. My duffel is orderly because my Battle Buddy Shelly Weisengard folded my gear so nice and neat when I was in that medical tent waiting for take-off. Thank God for Weisengard. She's still deployed back in Kuwait. I'd be dead without her. Really, I would. She didn't take away my control–she held my hair back as I barfed.

❧

IT'S LATER NOW. I'm sitting in a large room they call the "common space." Twenty of us sit in stacking chairs arranged in a large circle so we can see each other. Stubby gray carpet covers the floor, which matches the gray walls. This room feels more like a scientific laboratory than what I imagined a therapy space would be. Fading light streams in but what I don't know is if the light is real or not. Could be stadium night lights that surround the building, who knows.

Mrs. Gowan and Black Forest Cake sit with their backs to the windows. Mrs. Gowan's clipboard sits on her lap, and she smiles wide. She's been happy since I got here, so I know already that I can't relate to her at all. Black Forest Cake's a grumpy fusspot with his arms crossed over his dowdy uniform. A pink-ish smidge of ketchup is smeared under his collar. I don't trust the horse's ass, either, so I hope those two don't expect much from me.

I feel that fluttery nervous butterfly feeling in my stomach. My palms are sweaty, so I run my hands through my wet hair. Mrs. Gowan gave me coconut Holly Day Shampoo and Conditioner that somebody donated to Support the Troops. Discarded hotel shampoo is nothing to some people, but it's everything to me. I smell like a My Little Pony instead of a gas station bathroom. Even still, I'm not calm.

All of us wear our stiff blue pajama shirts and pants. It's like wearing a cardboard box. My drawstring is missing, so I cinched the waistband with my hair tie. The robe is thinner than the jammies. It's freezing in here. As Dad would say, it's colder than a witch's tit.

I'm on the end of our side of the circle, after Skittles and our other roommate, LaTonya, who's Army like us and arrived two days before. Up close she looks about eighteen, with bright eyes, silky brown skin, and a constant smile. The two of us share a big bed, which was decided when Skittles complained she couldn't share a bed with nobody. LaTonya pulled a cot from the closet and told her to set it up for herself. That move shut up Skittles real quick.

Out of the corner of my eye, I see one of the double doors fling open and a lean Hispanic Sergeant floats in. He's in a squared-away starched uniform. Black Forest Cake glares at him, pointing to his watch but he gets a smile from Mrs. Gowan, which he returns. I try to look away but can't. Dark hair, dimples, and super cute, so he's hard to ignore and seems to know it. Not that I'm looking. Manolo is hotter than anyone.

"Welcome everyone," Mrs. Gowan says as the sergeant sits down opposite me. "My name is Mrs. Gowan. This is Staff Sergeant Zelder and Sergeant

Cortez just walked in. We want to tell you about your upcoming visit for anyone that arrived today."

Visit is an interesting word. I eye the other tourists to see their reaction. Nada, Zero, Zippo—no reaction. Are they listening? Some flick at their nails while others look at the carpet. Skittles' nibbles a cuticle. Guess it'll just be me who buys a Cuckoo clock in the Gift Shop.

Mrs. Gowan says, "It's been a busy day and some of you are jet-lagged, so we will keep this short. We have team meetings every night where you can share your problems or concerns. We support each other here without fear of judgement. This time is for *you* to help *each other*."

I don't like this idea. Nobody responds but one guy nods. She takes this as a win.

She sits up straighter. "Okay. Great. Let's go around and share our names. No reason to say your diagnosis if it makes you uncomfortable. Let's start with our elected President, Robert."

Elected President? Now I know I'm in a nut house.

Mrs. Gowan smiles at the Black muscular guy a few patients down from me. He sighs and looks up from the floor. His wavy, thick hair sticks out high on his head and his beard is all chin stubble. He's got his elbows on his knees and his hands come together in a peak to his chin. One knee shakes fast, but his face shows no concern.

"Yeah, sure, no problem." He leans back but his knee keeps tapping. "I'm Robert. The doc's got me pegged with PTSD, some anxiety, depression. You know, the usual."

So much for secret diagnosis.

Mr. President rambles on. "Been here thirteen days and ready to get out in two. Depends on my chain of command, they're here in Germany. First AD. Army's kicking me out, which I ain't got a problem with. I can't take scooping up body parts no more. I'm done with it. For real. That's all I got to say, guys."

Mrs. Gowan smiles at him. He returns a sheepish look. She nods to the next victim, a boxy Filipino-looking soldier slumped down in his seat, eyes on the ground. A pair of crutches lean on the back of his chair. Looks like the quiet, caged type.

With his eyes on the ground, he growls out, "First Sergeant says I got survivor's guilt. I was in the turret, covering for my buddy Smitty who sat shotgun. We hit an IED, whole vehicle burned up quick. I jumped. I thought they followed me out. Swear to God. I swear I thought they were right behind me..."

His voice cracks and the pain leaks out his eyes. He's screwed up because he survived. I swallow hard. I understand that. I think all of us in here understand that.

President Robert sits up and fixes his gaze on him. "You didn't kill 'em bro, the IED did. You gotta release that guilt, it's gonna kill ya. Then y'all dead, every one-of-ya."

The slumped soldier wipes his eyes without a glance up. Robert doesn't look away. Eventually the slumped soldier looks up and their eyes meet. Tears in both their eyes. He nods at Robert then looks down again.

"Thank you for sharing," Mrs. Gowan says gently, "As you can see, a lot of others in the circle have similar experiences, that's why we share. Next, please."

Next Please doesn't move. Black Forest Cake sits up straight as he clears his throat.

"Hernandez. JUAN. Now!" he barks.

Patient Juan yawns. He might be Mexican, maybe Dominican. Could be Puerto Rican. Looks goofy with big ears, buggy eyes, and paunch—a Hispanic Bart Simpson.

"Sorry, Sarge. Hey guys," he says as he sits up, "It's my third time here, let me tell ya, this place is easy, I'm not complaining, no sir. We get our paychecks to do nothing 'cept for take naps and make crafts. We go to the gym. Draw. And they bring us meals on trays. You don't have to do shit. Still get the same paycheck."

"Hernandez, that's enough of that," Black Forest Cake says. Sharply, irritated.

"Just speaking the truth, Sarge." Juan wipes his nose on his sleeve.

"You're speaking trash," Black Forest speaks over him and points to the Next.

Next is an older white lady with wrinkles around her blue eyes—maybe forty or so.

"I'm Allaine and like to get really high," she says as she bats her lashes. She speaks in a light British accent, trilling the r. "I do it by buying cantaloupe at the Commissary then selling it door-to-door to Germans. I sell it every day, rain or shine. If it's on sale, I sell the Honey Dew."

She goes on and explains how the Germans pay her for the cantaloupe or they pay her to go away. Either way, she gets enough for her drugs. "I'm a business woman."

Mrs. Gowan says, "It's time to take responsibility for yourself and stop using."

I frown and look at the others, who aren't looking at me and seem to have no problem she's a druggie. What the hell. I can't relate to this lunatic. I never tried a drug stronger than cough syrup. Why on earth is a civilian with a drug problem mixed in with us from the war? I scan the room with more intensity. I realize that we are a mix of civilian and military and this doesn't make me feel good. I'm starting to think nobody in here will understand me at all.

On we go. One solid-as-a-rock built-up Black female says she tried to commit suicide three times but gives no details. Why she wants to kill herself is something I'll never ask. On her left is a lean, balding, bi-polar white dude who holds up a shaking hand to show the side effects of lithium—a nonstop tremor. There's no way he could pull the pin on a grenade, he'll be chaptered out for sure.

"Don't worry," he says in the direction of the three of us roommates as he motions to his crotch, "No erectile dysfunction over here."

Gross. I twist my body into a pretzel on the hard chair and shift away from him.

"That's not appropriate," Mrs. Gowan warns him, but he continues to give our corner a ridiculous smile while pointing at his weenie. My temper flares and I mock cut up his weenie.

"*That's* not appropriate," he whines, flustered. I shake my head at him—I just want guys like him away from me. LaTonya *tsks* as I twirl my damp hair around my finger over and over.

The next one was on the C-130 with us. He slept the whole way. Guy's a short white dude, but super-stacked with a wide, red runny nose and thick black glasses. He looks us over.

"I guess we go by first names. I'm Peter. Don't say Pan, that shit ain't funny. Marines."

Someone in the circle gives out the Marine battle cry, "Oorah."

"Oorah," Peter says back as he leans forward in his chair. "Anyways, me, well, I was poisoned before we deployed and I…I…I told the cops to arrest the whore bartender who served me. She's a spy, trying to sabotage us, all of us, so you better be careful, guys."

"We're here to help you with these ideas," Mrs. Gowan says with sincere optimism.

He looks at all of us and wags a thick finger. "I ain't sweet, neither. I'm no gay bastard. If anyone calls me Kool-Aid, I will fuckin' bust your shit."

I hear this and stop twirling my hair. I feel him, big time. His reaction to being called Sweet is how I feel about being called Jelly except without the prejudice.

Juan wakes up to this and smiles a big grin at him. "Betuwon't."

"Guaran-fucking-teed, man. Ask anyone. One of those sand monkeys was calling me Sweet. Shot the shit out of him and the whole soccer field."

President Robert sits up, very pissed, "Watch your fuckin' mouth, bro."

"Enough! That's enough, Peter, be careful of word choice. We are respectful here," Mrs. Gowan says as Black Forest Cake glowers at Juan and spits out, "Moving on."

Skittles. She sits with her arms and legs crossed. Grumpy, but talkative.

"Right. Okay. I shouldn't be here, like not at all. I need to go back downrange and prove this is all one mistake. I was joking when I said I wanted to shoot my Platoon Sergeant. I mean, everyone was thinking it, but I just said it out loud. I should go back and get it straight, right?"

Nobody answers that sort-of question we know the answer to. We keep going.

LaTonya's been diagnosed with a personality disorder.

"I'm unsure what that means," she says to Mrs. Gowan. "The doctor didn't say."

Mrs. Gowan says not to worry. "You'll have a new doctor on Monday to explain your diagnosis and discuss your treatment plan."

The room is quiet.

It's my turn. I sit up straight and try to take a deep breath, but my throat is so dry, it hurts. I cough and cough. It turns into a coughing jag and I can't stop it.

Mrs. Gowan has sympathetic eyes. "Would you like some water?"

I nod my head and she jumps to her feet. I'm a little mad she's leaving me, but I can't talk otherwise.

Black Forest Cake taps his fingers against his large knee and looks around as I cough.

He asks, "Anyone else got something to say?" Nobody raises their hand.

My cough lessens a smidge as the door shuts behind Mrs. Gowan. I loudly clear my throat to break up the dryness and cough again. Numbskull Black Forest Cake doesn't look at me but comes to life, fists on his hips, and speaks.

"Listen up. Mrs. Gowan forgot to mention that talking in group is important for two reasons. One—it helps us all get to know each other. We're a team here so we should know each other. Second, sharing means admitting you got a problem. None of you would be here if you were normal. Each and every one of you has a problem and I've got lots of experience with you people. You'll all do what I say, got it? If you're thinking for a minute you don't got to follow my rules, it will make your life real hard. I'm the team coach. Hear me, Ashe? I'm talking to you, you know."

The room gets smaller. I'm too shocked to try to respond. He's got no right to say this, especially in front of the whole room. I feel everyone looking at me, the most messed up one that needs a good talking-to.

Mrs. Gowan re-enters the room right after his little rant and hands me a bottled water. I hold back hot tears as I unscrew the cap and take a swig. She takes a seat. Her face twists into a frown. Even she can tell something happened.

Go fuck yourself is on the tip of my tongue but I suck it inside and plaster on my resting bitch face. If *this* is a team and he's one of the coaches, I'm getting off this team.

"*No hablo inglés*," I say, straight faced. This is followed by the longest second on record.

"Speak English, Ashe," Black Forest Cake says as his face darkens, "Then we can move on to people with real problems." Mrs. Gowan looks at him, her lips pursed tight, but averts her eyes when he looks at her with a scowl.

Mrs. Gowan leans towards me with a sweet smile, "Part of recovery is sharing with others, Private Ashe, so we can all help each other. That's why we're here."

Ten to fourteen days of *this*? Ten to fourteen days of making me feel like crap and taking it? God help me. I'm no doctor. I'm no nurse. If me helping others is the plan, we're all fucked.

"*No entiendo, Señora.*"

"Aw shit," Juan says loud enough for all to hear. Black Forest Cakes lets out a *pfff.*

"Sergeant Ashe," Mrs. Gowan emphasizes my rank, promoting me in seconds.

I refuse to cooperate, even with her. *"No soy yo."*

"Cortez, take her out," Black Forest Cake growls with an impatient flick of his hand.

"*Ven conmigo, por favor*," Cortez says and stands.

I cock my head to the side and narrow my eyes at him.

I hear Juan say under his breath, "*Es un buen guey. No te preocupes.*"

He's telling me that Cortez is okay. I don't trust anyone but between the two in here and him, I choose Latin Vogue. I get up and follow him into the hallway. I expect a scolding or speech, but he doesn't stop. We walk along the hallway until we stop outside a large door. He pulls out his dog tags, finds a key, unlocks it and opens the door to the stairwell. We head down the cement stairs. I jam my fists into my robe pockets. The last few times I was alone with a male flash through my mind and my heart races. I feel a panic rising but he doesn't stop and I follow.

A few steps in front of me, he reaches the first level and shoves open the thick metal door. In less than a second, we're outside. It's warmer than upstairs and I lower my hunched shoulders. What a relief. I look around to see the large lawn illuminated partly by stadium lights, partly by the moon, and partly by all the vehicle lights that pass by. Way in front of me, a little vanilla-icing-white rotunda connects to a tiny bridge over a sea of flowers. Purple, lush lavender plants stand in perfect order. It's like the setting of a fancy wedding where the bride walks over the bridge to meet her new husband. This idea makes me depressed and I regret looking across the yard. I turn my back to it.

Cortez fishes out his cigarettes from his breast pocket, slaps his pack, and lights up.

"*Fumas*?" he says. I shake my head.

"Gotta tell you, that's a new one—*no hablo ingles. Hablas espanol*?"

I ignore the question and shrug. He seems nice enough, but that doesn't mean anything. He could be a serial killer or a rapist or the type who rolls his boogers and eats them or even worse, a former MP. Worst of all, SF. So the less he knows about me, the better.

I play it safe and change the subject back to him. "You're paying to kill yourself."

"If you don't smoke, you don't get breaks," he says and coughs that rusty smoker cough.

I involuntarily take a few steps back. I don't love the smell of smoke.

He watches me. "Hey, *amiga*. Don't even think about running; you won't get far."

"No place to go," I say with another shrug.

He breathes out his smoke high above my head. We stand a few feet apart as he smokes in and out. I say nothing, but think everything.

"Zelder's as useful as tits on a bull," I say, which sounds weird out loud.

He shoots me a worried look. "He's powerful," he says. "Piss him off and you'll have status checks every fifteen minutes. No joke, sometimes even five minutes if he's really pissed. He's not a doctor but he's the real boss, if you know what I mean."

I nod. I do know what he means. There's always the guy that assumes the role of commander in the absence of real leadership. They're in charge based on their own say-so, and nobody wants to challenge. It's easier to just go along. I nibble the bottom of my lip as it sinks in. If he's the boss, I'm dead meat.

A gentle breeze scatters the flowers in front of us, and my damp hair blows into my face. I shiver and pull the thin robe around me tighter. I see him studying me. He smiles. Reveals a deep dimple. I feel my face flush and look away then return his gaze. I see sympathy in his dark eyes, which makes me feel better somehow.

He says quietly, "I heard that you shot a Special Forces captain. Normally you'd be locked up doing something like that, but you're here under psych eval. Was it a flashback?"

The question is a surprise. I cringe inside. Truthfully, I'm not certain how it went down.

He continues to smoke and look.

"I—-I don't know, it just went so fast," I admit with hesitation. One second, I was listening to Privates complain about guard duty. Then I lost all awareness. Next thing I know; I'm tied up with Butler's ugly face staring down at me. A whole bunch of time is just gone from my mind, like it never happened. Except that it did happen because I have the aches and the bruises to prove it. I had the pee in my hair to prove what happened with Shorty and now it's Black Forest Cake, who I *hope* doesn't come near me again. My whole body starts to panic and get hot.

I take a step closer to Cortez and ask, "How do I get out of here, fast?"

He looks at me and I mean *really* looks at me, up and down. Our eyes meet and he stares hard. "You happen to be pregnant?"

The question hits like an explosive. I'm speechless for a few seconds. Then fury. Rage. Finally, I speak—no, *yell*—out my response.

"Whatever you heard, it's *false,* okay. Made up bullshit. And it's so crazy that you'd even ask…you can't ask any woman, not even a soldier."

He says nothing, but pulls back a few inches. He has no idea the nerve he hit.

"Woah," he says.

I'm not done. Still mad. I wrap my arms tight around myself and play with the layer of fat in my middle. "You're basically calling me a lard ass with a flabby stomach."

I realize I'm shouting but I cannot help it, even though my voice shakes. He makes a time-out sign with his hands as he takes a drag, raises his chin and blows the smoke above me.

"Calm down, Ashe. That's not what I meant."

I am *not* calm. I am trembling all over. I look down at my stomach and slide my hand across my belly—it's still flat. I'm not pregnant. Manolo and I were always super careful about that and besides—well, no. Answer is no.

"Do I look fat?"

He laughs. "No. Jeez. You need to eat *more.* But soldiers with other medical conditions that we can't treat on the psych ward get sent to Walter Reed as soon as possible. You just said you want to leave, that's why I asked. We always send the pregnant ones to Walter Reed ASAP."

I feel a twinge of hope, and a shit load of embarrassment. There I go again. Getting wound up tighter than a tick's ass. I stop myself from saying anything other than, "Who else?"

He shrugs. "Lots of soldiers move after a few days, not just in this ward. Most of the injured are first operated on in country, sent and stabilized here, then on to Walter Reed for follow-up care. Landstuhl keeps the guys with heart attacks and kidney stones until they recover, and then we send them back to Iraq or Afghanistan. Only the soldiers actually stationed in Germany or Italy don't get sent on to Walter Reed."

Cortez squashes the cigarette under his boot. I say nothing. My unit is stateside. This is the one of the few times I've ever been glad to be assigned to Fort Shithole.

I'm curious. "Have you been to Walter Reed? Or know anyone?"

Cortez tilts his head to the opposite side of me, spits, then wipes his mouth.

"Sorry," he says, not giving an answer to my question.

I have to know. "Is it better than here?"

He meets my gaze and sighs. "Here's not bad, but it's small. Walter Reed's bigger with a lot more staff. It's a training hospital so there are loads of doctors, mostly military but also civilians, which means more females. It has a good reputation, but I don't know personally."

So I need to get there, then. But…my breathing stops.

I feel sick as I ask, "Patients fly in the C-130's to the States?"

He shakes his head. "If you can walk, they'll give you civvies to wear and get a group together for a commercial flight. They leave every day, even on weekends."

I am very happy with this conversation. Staying here will be another catastrophe in my long list of recent disasters. This whole mess of my life shouldn't have happened. I'll have to take a chance…can't live life here. I try not to get worked up, but my heart races.

"I shouldn't be here." I blurt that out louder than I intend.

Cortez shoots me a look. "Too late for that, *amiga. Comprendes*?"

I nod, but look away and wrap my arms around myself even tighter. I have a full view of the meticulous, green landscape that surrounds the buildings. Each structure is lined with full flower beds of thriving, leafy plants. I catch a whiff of lavender, and know I smell rosemary and sage. Freshly cut grass. I breath in those scents, the smells of the prior-to-Army era for me, before my service. Countryside scents. Cute kittens and fluffy bunnies. Happiness.

He looks at his watch. Casio. Rubber-y looking band. I can't wear those, ever. Latex, rubber, whatever. I unwrap my arms from around my waist. Deep within my exhausted brain, an idea starts to form. I may have a way out of here, and soon.

He says nicely, "We'll have to head up again."

I nod. My new plan may work…if things go right. I almost forgot a few things about myself that existed prior to joining. But those things are exactly what I need now.

CHAPTER 7

Amanda, H-Status

"CAN YOU STOP moving, please?" Skittles says super polite, like she thought about asking for ten minutes before she snapped inside and finally did.

I freeze. "Sorry."

I don't want to be noisy but these stiff sheets make a swishing noise every time I move, which is like every three seconds because I cannot get comfortable. Not only are there no locks on the doors, we have new staff members coming who could be *anyone.* I tried to make a bed in our small bathroom that actually locks, but the staffer on duty said no can do.

My roommates both got strong sleeping pills for their night meds, but not me. I didn't come with any prescriptions and doctors prescribe meds, not nurses. It's for the best, though, so I can keep watch as they sleep. I press my face into the pillow. No use. I roll on to my back, stare at the ceiling, at the dark corners of the room.

It's useless even *pretending* I'm going to sleep. I figure I'll just annoy my roommates. I kick off the sheets and slink out of the room. I stand on the other side of our door and hear the new nurses and staff shuffle in for shift change. I peek my head out and see Mrs. Gowan's back, her small shoulders slumped over. She wears a pastel pink sweater on top of her scrubs and a large silver coffee mug hangs from her right hand.

"A new patient named Ashe is on H status," I overhear Black Forest Cake announce to the new nurses. I see him swinging a massive blue cooler in his hand and he points with his bear paw thumb towards our direction. I jump back so they can't see me, then lean back to hear more.

"Already on H Status?" a female nurse says, raising her pitch, "What for?"

"Let me tell you…," he trails off as he points at the clipboard in his hand. They get quiet so I can't hear. Time to boogey. I tiptoe into our room and lay on the rigid bed. Can't even imagine the shit he's spreading.

I whisper my warning to the others, "I'm on something called H-status."

Skittles lies on her stomach with her head stuffed into her pillow. She turns towards me, on her side. Without her purple eyes, she seems softer and prettier. More real.

She says in a calm way, "Maybe it means health or happy." She's an optimist like Weisengard.

I stare at the ceiling thinking of H words. Hero. Helicopter. High-value target. Hazard. Hate. Hygiene. LaTonya turns over onto her back and smashes the pillow over her face.

"It will suck," LaTonya says from under her pillow. "H stands for HELL."

I wince and rub my wrist back and forth. I whisper, "Hope not."

"Nothin' you can do 'bout it," LaTonya says still under her pillow. "Go to bed."

In a few more minutes, both snore. Soft. Not the saw-wood racket Dad makes. And Connor. God, I'm really alone.

Maybe meds are the only way to sleep in here. It's so cold in my thin pajamas and the sheet is as thick as a tissue. I run my fingers over my ribs, still thinking about what Cortez said. I pinch a roll of skin between my fingers and thumb, squeezing hard until my nails cut flesh. That's what I get for being a chunky Brewster, no wonder he thought I was pregnant. Manolo would hate how fat I got in Kuwait. I have enough ass for six women.

I try to stay up but I'm tired. Sometime later I drift off to sleep. Doesn't last long.

In a couple of hours, I learn what H status means.

It means that in the middle of the night, the doors are thrown open, the lights flipped on, and I'm told to move my ass out of bed. I squint to make out the time; I'm confused and disoriented. Oh, God. I look around and see my roommates slumbering on, eyes closed and dreaming like innocent little kitties. Oh, yeah. I'm *here.*

"Ashe. Blood draw, now," a squat, white female staffer from the doorway shouts.

I jump up and switch the lights off. I wrap my robe around me and scoot out.

I follow the short grouch down the hallway and into a small room at the end of the hall. Vital-sign machines line up against the wall like soldiers at attention. I take off my robe. She points where I need to sit and wraps a rubber tube around my left bicep. I don't even have to look at her to know she's scowling as she inserts the long, hollow needle into my arm. I'm dehydrated, and it comes out of me at the rate of thick manure through a thin pipe.

"What's H-status?" I ask her as I watch the skin around the tube turn red. I don't want her to notice this skin reaction so I pull my shoulder as far back as I can in the socket, making the sleeve cover part of it.

"Why?" she says as she drums her nails on her leg. She's wearing mint green scrubs for a top but BDU pants on her legs. She *must* be a soldier. Nobody else dresses like that.

"Is getting blood drawn at 2 a.m. H-status?"

She doesn't make eye contact and sighs dramatically.

I lean forward. "Come on, just tell me what's going on. Nobody tells me nothing. It's not like this is a deployment and everything is top secret."

"Kuwait isn't a real deployment," she says without looking up from the needle. So. She must have heard some talk about me, if she knows that fact. I can imagine what else she heard.

I lean back, not flinching at the twat's words. "Before this, I was in Iraq for a year. Eighteen months, actually."

She says nothing and suddenly I get an idea why she wears scrubs on the top.

"Where'd you deploy?" I ask but I already know the answer: nowhere.

She shrinks back and avoids eye contact. Her voice shrivels up as she states, "I almost went to Iraq but they needed me to stay here."

Ha! Knew it. The soldier has a needle in my arm, so I'm not saying anything, but I smile inwardly, a slight upper hand on her. Everyone hates the *I Almost Went to Iraq* guy, the one who is all smoke and mirrors and bullshit. I might be the one considered crazy between the two of us, but I have what she doesn't: a combat patch. This shouldn't make me feel good—at all—because the Army sucks, but it's nice to one-up her, since she is being a bimbo.

I glance around the room and then at my arm. It's starting to itch so I make a tight fist to rush the blood along. Four vials later, I finish and she slides the needle out, holds gauze over my arm but doesn't stand up. I pull the tube off my arm and take over pressing the gauze.

Arrogantly she points her finger in my face and says, "I don't need to deploy, I've seen a lot. When I get out of the army, I'm gonna write a book about all of the losers coming in here. Complain about everything, always whining. I can't believe they're in the Army."

I am angry. Rage, I feel it boiling inside of me. But I purse my lips tight and keep it in.

Instead, when I speak, I am inches from her face, making sure she hears me.

"That's called an autobiography," I say and then stand up.

Ah, man, she pisses me off but anything I do can and will be used against me. The clock on the wall says it's 2:45 a.m. and walk out of the room. I hear her say *hey* to get me to stop. I don't. So she speeds past me, like I planned she would. Halfway down the hallway, I stop.

"I forgot my robe," I tell her, but to her back.

Before she can turn or say anything, I rush back to the room. My robe is where I left it—right on the chair—and the box of latex gloves is on the table next to it. Latex doesn't seem to bother me as bad as rubber, but they both cause me problems. I rip as many out of the box as I can, squash them into my pockets, and walk out to meet her at the doorway.

"Let's go," is all she says as she leads me back to my room. I creep stealthily back into the room and lie down, careful not to wake up LaTonya or Skittles.

I put two of the gloves on my hand, over my legs, and on my stomach. I lay another on my pillow and roll my face into it. With any luck, I'll have a scaly skin rash soon. Maybe even some swelling. With any luck, I'll look good enough to evacuate.

❧

I'M CONFUSED. I hear a loud bang. The door flies open and the florescent lights switch on. My body jerks awake and I squint my eyes open. For God's sake, what time is it? It's still dark outside, so I don't know. I'm mixed-up, lying on my back but know soon it's about to end.

Black Forest Cake bounds into our room, clipboard in hand.

Shit.

"H status checks! Checks, *ladies*!" The last word sounds patronizing, like we aren't ladies at all.

Why are you still here? I want to shout. His shift should be over by now.

He doesn't look at me as he speaks loud enough for the whole hospital to hear. "Get up. Up."

Skittles and LaTonya open their eyes, confused. They shimmy out of bed and I scoot off the side, clutching the gloves under my robe. Nobody's looking. I stuff them back into my pockets and make fists to hide the bulge.

"What's wrong with your face?" LaTonya mouths to me. I pull my hand out of my pocket and look down at my right hand to see raised red, scaly bumps on my palms and back of hand. I touch my face and feel the same. My nose is running and I feel my eyes watering. Good, but not good enough to leave and get away from this jerk.

"What's wrong?" LaTonya mouths again. I shrug.

As he throws open our drawers and flings our undies on the floor, he talks to himself about *soldiers these days*, meaning us. *Too lazy*, he murmurs. Sleep too much. Complain too much. Eat too much. *Too much*, he says. I squeeze my hands tight around the gloves, thinking.

As he walks over the pile, he kicks a pair of socks. Complaining we have too many clothes. That's enough for me. I rip a finger from a glove and slip it into my mouth. Almost immediately, I start to gasp as my throat closes.

Shit, this isn't my plan! I try to spit it out, but it's stuck between my lips and gums. My swollen tongue isn't able to get it free. My throat is closing too fast, way quicker than when I was a kid. Like breathing through a straw. Panic rises quickly.

I see him dig his arms under the bed so his chin hits the edge of the mattress. Then he pulls himself free, loosening our sheets. Both of my hands clutch at my throat and I can't think straight. I know that I have to get the latex out of my mouth, but my hands are frozen.

"Sergeant, something's wrong with Ashe!" LaTonya shouts.

"Clear," he says without acknowledging her. "Pick it up and put it away. Next check starts in fifteen minutes so get going."

"She can't breathe!" Skittles yells and rushes towards me.

He crosses his arms as he cocks his eyebrow. I watch him watch me, then I can't stand anymore and slink down to the floor. Skittles slinks with me and holds my sides.

He takes two swift steps forward as he growls, "What's wrong with you now!?"

LaTonya rushes to my side. "It's okay, just relax. Breathe, okay?"

Get it out of your mouth, is all I can think but I can't move. Suddenly, I wheeze too hard and accidently swallow the little piece of latex in my mouth. I gag, then cough. Someone is rubbing my back but things are blurry. Snot is running down my face and my vision is turning on and off. Out of the corner of my eye, I see Skittles run out of the room, screaming for help.

This is bad. Sweat runs down my back and pools into my undies, my hands shake and my lips tremble. I feel my stomach quench and I crawl over to the garbage can, my only hope to get the latex out. I've been doing this for years now and don't even need to stick my finger down my throat anymore; hopefully, my windpipe is still wide enough. I close my eyes and imagine a milky-white glob in my stomach that must come out. I tell myself like I always do: *Get it out, Amanda! Puke!*

Water mixed with bile heave up and clear trickles of spit land in the garbage the second that Skittles rushes back with two nurses on duty. I hear Black Forest Cake's voice, loud and angry. I hear a nurse give orders clearly, enunciating her words and more and more people come into our little space, all in scrubs.

Skittles screams, "Oh Lord, don't let her die!"

Soon, I'm lying on the floor, then two guys lift me and heave my body on to a gurney. I want to ask the one on my right what H-status is, but I don't get the words out. In an instant, my swollen eyes close and the whole mess of the room disappears to black.

CHAPTER 8

Amanda, Way Out

A PRETTY NURSE dressed in pink and white polka dot scrubs stands at the foot of my bed. She's reviewing a clipboard. Her hair is slicked back into a tight bun, but I can tell by the gigantic diamond stud in her nose that she's not a soldier. Her high cheekbones and full lips remind me of Jo, but her skin is a shade of warm, wet sand, while Jo is the same shade of pale as me. The angled glasses perched on the tip of her nose make it look like she's reading a book and not my chart.

I know this is not the psych ward. A white curtain hangs to one side making a sort-of privacy wall. Sun shines dimly through a small window. TV is off, tucked up near the corner perpendicular to the window, and the walls are a bright, glaring white. It smells like cold syrup. A needle attached to an IV is stuck in my right arm. My mouth is dry. I'm thirsty.

Nurse notices me looking at her.

"Good afternoon," she says, pushing her glasses up and smiling.

I try to clear my throat, but it's scratchy and hurts like hell. Nurse comes up to the side of my bed and holds up a pink plastic glass filled with ice water and a straw. She holds it steady as I take a long drink. Reminds me of bottle-feeding calves on the farm, except I'm the calf in this situation. It feels terrific going down with this nurse holding my drink, her being nice, but then I remember what happened to get me here. Pressure builds in my head and forces me to sit up and stop swallowing. I shake the water down my throat. Cough.

"Thanks," I manage to croak out. I feel shame.

In spite of my situation, I understand something terrible. I did this.

I almost killed myself.

Over what? Black Forest Cake. I really am going nuts. *I'm such an idiot.* I should never have put that in my mouth. I took it too far.

I hold up my hands and look at myself. Rashes are clearing up. Thank God.

Nurse sets the water on a small side tray table.

"Don't send me back," I beg, but in a whisper, so I'm not sure she heard me.

"You've had quite a day," she says smiling in a way that makes me understand she's glad the morning belonged to *me* and not *her*. I notice the clock on the wall. It says almost five o'clock, which must be in the evening. I've been asleep for hours. She steps closer.

"I need to ask you some personal questions, okay?" She has a pitying look on her face, almost like she doesn't know where to start.

I nod to say it's okay but feel a little sick. My pulse quickens with worry.

"Earlier today, we noticed that you have some severe bruising in your pubic region. Lacerations, cuts. Amanda," she says very gently. "Amanda, were you sexually assaulted or raped in the past 24 hours?"

I turn to look at her, not even able to hide my surprise. I thought she'd ask me about the latex, instead she's worried I might have been hurt. Tears fill my eyes, but I shake my head. I see relief wash over her pretty face.

She continues in a serene voice. "Are you hurt anywhere else that maybe we didn't see?"

"No," I lie because she can't see inside my head. Physically, though, that's it.

"I'll let the doctor know that you're awake, okay? Give me a quick minute."

She steps past the curtain, and I hear a door open. I reach up to my face and feel my puffy, swollen cheeks. I stick my tongue out of my mouth but it's a normal size now. I lie on the bed and cover my face with my hands to hide the tears swimming in my eyes. *Stop, Amanda, you're fine.*

The curtain swooshes open and youngish blonde guy with a high and tight haircut enters the room. He looks like he belongs on TV with his stethoscope, faded blue scrubs and bright white tennis shoes. The nurse follows in behind him. I wipe my eyes.

"Sergeant Ashe, nice to see you awake." He flashes a smile at me as he grabs my chart from the nurse.

"I'm a Private."

"I see." He pulls a rolling stool next to me so we are almost at eye level, which makes me think he's really short. He flips the page, reads, then looks down at my hands and up around my face, but doesn't mention how puffy it is, which I appreciate.

"You had a terrible allergic reaction this morning."

I nod my head and grasp my sheet.

"What we're trying to figure out is from *what.* Your chart indicates you have no known allergies. Upstairs told us you didn't take any medicine from the hospital. No creams. Lotions. Nothing. But think about it, okay? Really think back to this morning. Did you use a new type of soap? Did you take any type of herbal supplements or vitamins or maybe you ate something out of the ordinary?"

I shake my head. "They took everything from me when I arrived. And I showered yesterday afternoon, so no."

"Right." He considers what I said. "This is deathly serious. We had to give you a shot of epinephrine. Have you ever used that in the past for an allergic reaction?"

I cough and cover my mouth. Two answers to that question exist: the truth and what the recruiter told me to say. When I signed up, I really did tell him about my rubber allergy. He asked me if I can control it and I said yes, which I can. Recruiter said that under no circumstances should I ever admit I had this allergy prior to service. *Repeat after me, Ashe: No medical illnesses existed prior to service.*

"Never," I lie.

Actually—five or six shots, at least. First real reaction came when I was five and had chewed the arm on Connor's Jesse "The Body" Ventura wrestling action figure. He owned all of them: Hulk Hogan, Macho Man Randy Savage, Junkyard Dog, Mr. T., Andre the Giant, Hillbilly Jim, and even the hard-to-find Brutus the Barber Beefcake. He went tattling to mom as my throat started to close.

The doctor stands up, worry on his face. "That's what I was afraid of. Listen, I'd like to send you on to Walter Reed. It's vital that we determine the cause of your reaction and they have a wide range of medical specialties, often the best in the world."

"Just like that?" Once again, I can't hide my surprise. Besides the almost dying part, getting out of Landstuhl and away from Black Forest Cake is almost too easy.

He flashes a Hollywood smile. "Walter Reed is a larger hospital."

"When do I go?"

The doctor and the nurse exchange a glance that I don't miss, and instantly I remember that I shot at shit-for-brains, so maybe going to Walter Reed will take some time. Maybe this plastic/latex allergy isn't my biggest concern. My mind races. I get there, get treated…then what? Getting medically discharged might be the best option out of all of the bad options. I re-upped in the first few months of our Iraq deployment for the cash bonus. I hate myself for that dumb decision, which added years to my enlistment. Man, if I'd have thought straight, I would've had this allergic reaction years ago and got out sooner. Stupid, stupid me.

He forces a smile. "Let's see what happens. If you have no concerns, I'll ask the team here to prep you for the first flight out tomorrow. That sound okay?"

I nod, hiding how happy that makes me. I should be even more excited, because it's exactly what I want…but it was too easy. Nothing is ever this easy in the Army.

❧

TV'S ON BUT I'm only half-watching. Overseas, all stations aired are from the American Forces Network—AFN. It's controlled by media dictators that pick and choose what they allow us to see. Worst part of all are the god-awful cheesy AFN commercials shown in between pre-cut shows saying crap like *Bam! Styrofoam can't be recycled, Yo!* and *Drink more water!* Seem to talk down to people worse than a new Atkins dieter.

Today, at least they got on *Friends*—the one with Rachel's sister saying that she's supposed to learn the value of the dollar from the "one daughter that dad's actually proud of."

That would be Jo in my family. Definitely she's the one we're proud of. In August, she won Grand Champion showmanship at the Waupeekie County Fair with her pig. Dad was super pumped and I'm sure Mom was, too. Imagine Mom knowing where I am right now. Disgrace.

I turn the volume down because I hear the metal curtain rings scratch along the metal rod making a *ting-ting* noise and see it move. I sit up straight and clutch the remote in my hand.

It's Cortez.

"Hey, sunshine," he says and pulls up a metal chair. Sits at my bedside. Looking good in some civvies—West Coast skater vibe. Baggy jeans and a graphic t-shirt. Black and white Vans. Musky cologne. He's holding a grey bag from the Post Exchange.

I feel the opposite of sunshine, but he comes in full of smiles, which he must know show off his dimples. I smooth the sheet down on my bed.

I smile, too. "Hi."

He leans forward. "You scared us this morning. How are you doing now?"

I shrug. "Fine. How are you?"

"Fine as well, thanks." He has a funny, forced smile. He adds, "It's my day off but I thought I'd swing by to see how you are."

My smile fades. Days off are few and far between. "You didn't have to do that. *Totally* not necessary."

He rubs the back of his neck with his free hand. "Really? Because I think I did. I feel like part of this is my fault."

I take a breath and let it out, my nerves on edge. Guilt. An emotion I understand. But he's not guilty of anything. I'm not sure what he means and I don't say anything. I switch off the TV for something to do.

He holds up the grey bag in his hand and sets it on the foot of my bed. "Some civilian clothes for your flight tomorrow, courtesy of the USO. Nurses picked it out for you, so don't blame me if you don't like velour tracksuits and white tennis shoes. We got your gear ready to go as well, so now you just have to wake up and get on that flight."

I nod. "Thanks. For the clothes and for checking on me. I appreciate it."

Silence. He regards me for a minute then reaches into his pocket and pulls out a wad of smashed up, used latex gloves. He sets them on the tray table next to the water cup.

Shit.

I swallow and hope I am keeping my face even.

He speaks low but looks me in the eye. "When I found out about what happened to you this morning, I went to the ward. Spoke with your roommates. Looked into the trash and found these gloves. They said they found them when cleaning up from a Health and Welfare check. I thought maybe you'd know *why*."

He pronounces the last word very clearly, but I'm focused on the word *Health*. I suppose that's what the H-status was, but you'd never know from what happened. I look away.

He's persistent. "Ashe. Do you know anything about these gloves?"

I want to ask him what he is trying to accuse me of, but I am afraid he will actually tell me. I chew on the inside of my cheek and think. I have to stick with what I said before.

I say as convincingly as I can, "I don't know."

He looks at me and lets out a loud sigh. "I'm no detective, okay, but this is what I think. You were a sergeant on gate guard. You shot at an SF officer from close range—didn't hurt him but could've. Seems like you got a beating after that, then you were sent here instead of taken by the MPs. Not sure why, but whatever. I don't know what happened on the C-130 that made you stink like a porta potty and put into Isolation upon arrival, but I suspect that's why you've had problems with Zelder and why you didn't cooperate at the meeting that got you sent outside with me— where I thought we had a decent conversation but seems as if I gave you a bad idea—and then this morning you almost died of anaphylactic shock. From what I gather, your allergic reaction was from these latex gloves, which seemed to have come from the blood draw room. I suspect you knew that you'd have a bad reaction, and so you snuck some out to use at night. What I'm trying to figure out is *why*. You don't act suicidal. Your intake form indicated that you don't have thoughts of hurting yourself, although it did say that you don't eat which I guess is part of what's happening. I've been trying to figure out *why* you almost killed yourself to leave here? *Why* shoot at an SF officer? *Why*?"

Why? For a second, I think of telling him, truly. He's been a good NCO, so caring and concerned. To see him looking so serious gives me a kind of a jolt to tell the truth. But it's too hard and I'm too tired.

I turn and face him. "So, did you?"

"Did I what?"

"Did you figure out *why*?"

He frowns, a look of disappointment on his face. "Ashe, I looked at your Enlisted Record Brief. High speed until the end of your Iraq deployment—below the zone, top block NCOERs. Then...not even mediocre. I've been a behavioral health specialist long enough to know it's related. What happened in Iraq that got you to take that shot?"

I hold in the hot tears forming in my eyes. Every emotion I've suppressed floods me: anger, sadness, shock, pain, humiliation, disappointment. My heart pounds hard in my chest.

"Forget it, okay?" I tell and ask him at the same time.

"I'm not trying to get you into trouble."

"I'm leaving anyway." I'm not sure how to feel right now.

He insists. "How did you know the SF officer?"

I look up at the ceiling. "I know what you're assuming and no, he wasn't my boyfriend. I barely talked to him. Just know that he deserved it. That's *why*."

"I'm sorry," he says, "I get your feelings, your resistance to talking. But help is available to you. Don't try to take things into your own hands."

I clutch my hands together, finding strength. I *wish* his words were true. He has no idea what he's talking about. It drives me crazy enough to argue.

"No, no, Cortez. There isn't *help* for me. The sad thing is that I tried to report him, okay? It all got swept under the rug. Reality is that he gets away with it and I got to deal with it alone." My voice sort of quivers. I bite my top lip to control myself.

"And how's that going for you?"

My eyes fall down to my hands. *He has no idea.*

I shrug without looking at him. "Fine."

I know he's a good dude and maybe even wants to help me, but what's the point? I'm leaving, he's staying. The army's full of people coming and going. It's a transient life that lets soldiers hide—in some cases—or move up quickly in the ranks in others. No wonder we keep our problems inside, not knowing who to talk to.

He sits there, not moving then gives a brisk flick to his baggy jeans. Wipes off imaginary crumbs. I know he feels bad for me, but I'm used to doing things on my own.

I feel like I have to defend myself. "I'm totally fine."

"Sure," he says. "Go ahead and lie to me as well as to yourself."

I stay silent.

"Well, I guess you should know that I lied to you, too." I turn suddenly to face him.

I'm surprised. Can't help but ask, "About what?"

He looks me directly in the eyes. "I know people at Walter Reed. My battle buddy is stationed in the Burn Center. A friend works in Ward 53, the Mental Health outpatient clinic. Last night I thought you were gonna ask for a favor, so I lied. I wish I hadn't. Seems like you're not the type to ask for favors anyway."

I feel the pit of my stomach clench. "I didn't lie. I. Am. Fine."

"Whoever it is that you'll be working with, I'm calling them up. I'm telling them about your allergy so you can't try that again. I'm letting them know you don't eat. I hope to God that you get a good treatment plan and a decent therapist."

I wince. Okay, fine, he can call up whoever he wants but it doesn't mean anything.

I shake my head.

"You're not alone in this, Ashe."

"You don't know me, Cortez."

"I know enough."

"What I did…" I trail off. Words fail me.

"What you did was a reaction to someone who hurt you."

The mention of that 'someone' taints everything. I shove aside the thoughts forming. I don't want to talk about any of this. To anyone. Ever.

"My life isn't your business, Cortez."

He sighs. "I'm an NCO. The second you got off that C-130 and became our patient, your life became my business, Ashe. I take my job seriously. Most of us do—including the doctor that unfortunately you never met. My team helps treat mental health disorders. Soldiers get better. You're not going to be able to do it on your own. Nobody does."

I sigh.

Nobody, he said. I'll show him. Nobody until me.

CHAPTER 9

Amanda, Hospital Nummer Zwei

IN 2006, WATER Reed Army Medical Center is the flagship army hospital. It stands at solemn attention in the middle of a sprawling campus behind black iron gates, six miles from the White House. Hospital has nearly a century of treating soldiers—and Presidents, too—under its belt and it looks it. Old and hardened.

Spread out over one-hundred thirteen acres, the base grew rapidly after opening in 1909, and by the 1970s a new hospital facility opened. Now they are known as Building 1 and Building 2. You can tell the difference in many ways, especially by the landscape. Original Building 1 is red brick, flanked by tall trees and shrubs. Building 2 is surrounded by concrete.

Civilians, patients, military members and families of all types and ranks buzz in and out of the main entrance of Building 2—day and night. Over 10,000 people live and work on the campus where the country's wounded warriors come to get fixed.

I know this all before I even see it.

Info like this was part of my knowledge test during the Soldier of the Quarter interviewing process. I studied for hours to prepare for that board; helped me get promoted.

Ride across the ocean was alright. Arrived in the middle of the day at Andrews Air Base on a clunky C-17, which turned out to not be a commercial flight at all. We still wore our civilian clothes. No Shorty Airman, thank the Lord. I was mostly ignored.

Tranquilized to prevent movement, I sat next to a sweet nurse who wiped drool off my chin along with her other duties. A bunch of physically injured guys were on the flight, some laid out on gurneys, others strapped down with blankets pulled to their chins. For sure, soldiers were in pain, but it appeared as if they were all going to live some version of life.

As we pull up, the hospital looks half super-villain fortress, half-hospital. White school bus we've been riding drops a group of us ambulatory types off in the front of it. Fresh cut grass in front smells so good, almost as nice as the smell of a large combine running through a wheat field. Large American flags above us, whipping in the wind. Weather's warm and sticky.

A heavyset Black nurse meets us. She calls out our names from her clipboard. I follow along with everyone else, all of us half drugged and slow. We pass banners saying "Welcome Warriors." Definitely gives me a feeling of shame. I'm walking while others are physically injured. There was a guy with no legs on our flight. I bite my cheek and follow.

Nurse leads us down a flight of stairs that connects to a completely empty space with large windows and posters proclaiming how great it is here. Thinking about it, maybe the bus dropped us off on the second level, although I can't figure it out. Is this the first floor? Nurse is fast, so I don't exactly look around. Eventually we arrive in the ER.

We sit and wait. It's not long until my name is called. I get a temporary bed. A tech says this as she leads me towards a tiny room big enough for an exam bed and equipment.

It's quiet where I am. Smells like pine sole disinfectant but the room isn't exactly clean. The first thing I notice about Walter Reed is the dirt. Not that I didn't see the water spots dotting the ceiling or the cracks in the floor, but the dirt is truly outstanding—whole pieces of crud waxed over by the janitors, creating fossils of gunk. Landstuhl sparkled like new chrome rims on Manolo's Mustang. Walter Reed is a dirty Humvee with broken tail lights.

There's not even a TV or an old copy of Soldier magazine. All I got are thoughts, as broken and cracked as they are. Every time I feel my eyes shiny with tears, I pinch the inside of my arm. *Shut up, Amanda*. I have nothing to cry about. I'm here, just like I wanted. I lay on my back and count. 142

ceiling tiles. 568 corners of ceiling tiles. 94 of the ceiling tiles have wet marks. Fourteen look gray. I think I sleep 'cause I'm startled when the door opens.

A bouncy Filipino nurse about my age comes in, humming a song I don't know. Her high ponytail sashays as she moves.

"Hello there," she says bubbly and cheerfully.

I clear my throat, "Hi."

"My name is Andrea and I'm a nurse. I'm here to take your vitals," she says and I nod in return, "Can you tell me your full name and last four of your social?"

"Amanda Ashe, 1-2-3-4."

The nurse is perky. Prances around the room, opening cupboards, washing her hands, and pulling on gloves. She moves to her music, swaying as she prepares herself. After the past 24 hours, I'm beyond glad to have someone like her helping me. Nice, kind. Happy. Lord, the memory of Black Forest Cake churns my stomach.

She takes my blood pressure and asks, "How was the flight?"

"Fine." I yawn. "Jet-lagged."

"I bet." She smiles at me, "I hope you stay with me for a while. We'll get you some good rest and a decent meal. I can roll in a TV for you, later. If you want."

I smile and nod. Carefully, she takes my temperature and draws blood, without the rubber band-thingy around my arm. She pulls out a warm blanket. I'm comfy and cozy.

There's a knock on the door. She looks quizzically at me then steps into the hallway.

A few minutes later, the nurse re-enters followed by a pudgy, male white orderly wearing Snoopy scrubs. She fakes a smile at me, while he doesn't hide his scowl.

"So that's it for now," she says. "He'll take you upstairs and when we need to run more tests, we'll come up and get you."

No! I'm finally comfortable and I want to stay here. I can't help but protest. "What about my rash?"

"It's under control at the moment. Don't worry. We'll make sure to monitor it," she says with forced enthusiasm. "It was so nice to meet you. They will take good care of you upstairs."

I nod. "Thanks," I say, and she smiles at me with her mouth, not her eyes, which makes me realize that upstairs might not be what I think it is.

Reluctantly, I leave the warm blanket and the nice nurse. Outside the door the orderly has a wheelchair ready for me.

"I can walk," I say.

"Better if you don't." Makes zero sense but I don't question Army wisdom. Better for him, probably, so he has a job. I get in the wheelchair.

"Ward 54, here we come," he says as he presses down on the brake release.

The way he says it makes me think chances are slim it's a desirable destination. Even with his grim expression, it can't be worse than Landstuhl. He pushes me through hallways full of young soldiers, nurses, doctors, Chaplains, and administrators. All going someplace. Easy listening music plays in the hallway. Stuff I've heard a zillion times because Dad played it in the barn. He swore music helped cows produce more milk. I told Manolo that once to make him laugh. God, I love his laugh.

I close my eyes. In the back of my brain, I feel a pulsing sensation of a headache.

Elevator *bings* and I open my eyes. A man walks off and the door closes again. I didn't know we were inside it; I'm so checked out. Good thing. Small spaces with dudes make me anxious. I look at the ceiling, but there are no tiles to count and calm down. The orderly looks at me with a deep frown. I jerk my face down and slump in the chair. *Bing!* The elevator opens. He pushes me out and we wheel along another hallway.

The pulsing sensation turns into a massive headache, spreading fast. The shockingly harsh fluorescent light in the hallway makes it worse. Shutting my eyes, I hear light piano music, which is nicer than the easy listening. We stop outside a thick set of double doors at the end of the hall. I peel my eyes open as he brakes and pushes a large button. I hear an awful, loud horn noise that pounds in my brain.

He speaks into an intercom. "Got another one for you."

"Roger," a voice crackles. Can't tell if it's male or female. "Bring her in."

The electronic double doors click slowly open. Gripping the wheelchair handles, he shoves me inside. Hard. My head jerks back. We enter and this gigantic wood-paneled nurse's station stops us. It's front and center. An odor burns my nose and I cough—it's stronger than the antiseptic iodine udder wash we use to clean up the cows before milking. I sneeze—hard. Look around to see chairs and a plastic couch next to the doorway. A Christmas tree stands without lights. It's September. Either they are super early or late. There's no music.

It's set to below freezing in here. I cross my arms and clutch at my sides. Two nurses in scrubs sit behind the desk. One hefty Black lady has her hair pulled back so tight I see her scalp. She's typing and focused on the computer screen. The other nurse is Black, too, with blue cat-eyed glasses perched on her small nose. Her hair is perfect ringlets, which are brown and gold–swirls of milk chocolate caramel. She eats orangish dusted chips as she talks on the phone. I suck down the drool forming in my mouth and rub my temples. This headache sucks.

"Thank you. Leave her there." The one typing on the computer yells, glancing over and waving. The orderly puts on the break and rests his hand on my shoulder like he's giving me my last rites. He squeezes my shoulder and splits a nanosecond later. I hear that god-awful noise of the door again, as it closes behind him.

Nobody says a word in my direction or even looks at me. Okay, this is not the reaction I expected on minute one of a psych ward. Clutching the sides of the chair, I stand. If the Army teaches you anything, it's to keep moving. Shifting targets are harder to shoot. I shuffle towards the faded noise of a television–where there's TV, there's soldiers, guaranteed. I need information about this place and the soldiers will tell it to me straight.

Lord, it's weird to be in here. I see six patients in green pajamas and blue robes along the walls of the hallway. They're standing and sitting. None of these soldiers does anything strange, they're just muttering, sputtering, talking, and laughing. One lady with long blonde hair faces the wall, completely motionless. Her hair looks like Allaine but it's impossible. Allaine is back on the streets of Germany selling her cantaloupe and this lady is here looking very medicated, as I was on the plane. Legal drugs versus Allaine's illegal ones. Same, same, but different.

The long, beige hall leads into a big, open room. Rows of plastic chairs line up against one of the walls that lead to a red touch-tone phone sitting on a table, unused. Three guys lounge on overstuffed chairs, staring at the TV. It's AFN. American Forces Network. Damn. There should be some type of American television since we're stateside. Not this lame garbage.

I quickly about-face. Too fast. As I spin, I run smack into a tiny *Don't Fucking Touch Me* who was trolling the hall to my rear.

"Hey," she says loudly as we smash together. "Fuck you."

I stumble but catch myself, and stare at her. I'm 5'2" but a monster compared to this small pale white waif. Black eyeliner rims her bloodshot, green eyes and she has crusty falling-off mascara bits on her cheeks. Stringy, long black-dyed hair falls down her face. Her roots are a dirty blonde. She scowls. Bitch isn't just punk, she's *Stay Fucking 1,000 Miles Back Punk.*

I recover. Stand up tall and cross my arms. Say, "It was an accident."

Bitch crosses her own arms to reveal a tattoo on her forearm, a crucifix made of snakes. Looks more like a tattooed, pissed off toddler than a soldier.

Blue cat-eye glasses nurse from the front magically appears between us. Her ringlets frame her smiling face, revealing a big gap in her teeth. Up close I see she wears winged eyeliner that compliments her Cat-Eye glasses. Her hands are formed into a prayer between us.

Firmly, she orders, "Ladies, separate. Katie, please return to your room."

I step back, relieved. The punk stays put.

She whines and points. "Why does she get to wear civvies?"

"She just arrived, Katie."

She scowls. "My name is fucking KAT-IA," she says louder than before. "But call me Private First Class Moon. That's my fucking name, got it?"

Who in the hell is she? Talking shit like this. Cat Eyes keeps her cool.

She stands firm. "I'm not asking you again. Return to your room."

The shrieks are awful. She jerks her thumb towards me, "Fuck you. I didn't do *nothing*. It's this bitch here who ran into me."

"Darrell!" Cat Eyes shouts out, not rattled one bit.

A stacked, Black bald man appears from around the corner. Looks like he lifts cars for fun. My God, he's got muscles in his pinky toe. Ears the size of cauliflower. Neck thicker than a bull. He stands tall next to Cat Eyes in starched blue scrubs. He's not smiling but not frowning, giving his eyes the look of two crescent moons. The punk girl scowls at big Darrell. She's 80 pounds soaking wet, and he's easily 250, and not an ounce of it is fat.

"Well, then, let's go PFC," Darrell says, waiting.

Clearly, she wants a fight. Fucking Katia gives me a hard glare, her frail white body pulses red. A blue vein throbs in her forehead under her translucent skin. Turning, she drags herself and her moccasins along the dirty floor. I can't help but stare. *How the fuck did she get in the Army?* Darrell guides her away but the awful feeling that began a few seconds ago stays.

"As for you, let's get your vitals," Cat Eyes says.

I stare at her, wide-eyed. "Literally just had 'em done in the ER."

She smiles. "Follow me. Won't take long."

Christ. I rub my pulsing forehead. I think about saying no and what that might look like. Would Darrell come and get me, too? And then what? I will follow her, I know this, but my imagination is running away with ideas. I'll run to the front doors, wait for the next sucker to be buzzed in, and bolt. Sneak out of this hospital and hitchhike to Mexico.

But not now. Not today. Instead, out loud I tell her, "I got a bad headache."

"Vitals first, then I'll get you Motrin."

I follow her. My bones feel rock heavy. Remnants of the massive dose of sedatives they stuck in me before the flight remain deep inside. A rotten thought overtakes my pounding brain.

"Wait," I say as I catch up to her. My knees are suddenly shaking.

I lean forward and whisper, "Am I on H-status?"

"What's H-status?" she asks, head tilted.

Good fucking question.

"Never mind," I say, "Let's go."

❧

PSYCH WARDS LIKE signs, but they really like to ask you about your own death. Intake is a bunch of questions, over and over again. *Are you suicidal? Do you want to hurt yourself? On a scale of one to ten, rate your mood. Rate your pain. Rate your life.*

"Do you have the feeling or thought that you don't want to live?" is the exact question.

"No," is my exact answer.

The staff says that they are here to protect the patients, but by these questions it seems like they just want to make sure we don't stab ourselves with a plastic knife. That would be a lot of paperwork, a lot of blame to go around. An officer might even get his hand slapped.

Cat Eyes fills out my forms but keeps flipping back to the documents from Landstuhl.

"What about this note that you didn't eat? You're gonna have to eat."

"I will," I lie, ashamed it's out in the open.

She sets down her pen, leans back in the chair, adjusts her glasses, and crosses her arms. Matter-of-factly she states, "I imagine it's not so easy, otherwise it wouldn't be in your file. Look at you. You got no meat on your bones. What'd you eat since yesterday?"

I lick my lips and shrug; I'm not admitting to her it was next to nothing.

"Uh-huh," she says, her eyebrow arched high.

"I do have safe foods I eat." I twirl my hair as I search for the words to explain, but I can't, so I say instead, "It's complicated."

She uncrosses her arms. "I'm sure it is. Listen, honey, I'm sorry to say I don't know much about recovery for eating disorders. It's not a common diagnosis here."

My heart starts pounding the second I register what she's saying. She's got me all wrong, since I am definitely not some emaciated teenager trying to get attention. I am just very selective and like to control what goes into my body. That's not an eating disorder, it's being healthy.

"I don't have an eating disorder," I inform her.

"Uh-huh."

She waits for me to say something, but I don't. It's hard to explain to someone else.

She sighs. "These safe foods you mentioned. I can get you a menu so you can pick what you want for each meal. There aren't too many options, but I'll call down to food services."

I nod. Unlike most people, I know exactly how many calories are in each food. It will be easy to fool the staff if I can order myself. "Yeah, that'd help a lot."

She nods. "Let's take it one day at a time. Getting better–it's a process. How else can I support you today, hon?"

Support me? She's being too nice. Like Mrs. Gowan was.

She repeats herself, "Need anything else?"

I choke out, "I...could I get a robe? It's cold in here."

She shakes her head. "No robes in Ward 54," she says back with a sad smile. "We're ordering new ones. Without belts."

That news makes me sick. I look up at the ceiling tiles. I stop myself from wondering how a soldier did it, but *me* of all people, know that where there's a will, there's a way.

After our chat, the inventory goes fast, everything nice and neat from a few days ago. When she's not looking, I palm my tweezers from my toiletry bag. I clutch it in between by thumb and my palm. I may need some type of protection in here. Black Forest Cake didn't do nothing, but he could have. A tweezers isn't much, but it's something.

After all, it is my property so technically it's called 'tactically acquiring what's mine.' When I was a kid, I stole one Root Beer barrel from Top Hardware. Mom saw the candy in the car, swatted my butt, and marched me back in there to apologize to the cashier as she squeezed my neck from behind. Stealing is wrong, she said. True, mostly. In the Army, it depends on your point of view. Soldiers know there's one thief in the Army and the rest of us are trying to recover our gear.

I follow her to my sparse, small room with two beds, a sink, two dressers, and an adjoining musty, tiny bathroom. She points out the shower settings and how to flush the finicky toilet. Jingle jingle, hold down for three then pull up.

"Now if I do get you some of your 'safe foods' is this latrine gonna be a problem?"

She's no dummy. Starvation and barfing do go together.

I shake my head. Hell no, not at all.

❧

WHOEVER SAID "TIME flies" never spent any in here. I'm sitting in the dayroom for chow. Showered and changed into the uniform of the ward—blue and green pajamas. I have on two pair, but I'm still cold. Army green socks. My civilian-USO-clothes were considered another form of contraband.

Dayroom is the same room as the room with the TV but on the opposite side. The divider that separates the two sides is pushed back so it's one long, continuous space. I see a ping-pong table and a bookshelf containing a few games and volumes in the same area as a TV. This side has round tables and folding chairs, a card table near a locked chest, and soldiers ready to eat.

Cellophane wrapped plates wait for us on a rolling meal delivery cart which must hold at least fifty meals, even though there aren't twenty of us. Smells like warm potatoes.

Staff told me to sit at a table with two male gym rats. Not as big as Darrell, but stacked enough. I stand here now, wishing that it was any other table. They look like former Green Berets. Great. Just great.

"We don't bite," one says and pushes the chair out for me without standing. I hesitate and look around. Slim pickings. Very few open seats and none by the few other females. I pull the chair out further and sit down. With my eyes, I say thanks. With my mouth, I say nothing.

Staffers start a head count.

"Not yet, hold up. Still waiting on Addictions 1," says one to another loud enough for us to hear and not ask questions.

"Here's most of 'em, so keep the flipping schedule," the other says, rubbing his brown buzz cut nervously. He stands, pulls trays from the cart, and delivers them to the closest patients.

A tray is placed in front of me. I didn't get to order because it was too close to meal time. Definitely, I don't want to eat this, but there's lukewarm coffee. My hand shakes as I grip the half-filled Styrofoam cup and sip. It's church coffee—watery but caffeinated. Warm. Dudes across from me inhale their chow. One chews his cud and I can see the chicken and peas all mashed together, rolling around on his tongue. *Close your damn mouth* I want to say but don't. I gag inside. Peas are a safe food, but not like this. Guy chugs his milk, smacks his teeth and digs out a stuck piece with his pinky nail.

The other soldier, the nice one who pushed out my chair, scrapes his food into four equal quadrants. Nothing touches. He's got tattoos on his hands and neck and a hole in his ear from a former plug. I don't know what his background is—a cross between a Filipino and a Hawaiian or hula islander of some type. No matter what it is, he concentrates laser-like, as if the pain from butter touching the chicken would be worse than a needle. He's a tattooed, buff Obsessive-Compulsive by the looks of it.

"What's that taste like?" Tattoo points to the peas on his plate with a spork, trying to keep the slippery balls from hitting the potatoes.

Cud Chewer smiles wide and shows off yellow teeth. "Them's peas. They taste like *peas*, bro. You know, vegetables?"

"Ah, hell no I don't know. If it didn't have no face, I avoid it," Tattoo says with a frown.

Cud Chewer gulps his milk. Tattoo moves the peas around with his fork. Finally, he stabs one and holds it up to his dark eyes for inspection. It's a fair question. What does a pea taste like? Mom grew peas in the garden. I spent hours canning the damn things but never thought about how they tasted. Grass? Slippery green dots of mush? A farm girl who spent her childhood eating them should have a decent answer, but I don't.

I look around the room. Not that my past matters. Nobody here knows me, and I don't know them. I can be anyone I want in here, with restrictions, of course. Like Weinsegard said, my choices are slutty mcslutster, frigid bitchinator, clueless airhead, butch gay or plain gay, and sleep to the top on-topster. Maybe I can be invisible.

I unwrap my tray. The plastic is wet with droplets of un-escaped steam. I set the plate filled with fried chicken, potatoes, and peas in the middle of the table. My favorite meal—before. I carefully place the vanilla cake and package of condiments next to it. The sweet vanilla aroma hits me hard – smells like candles in Manolo's apartment. I suck down the coffee to cover up my face. Clear my throat and look at Cud Chewer and Tattoo.

"You guys can eat this."

They look at me, mid-chomp.

"You sure?" says Tattoo. I nod and he takes the cake. Sets it off to the side, dress-right-dress with his own.

"That's really nice of you," he adds as he looks me over. "What're you gonna eat?"

"I'm okay," I say and sip more coffee.

People used to tell me I was nice. They always had that idea about me and they were right. I'm not being nice *now*; I want that away from me before I get the urge to eat it. I'm jetlagged and anxious. If I eat, I know I'd have to puke and it's too much effort.

Cud Chewer mumbles thanks and stabs the chicken with his spork. I set down the coffee and sip my water. I avoid looking at the potatoes and peas.

Giving away food may help me later if I need favors. In the field, best friends are made over MRE trades. I would've field stripped a cigarette for a Chili Mac MRE during Basic. There's no debate—that's the best Meal Ready to Eat; has jalapeno cheese spread as a side.

"What's your name?" the Tattooed one smiles as he asks.

My mouth turns dry. I sputter out, "Ashe."

He raises his eyebrows. "You okay?"

Does he honestly think the answer is yes? I try be cool. "Um. Yeah, thanks. Let me guess – your nickname is Tattoo."

His face reddens. "How'd you know? You from the 101st?"

"Lucky guess." I gesture towards the angel wings wrapped in a pair of dog tags on his forearm, almost a complete inked sleeve. He lifts his forearm and takes a look at what I see.

"Yeah, that's a new one," he says. He settles back in his chair, then stabs a mushy pea.

I sip my coffee until it's gone, swallowing down my unease with each swig. It's quiet. Minutes crawl by until a shrill voice interrupts like a whistling mortar. Impact—boom. It's *Don't Fucking Touch Me Katia* flying into the room.

She stands in the entrance. "Ya'll better have my fuckin' chicken."

"Sit down, we'll bring it to you," says a seated staffer, flustered. He stands as he sets down his crossword puzzle on a table. Ignoring him, she rushes the room, finds the tray with her name written in block letters, and smiles a wide grin as she pulls it from the metal cart.

"Hell ya, my fuckin' chicken."

I see the cellophane tightly wrapped around a bulging leg of some kind, as big as it is, it could be ostrich. Our table has two free chairs and I shift my eyes away from her, so it looks less inviting. I didn't need to. She crisscrosses her legs and plops down on the floor. Does it without spilling a thing. I can still see her and something won't let me pull my eyes away.

Katia rips off the plastic and holds the chicken leg suspended between both hands, like corn on the cob. She eats it that way, too, chewing up and down and up and down, one row at a time. Sucks on the bone until it looks bleached. I have never seen anyone eat like her, not even at the annual Breakfast on the Farm. My stomach growls and my tongue drools as I watch.

Other soldiers start to arrive. Buzz around each other like flies, laughing and talking. I pull my eyes away from Katia to watch them stroll in.

Oh shit.

Room spins as my legs go weak. My heart pounds against my ribs. I want to scream at him. At the world. Why is he here? Why, why, why—

I'm dizzy, so I grip the table. I grab the open milk carton on my tray and stand up tall.

I scream. "Jackson! Over here! *Asshole*!"

I lock eyes with the dumb-fuck mechanic. Butler's dopey sidekick. His mouth hangs open and fear flashes over his face. I fling the milk and it hits his chest. Bullseye. Splatters and thuds to the floor. He flinches but doesn't move, his gaze locked on me. I need that loser to suffer. I want him to feel pain like I did.

I grab the cake from Tattoo and reel my arm back when Darrell grips my wrist and shakes it free. He lets go. A ring of frosting remains in my hand. Cat Eyes appears at my side.

"What's the problem here?" Her tone is even but I am crying now. Big, fat tears.

"Him," I say and point at Jackson. God, I feel as if I might explode. I run my hands through my hair. Forgot about the frosting. Now it's in my hair. On my cheek. *Fuck.*

Katia jumps to her feet, hops foot to foot. Waves the mauled chicken and chants Jerry Springer style, "Fight, fight, fight."

"You sound upset. It's okay," Cat Eyes says to me. Then, sternly, "Sit, Katia."

Jackson whines like the baby he is. "Wasn't me, Jelly."

He calls me *Jelly*. It's like he hit the fast-forward button on my anger. I have to stop him from repeating it.

Cat Eyes and Darrell flank me, so I jump on the table, and soon I am hurdling over it, lunging over anything in my way to get to Jackson. I need to beat his ass. I zero-in on him, blind with rage. I want to bash his head with a tray until he bleeds out his ears. I want him to be as miserable as I am.

Nobody stops me. Patients clear the way. I'm getting close. A few more strides. Jackson is frozen in place. His face turns white. Puts his hands up, like *hey buddy*. And I almost make it to him on the other side of the room. Except.

As I'm close enough to dropkick him, Darrell grabs me from behind. I slam into his plank-like shoulder. Holy shit—OUCH. I scream as pain bursts throughout my body. I thrash wildly and he holds tighter.

"Let go." I demand of him, which he doesn't do.

He hauls me away, saying nice things in a quiet voice. I don't hear because my ears pound angrily into my skull. Soon I'm sobbing.

Life went from bad to much, much worse.

CHAPTER 10

Amanda and Friends

BIG DARRELL SETS me down at the exit of the Dayroom. I stand there, panting and sobbing. He herds me gracefully down the hall and into my room. He opens the door and we step in together. I look at him, stupidly, as I try to stop crying

"Stay here," he says in a stern growl, as if I'm a dog. "Stay."

Shuts the door with a soft click. I stand in the middle of the bare room, arms crossed. My tears turn to uncontrollable shivers. I squeeze my eyes shut. I hate Jackson but I really need to get a grip. I reach for my ear lobe and pinch it so hard between my thumb and pointer that my earring hole bleeds. I keep pinching until I feel a drop of warm blood on my thumb. Pain calms me down enough to breathe.

Then.

A terrifying thought hits me: What if Vincent is here? Jackson and Vincent were mechanics together in the same unit. Could he be—? Pain shoots into my left arm and my limb tingles. I'm shaky, unsteady. Cold. Hot. Panic attack. I cross my right hand over my chest. Damn heart is beating harder than a milking machine.

Bury it, Amanda, bury it.

I grab my clavicle, like Katia grabbed her chicken leg. I squeeze hard. It's not working. Jackson's face flashes in my mind. My insides curl up tight, my body is hot, and I feel as if I'm cracking in half.

I manage to take a few steps and collapse over the sink, turn on the cold water, and stick my head under the faucet. Fumbling, I do my best to rinse out the frosting and the blood. To cool off my hot head. Running cold water over the back of my neck soothes the violent rush of pain. Drip by drip, I can breathe again. I can think. I turn off the faucet and dry off using the washcloth near the sink.

I sit down on the bed, wrap myself in a sheet, curl up and face the wall. For a very long time, I've tried to ignore what happened in Iraq with Butler, Jackson, and Vincent. Cortez was right. Ignoring isn't helping me. I feel worse and worse and now here I am, face to face with Jackson. My shoulders shake and huge tears spill down my cheeks. I wipe my eyes and nose with my sleeve and roll over to face the ceiling. I count the tiles, again and again. Math is the best subject there is because it doesn't depend on feelings.

In second grade Mrs. Star taught us the math symbols for Greater Than and Less Than. Nine is greater than five, but four is less than eight. These symbols are everywhere. Elementary school, high school, the Army; it's all the same. We interchange the numbers with people. Tooth-brushed kids are greater than smelly kids. Football players are Greater Than Pot Heads. Infantry is greater than Finance Corps. Warfighters are greater than service support. Special Forces are greater than everyone. That's not my opinion, just one of the many irreconcilable differences I got with the Army. Irreconcilable differences don't have a symbol. Maybe I'll invent one.

On the other hand, equal signs exist, but that's usually between the really smart or the really dumb. Or the really screwed up.

I hear a knock at the door, my brain reactivates and snaps me to the present. I fling myself off the bed and rush to the bottom drawer of the dresser to find the tweezer that I hid. The door slowly opens.

It's Katia. She's got one hell of a wicked grin on her face.

"Yeah?" I half-ask, unsure.

"Can I come in?"

She doesn't wait for an answer. Katia shoves the door open with her bird elbows. She clutches the mauled chicken so tight her knuckles are grey. Shiny grease stains her nails.

She's still grinning. "What was that about?"

I grunt. "Why do you care?"

Just a couple hours ago, she damn near clawed my eyes out for *her* running into *me*. She shrugs and slumps to the floor in the middle of the room, careful to keep the chicken high above the floor. She sucks her thumb and smacks her lips.

"Was Jackson in your unit?" She ignores my question.

I ignore her's. I don't want her to stay in my room, but I know she won't care what I want. Shit. I need to get my thoughts straight and her asking me questions won't help. I watch as Katia cracks open part of the bone that's still in one piece and pulls the two pieces apart.

I see the blood marrow and look away. "Gross."

Between the grease, the skin, and now the marrow, I'm sure she ate close to 800 calories for dinner. I'd have to run for over an hour to burn it off. I'd rather avoid it altogether.

"Delicious," she says and reaches for the bedsheet to wipe her hand. "I don't like him neither. Gives me the creeps."

I step to my dresser and, glancing back, hide my tweezers. I walk towards her and lean against the sink. "They take him away? Ask him questions?"

She shrugs. "No, he got to eat."

"*What*?" Disbelief. I kick the bed frame. Fucking great.

She rolls her eyes. "God, that was like an hour ago. Why're you still so pissed?"

"An hour?"

"Everyone's watching TV now. Meeting after."

"An hour?" I repeat.

Didn't feel like an hour. I was afraid time would drag, but no—I lost an entire hour. I squeeze my eyes shut and scream. Release the pressure raging inside of me. She shushes me.

"Calm down or Darrell's gonna come in," Katia says. "That's all we need, have big boy as our constant babysitter. You don't get away with nothing with him."

A knock on the door.

Katia purses her lips and tosses the chicken bone in my trash. "See? Told you."

The door opens and Cat Eyes enters the room. She shakes a bottle of chocolate meal supplement in her right hand, left hand on her hip. I cross my arms. I'm *so* not hungry.

"Brought you dinner."

My stomach makes gurgling noises, which I ignore and squeeze my arms tight together. I start to feel anxious and breath heavily. I barely moved today, I could go another 24 hours without food and I'd be fine.

I shake my head. "Not hungry."

"Uh-huh."

She surveys the room, sees Katia and raises an eyebrow. Cat Eyes says nothing but walks towards me, unscrews the cap, and hands me the bottle. I take what she's holding out because she looks like she won't take no for an answer. She walks to the empty bed and sits.

I grit my teeth. "I'm a slow eater."

Her eyes are as still as glass. "I'll wait."

"Do I *have* to?" I hear the whine in my voice. She ignores it.

"First, I watch you drink," she says as she clears her throat. "Then we wait twenty minutes. So, whenever you're ready."

"I'm out." Katia wipes her greasy hands on her bottoms, "TV's better than this."

I sigh. She's right. How ridiculous—I'm a grown ass woman getting watched as I sip a premade mix of calories. Is this what I am now? I shake my head, clear my thoughts. *Fine.*

Katia hops up and walks towards the door. "Later, Martinez."

I freeze. Time stops. I speak slowly. "What did you just call me?"

She rolls her eyes. "Martinez, dumbo. As in Pedro Martinez, pitcher for my team, The Mets. It's a compliment. You got a pretty good arm."

Cat Eyes notices my tone and stands up. Walks between us. Katia doesn't. She opens the door and walks out. My body shakes—how? Why? It's all too much of a coincidence to be one. My hands are shaking so hard, I set the meal replacement down on the sink counter before I spill it all over. I confront Cat Eyes, my finger in her face.

I shout. "What the hell is going on in here? What the *fuck* is going on here?"

I scream loud enough to drown out my pounding heart. I'm dripping sweat but my body trembles and shakes. First, Butler appears at my gate in Kuwait. Then, Jackson strolls into the dayroom—*which, what are the odds?* —and now a comment about Martinez. As in, my Manolo. She just said Pedro to throw me off. Something fucked up is going on. I grasp my head, pulling at my hair, my knees go weak.

"Where in the hell am I?"

Cat Eyes steps closer. "Ashe, stay with me, honey."

I swat her away. "What the fuck is happening? Who's in on this?"

I have a lightbulb moment: a conspiracy to make me crazy, to shut me up forever. I know that's what it is—someone knew I'd be gate guard and that I'd go crazy on Butler. Then they planted Jackson in here just to fuck with me. Katia's no soldier. She's probably an actress…I should've expected something awful like this, but holy shit. I can't believe it.

Cat Eyes is making a *sssshhhhh* noise and telling me to calm down, that I'll be okay, and that everything will be okay. No, no, no it won't. I look at the ceiling with a new interest. Nothing—no cameras. I rush to the mirror to see if there's a camera…no. I open up the cupboard but it's empty. I look around, trying to figure it out.

She follows me closely. "Ashe, what are you looking for? Talk to me, honey."

I whip around to face her. "Please. Just tell me what in the hell is going on… please…"

"Tell me," she says. "Who is Martinez?"

Suddenly, I'm crying so hard I can't breathe right. I gasp and cough. My throat feels full of bile and I dry heave but nothing comes out. I choke on my tears.

Cat Eyes restrains my arms and leads me to my bed. She keeps a tight but gentle hold, like she doesn't want to hurt me but if she lets go, I'll hurt myself. Which may be so. I can't deal with these raw feelings, they hurt too much. Somehow, my head ends up on her lap. She strokes my hair as she holds me down with her other arm.

She orders me, "Breathe in, breathe out."

I let out the breath I'm holding. It exits too sharp, as if it's cutting me from the inside. I cry harder and snot runs from my nose. My headache crashes into the front of my skull and I let out a little scream. All the while, Cat Eyes shushes me and strokes my hair.

"Who is Martinez?" she asks again, calmly.

With her stroking my hair, I feel safer than I have in a while...since the night before we deployed. If there is a conspiracy, she's not in on it. The words come from somewhere deep inside me. I cannot stop them from pouring out.

"My boyfriend…" I say, "actually, my fiancé…an IED."

It had so much blast the aftermath looked like insurgents were trying to launch him into space. From what I heard, the funeral was closed casket.

I didn't get to go since we weren't married. Not being there for him was another failure on my part.

"I'm so sorry," she says. "What an awful, terrible tragedy."

My chest tightens. "Worse part is…it's my fault," I whisper and cry harder.

She continues to stroke my hair. I deserve to be slammed against the wall, raked over a hot fire. I deserve to be the one blown up. Not this. She's too nice.

"How could that be?" she says as she continues to stroke my hair.

I sit up so we're side-by-side. My eyes are so puffy, it's like I'm looking through slits. Tears flow again and I wipe them away with the back of my hand.

She says, "Honey, how could that be?" Her eyes are full of genuine worry, and something else. Sadness? Panic?

I stand and cover my face with my hands. I pace back and forth. *Control yourself, Amanda. Control.* I try control myself, but the words rush out.

"I killed him. He's dead because of me." I look and see the worry in her eyes, but also disbelief. I'll make her see. "He came to BIAP—the Baghdad airport where I was—from an FOB just a few klicks away about once every couple of weeks to see me. Stayed for a couple of hours to refuel and get mail. It wasn't his *real* job. I should've told him to not risk it, but instead I asked him to come more. I was such a selfish bitch."

I stop pacing and flop on the bed opposite of her. Swing my legs onto the mattress and look at the ceiling. Run my fingers through my hair over and over, working out the knots and trying to calm down.

"Oh, honey, I'm so sorry," I hear her say.

I go on. "He sat shotgun…his whole side was destroyed. Only the driver lived."

I close my eyes and cover my face again. A disgusting glob of bile is building up in my throat which makes me want to puke but I force it back down.

She says soothingly, "Every day patients with injuries from IED's are sent to Walter Reed. So many victims come through here once their bodies heal, many feeling the same as you. Bad for getting out alive. Ashe, you didn't put the bomb on the side of the road, it's not on you."

Yeah, right. I begin to cry again. "Don't you see? He would be alive today if…"

"If *what*?"

Oh, God. These awful feelings are choking me. I jump to my feet. As I pace the room, I burst into tears. I say, "If *everything*. *If* I had enough courage to take him home and make my mom meet him. *If* I wasn't such a coward and asked him to get married in Wisconsin years before we deployed. *If* I didn't whine and beg him to visit me. Everything is my fault."

Tears roll down my face, but I don't wipe them. I sit down on the bed, hands between my legs and stare at the floor. "Isn't fair," I say, "Nothing in this stupid Army is fair."

I don't look up, but I hear her sigh. "You got that right, honey, life sure isn't fair. As I'm driving to work and listening to the news, I get the feeling that being here in Ward 54 is the sanest place to be."

Wrong, I think. It's a cage. Anyone living in a cage will be safe—until they aren't. Cows feel secure in their protected fields. Up until the day they get carted off to make dog food. Damn. If it weren't for the facts that I'm tired and she's nice, I'd scream until the mirror shattered.

I hear Cat Eyes talking and tune in. "And I'm so sorry to hear about your fiancé. What a terrible loss. I can't imagine."

I look up to see Cat Eyes staring at her hands, which are in her lap. Her nails are a purple-pink color, which I didn't notice before. She looks at me, stands, and walks to the sink. She brings me the meal replacement drink.

"Starving yourself won't bring him back. You got to eat."

I feel too drained to drink it, but I'm not up for another fight. I take it from her and sip in silence. Although it tastes like chalk dust, I drink the whole can. I hand the empty bottle to her. She fills it with water and brings it back. I drink the cloudy water.

I manage to think of something other than Manolo for a second. I'm curious and have to know. I ask her, "Is Katia really a soldier?"

She nods. "Fort Drum."

"So this is all..." I start but don't finish.

"A coincidence, honey. Not a nice one, but it's a coincidence."

I trust Cat Eyes. Maybe Katia calling me Martinez was nothing more than a fluke.

"Now what?" I ask.

She's standing. "We wait. And you either tell me about what happened with Jackson, or you can rest. Jackson is a part of a story you haven't even begun to tell. You have too much on your shoulders, honey, they're sagging."

I shake my head. Can't talk about that scumbag today.

She sighs. "You must be tired, it's past 20:00 and we're six hours behind Landstuhl. You should try to get some rest."

I don't say anything, but I know she's right. I pull back the sheet and climb in. It's cold, yet soothing. Tears well in my eyes so I slam them shut. She speaks but I don't hear her again. I keep my eyes closed until I somehow fall asleep.

CHAPTER 11

Amanda and the Wolf Pack

I'M STANDING ON a cold, white marble floor. My bare feet are icy and clammy. Floor's sticky. Air smells like stale sand. Somehow, I know this place. *Oh, right.* It's an Iraqi palace, a former Ba'ath compound that Special Forces made into their fort. I remember it as loud and full of people, but now it's empty and dark. Only the moon gives off any light, which glows in from the many windows, some broken and some not. Moonlight reflects off the skin on my feet, which makes them look translucent. Legs, too. *Damn, why can I see my legs?* I look down. I don't have pants! I freaking need them. My brown, issued t-shirt barely covers my butt.

I try to turn, but fuck. I'm stuck. I squirm, twist and shake until *POP.*

I feel as my body transforms itself into an inflatable balloon. I float higher and higher until I hit the ceiling, way above the marble floor. I'm stuck near a gold light fixture high up in a hallway of the palace.

Hovering above, I can see everything below. The grand, golden hallway is fortified with sandbags, which is the only decoration at all. Floors are dirty. No mirrors, paintings, or furniture anywhere. Everything must've been stolen or removed.

Captain Butler walks out of his room. I know it's his room by the American flag draped over the door, but I'm not sure why I know this. He's shirtless, buttoning up his cargo pants with a smirk on his face. His shaved head shines in the moonlight and I start to remember. Something bad happened, but I can't think of what. His flip flops slap against the marble floor as he struts down the hallway. My balloon bangs against the ceiling with every step. Thump. Thump. Thump. I can't see him anymore when he makes sharp turn.

Minutes pass. *Think, Amanda…what happened?* My memory is hazy. I watch the mice zigzagging between the empty bags of chips littered across the floor. A portable fan whirrs.

From the opposite direction, Sergeant Vinny Vincent appears from a side hallway. The hairy bastard slinks over to the room Butler came out of. I feel a sickening, terrifying dread. He's the awful Special Forces mechanic who…*did what?* He's in and out of the room quickly, carrying a dirty, limp body in the hallway towards the entrance door.

Oh my God. That body he carries is *me*.

The Other Me looks awful. So pale and scrawny. At least I wear pants and top, even though they're a crumpled mess. My head's rolled back, bouncing against Vincent's massive, shaggy arms. My eyes are shut but my mouth is open

My balloon body bounces on the ceiling. *Hey,* I yell, but nobody looks up. *Hey!*

Jackson comes from…where? I don't know, but he sees the other me—and follows Vincent. Balloon Me slides along the ceiling, following their movement towards the entrance.

Jackson speaks up as he tags behind. "Vincent, what happened?"

"Get her weapon from Butler's room and bring it out to the van."

"You taking her to the TMC?" Jackson says.

Yes! Great idea! My mind screams, but no words come out.

"Open the door and shut the fuck up," Vincent says. "That's an order."

Jackson obeys and opens the majestic door. A swoosh of air somehow carries my balloon body out and into the open. Drifting above, I see Vincent carry me over the white gravel to the mini-van parked a few yards away. Jackson catches up and slides open the side door. I have a good view of Other Me, but my body looks almost dead. As the wind carries the balloon me along, I see Other Me flinch. Not dead, then. Vincent lays me on the seat in the second row.

"Maybe she's got alcohol poisoning," Jackson says as lays my rifle on the floor van's floor.

Vincent tosses the keys to Jackson. "Drive. Tent City."

Okay, not as good as the TMC. But still, I live in Tent City. Weisengard can help me.

They both enter the vehicle. From above, I can't see inside. Jackson turns on the van and backs out of the driveway, but keeps the headlights off. Light discipline. Vehicle drives on the rugged, desolate road towards Tent City, leaving behind the marbled Special Forces compound. I remember this route, as I rode on it a few times. But...this doesn't feel right.

Minutes later, the van stops. Engine turns off. Hovering above, I hear the men argue.

No. This is bad. VERY BAD. Other Me needs to go to Tent City. ASAP.

Jackson flings open the driver's door. Gets out and storms away. When he's close to fifty feet away, he pauses, turns around, takes a few steps back towards the van. *Yes, go back.* He stops. He walks further away.

Fuck. Get back there! I try to scream from my balloon body as I float over him. *Don't leave her. Don't leave ME.*

Jackson sits down on the side of the dirt, pulls out a cigarette. I focus on the van. Dread fills every helium molecule of me and I start to drop as the wind blows. The swirling wind pushes me until I'm low enough to look into the side window.

The moonlight is bright enough to light up the scene inside. Vincent jumps from the passenger seat over the middle console. He crashes down onto Other Me, who is sprawled on the long bench seat. Other Me shudders as Vincent sits up, quickly unbuttons her pants, and flings off her belt. Grabbing hold of her waistband, he tears the pants down past her knees and rips the lace panties in half. Throws 'em under the seat. Slides off his own running shorts. His disgusting hard body is on hers. On *mine.*

Stop it. I yell as I bang my balloon body against the window. I slam myself against the window over and over, catching the string tied to me in the door handle.

Nothing I do is heard. Vincent holds his right hand over her face. With his left, he presses hard on her windpipe, muffling all noises. Mounts her and slides himself inside. I can't look away now, even though I desperately want to. Pure panic inflates me.

Wake up. I'm screaming from inside. And I don't know what it is—maybe adrenaline, or maybe she heard me—but her eyes open and she thrashes underneath him. They're struggling, even though he's too heavy for her to move. She tries to claw his eyes, but he grabs her wrists so tight I see red immediately. He screams as she sinks her teeth into him—an honest to goodness feral bite. In response, he head-butts her—*hard*—on the forehead. She screams and thrashes her head around. He pulls back his thick arm back and punches her square in the face, calling her a bitch and a whore as he makes impact. She tries to twist away. He punches her again. Blood pours out of her nose as she cries. He bashes her nose, like he wants to split it. I hear a crunch, so sickly loud and clear.

A brief silence. She's still, but breathing.

Terror blows like wind through me. I want to fly away. But goddam it, my balloon string is still caught. I'm forced to watch.

He slides himself back in. Her whole body lurches away, but he's got her trapped. He says out loud: *"I'm gonna ram you like a tent peg, you bitch."* Over and over again, he keeps going. I'm frozen. Sick with disgust and unable to fly away. I see him pull out and brusquely forces her face to meet his hips. He fish-hooks her mouth open and jams the tip of his dick inside, ignoring her gag. *But I hear it. I hear her screaming on the inside.* He clenches his body tight and forces his cum in her. Pulling out, a clear glob over her face mixes with the blood. *Jelly donut*, he says. *Fucking bitch is a jelly donut.*

Just like a Jelly Donut, the bastard repeats again, as if I didn't hear the first time. I try to yank my body away because I just can't watch anymore.

She tilts her head to the side seconds before...

The balloon pops.

I wake up. Lean over the side of the bed and vomit. Globs of chocolate bile launch from my mouth and nose. I spit.

Lord, God. Why did I have to relive that? Wasn't just a nightmare, but my life. Vincent's body on mine...I gag again. Roll over back on to the bed and rub my face with the sheet. My heart slams in my chest, each beat a balloon popping. I feel gross. I feel exhausted.

I hate nightmares.

Tears slide down my cheeks. Seeing Jackson dredged up everything I'm squashing down. First, Captain Butler drugged me, took advantage of me while I was passed out. Vincent was supposed to take me home—to dispose of me—but they got into some hot argument before he left. Halfway back to Tent City, Vincent decided to take it out on me. I was drugged, but I was in and out of consciousness. I knew that things were happening. When he came and...Oh, God. I can't even think about it.

Jackson knew what happened. I watched him come back into the van, look at me, and say zilch. I was bleeding, for cripessake. He drove me to the edge of Tent City and dumped me on a pile of sandbags. Threw my weapon out the window. I had to low crawl to my tent.

Please, stop thinking, I tell myself. *Fuck these memories.* I roll my head back and forth, press my eyes open. It's dark in my room, but I have no idea how late it is or how early. I jump out of bed and flip on the lights.

I cannot be in here with Jackson. Allowing a bad situation to continue makes you responsible for it, and that's what he did. It's him or me.

❧

I WIPE UP my puke with toilet paper and flush it down. I make my bed, wipe my face with cold water, and slip on my socks. Turn off the lights and slowly open the door to the hall. It's quiet and empty. I have no idea what I'm doing—yet. I just can't stay in my room anymore. I pause—*should I bring my tweezers?*

I hear a raspy voice. "Where're you going?"

I'm busted. I jump and turn around. Katia is sitting in the door frame of her room, biting her nails and spitting out the shards. I breathe out. Not busted.

"Don't know," I say, because it's the truth. "What time is it?"

"1:30." She chews on her thumb nail. "They just did room checks."

Checks are every thirty minutes. An idea hits me that will get me away from Jackson. "Where's the phone for patients?"

"Dayroom. You need permission and a calling card." She air quotes "permission." I don't have either.

I look down at my socks and think. I say, "I saw two nurses talking on phones before at the front desk. Is that staffed at night?"

She doesn't look at me, even though I stare at her. She clears her throat. "I guess you could try. I mean, maybe, if you knew what you were doing. I don't suppose you know how to call out. It's not DSN. Me, on the other hand. I know."

Fine. I ask, "Are you gonna tell me or what?"

She picks under her cuticles, "I want some of your tray at chow."

I shrug. "That's easy enough."

She wiggles on her bony butt cheeks for an endless second.

"The nurse's stations got two phones right underneath the counter. You can reach under and grab one. Dial 9 before the number to get out of the hospital and 0 for operator."

"Got it. Dial 9." I step away from her.

She grabs my ankle. "They won't just let you."

I look down at her. Reach out my hand. She grabs hold and bounces to standing.

"I know how to open the locked outside area. This guy Chimney showed me. Two staffers called in sick, so front desk bitches will have to get off their asses to see what's up."

Whoever Chimney is, I don't know.

"You're helping me." It's a statement, not a question.

She cocks her head and grins. "Yeah, damn straight."

"Right now?"

"Now or never," she says with a wink, "Fuck Jackson."

Finally, an equal.

❧

I'M NERVOUS AS we move. Halfway down the empty hall, Katia and I split apart.

"Cover me while I move," she says in a laugh-whisper and hustles towards the forbidden glassed-in outside area known as the atrium. I slink next to the wall and wait for my chance. Heart pounding, I'm *this close* to barfing again.

I hear a commotion, like a rusty door opening and a nurse from the desk hollers out.

"Get back in here. PFC. That is *unauthorized*. That's an *unauthorized* area."

I can hear Katia yelling loud enough to wake the whole hallway. "I'm up. They see me. I'm down." I imagine her executing a combat roll and dropping in place, just like we were taught in Basic. The idea of her somersaulting makes me smile and I feel less nervous.

There's under-breath mumbling and grumbling from someone, and squeaky shoes dash down the hall. I peer around the corner. The coast is clear. It's now or never.

Looking behind me, I hustle on tip toes to the giant desk. I reach over the counter, find the gray landline, lift it as quietly as I can and turn the phone towards me so I can see the numbers. I dial "9" followed by the number. I remind myself to breath.

A clear, crisp woman's voice speaks. "911. What's your emergency?"

Relief. I stumble over my words. "Yeah, hello. It's this…guy. I have to report on a guy that's a soldier."

"Ma'am, please slow down," she says. I realize I sound like an idiot. I have to get my shit together so she understands this *is* an emergency.

I lick my lips and take a breath. "He…like…attacked me…or not him… he let it happen, you know. I – I can't be near him. Can a real cop come to Walter Reed and get me?"

The dispatcher is composed. "Ma'am, can you tell me your name?"

A thick knot forms in my stomach. "It's Ashe. I mean, Amanda. Amanda Ashe. You want my Social?"

"No. Ms. Amanda, that's okay. What's your address?"

My throat tightens. "I'm in Walter Reed Hospital, on the base. Building 2, I think. They put me in here with this creep. He's gonna do something to me, I know it."

As I say the words, sweat slides down my back; my pajama shirt sticks to my back. I realize: yes, he will be a constant threat. Maybe he'll start rumors again. Worse, tell guys what really happened and get everyone to call me Jelly. I see myself held down, covered in my own blood and glop. I dry heave into my shoulder.

"Ma'am, stay with me here. Did you just say—"

I slink down to the floor, gripping the phone as she repeats my words back at me—Walter Reed Army Medical Center. My shoulders shake as I stop the tears from pouring out of my eyes. *Amanda, you can do this,* I tell myself. The knot in my stomach loosens a little and I cut her off mid-sentence.

"Listen to me," I wish I didn't sound so desperate. But I can't back down, regardless of how shrill I sound. "Send the police, the real police, not the MP's. Military Police are fake cops. I need him arrested."

"Ma'am, calm down." She says *calm down* like Shorty Airman said *Drink Water*, as if she knows better than me then says it again, "Please calm down…"

Rage pours into me. I can tell she's not taking me seriously. "I AM CALM. Listen, just listen. Send some cops. I'm in Ward 54, okay? Think it's the second floor, or the third. Ask at the front desk where the inpatient psych room is."

"Ms. Amanda…"

Everything stops. Then, two things happen simultaneously. The 9-1-1 lady says something as a female nurse I've never seen before runs towards me, followed by a male nurse, who could be Darrell's little brother. I jump to my feet and turn my body to avoid them, but the cord is tangled so I can't get away. She rips the phone from my grasp, but I don't hear what she says after the initial shout. My ears are stuffed. The big guy holds my arms behind my back as if we were on an episode of *Cops*. I pull to get away from him. His loose restraint tightens. My stomach sinks. I can't get away. With this grip, my chance for help is gone.

The nurse talks rapidly to the 911 lady. I'm not looking, but I hear her get madder and madder because her voice rises just like Mom's does. Katia howls somewhere down the hall. *I'm up. He sees me. I'm down. Just practicing, bitches. There's a war going on.*

It's a big racket. Patients open their doors and peek out at the commotion.

Jackson is one of them. He sees me then tries to back up into his room. Too late, asshole.

"Chicken shit." I yell at him. "You're nothing but a lousy chicken shit."

"I didn't do nothing," he says, holding up his hands. "Wasn't me."

"What's she got against you?" I hear him get asked. The lying bastard repeats his words.

"I didn't do nothing."

Tears well up. Stinging, angry.

"Exactly," I whisper. He didn't do nothing that night, or later, when Vincent and Butler threatened me. He didn't do nothing when my photos got smeared across the internet or when SF spread rumors about me. He didn't do nothing.

I bite into my cheek until I taste blood. My blood, the blood that dripped from my head that night and pumps through me, keeping me alive. I wish I could switch places with Manolo.

CHAPTER 12

Jelly

I SURVEY THE therapy room: one office desk in the middle, four plastic chairs around it, one of which I'm in, two on each side. Only window is the door window that's streaked and cloudy. Clock above the door tells me it's 07:00. No bookcases or personal touches. A single sign: *Big Things Often Have Small Beginnings*. Great. More advice from signs. I put my head down on the table. Wait.

I hear, "Rough night?"

God, that's an understatement. I look up.

Cat Eyes leans against the door frame. Her hair is pulled up this morning. I'm a bit sad because her ringlets were so perfectly pretty. Remembering what she said yesterday, I imagine her driving in to work and listening to news so bad she'd think Ward 54 is the safest place. Now I know for sure it isn't. Didn't have these nightmares anywhere else.

I exhale in a rush. Nod.

She smiles. "Doctor came in early to meet you. Gonna prescribe some medication, which you need, honey. Make sure to tell him what you told me, alright?"

I nod again and let my head fall against my palms. I'm dead tired. Couldn't go back to bed with an orderly watching me all night. Katia spent the night in the one Isolation room. Cat Eyes has some type of psychic ability to know how I feel, 'cause I feel her shift and sigh.

"Honey, things will get better."

I try to smile. She drops her gaze, pushes herself up, and backs out of the room. Doesn't get far. Outside the room I hear her talking with two other voices, one male loud mouth and a softer toned female.

Loud mouth is practically shouting. I hear him ask, "How did he die?"

No. Hell to the no. I jump up and bolt out of the room.

"How did *who* die?" I say this to the three of them, accusingly. If they are talking about me, why don't they just ask me?

I startle two of them. Cat Eyes looks like she expected me. Soft toned female is a pretty Black Lieutenant: 100% physically fit, full lips, large bronze eyes surrounded by thick lashes. Short, curly afro-like hair and the stance of a judo champion. Loud mouth Major is her polar opposite: white guy, fat-bellied, jowly, pointy nose and thin lips. Wisps of formerly blond hair and the posture of a slump-shouldered man who sits behind a desk. He holds a hot coffee and bag of donuts.

"Good morning," the Lieutenant says softly. Then she glances at the Major who turns and faces me. I suck in my breath, hold it. *Please* let him be a good guy.

"Sergeant Ashe," the Major says without a smile or kind eye. "We'll be in soon."

Not a good guy. Shit. He turns away from me, as if dismissing me.

"I'm a *Private,*" I say, emphasizing the rank. I'm so frustrated right now, I'm this close to reaching out and turning his fat body to face me. He looks over.

"Go back in. Wait," he says with more force. "Now."

I stand for about ten seconds and look him up and down. He does the same, frowns, and says nothing. Looks away. Dismisses me for the second time. I give him one last dirty look and step away from the trio. When can I catch a break?

I obey. My heart beats so hard I want to puke, but I go sit down. Another jerk, but this one is expected. I've met more mediocre bozos for officers than great ones. This bozo's name tape says *Muscrat.* Major Muscrat is the perfect name for a man who dismisses me so easily and who doesn't even say *please.* The correctly spelled way—muskrat—means a large rodent and we got lots of them in the marshes near the farm. Carry diseases and all sorts of filth.

I sit on the edge of the chair, agitated. What nerve. My heart rate's tripled by the time I hear their shoes squeak on the linoleum.

The officers come in. Muscrat plops into one the plastic chairs opposite me with LT next to him. He tosses the brown donut bag on the table between us and takes the lid off his coffee.

"Good morning, Sergeant Ashe," he says as he crosses his right leg over his left knee, then reaches down to keep it there. His belly is in the way.

"I told you, Sir," I say, to keep the record straight, "I'm a Private."

He inspects a document and frowns. "Paperwork says Sergeant." Muscrat pops open the bag and places two white-frosted-jelly-filled long johns and one apple fritter between us. I start to salivate excessively. Because once upon a time, I loved donuts, their sticky-sweet dough fried in deep fat. Their sweet aroma. My tongue adores them, but my mind hates 'em. I'm not weak, but I can't control the drooling. I fake a cough so I can swallow.

He purses his lips. "My name is Major Muscrat. Walter Reed is a learning hospital, and so you'll have different doctors and staff during your time here, but I'm your primary psychiatrist and Lieutenant Faulkner here, she will be your therapist."

"What?" I recoil at his words. Sit straight up in panic. Without waiting for an answer I continue, "I can't stay here. Absolutely no way. No, no, Sir. Jackson is *here.*" I slam the table open-palmed as I say the last word.

Muscrat makes sort of a gruff snort. Tilts his head. "Staff told me about the little altercation."

My cheeks feel on fire.

The.

Little.

Altercation?

"No." I pound my fist. "Get me to another hospital. Send me back to Kuwait. Anywhere but here."

My eyes plead with the LT. She frowns.

Muscrat shakes his head. "You're winding yourself up for no reason, Sergeant."

My mind screams. "I have a *hellava* reason, sir."

Dr. Muscrat sips his coffee and shifts in his seat. "Disagreements happen on occasion in such a closed environment like this. When soldiers stop avoiding their problems and start to resolve their issues, they get scared. Soldiers lash out. Fights happen."

I shriek, "It's only *him* I got a problem with."

"Is that so?" Dr. Muscrat looks at me, unconvinced. He re-inspects the paperwork in front of him. "You were evacuated out of Kuwait because of a serious altercation. You pointed your weapon and shot at an unarmed, highly decorated officer. Seems to me that fighting is in your nature. Anger issues like yours have to be controlled. We can help you control it."

I get a sharp feeling in the base of gut, like I'm stabbed. I ball up my fists, study him. I speak as evenly as I can.

"Jackson," I spit his name for emphasis. "He's the same as Butler, this so-called highly decorated officer you're talking about. Both guys hurt me, they are total trash. I *cannot* be in the same place as Jackson, I can't do it." Period.

Muscrat leans in. "Did he ever physically touch you?"

I turn hot. "Um. No, he didn't. But he *let* something happen. Him and his friends were out to get me the entire deployment in Iraq."

Muscrat scoffs and leans back. Sips his coffee as he opens up a green notebook, and makes some scribbles. I try to look at what he's writing, but he cups his hand around, making it impossible. I see myself stabbing him with it—since I've got anger issues—but I breath in one and out one to slow down my jumping heart.

"Do you often think people are out to get you?"

I swallow, trying to stay calm. "Jackson *is* out to get me."

"Do you also feel anxious, worried, or scared about a lot of things in life?"

I pound the table again. "*Jackson* makes me anxious."

He doesn't look at me. "Do you purposely avoid situations in which you might experience anxiety?"

My face is hot, my mind is a mess. I cross my arms. "Everyone does."

Muscrat sips his coffee. Doesn't look up. "Any current or prior plans of hurting yourself?"

Once again—will I kill myself? That's his real question, what an asshole. He needs to ask me about Jackson. "Not me, I'm not hurting me. Jackson better watch himself, though."

Muscrat shakes his head and finally looks me in the eye. "Enough. I understand what you are implying. You're in plenty of trouble as it is, don't you agree?" I don't answer. Grind my teeth. He continues. "We work things out in *this* ward. We move patients when we discharge them to Ward 53. You'll stay. He'll stay. It's fine."

And the fountain of anger inside of me erupts. Jumping to my feet, I kick the chair.

I scream. *"FUCK."*

It startles them. The LT jumps in her seat. Muscrat leans over to protect the donuts.

I pace in front of them. Run my fingers through my hair, but I hit a knot and it makes me madder. I yank at my hair, pull it out. Kick the chair again.

He looks at me, as if he's trying to decide what to do.

I don't want him to call for help. I cross my arms. Say, "This sucks." Stay still.

"You're *acting out*," he shrugs. "If you keep this up, there will be consequences."

"I'm *angry*." I'm shaking with fury. "Sir, this isn't fair."

Muscrat continues as if I never spoke, "Inpatient has three goals—to medically stabilize patients, normalize behavior, and understand the role of your diagnoses in your life. Right now, we only know what's on notes from Kuwait and Landstuhl, plus a few observances from our staff. I'm asking questions to make a diagnosis so we can begin to medicate you properly. From your behavior with Jackson and accusing a staff member of conspiring against you, I'm including 'paranoia' on your assessment. If we could talk for a few minutes, I can learn more."

LT adds nicely, "Can you please sit down?"

She says please and it's the only reason I do. She exhales in relief as I sit.

Fine. He wants to talk, so I'll talk.

I say, "I'm not paranoid, Sir. Here, let me show you."

I point at the three donuts. "Can I have one?"

He nods. "That's another point to clarify—you have eating issues."

I scowl. So nice to be told about *me and my problems* by complete strangers.

"A jelly donut," I say as I pick one up and hold it in two hands.

"My favorite," Muscrat smiles. I suck my drool in again.

I shudder. I rip it into two parts so the raspberry filling bulges out.

I go on. "Jackson, Butler, and some other asshole in Iraq, called me Jelly. Got all of BIAP to use that nickname. Laughed about it, but it wasn't funny, sir. There's a big story behind it. The SF officer—you know, Butler, the one you called a highly decorated hero—drugged me, did what he wanted when I was passed out, and took pictures. Another shit-for-brains head butted me and blood got on my face after he came all over me. Jackson was there, understand? Saw everything. Did nothing. He let it all happen."

My heart speeds up. I shakily set one half down, scrape the white frosting on to the table, then flick out the bright red jelly. Mixing it together, I force myself to show them. Make them understand how bad it was.

"When white cum, like this frosting glob, and the blood from my face, like this raspberry here, came together, the guys say it looks like a jelly donut. That's why they called me Jelly. SF team told me to watch out 'cause they'd do it again, too. Reminded me that they had all sorts of weapons to keep me quiet. Joked about it, like it was nothing. But it was…horrible."

Across the table, the LT's cheeks are burning red. Muscrat's mouth snaps shut.

He stares at the ripped and smashed jelly donut all over my hands.

My voice quivers. "I told on them, Sir. I asked for help from my commanding officer."

LT leans forward towards me. Whispers, "What happened?"

"Nothing to the guys. I'm the one who suffered."

I swirl the frosting and jelly together as I speak, over and over. Making swirls in the angry sugar blob slows down my pounding heart. Part of me wants to say more, but most of me wants that to be enough for him to write down and make some diagnosis. I meet his eyes. Will he ask me about Manolo now? I brace myself with a deep breath.

"Go wash your hands," Dr. Muscrat requests, his tone as flat as his eyes.

Huh? What the hell? *That's* his response? Another wave of anger pulses through me.

LT leans back and double takes her boss. Looks like she wants to speak but keeps it in. She closes her mouth but continues to stare at him. He won't look at her.

He says with more authority. "Two doors down. Rest of the patients are in therapy sessions now. No one else is in the hallway. Go."

LT stands slowly and gets the door for me. I'm so confused.

"Now," he says without averting his eyes.

I don't know what else to do. I force myself to stand, scoop up as much of the mess in my right hand and pick up the other side of the donut to throw in the trash.

"Come right back," LT says in a soothing voice as I exit.

I walk a few steps. Stop. Creep back and listen at the door.

I hear her sit back down in her chair. It squeaks.

"Really a shame that such a pretty girl is so vulgar," Dr. Muscrat says, "I'll put her on twenty milligrams of Prozac. I'll prescribe something for nights that's strong enough to knock her out. She shouldn't be prowling around making trouble."

There's a pause. 1. 2. 3.

LT speaks up. "Sir, we should have let her finish her story. That's what they—"

"That was enough for me," he cuts her off, sharply.

She clears her throat. "Sir. She's really terrified to be here. The call to 911 was genuine." I feel as if she searches for the right way to speak to this clown. I hear her plead, "Can we move Jackson? I can call Bethesda."

He speaks quickly, almost hissing. "She's our soldier and we'll take care of her. We don't need the Navy involved. I can't even imagine what the Colonel would say about that."

The Colonel? Shit. Well, now I understand. I see Muscrat for what he is: a coward who doesn't give a shit about me. He cares what his boss thinks instead of what's best for his soldiers.

God bless her, the LT tries again, "Sir, she's obviously had deep trauma… if this situation, plus what the death of her long term boyfriend…"

Dr. Muscrat cuts her off. "Everyone in here has had deep trauma. She's playing to our sympathy. We have no witnesses, no statements. It's one word against the other. Jackson's side of the story would be different. Talk to his therapist—I think it's Wilson—see what he says."

I sense her frustration as she tries again. She says, "What about outpatient? He arrived before Labor Day. It's been months, and he's not exhibiting any of his old behaviors."

She's not giving up yet, this LT. She's pushing back, trying to help out a soldier. Thank God one of them has a brain.

I hear the metal legs of his chair slide against the floor.

His voice rises. "We don't even know a date that all this supposedly happened," he says, "Or any of it. At this point, we have to be suspicious. I don't have a name of her deceased former partner. I don't have a time frame of her deployment. Did Jackson even deploy at the same time? Were they in country at the same time? LT, *think*. She never gave specifics. Never said a date. An actual date would make it believable and then maybe I'd give any credit to this whole *fantasy*—"

A loud smash stops him.

Me.

I smear the red jelly from the half of a donut over the window, like a semicircle of blood from one side of the door to the other. I wipe the mixed frosting and jelly from my hands on to the glass pane and write the date of the shit-storm assault: 01 – 04 – 2004.

Manolo died in November. I started to numb myself out after that.

I place my handprint in the middle of the jelly. I drag lines down, down like death.

Dr. Muscrat scrambles to the door and we stand face to face.

I stand tall. "How about this fantasy, Major? My *fantasy* is that female soldiers are raped a lot less. Or ideally, not at all. How about that?"

"Go and wash your hands," he says slowly. Dumbfounded may be the way he looks.

I point up at the door. "Here's the date it happened. Ask Jackson and call my chain of command. You'll find my story checks out. I got names, I got dates, and I got times. And after you write this shit down, call a cab so I can get the fuck out of here."

I whip around, not waiting for a response and stride towards the bathroom.

CHAPTER 13

Amanda, Ward Hero

KATIA SMILES AT me from across the table. "You did *what*?"

"Took some balls," Tattoo says, sitting next to her. He nods approval.

"He wasn't listening to me," I say, "LT seems to be okay, though."

"Yeah, she's alright," Tattoo agrees.

Katia shrugs. "Wish I had a donut."

We're in the Dayroom now, waiting for Arts and Crafts. Meeting with those two went long so I didn't have to avoid breakfast, I missed it. Katia gave me the coffee I had on my tray and ate the rest. Jackson is nowhere in sight.

A lumpy, white civilian lady with a halo of short, frizzy hair pushes a cart. Wears a flowing peasant skirt and chunky jewelry. Patients seem to know her as she stops to talk with each person she passes. Standing before us she announces in a booming voice, "Now we're going to make moccasins up in here. Pick a kit, check the size, and let's get to it."

She passes around giant plastic tubs of slipper kits. I like her enthusiasm. I'm sick of sliding around in socks, so I want to participate. I dig to the bottom of the box and find my size in a dusty brown and red kit. I rip open the plastic and read the small slip of instructions.

I sit next to Tattoo, who also took a kit. Katia takes a magic marker from her pocket and colors her long nails black.

"Don't you have some?" Katia says to Tattoo. I look at his feet, sure enough.

"Too loose," he explains then looks at me. "We did this two weeks ago but they get loose quick, so you got to make sure to tie it all up tight."

Tattoo and I work side by side. He watches and advises me, "The way to get the bunches tight is to go around after the first lacing."

I do as he says, happy to focus on something.

"Pinch and pull through each hole again," he says motioning how. The material is stiff and it's easier said than done. My hands feel so brittle. He takes mine and pinches and pulls.

As he works, he says, "You know, I think the reason Muscrat acted like that is 'cause he's trying to save face. Makes him look bad if he shifts patients around."

I'm irritated. "Yeah, no shit. But not my problem."

"Just sayin'. He should've moved Katia somewhere but didn't."

She looks up from her nails, darts her eyes between us. "Keep me outta it."

He leans in, narrows his eyes. "What I'm sayin' is you and her got things going on that are different. I mean, most of us are guys, so it's gonna be different. Makes him look dumb if he admits he doesn't have a clue on how to treat you."

I think about this for a second as I look around, suspicious. "Everyone else in here, he can deal with? Except us two? Come on. We aren't the only females."

"There's only unofficially two basic types in Walter Reed's Ward 54: PTSD and the rest," Tattoo says. "Call it what you want—shell shock, battle fatigue, combat stress reaction, or whatever—that's what the docs got most of their training in. Everyone's got PTSD here, in all the wards. Burn victims. Bullet wounds. Head Injury. Brain injuries. All their secondary diagnosis is PTSD. You probably got it, just other stuff, too, that he can't figure out."

"What about that brain dead one?" Katia points over to a thick, Black female with two large braids framing her face. Sits alone, talks to someone we can't see.

"She's schizophrenic, you idiot," he says. "Not brain dead. And of course, they know what to do. Schizophrenia is all psychiatrists read about in their real med school."

Katia rests her chin on her hand. Doodles on the table.

I gaze at Tattoo. "You have PTSD?"

"That's what they say. IED got me."

I turn my full attention to him. "Where'd you get blown up?"

"Afghanistan." He holds up his arm and shows me an angry red scar on the soft underside of his bicep. I saw it before. It's near his American flag tattoo. He wears short sleeve pajamas so I know he doesn't care who sees it. I make a *hmmm* noise, which means I'm glad he didn't say Iraq. I feel protective of Manolo, as if he's the only one allowed to be blown up there, which is twisted, but it's what I'm feeling.

"How long you been here?"

"Walter Reed?"

"Yeah."

"Year and a half," he says. "Stayed in the hospital for a while, then got a room in the Mologne House next door. It's a hotel next to the hospital. Was about to go home when I got sent to Ward 54. Caught drinking and driving without a license in B-more."

Katia stops for a second. "Shit head, you never told me that."

I try to hide my surprise but can't. "Seriously? Did they bust your rank?"

"Nope. Still a Staff Sergeant. Caused by PTSD, they said, and I'm telling you. It was."

Katia says, "Why don't they got you in Addictions with me?"

He shrugs then hands me my moccasin. "One minute, I'm in a bar. Next thing I know I was driving 110 in a 45 zone, trying to save my best friend from a roadside bomb. Muscrat said I had a flashback, so not technically my fault."

My chest tightens. "Jesus, I'm sorry. Did he make it?"

Tattoo shakes his head slightly and turns over his other forearm, the one with the dog tags and angel wings. We're both quiet.

I don't know what to say to him. Tears prick my eyes, so I press on my lids. The moccasin laces blur. It's shitty to share a connection like this—both our best friends died in war.

"Bunch that up tighter or they'll slide right off," he says.

I work without talking. Focusing on something takes the pain away, at least for a little while. In less than twenty minutes, I'm finished. I slide on my new slippers. They're tight and look nice, just like the accompanying picture. I cut off the surplus of the nylon laces with kid scissors. It would be better to melt the ends, so they don't fray but if anyone had a lighter, it's been taken away. Contraband.

I'm tired. I look around.

I look at other soldiers' arms, their tattoos. Wonder the meaning behind them. By the number of nicotine patches I see around here, looks like every last goddamn one of the soldiers' smokes. It's not rocket science *why*. Soldiers needed the predictable habit of packing, lighting, and inhaling when the rest of wartime was so unpredictable. Technically, the Army doesn't approve. The Army's got itself a War on Tobacco like it's got a War on Terror like it's got a War on Women. By my experience, it's losing. Me and Manolo never smoked. I told him he'd look sexy smoking with his little mustache puffing away, he said if I want to lick an ashtray, to go right ahead.

I look over at Katia. She's still drawing on the table. A smoking donut.

"A fucking Rembrandt right here," I say.

She rolls her face towards me. A familiar smirk on her face.

"Passes the time, bitch. You'll see."

CHAPTER 14

Amanda and Katia

KATIA MOVES INTO my room. She carries her underwear in her hand through the hall, throws open the door, and shoves them directly in the empty bottom drawer. While I'm peeing, she takes a look around—which are *her* words. My words: she snoops. Nosy little thing.

When I return, she's holding my tweezers in her right hand, eyes wide.

Looks at me. "Jesus Christ, how'd you get that?"

I take a deep breath. "Palmed it during inventory. It's mine."

She touches the tip. "Motherfucker, that's sharp."

I step towards her and snatch it away. "You don't even have eyebrows."

Katia brings her hand to feel her itty-bitty pencil-thin brows. The little wisps of blonde above her eyes are in contrast to mine, which are too thick and too dark. Manolo bought this thirty-dollar tweezer with razor-sharp edges for me as a Christmas present. How romantic—I mocked him. I should've shut my fat mouth. Next gift was a pair of high-quality, handmade calfskin boots, all the way from Leon, Mexico.

"Let me see it," she says. She grabs it back. She pushes it hard into her thumb.

I snap my fingers. "Stop it," I say and reach for it.

"Chill out, just testing." She keeps it in her hand. "I can pluck yours. I used to do eyebrows for extra cash. You're looking like Frida Kahlo."

I don't hide the surprise. "Shut up, you know about her?"

She mocks me. "Everyone knows about her, idiot."

I admit, "I-I didn't about know her 'til a few years ago. She's Mexican."

"No shit, Sherlock. Here, lie down on your bed. I'll at least get the ones in the middle before we got to go."

I stretch out and she pulls a chair from the corner and sits next to me. Serious looking, she pushes the tweezers down to catch the hair root and pulls up. She's gentle. Using her fingers, she brushes the hairs away from my eyes. Seems like she's done this many times before.

"Hey," I say. "Can I ask you something?"

She looks at me then goes back to work, "Maybe I don't answer."

"Tattoo said they should've sent you somewhere else, too. Like, where?"

She hears the question but doesn't meet my gaze. She works her lips into pucker as she concentrates then pulls again.

"Ouch."

She pushes her chair back and I sit up in bed.

"Wimp." She stands and turns her back to me. Walks to the mirror and plucks her own.

She bends at the waist over the sink. Stares into the mirror. "I'm getting kicked out for a personality disorder due to PTSD. Not from the war, but from my PL. You know what I mean. But the thing is, there's not enough proof to convict him. I kept evidence, but my CO said I was just calling rape. Blamed me, like I wanted to get with him or something."

"I totally understand." My voice comes out more pissed than I want.

She turns around, butt against the sink. Talks to the floor. "PL's dick was soft and curved, probably why he had to force to get what he wanted. Jackass."

Oh, God. Someone got Katia, too. I can't hide my anger as I say, "Fucking gross."

"Yeah, well, I'm the one considered mentally fucked and ruined for further service but since the rapes never officially happened, because there's no evidence, he stays in. Basically, they said to me, thank you for your service, now get the hell out. Like it's my fault for everything."

She turns around. Faces the mirror again. Pulls out some of her light mustache hairs.

She sighs. "I knew the second I reported to the unit, he was a sack of garbage who wouldn't take no as an answer. Grabbed my ass, day one. *Day one.* Imagine. Got worse fast, and I wasn't the only one who had to deal with him."

I listen to her breath as she plucks, getting angrier and angrier.

"Stupid fucker went to the range twice to get Marksman. I was Expert. Nobody had a tighter shot group."

I sigh. Asshole. If she was good, then he might have ended her career out of spite, but probably not if he hit on her day one. If he touched her on day one, he was a plain shithead. I stand up and meet her at the sink. I look at myself in the mirror. I hate being powerless.

"What's your MOS?"

"*Was* a Signal specialist. 25U. Commander stripped my security clearance so that makes me nothing. I don't got a job."

We're quiet, but our eyes meet in the mirror. She looks down, so I scratch at an ingrown hair in the mole on my eyebrow. "Hey. Thanks for doing my brows," I say, genuinely impressed with it. "Too bad that's not a job we could get in the Army."

"No worries, Frida."

"Hey, they weren't that bad."

She laughs at me. "Says you. And nobody here believes *you.*"

❧

I'M STARVED FOR sleep by the time it's lights out. I shut my eyes in my own bed. Katia's is a few feet away, tight against the other wall.

I like the little punk, but she's loud. The overly starched sheets crunch every time she shifts, which is every other second. Rustles like a pile of dry leaves as she twists and turns. Bed coils squeak. I roll over on my side and see her small rear facing me. Under the white sheet, she looks like a baby lamb I once raised that I called Sheila. Dad said never name an animal 'cause more than likely they'd end up on the plate, but she grew up to be an ewe. Sold her milk and wool instead of her meat. Sheila had a decent life, and so can Katia. I know it.

"Hey," I say in a loud whisper. "Where's home?"

She turns towards me, eyes wide open.

I watch as she contorts into an even smaller version of herself. She's the size of a bullet.

"Nowhere."

Nowhere sounds drastic. Maybe nowhere she'll admit, or nowhere she feels at home. I know a few soldiers who say they don't feel a connection to any particular place, especially after a deployment or two.

"Not sure where I'll go, either. I mean, I'm not sure what's happening, so who knows."

She sits up a little, like doing a crunch but lays back down. Stares at the ceiling.

"You got a family?" Katia asks.

"Yeah, a sister and brother. Parents are still married. What about you?"

"My family's either dead, missing, or not interested. One's in jail."

"Shit, I'm sorry." I mean it.

She blows out her lips. "My dad's the one in jail. Not like I knew him. He was one of those shit-bags that paid my mom five bucks once in child support. She spends her time marrying and divorcing chumps with short-fused tempers. I've been on my own for a while."

"I see," I say. I mean, I really do. Because it explains why she might have joined. Everyone's got a reason—for country, family, honor. Running from something or running to something are the top two. Thinking about itty-bitty Katia taking the brunt of middle-aged men's tempers makes me angry and is a perfect reason to join the military. I took Mom's but she's my mother. My blood.

"Don't get the wrong idea. We weren't poor or nothing like that. My mom had a decent job and she always bought me new jeans, label shirts. Tons of shit to make up for spending all her time with her boyfriends. I never had curfew or rules. I could eat frosting for breakfast, no one noticed nothing. My mom was usually hungover anyway. I didn't want to be like that, working at Kwik Trip, going nowhere."

I stay quiet. We are equals in lots of ways.

"When'd you graduate?"

"Year ain't important. But I graduated. Top 100 in my class."

"Really?" At my school, that would be a decent stat. We had 200 kids.

She snorts. "There were 101 kids in my class."

I try to suppress it. I suck in the bubble forming in my chest. It bursts. I laugh out loud from deep in my belly. Katia giggles. We cross the line from giggling to laughing. Tears roll down my face and big guffaws—deep and loud—come from my mouth. I'm breathless. Katia joins in with her own cackle. Our laughter floats out of the room.

The door swooshes open. It's Ponytail—the night nurse with buttery highlights and pink sparkly blush on pale cheeks who's always smiling. She says calmly, "Lights out, ladies."

"Lights are out," I say.

"Get some rest," she says and sticks out her tongue.

What is this? Middle school? It has the right effect—I giggle and stick mine out.

"Hoohah," Katia says, and we both laugh. Real laughs.

Ponytail stands for a few seconds, then shuts the door as she whispers, "*Shhhh.*"

Laughing makes me tired. I shut my eyes as I let out the last giggle. For not doing much in here, it's draining. I feel my ribs then look out over at her. Katia is motionless across me. I close my eyes. I feel myself falling asleep as my breathing deepens. I can sleep with her in here.

"You ever go to Indiana?" she whispers, and I crack open my eyes again. I see her wipe her forehead with her sheet.

I close my eyes again. "I never really been much of anywhere."

"Worst state ever. Left when I was seventeen."

"Hoosier state." Just a few states away from mine, the Dairy State.

"Loser state. When I was seventeen, my mom's boyfriend was a total clown puncher. Picked on me all the time, and my mom didn't do nothing. So I packed up my jeans, t-shirts, and swimsuits in one big-ass suitcase. Had this stupid idea to hitchhike to Florida and be a waitress. Got as far as an I-70 truck stop in Ohio. Stayed until I turned 18, seven months later."

The real story. I got the sense that she's about to trust me with something important. I don't want to say or do the wrong thing, so I stay still. I bite my tongue to stop the million questions forming in my mind, which I probably know the answer to. I've seen the Missing Persons ads on milk cartons.

She cracks her knuckles. "Eventually I got this regular. Pudgy white guy with a bald, lumpy head. White yogurt raisin forehead. Ugly as hell. Always in uniform."

"Jesus," I say. "Lazy bastard didn't even change his clothes?"

"He was alright. Brought me Otis Spunkmight blueberry muffins and gallons of apple juice. Think he was lonely 'cause he wasn't at a base. Guy talked all the time about his good old Army days, talked about his buddies. Told me on repeat about Desert Storm. Him and his unit were forced to eat these anti-nerve agent pills every day. Made them so sick he said they shit themselves. Told me that's real friendship, guys wiping each other's ass when they crap all over each other. Put their asses on the line for each other. Literally."

She laughs a little. I gag but keep it inside. "That stuck with me, you know?" Katia says. "I was all alone. I lost touch with everyone during those months. I wanted friends like that."

I get it. "So that's why you joined."

She snorts forcefully. "Hold your horses, Ashe, I ain't done yet." She clears her throat. "Ohio gets hot. It was like 95 degrees for a whole week, and he paid for me to have a motel room with clean sheets. Sure as hell beat the Truck stop. I had A/C and took hour long hot showers. He brought all sorts of fast food. On the last day when it cooled down, I said, hey you know what? It's my 18th birthday. He was scared shitless. Didn't know he was fucking a minor this whole time, though anybody could see I wasn't barely above sixteen. I've always looked twelve. Panicked, he thought I had a video or pictures. Nope. I said, *hey don't sweat it, you inspired me. I want to join the Army. Be all I can be.* He was all for it. Proud of me. Went out and bought us a sheet pan of lasagna and red wine that gave me a headache. Best part of it was that he took me to the Recruiter's office because he *was* a Recruiter."

"Funny." But I don't laugh.

I listen to her breathe in and out. That was quite the speech coming from her. Maybe Katia tells me this to get sympathy, but she has no reason to do that. She knows I believe her. Maybe she just wanted to tell the truth, get it all out. I feel my hands tremble as I rub my ribs.

"That's a lot to think about." Which is an understatement, but it's all I have.

"Now you understand I don't got a place to go back to."

Sympathy wells up inside of me. "You can go with me," I say. "When I get out."

Katia snorts loud and hard. "Who the fuck you kiddin'? Don't take this the wrong way, but how can they let you out if you don't eat? Maybe you don't ever get out of here."

"How am I not supposed to take that the wrong way?" I curl protectively into a ball on my bed, the pulse in my stomach beating strong. I clinch the fat roll around my stomach.

She smacks her lips. "Okay, well. You know what I mean."

I say quietly, "I eat when I want to."

"Yeah, sure. Then show me."

I give her a hard look in the dark. "I thought you wanted my food."

"Well, I don't want you to starve to death," she says, nicer this time.

I let out a snort. "I'm so far from that."

"Not really. I could stuff you into an ammo can."

I'm not talking about this right now. I just. I can't do it. I pivot, make an about face.

I ask, "So was the recruiter really the PL you told me about before?"

"Nope. Recruiter was a nice guy. It took a while for my paperwork to sort itself out. I spent a lot of my time at his office, and I got paid, legit money. Filing papers, making copies. I learned how to do push-ups. Studied for the ASVAB. We went out the night before I left for Basic. Honest, I never even *thought* about him 'til months later when my PL started hovering over me, demanding all sorts of favors. Kept reminding me that I can't say no 'cause he's the boss and I'm a whore. I thought maybe somehow the Recruiter had told somebody, but I never saw him on base, never heard about him again. PL was just a creep. I knew he'd go unpunished, but I couldn't take it anymore. Told the CO. You see where that got me."

Such bullshit—I'm *mad.* I can't let Katia take the fall for her PL's actions. I shake my head back and forth over my pillow. "I promise you, he won't get away with it. He deserves..." I'm at a loss of words, I'm so furious. "You know what? I'll throw him in the manure pit for you. What's his name?"

"Jimmy Wright. What the hell is a manure pit?"

"Exactly how it sounds. Giant swimming pool-like hole filled with manure."

"Shit?"

"Yeah. Too many cows in one spot without any way to get rid of all the crap. Can only spread so much of it on fields. The methane gas that builds is toxic and he'll pass out before he drowns. Wright'll be dead in ten minutes."

"Shitty way to go."

I snort down a chuckle. "Yeah, it really stinks."

Katia laughs, but it's forced. Empty, not like with Ponytail. I want to cheer her up. To let her know it's going to be okay. I sit up on the bed and look at her.

"When I get out of here, you and I will live together, okay? Trust me. Just wait a few weeks. The Army is just a part of our lives, not all of it. We'll look into the GI Bill. Go to college and get a real future. Don't forget: New Manchester, Wisconsin. Look it up and ask around. Everyone knows the Ashe farm."

I watch her silhouette in the dark. She chews her bottom lip. Doesn't look over.

She mumbles, "I heard you shot at SF."

Yeah, well. This makes me pause for a second, my stomach flip flips. It's all or nothing. She trusted me with her story, and I will give her the same respect.

Deep breath. In. Out. I say, "I did."

"Did you kill him?"

"I didn't even hit him."

"Should you have?"

I blink. Nobody's asked me *that.* "Yes. I mean, no. Maybe. I blacked out. It wasn't even me shooting. It was my memories."

"So you probably should have nailed him."

She's not wrong. "Flashback to my first deployment. It was rough."

"Why?"

I lay back down. It's now or never to tell her my whole story. I start by telling her about Manolo. I tell her about him dying and me drinking to numb out and getting alcohol from the only source—Special Forces. I tell her about Butler liking me, but me not wanting to go near him. He wouldn't take a no, so he drugged my punch. I tell her about the awful ride home with Vincent I wish I could erase from my memory and Jackson not stepping in to help. About the photos they took and how Butler sent them all over when I tried to tell on him. I tell her—start to finish—letting her know everything up until the rubber gloves. It's the first time I ever get it out, to anyone. Reliefs rushes through me, top to tail.

"Sounds like that manure pit will be full," Katia says.

I can't speak for a few seconds. Since I'm being honest, I let her know my biggest secret. Something I haven't even admitted once out loud, it's too rotten and horrible. I feel myself shaking as I open my mouth.

I close my eyes as I admit, "I'm so mad at Manolo. Furious, really. Before we deployed, he bothered me for weeks about staying safe. Then *he* died. It's like he cursed us with his stupid worrying...it's dumb to be mad at the dead, right?"

Tears spring to my eyes. I know I should only be sad or depressed instead of being so pissed at him. Holy shit, I feel so pathetic.

She sighs. "Normal. I'm angry at everything. Blue sky. Rainbows. Singing birds. Happy people. Usual lame-ass shit. People who die without me wanting them to would piss me off enough to want to shoot at something, too."

Her support makes me feel better. Understood.

I agree. "Too many jerk-offs get to live and good people die."

"Don't even get me started on that," she says.

We both stay quiet. Thoughts of Manolo and what I just admitted run through my mind. Sure, I get sad and cry, but anger is pretty much the main emotion I have towards him right now. If he lived, life would be perfect. I'd never have met Butler, Vincent, or Jackson. I'd never have been drugged or any of that other bullshit. I certainly wouldn't be here.

CHAPTER 15

Amanda and a Battle Buddy

I WAKE UP in the dark, sweating. The crushing weight of last night presses against my brain and I have a splitting headache. I turn my head to see Katia, who kitten snores on the next bed over. Shame burns my cheeks at what I told her. I dodged a bullet—literally and figuratively—so why can't I just let it go? Being mad won't change that Manolo is dead. God, I'm a gigantic brat with my head stuck so far up my ass that I can't stand myself right now.

I kick off my sheets, roll off the bed, and tip toe to the small bathroom. I peel the sweaty pajamas off and stuff them in the corner on the floor, near the shower. I'm in my undies and sports bra. I pee and shut off the lights before I open the door to sneak back to bed.

Except she's up and the bright fluorescent lights are on full blast. Stands directly in front of me, her eyes twitching. "What happened to you?" She's looking at the deep blue and purple bruises, courtesy of Special Forces.

My heart sinks as I remember. Embarrassed, I turn towards the dresser for the pajamas. "They're getting better."

"Compared to what?"

I start shaking. God, I feel sick. "It's not bleeding."

"And you ain't dead. But still."

Katia looks me up and down with a huge frown on her small face. She focuses her eyes as she asks, "They know about that?"

I shake my head. "ER nurse asked me, but nobody here."

"You should show the LT. If they got balloon surveillance of you shooting him, then they got surveillance of them kicking the shit out of you. But maybe not. Shit goes missing all the time. Evidence disappears. You know that."

I sigh. "Maybe. But what good's that gonna do?"

She frowns. "Reality? Probably not a goddamn thing."

❧

KATIA AND I are instant battle buddies. She's my guide to this place. Staff lightly knocked on our doors at 0500 for vitals check and meds distribution. We were already up. In line, we stood together behind the schizophrenic and Katia tried talking to her the whole time. Something about the moon being an eye that is actually watching all of us.

"Don't make fun of her," I say.

"Not. How the fuck do we know she's not the sane one?"

My vitals are normal, but my head still hurts.

"What pills they got you on?" I ask Katia as we wait in the meds line.

"Fuck if I know. I don't take 'em."

What? I feel anxious instantly. I swallow hard. "Who's your doctor?"

"Muscrat, same as you. You trust that annoying turd?"

She has a point. I step inside the small closet lined up with bottles of pills and give my last name and last four of my social security number. Staffer hands me a small paper cup and waves the next patient in. Without thinking too hard, I pretend to put them in my mouth but actually stuff the meds in my pocket like Katia suggests. As I walk out, I throw away the little cup in the overflowing waste basket. She's right. Katia is absolutely right.

Why should I trust Dr. Muscrat?

Nobody sees me do it. It's the end of night shift and even Ponytail looks tired as she helps an older guy out of his wheelchair. They should be checking, but it benefits me they don't. Rule is: trust but verify. That rule saves lives in Iraq. Doofus soldier of mine put DVD cases in his Flak Vest 'cause he didn't want to wear the heavy plates. I punched his chest, and it was as soft as a muffin top. Ordered him to show me and he pulled out six seasons of The L Word. That show is terrible, I said. It's about lesbians, he said, so it's glorious.

Katia gives me the daily report as we get our sharps and brush our teeth in our room. She says that Cud Chewer, the loud eater I sat next to on my first day, was replaced by a soldier from downrange who shot himself in the stomach a few months ago. Two operations later, he's coming to Ward 54. A white, tall soldier from the National Guard, who is assigned to Fort Meade, insists he's General Pershing and makes rat-ta-tat tank noises on the walls.

She also says, "Oh, and Jackson is here."

My stomach drops. Shit. Shit. Shit. Every muscle inside me is on guard. I stop walking alongside her and grip the wall. My Sharps bucket almost falls.

She grabs my elbow and takes my bucket. "Sit with me and Tattoo. Nobody's gonna bother you."

I don't move, unsure. So she gives me a squeeze and pulls me along. I decide to believe her. We return our Sharps bucket and then into the Dayroom. We sit down.

I see him immediately. Dumbass Jackson's at a table full of guys. It's 0600 but he's laughing and shooting the shit like he's got zero fucks. He never once looks over but I stare *hard* at him. My mind spins, taking me to the past. I see myself back inside the van, Vincent's hot breath. My face slicked with blood. I'm getting so worked up, I don't hear Tattoo or Katia talk, even though I see their mouths moving. How long do I chew *my* cud over this? Could be ten minutes, could be ten hours. My mind stops its endless loop only when I smell stale cigarette smoke. A small Indian man, middle-aged with a paunch, slowly pushes in a large cart stacked high with sealed trays. From twenty feet away, I can smell him. Reeks of old fumes.

He leaves the cart in the front of the room and steps back. Gives us a bow, then turns.

"Thanks, Mr. Patel."

I know that jowly voice.

Major Muscrat's stands near the trays with one hand on his hip, fancy coffee cup in the other. He leans against the wall and scans the room. A guard lording over his prisoners. We make eye contact and he raises his eyebrow into an expression that says, *I'm the boss, so fuck off.* My pulse quickens and my tongue turns to sandpaper but I don't look away. He does.

Luckily, Cat Eyes is present. She's all business, moving with a purpose and directing the staff to hand out trays. Breakfast is much earlier than yesterday, I think, but check the clock and see I'm wrong. They're on schedule. I'm the one mixed up.

Staff sets down our trays and Katia and Tattoo unwrap their food.

Cat Eyes crouches next to me. "Honey, we ordered what you asked for."

I take a deep breath and pull off the saran wrap. It *does* have the corn flakes and 2% milk I requested. Banana. Plus, paper plates piled high with food I *didn't* ask for: eggs, toast, oatmeal, three pancakes, a Danish. Holy crap. All this extra food causes a wave of panic in me.

"I didn't ask for this stuff." I point to the added items in terror, "I can't—." I can't eat this. Not exaggerating; I'll barf without even wanting to.

She nods and stands up. "Eat what you actually ordered. That'll be enough."

"Roger that." I feel better. Corn flakes and milk with bananas on top was my usual. I relax: I can do that today. First things first. I take a sip of coffee and the steamy liquid warms me up. Tastes dark, bitter, and watered-down. Like Army coffee does.

Cat Eyes stands behind my chair. "None of this gets thrown, honey. Got that?"

I nod, embarrassed.

"I'm taking that Danish," Katia says and helps herself. Takes a bite.

Cat Eyes chuckles, "Caring is sharing." Without another word, she pivots and moves towards the tray cart.

I focus on my task. The spork makes it difficult to slice the banana, but I manage to cut up half of it onto my cereal. I open up my milk but spill a few drops, so I take Katia's napkin. She kicks my foot under the table. We lock eyes. Her surly smile fades and she nods in the direction behind me, eyes wide. I sense someone standing above me and turn around. Immediately my skin starts to crawl. I whip my head back around, stare at my spork.

I feel him bearing down on me. Muscrat's voice rings out, "There are hundreds of starving Iraqis who'd be happy to eat this."

I think: More like thousands, or millions, all of them stuck in a fucked-up situation, getting blown up same as us. I don't correct him. He never saw an Iraqi in his life.

In the same loud voice, "Very nutritious meal."

Unbelievable. Asshole needs to leave me alone. Instead of responding, I fix my gaze on the square pat of margarine on top of the pancakes. The meal I ate in the DFAC on date of 01-4-04 was pancakes and syrup. I barfed so hard in that van, all the food I ate *that week* came up. I felt morsels of fluffy buttermilk pancakes in my nose. I'll never eat a pancake again.

"Take a bite," he says as moves in closer.

I feel him looming over me. I shiver as I say, "Sir, I don't like pancakes."

"You don't like the *pancakes*?" he asks loud enough that I feel some eyes on me.

Katia steps in. "Sir, she's not the only one. Your momma don't."

He speaks again. "Not appropriate, Private Moon."

"I'm a PFC, Captain."

Muscrat ignores her and inches closer to me.

He speaks low. "Private Ashe, I've been patient with you, but now you need to eat. You have thirty minutes to consume the full meal of 958 calories. If this tray of food is not eaten in that time, you will be offered a liquid supplement worth 500 calories, which you will drink. If you continue to refuse and disobey, I may need to consider a nasogastric tube insertion into your stomach. It's been days since we've had a record of you consuming food."

My face feels hot. My hands tremble.

He pauses, sips his hot, designer coffee. "It's your choice."

I shift to sit on my hands. I feel like I'm choking. I need him to leave me alone so I can think. I look across the room to see Cat Eyes, hands on hips with a frown. Her and Muscrat are making some eyes at each other, but I know what they know, too. Muscrat is the decision-maker, no matter what.

My instinct is to yell *FUCK YOU*, bolt to the double doors, and scream for help. My instincts are what got me in here. I keep my mouth shut.

He leans over the table and repeats his words, "It's your choice."

I snort. Bullshit. Nothing is my choice.

My thoughts are a mixed mess in my head. Even if I eat now, he can hang that tube over my head to get me to do what he wants. I know I'm still normal weight for a bulimic anorexic. I read up on it weeks ago. Feeding tubes go in if someone weighs less than 80 pounds for my height. I'm way above that.

Muscrat stands up straight. "PFC, place that Danish back on Ashe's plate."

Katia protests. "I already ate half of it."

"Then she can eat the other half."

I look across the table at her. Katia takes the Danish in her hands, then rips it apart into four pieces before she crams all of it into her little mouth, chipmunk style. Her big eyes declare victory and I suppress my small smile.

He looks down on me. "I expect the rest of it gone. Eaten by YOU. Thirty minutes."

We both glance at the clock. He walks away, and talks to the guys at the other tables. Every few seconds, glances back at me. My stomach twists painfully. God, I feel sick.

Tattoo says quietly, "You don't have to eat it. He won't put that gas tube in you, I bet."

"Hell he won't," Katia grunts, drinking the milk.

I lower my eyes to the unappetizing tray plate in front of me.

"I can eat the eggs without him knowing," Tattoo says but I hold my hand up to stop him. I shake my head. No use him getting into trouble.

I place my coffee in the middle of the table. "Save this for me."

I take the spork in my hand and scoop up my first bite of the coldish, congealed plain oatmeal. I force myself to swallow. The icky lump slowly slides along my throat, a slow-moving landslide of sludge.

I hear Muscrat loudly guffaw to another, "You don't say."

I stare at him. How does he manage to look so caring when I know he isn't?

He moves to Jackson. Starts chatting. Makes my skin itch.

I use the spork like a bulldozer and scoop up a gigantic spoonful of food. My goal is minimal chewing time. One thing a bulimic is good at is scarfing; I can shove anything in my piehole—hot, cold, lukewarm, thick, thin, you name it, as long as it's not too sharp or too dry. Lord, it has to be the correct consistency, otherwise half won't budge and stays in the stomach while the other half of that shit blows back up through the nose and it's picking bits from the sinuses for days. I inhale the entire tray in minutes. In no time at all, the 958 calories churn inside me—eggs, pancakes, margarine, cereal, oatmeal, banana—all of it.

Major Muscrat glances over. Turns his nose up at me, triumphant. Another pawn has fallen, and he smirks his approval. I don't blink. He shifts his focus away.

I'm not done.

I stand up. I wobble over to the tray cart and slide my own on top. I reach under the cart, grab a small bottle of liquid nutrition, and hold it up for him to see. He nods—clearly pleased that I am going for extra credit. I crack it open and take a swig, although it tastes like chalk dust. I chug it down.

The others are back in their own world, no longer interested. Major Muscrat summons Cat Eyes and I hear him give her orders.

"She needs to sit under observation for thirty minutes."

Ha. The bastard said *eaten*, he didn't say *digested.*

A moment passes, then another. My head is dizzy. I feel nauseous, but I can't stop now. I forge ahead. My gaze darts around the room. I look for a garbage can. I spot the plastic-bagged rimmed garbage can on the opposite side of the room. I stand up and waddle towards it. Jackson cowers like a baby as I do, but I stride past him. Garbage can is on wheels. The sturdy plastic bag inside is tied tightly around the edges. It's the hefty type that can handle messes. I roll it so it's directly behind Jackson.

"Ashe, what's happening over there?" Muscrat hollers.

Observe *this*, motherfucker.

I bend at the waist, grip the sides tightly, and let out a wet, gloppy heave. Half the contents of my stomach project forth into the trash can, splattering the sides. Bits of oatmeal stick inside my nose and I farmer blow to dislodge it.

"Nasty." Jackson's buddy sitting next to him yells.

"Told you," I hear Jackson say, "Crazy bitch." He's pushed himself away from the table. Sits there, sneers at me. I gape at his ugly face. *Now*, my mind screams!

This time, I make it to my target. No Darrell here yet. I stand over him and look down. He whimpers but doesn't move. I heave again over his stupid body. Beige globs of pancakes and eggs land on his lap. He recoils, chair tips over and he falls flat on his back, bawling the whole time. I watch him and do nothing.

"Ashe, stop it!" Fucker whines, sprawled out on the floor. "Help."

Pathetic. A laugh bursts out from me.

"Help? You want help?" I say. My throat is constricted making the words hard to say. "I asked for help, too, you…stupid horse's ass."

I feel arms around me. Cat Eyes and another staffer I don't know flank me, arms fastened tightly around me. My knees shake and I grab for them, but inside, I'm calm. Puking makes me feel strong. I love being the boss of my own body. I love the empty feeling. Pure peace, pure bliss.

My peace is short. My head spins, knees go weak, and I cling to Cat Eyes. My head hurts and my mouth tastes metal. I tumble back from the trash can, Cat Eyes and the staffer holding me up.

My eyelids flutter and I see the blurry ceiling. I'm pretty sure I see Manolo right before I close my eyes, looking down on me as the moon.

CHAPTER 16

Amanda, ER

MY FOOT HITS a sandy bank, but it doesn't stop on the surface of the sand. Quicksand. Soon I'm up to my shins in soil. I try to pull it out, but I sink further down and now I'm up to my knees. Harder I pull, quicker I sink. I hear someone laughing behind me and I twist around but my legs sink again, now up to my thighs. It's like a huge vacuum pulling me back down and every time I breathe my body sinks down more. I panic. I'm sunk close to my waist. I know someone is lurking behind me. Quicksand turns into thick manure.

"Help me!" I shout to whoever it is. "Help!"

I wake up.

"Ashe, it's me. Relax," LT says. She stands next to me, trying to smile but the corners of her mouth don't curl. I wonder why she's here, but I don't mind. Part of me wants to ask her about the sand, but I realize it's a nightmare. I'm still in Ward 54.

Oh, no. No, I'm not.

This room looks like the ER I started in a few days ago. It *is* the same room, or close. It catches me off guard, this new room. I shiver from the cold. I touch my fingers to my face, then my neck. I want to touch my stomach but an IV tube stuck in my right arm makes it difficult.

"You know where you are?" LT says. She touches my arm.

I shake my head. Locking eyes, she nods and keeps a sad smile, which I now see as not only sad but fake. It's the type of smile that tells me she has bad news but doesn't want me to freak out.

LT starts slow. "You are in a recovery room in the surgical suite. You have a gastronomy tube in your stomach based on the medical emergency you experienced."

I move my hand under the thin, white sheet and over my stomach with my left hand. Somebody put granny panties on me that stretch over my middle. A wide gauze patch covered with sticky tape presses down on the tube bump.

"What emergency?" I can't speak well. My throat is raw and raspy.

"A decision was made to insert a gastrostomy tube. It's used to deliver nutrition directly into the stomach when patients can't eat for themselves."

I'm stunned speechless for a second. "Oh, my God."

I close my eyes. Oh yeah. I remember. I didn't have trouble *eating*. I had trouble with Jackson and Muscrat. Hot tears form in the corners of my eyes. I cry, which hurts my body but not as much as my brain. I've been *ambushed*. Sneak attack while I was drugged up.

"Who?" I demand as I wipe my dripping nose, "Who ordered it?"

Reluctantly she answers, "Major Muscrat spoke with the ER doctor… they checked your vitals…and…I guess your electrolytes were almost non-existent, and your system was weak. I'm sorry."

I let out a cry. Tears continue to sting my eyes.

LT says, "You should know that the G-tube insertion means you'll have all the nutritional support you need. I've read about many young people who need it for just a short amount of time. Eventually they go back to eating normal and it's removed."

"Stop, please stop," I hold up my hand. I don't want to hear the excuses.

Lord, I'm tired. My brain aches, my heart hurts. I don't know how much more I can bear. My body, invaded and violated. Again.

"This morning?" I say.

She's nervous at this question. Interesting. LT pauses for a few seconds before answering. "Yesterday morning." She sees the look on my face and speaks quicker. "Sergeant Ashe, you were dangerously dehydrated. Like I said, your electrolytes were severely off-balance which could've made you a candidate for a heart attack. I saw myself yesterday that they needed to put three I.V.'s in you just in the few hours I was here. Doctors decided you needed twenty-four hours of rest and proper nutrition prior to surgery to make you strong enough for it."

"For a surgery I don't need," I cry out.

"I'm sorry," she says.

I close my eyes. For fuck's sake. I exhale. This feels like part of my nightmare. I open my eyes, but she's still there. IV is in my arm and the granny panties are on. I look at the one foot not under the tucked-in sheet. I look at the toes wiggling to prove I'm alive and not stuck in quicksand.

A muscle twitches in her mouth. "Your throat's going to be a little sore. The doctor used numbing medicine for the endoscope, but it *does* irritate the throat. You can have as many popsicles as you want."

I lick my lips, want to say something—but what? I know it's not her fault. She's the unlucky one Muscrat made stay, in case I had *anger* issues.

She continues, her voice tinier than before. "I heard the doctor and nurse. It's easy to care for, they said. They pushed it right through a small slit in the skin and your stomach wall. All you have to do is keep the incision and tube clean so it prevents infection."

Wait. My mind is churning. I shake my head. I clear my throat.

"What's the tube made of?" My voice cracks.

"What do you mean?"

I fumble at the granny panties to push them down and start to claw at the bandage over the wound. The IV pulls on my arm.

I'm frantic. "The tube. You said tube. What's it made of?"

Alarm spreads over her pretty face. "I'm not sure. Ashe, don't touch it."

"I have to." I shout at her. Wriggle the hospital gown off. Peel off the gluey tape. Reveal the tube. It looks like some skinny creature busting out of stomach, horror-film style. My skin around it is red and irritated, bumpy and raw. I pull everything off to expose my skin to LT, so she can see. Her face bunches together, scared.

"I'm allergic, LT. That's why Landstuhl sent me. This thing they shoved into me, it's gonna give me a reaction. It's not stopping me from dying, it's making me sick." I make it sound very dramatic.

She steps towards the door. "Let me get the doc…"

I lay at an angle and stare at the ceiling for a long time. I bite my numb tongue. I finally feel pain and the hurt settles my nerves. The insertion point and tube don't hurt, even though they're inflamed. I'll act like it does, just to show them. Treachery is what hurts. Betrayal of trust and a crack in this lop-sided relationship. I've got to figure out how to get the upper hand, or die trying.

CHAPTER 17

Amanda Returns

"MAKE A HOLE," Tattoo says as he walks towards me and Katia's table with his tray. Short staffed, so we 'get' to do some things for ourselves. Like fetch our own trays. It's our table now since Katia drew the smoking donut. Turns out, she used a Sharpie and not a magic marker. As dark as the day she drew it.

Tattoo doesn't need to worry about our table filling up too fast, as I'm the ward's outcast. Puking on people will do that. I feel all eyes on me, sitting here with Katia who's pretending to sleep. He sets his silver tray down and grabs a chair. Room is teeming with patients. Controlled frenzy. I hear some say good morning to Tattoo and he responds. Still sits with us, though.

"Managed two days out of here," he says to me as he settles in. "Impressive."

Katia's doesn't move her head. "Got Jackson kicked out of here, that's what's fucking outstanding," she says.

I look at Tattoo. He explains, "Moved him to Ward 53."

My breath catches in my throat. I exhale some stress. *Finally.*

I'm so happy with that news, I push my tray towards them, "Want this?"

Katia's head perks up.

Tattoo grunts, says, "What about you?"

Katia reaches over. "Shut up. We saw what she does when she eats. Total vom-bot."

What she says is true, but she has that playful look which means she's fucking with me. Soldiers fuck with each other all the time. That's what they do. The ones who can't do that are the ones you gotta worry about.

Tattoo sets one of the cereal boxes and milk near his tray, "If you want it, take it back."

Katia grabs a muffin and granola bar. Nobody wants the sludge peach yogurt cup.

Thanks to Cat Eyes, I got a list of choices last night before I moved back here. They gave me a calorie count to aim for. I'm aiming for zero. Instead, I filled it out with Katia in mind. If I wanted, I could order top of the line brands for every meal—real brands, no generics or off-brand. No bottom shelf crap. We're not gonna be less than if I can help it.

Katia goes to town, almost as fast as I can scarf.

"You shove your food down like that all the time? Inquiring minds want to know," I say.

Katia pours the Sugar Flakes directly into her mouth from the plastic bag. "Jealous?"

Shake my head. "You probably have a tapeworm."

"I'm a fat ass," Tattoo says. "I gained twelve pounds since I got in here. Couldn't hump a mile on a bet. Serosel at night and Noloft in the morning turned me into a slug."

"I didn't take my meds," I say. And I'm not going to, if I can help it.

I slip my hand into my pocket and close my fist around my morning dose of un-swallowed pills. Tattoo's mouth is full of my eggs, but he raises his eyebrows.

"You need to," he says as soon as he swallows.

"I don't trust Muscrat." I point at my stomach.

His expression thaws. Softer, he says, "Maybe you'd eat if you took those pills. Might make you feel better, then they'd take that thing out."

"Probably have to anyway. It's red near where they sliced me open." Red, and a little bumpy but 'not enough to raise concern' said the doctor who came back with LT.

Katia pulls my tray towards her. "Got any other good chow?"

"That fruity yogurt and fat free milk. Tastes like udder wash."

She makes a face and leans back.

Tattoo says, "Not taking your meds won't get you out of here sooner. Meds work. They helped me with my emotions, even if I got fat. You got 'em for a reason."

My brain knows he makes sense, but I can't trust Muscrat with anything, ever. Look what he did to me. Tattoo's eyebrows raise, his eyes wide. I feel like I need to defend myself.

"I mean. They probably gave them to me in the ER. I don't feel different."

"It wasn't long enough to make a change."

I shake my head. "I'm glad I wasn't drugged up with Jackson around. You don't know what he's capable of."

Tattoo says, "Dude's gone now."

I sip the coffee and ignore Tattoo. Katia sets hers on my tray as well. I nod a thanks.

"Quieter without Jackson's stupid voice," I say, although the rest of the patients are busy eating and chattering. It's not exactly silent.

Tattoo meets my eyes, "I never trusted homeboy, neither. He drank slug nectar."

"I like Highland Dew," Katia says. Which is the other name for slug nectar.

"Ah hell no. Every guy knows that Yellow 5 shrinks nuts. A guy not suicidal shouldn't try to shrink his own nuts on purpose. He might actually get to use them someday."

Cat Eyes creeps up behind us and hears the conversation. In a hush-it-up-man tone she says, "Change the subject, please."

Tattoo sits up straighter and says, "They're cool. They don't care."

This is supposed to mean that we don't care if anyone's talking about nuts and dicks and douches. Us women are cool because we aren't the fragile, offended types.

"It's inappropriate," she says, "change the subject."

Cat Eyes moves to the next inappropriate-talking table, raising her eyebrow up to her hairline, and corrects the next table.

I'm hopeful I never see those nuts, or the man attached to them, again. He should thank me. He's been sprung from the prison but he's probably bragging about the Jelly story, which makes me want to tell everyone he's got herpes. But that's lowering myself to his level, which I don't want to do, and I don't want to know if he has herpes, anyway.

"I'll be seeing that homo in Outpatient soon," Tattoo says.

At the word Outpatient, Katia shrinks as small as she can and sits still.

I'm alarmed. "Why?"

Tattoo answers. "Yesterday we had a group meeting. Staff said they nominated both of us to move to Ward 53. Said we were on the right track."

"I ain't on no track," Katia says, shrinking smaller.

"That sucks," I say, feeling a jolt of panic. I want them here with me. Which is unbelievably pathetic, but I guess I'm pathetic?

"Sucks big time," Katia says. "Second I get to Ward 53 they'll fast-track my medical board and kick me out in hours, not weeks. Prefer to stay here."

"Hell no, nobody wants to stay inside here all day," Tattoo says and shakes his head. "We get to wear uniforms over there. Look decent again."

Katia mutters. "Ward 53 is out-patient. We're forced to sleep in barracks. Rumor is there's mold on the mattress and rat shit in the walls."

"That's a lie. But so what? Even with rat shit, we're *free*," Tattoo says. "We can go off base, downtown, wherever. Think I'll get a tattoo."

I imagine Tattoo downtown D.C. and wish I could go with them. A new idea forms.

"Yeah, you can go anywhere," I say. "Know what you could do? You could go downtown and find us a lawyer. Or better yet, a reporter. Yeah. That's it. Some girl-power journalist." Thoughts rush through me. Yes, this plan is gold. We can get help.

"Lawyer?" Katia's voice rises in pitch, unconvinced, "Or a journalist?"

I'm talking fast. "You and me need a woman. A female who can write about all that stuff that gets swept under the rug. Know what I mean? Someone who reports all the Army secrets so nobody can cover it up any more."

"I guess." Katia says but doesn't look convinced.

For the first time here, I feel a sense of true hope. "I'm not messing around. We won't get kicked out or locked up if someone reports on this. We'll give them evidence. The more, the better. I'll tell the world what these so-called elites do when no one's looking."

Katia leans over the table, then sits up straight and looks me in the eye, "You think they wanna disrupt the *status quo*? Journalists get off on these hero worship stories. Nobody is trying to turn GI Joe into some type of creepy molester, Ashe."

I pound the table. I speak too loud, almost in a shout, but I can't help it. "They don't *know*. Only way for shitty people to stay in and do shitty things is because higher ups tolerate it. Media might give it some attention and hold these guys' feet to the fire if Americans *know*."

I look between the two of them. They stare at me in a thick silence.

I swallow hard. "Fine, then I'll just find me a good lawyer when I get to Ward 53. I'll sue all of Special Forces…it's Special Forces I'm going after big-time."

"Special Forces? Your big idea is to sue *Special Forces*?" Tattoo says.

I nod. Katia and Tattoo look at each other. Katia rolls her eyes and Tattoo stifles a laugh.

"What?"

They burst out laughing, full of fucking glee. Katia almost falls off her chair but catches herself as her whole-body shakes. Tattoo tries to hold in his laughs, but he doubles over on the table. I see his huge shoulders tremble with joy at my expense. I can feel eyes on us from around the room. I'm plain fuckin' furious.

"Shut up. Shut up and stop it." I'm blind with anger, but the words squeak out in a small whimper, like a pouting baby.

Neither of them says a word but Tattoo proceeds to sit up and wipe his eyes. Katia keeps her arms crossed and shoots me a look of pity that tells me she thinks I'm a genuine dumbass.

"For fuck's sake," she says as she leans towards me over the table. "Pull your head outta your ass. When you scream rape at SF, you got the whole country against you. They do all the dirty work for Bush. He needs them more than they need him. Bush'll call you a shameless hussy and send you to jail himself. Cheney'll throw out the fuckin' key."

I flinch at her words and shake my head. I'm upset that they are both so hell bent on doubting me and my idea. My plan isn't thought out, but it's not *bad.*

I try again. "It's…they don't know what kind of shit happens…"

Katia yells as her fist punches the table. "Fuck *yeah*, they do, Ashe!"

Out of the corner of my eye, I catch Cat Eyes booking it towards us. Hands swinging at her sides, lips pressed together. Her eyes locked on Katia. "PFC Moon. Ms. Potty Mouth. Keep the cuss words to a minimum."

Katia frowns, "You gonna tell me that we can't say *Fuck?*"

"I'm saying no need to yell it."

I look at the other patients and they're looking at Ms. Potty Mouth. They're also checking out Cat Eyes. I'm so confused about everything. I mean, who is correct? Me or them?

Katia says louder, "Good. 'Cause if we can't say *fuck* in here, we're all screwed."

"Keep it down," Cat Eyes orders. She waits a minute then walks away.

I stay quiet. Sag with unease.

I feel Tattoo lean forward and I look up at him. He glances at the staff over his shoulder.

"Listen, Ashe," Tattoo says in a low voice. "Consider this your Warn-O. It's okay to share these ideas with us, but if you accuse elite soldiers with what you consider a slam-dunk conviction, you'll be disappointed. You'll be labeled a barracks 'ho and sent to Leavenworth. Or wherever they send the females. Muscrat and LT Faulkner won't be able to help you. No one here will."

I try to get myself under control, but I'm pissed. "Then what the fuck can I do?"

"Not *that*," Katia says. "You got a death wish if that's your plan. And I mean that in a nice way, so don't get pissy with me."

Tattoo looks at her then exhales. "Sorry, Ashe, but suing the Army? That's a big, fat no, anyway. It's against the law."

"You ain't the first one to get that idea," Katia winks at me as she speaks. "Half the fucking losers in here, including me, would love to take some legal action. Probably why the military's got our own justice system—to prevent any real justice."

They look at me, but I look away. I feel as if a metal door slammed into my stupid face.

I keep my lips pressed shut. I look at my tray and grab what's left. I peel back the foil topping of the peach yogurt cup. I dig the plastic spoon down to the fruit on the bottom and scoop up a huge mouthful. It's tasteless and fake sugary. I scrape the sides of the container and take another bite. I eat the whole disgusting, drippy cup in seconds. It sinks into the growing pit in my stomach. I smash the garbage. I cradle my head in my hands. These two are wrong. I have to do it. For me and for Katia. And for the other ones out there, the ones who haven't even been hurt yet.

CHAPTER 18

Amanda and the LT

IT'S STILL MORNING, but it feels like a week since breakfast. A voice inside keeps asking me: *What if Tattoo is right? What if Katia's right?* They can't be.

Today's my first *real* therapy session with LT, ever. Katia and Tattoo went to Addictions, which was fine with me. I need a break from their smug mugs. My plan to talk to a lawyer or journalist is smart, not dumb. Ain't that the American way? I nibble on my nail.

LT's flipping through my chart, making some *hmmm* noises. She pulls out a sheet and her big brown eyes scan the page. Her uniform is sharp. No doubt she takes her gear to the dry cleaners and asks for pure starch. Her blouse is as stiff as Muscrat's personality. As long as she's not rolling around in the dirt, she can keep it crisp all week.

She flips the page over, then flips it again. What's it got on there, I wonder, but don't ask. I think of Dad. *Insanity is doing the same thing over and over again and expecting a different result,* he constantly said. Dad tried to turn everything we did into some kind of "lesson." Turns out, he was right about this. Flipping the same pages with the same words over and over again does make LT look crazy.

Finally, she finds what she needs and smiles at me. "Okay, so sorry about that. Here's what I was looking for." Gazing directly into my eyes she says, "From a scale of one to ten, how are you today?"

That's what she couldn't find? I have to admit, I thought it was something more important. I take a deep breath and lean back against my hard seat. I look at her with what I hope is a nice smile and say, "Negative one."

She writes it down as she says, "Sorry to hear that. Why do you say *negative one*?"

"LT," I say and point at the tube. "Can we get it removed?"

She nods, sympathetic eyes. "Does it hurt?"

"It's annoying."

"I can't imagine."

"Second, my paperwork is screwed up. About half the staff calls me Sergeant, about half says Private. I don't know what they got my pay grade at, but if they pay me too much, then they'll take it all back plus interest once they figure out they messed it up."

To screw up a personnel file takes seconds, to unscrew it takes forever. "Human error," is what the 42A Personnel Clerks call it, but it might just be job security.

She cocks her head to the side, eyes narrowed. "Can you say that word again—about?"

My ears turn red as I say, "About." I know to her ears it sounds like a-boot.

She grins. "Where are you from?"

My tell-tale accent. "Wisconsin. Where are you from?"

She leans back. "I'm an Army brat. My dad's retired."

"Retired what?"

"Colonel."

I can't hide my shock. "And he lets you walk around with *that* beret?"

We both look at the blob of black felt sitting on the table. The United States Army, in its infinite wisdom, decided to adopt the black beret as the official headgear over the patrol cap. They did that a few years ago and it's annoying as hell. Takes two hands to put on as you walk outside and doesn't block the sun. Worse, it has no structure and no guide on how to shape it. Soldiers learn from other soldiers who come from the 82nd Airborne how to position it on your head, but the lump next to LT is more cream puff than green beret. Hot water and a razor would fix it.

"What's so wrong with my beret?" She picks it up and turns it over.

"Now don't get defensive on me, LT. I got no idea how the Medical Corps runs things but in the real Army, someone shows up with a beret like that, they would have to beat their face."

She flips it around in her hand. "Nobody's said anything."

Of course not! She's an officer, and maybe I should back off. But why? In here, I have nothing to lose. I tease her. "You ever watch The Swedish Chef on the Muppets?"

She laughs a little. "I hate this thing," she admits, setting it back down.

"Everyone hates it. You need a razor and hot water."

"Sometimes I feel like I don't have time to even brush my teeth," she runs her tongue over her pearly whites. I understand that feeling. Never enough time in the Army.

"Spend a while on this side, LT, you get all the time you don't want."

She looks like she might say something but stops herself. Tilts her head. "How are your meds? Any side effects?"

Damn, damn, damn. She knows. She must KNOW I don't swallow them. I keep my cool and ask as calm as possible, "Like what?"

"Headaches. Nausea. Feeling tired. Abnormal dreams. Anything out of the ordinary happening since you started?"

Phew. She doesn't know. Thank God. But those side effects are my every day. Don't think that'll change if I take the pills. I shake my head. Pick at my middle finger cuticle.

"Could we start with you telling me about your relationship with Jackson?"

A flicker of irritation stirs in me. I dig at the sides of the cuticle until a nail splinters off. I chew at it until I taste blood.

She tries another way. "Or we could start with your boyfriend."

My heart drops into my stomach. Stop eating my nails. "Why?"

"I'm your therapist, *Amanda*. I need to know about you so I can help. We're both in the Army but our relationship is therapist to patient and not officer to soldier. Nurse Taylor told me about your reaction to the last name of your boyfriend, so obviously we need to talk about him."

So. Cat Eyes is really named Nurse Taylor. I'll try to remember that. Mentioning her makes me feel better and I relax for a second. If these two are allies, that's good news.

I clear my throat, feeling tears in my eyes. I blink them away. I take a few deep gulps of air. I'd love to talk about Manolo. It's been a long time since I have spoken about him and how we were, just a few short years ago.

"He was the best guy I ever knew. Smart. Strong. He was so amazing at everything. I loved him and we were...," my voice wavers. Tears come. "We planned to get married after deployment."

She hands me a box of Kleenex I hadn't seen before. I take one and ball it up, rub my eyes with it.

"How long were you together?"

I toss the used tissue in the trash. Look down at my nails and push the cuticles down.

"Almost three years. He died seven months into the deployment. We were supposed to redeploy after six, but we were over there a lot longer. Extended twice."

"That's a long time."

I sigh, voice wavering. "To be with someone without getting married or deployed?"

"Both, I guess."

I sink in my seat. Peel the skin around my nail. "Everyone teased us. A soldier in my unit got married and divorced in the time Manolo and I were living together. Twice."

I smile at the memory and look at my nails. "He said his soldiers got married way too fast and way too young, and plus with my family."

"What about your family?"

I swallow. "On the first day we heard about the deployment, I said we should get married. For me, it was a no-brainer. Buzz was, that married soldiers got separation pay, on top of hazardous duty pay—all tax-free. Telling my parents was my biggest hang-up, but turned out I didn't have to defend my decision. Manolo shocked me with a flat-out no. I felt seriously dejected and we had a huge fight. I mean, for us. I couldn't believe he shut me down so quickly."

She twirls the pen in her hand. "Why did he?"

"The thing is, LT, my parents." I stop, suck up my boogers, afraid to admit this to a Black woman, but the words don't stop. "My mom is kind of racist. She wouldn't even talk to me after I told her he was Mexican. Told me to get it out of my system, like dating him was just to get back at her. She never considered I loved him."

"And the rest of your family?"

"My sister and brother were cool. Dad, too. He said he didn't want me settling down so quick, like him and mom, but he didn't have a problem with Manolo being Mexican."

She nods that 'keep going' nod, but the memory upsets me. I wipe my eyes with the back of my hand, drag it over my nose and stop it from running. I cross my arms, then uncross them, careful of the tube. A long pause. I fidget over my nails.

I speak slow, quiet. "Night before we deployed, he told me he wanted to get married. Gave me a beautiful necklace as a promise. Started looking at rings online."

She leans closer to me. "Are you wearing it now?"

I feel my neck. Shake my head. My voice is weak. "It's gone."

I lost it in Butler's room. Never saw it again.

"Did you talk to your family about his death?"

"A little bit," I shift uncomfortably. "But I guess since they didn't know him, they didn't know what to say." It's the first time I really realize this. It really hadn't occurred to me until just now. Maybe I was too harsh on all of them.

She speaks with kindness. "Our time is almost up."

I look at the clock. Forty-five minutes gone. It felt like three.

She continues. "We'll work on individual therapy every day. There's group therapy, AA, occupational therapy, art therapy, family therapy and Cognitive Processing Therapy, we call it CPT. It's going to be hard, but we can work together to make things better for you, and to make sure your time here is well spent."

I rub the back of my neck. Time. We keep talking about time. That one time. That night. That night I drank. That night my life became an even bigger mess. I reach up and feel my neck again. As I do, my throat constricts. Suddenly I feel very, very tired and tears bubble up inside of me from the pit of my stomach. I try to hold it in, but fail.

"I'm sorry." I sob. "I hate crying." I can't stop.

LT touches my hand. "You can't really heal until you feel something, talk about him and come to terms with the loss." I cry harder.

CHAPTER 19

Amanda and Blue Falcons

"STUPID MOTHERFUCKERS," KATIA mumbles as she attempts to staple her papers together.

"Let me do it," I tell her but she pulls it farther from me.

We're making our own journals from scratch paper in a corner of the Art room with the frizzy haired Arts and Crafts lady. Technically, the schizophrenic is here, but she stares like she always does, drool forming in her lips and sliding down her chin. Found out her last name is Webber, so at least we can call her something besides schizophrenic. I don't even know my diagnosis yet, and I'd prefer it if people didn't name me by it.

Arts and Crafts lady has a name, too. Sally.

"Salmonella," Katia says under her breath.

My journal has a purple cover, which is really a stiff cardboard paper, with blue pages that Sally found in a printer. We have puffy sticker letters to create titles. Sally found us markers and crayons, too.

LT suggests it will help if I scribble down my feelings. After my big crying episode, she told me writing helps process emotions, and if I don't process them, I'll be stuck. Only problem is, I don't know where to start. So I'm taking my time and writing big block letters to avoid what we're supposed to do—write.

I look over at Katia. "What are the guys up to in the Dayroom?"

Katia staples for the tenth time. "Learning how to not beat their wives."

"I'm sure Tattoo loves that." I roll my eyes as I take the stapler from her. "You know, I bet he's a good husband."

"Are you stupid?" Her look tells me she already knows the answer.

"Ain't he married?" I give her a face that says I'm not stupid. Although I never saw a ring around his finger, I just assumed. Most military guys are married or going through a divorce. She still has that look on her face.

After a second she says, "You never seen a faggot before?"

My mouth falls open in shock. I get what she's telling me, but *what?*

I hiss. "Katia, *don't* say that word."

She shrugs. "Skeeter and Junes always called themselves faggots, it's no big deal."

"Who in the hell is Skeeter? And Junes?" I say the names with genuine bewilderment.

She winks at me. "Truck stop. Lots of faggots there."

God, she's loud. I shush her, "Katia. First of all, stop saying it."

"Faggot," she says with a sassy smile. Knows it ticks me off.

I stare at her with my eyes opened wide, brows up. Mouth pressed shut.

I whisper. "I like Tattoo and don't want to be the one who gets him in trouble. Ever heard of *Don't ask, Don't tell*?" I glance over at Sally and Webber as I remind her of the Army's current policy. They aren't looking at us. Katia flips her hand at me, as if to say she doesn't give a rat's ass about what I say or the policy.

"Gays are everywhere in the Army, stupid. Army needs 'em. Unless you see guys giving hot oil rub downs or sucking dick in uniform, they'll stay in," she rolls her eyes at me.

I stare at her, still shocked. "Did Tattoo tell you? He *said* so?"

"He don't need to tell me, stupid." She catches a glimpse of my confused face. "But yeah, he told me." She puffs out her cheeks, then holds out a hand. "Can I have that back?"

I hand her the stapler, trying to decide how to tell her to shut up about it. She's got to keep quiet. I like Tattoo. I like Katia. I don't want them kicked out for reasons they can't control.

My mind turns over this news. "Does Muscrat know...are they gonna chapter him out?"

She frowns. "Why should they? He's here for drunk driving and PTSD. Hard to prove a soldier's gay most of the time, unless they announce it to the world, which would result in a royal ass beating. Tattoo knows how to take care of himself."

"Yeah, I know." I reach for the stickers, for something to do.

She leans in close. "Don't tell me you're some type of gay bashing homo hater."

The accusation hits me hard. "No, not at all." I sputter. "I just never met someone who...was...*that way.*"

She *tsks* at me. "Then how do you know if I can say the word faggot or not?"

God, this girl. I say a little too loud, "Manolo and his buddies called each other *wet back*, but nobody else did. You can't if you're not..."

"A beaner?"

"—a Mexican." I flash her a severe look, as sharp as barbed wire. I know she's fucking with me, but I'm still pissed. I'm 1,000 percent humiliated by this conversation. Tattoo's been a blue chip, solid dude, and we're in here talking about his business.

"Gays are the best soldiers," she says. "Army fucks us all in the ass. They take it better than the rest of us."

I look away from her. I focus on my journal making for a few minutes, feeling stupid. I'm not sure if we had any gays or lesbians in my unit. There were rumors. As long as a soldier is a good soldier and not causing any trouble, no reason to investigate the gossip. Army needs dependable soldiers, so who cares? Policy is dumb. But—

"How'd it come up?"

Katia raises her thin eyebrows. "People tell me everything, Ashe. You did."

I flinch. She's right. "You tell him about *me*?"

She says nothing, but nods.

My mouth falls open. *What?* Why would she do that?

Truly mortified I stammer, "Everything?"

She shrugs and avoids my eyes. "Cliff notes version. I did you a favor."

"Oh yeah?" My heart hammers in my chest. Our conversation flashes in my mind and I feel ashamed that he knows about...well, everything.

She defends herself. "You were gonna tell him eventually."

My voice is sharp. "I make that decision. I didn't plan on telling him—ever ."

She rolls her eyes. "Yeah, right."

My words are choppy and panicked. "What if he tells someone else?"

"He won't."

"He *could*."

"Who cares? Keeping secrets is what makes people nuts, not talking," she says.

I am not getting through to her. God, I'll have to keep my mouth shut from now on. We have different ideas on privacy.

"Well. What'd he say?" I want to know.

She makes a face and shakes her head. "You'll get mad."

I swear she's trying to make me mad *right now*. "Tell me, goddammit."

"I will, but promise you won't get bitchy."

"Fine." I cross my arms in a huff.

She looks away. "He asked me, 'think she'll have sex again?"

"What the fuck?" My brain seems to explode. Now I'm pissed. What business is it of hers? Of his? It's nobody's goddam business! My heart's pounding. I want to hit them both.

"Think about it, stupid. First this great love dies, then these guys…"

"Shut up, Katia," I shout. "Just shut the fuck up."

She shrugs as I glare. "God damn, man. I knew you'd get all pissy."

I'm mad at both of them for talking about my problems without me. I'm mad at myself for opening my big, fat mouth. I peel the suns and moons off the sticker sheet and place them on my journal. Over and over. In a few minutes, it's completely covered. I don't feel any better.

Sally walks to our table and hovers over us, paint in hand. "Oh my, ladies. Guess you won't need paints. You got it all covered, don't you?"

I look at her. She doesn't wait for an answer. Takes the paint back. Katia sits up, places her finished journal on the table, and crosses her arms. Looks like she wants to say something. Before she does, we both hear the door creak open. Cat Eyes stands in a full pastel scrub set. Nails painted a hot pink. Hot pink hair band in her beautiful caramel curls.

Loud and clear, she announces, "PFC Moon, the Major wants a meeting."

Katia stands up, gives me the one finger salute. Grabs her journal.

"Stop pouting, bitch," she says. "You'll thank me someday."

"*Now*, Moon," Cat Eyes says and Katia slouches towards the door. Cat Eyes gives me a smile as she shuts the door behind them. I sit the rest of the hour in silence. Fuming.

❧

BACK IN THE room now. I'm curled up on my bed. We have free time and I'm supposed to be writing but I can't bring myself to do it. Every time I start, I think about Tattoo's question. I don't know the answer.

I wish my mind could slow down to the pace of my body. It's so easy. Therapy. Chow. Meetings. Journal-making. Resting. I haven't done this little in a day in a very long time. Maybe, ever. If Dad saw me now just lying on my bed, he'd tell me to *"Get off my dead ass."* Mom would tell me to help her, *immediately if not sooner.*

In the Army, I wasn't a Blue Falcon—Buddy F'er who shams and doesn't help out. I was always busy doing something. Makes me feel guilty to be doing nothing. I know soldiers are out there busting their humps on deployment. Juan from Landstuhl was right. I'm getting my paycheck for doing nothing. It's too quiet.

Or was.

The door slams open, striking the wall. Katia storms in. Greasy hair plastered to her forehead. Her eyes wild. She carries the newly made journal is in her hand. The other hand is clutching at her forehead. LT follows her, frowning.

"I maxed the APFT. Maxed it." Katia yells, "Every fucking time."

LT stands by as Katia paces back and forth in the room. I stare at them, uneasy.

Calmly, LT states, "Yes, we know that, PFC."

"Do you? Do you know that? Look at me. Never was taped, always made weight. Expert marksmen. Top twenty percent of Basic Training, do you hear that?"

"Nobody's arguing you weren't a good soldier," LT says.

"Am," Katia corrects her without stopping her pacing, "I *am* a good soldier."

"Right, sorry," LT says but Katia doesn't hear. She charges ahead, frantic in her steps and words. My breath is caught in my throat, afraid to breathe.

"Physically I was fucking perfect." Katia shouts, "Mentally, too. Emotional rock star. Not one fucked up thing about me, not one goddam thing. You got nothing to prove otherwise."

LT holds on to the clipboard like a life raft. We both watch Katia pace the room. With the few seconds of silence, I speak.

"Should I clear out?" I ask. I feel strange, seeing them. Suddenly they both look at me, as if they just noticed I'm here. Say nothing for a minute.

LT clears her throat, "That's up to PFC Moon." PFC Moon keeps pacing back and forth in our tiny room. She doesn't look over. There's something different, even for Katia. The way she's yelling is harsher than before, more desperate. I can't put my finger on it. Need to get off my *dead ass* and give them privacy, but I feel as if my body is in concrete and I stay.

"So this is *it*, huh," Katia yells, stomping back and forth as she grasps at her hair.

"PFC..." LT shakes her head.

Loud knock. Our eyes swoop over to the door.

"You need me?" Cat Eyes asks LT.

She doesn't wait for an answer and comes right in. Now there's four of us in this small excuse of a room. Stands near the opposite bed. I watch them, taking it all in, but a stone has appeared in my stomach. I feel sick, cramped.

Katia's voice booms, "Just let me get this straight. I come in here and answer all the questions, go to all the meetings, even make a stupid fucking journal."

She waves it in the air but continues to yell. "But because I tell you and Muscrat that my mom's boyfriends treated me like dog shit, like a million years ago, now I've got a fucking pre-existing condition that is getting me kicked out? I didn't have no fucking pre-existing condition. Just a shitty mom. And if that gets soldiers kicked out, then half the fuckin' Army's gone."

LT stays composed, looks at the floor then up again. Draws a deep breath. "A personality disorder, which is what Major Muscrat diagnosed you with, has a few causes."

Katia stomps over her words, "What is that anyway—a personality disorder? At least I have a personality. Unlike most of the ass clowns in here."

For the second time in a few minutes, there's a knock at the door.

Major Muscrat, in the flabby flesh. I haven't seen him since he gave his order to shove a tube in me. My skin crawls, heart pounds, and I feel like vomiting. I clutch the pillow in front of me. He's not even looking in my direction, staring only at Katia with a bored expression.

"What is the problem, PFC Moon?" he stands in the doorframe, taking it up.

Katia screams at him, "Don't think I don't know what you're doing, Muscrat? Kick me out with a pre-existing condition, huh? Guarantee the Army won't give me a cent for what happened. Disability benefits only for the service-related claims, isn't that right? Well, news for you, fucker—getting forced to suck my Platoon Leader's cock didn't happen before I signed up."

Major Muscrat puffs out his chest, standoffish and cold.

He speaks low, "PFC Moon, you are jumping to conclusions. A full medical board is being conducted and these are the preliminary findings. But you're absolutely right. Any medical condition found to have started prior to service will not be compensated. If that's you, then you still have options for healthcare. The VA can still help."

She explodes. "The fucking VA? You serious?"

"There is nothing *physically* wrong with you. No medical situation that needs to keep you here. The sooner we settle this, the better."

"Fuck that, sir!" Her journal flies through the air, missing him.

"Watch your language, Private."

She's not done. Faces him square on. "Who's paying you off, Major? Did that pathetic wiener Wright call you up?"

Major Muscrat clicks his tongue. Turns to LT and Cat Eyes.

Says simply, "We need a sedative."

They stand, helpless for a few seconds. Exchange looks, then walk slowly together out the door. They must follow orders. Katia stomps to get their attention back on her, but too late.

"No we fucking don't." Katia yells. "We need justice!"

Katia storms out of the room after them, the same way she came in.

"Get Darrell," Muscrat hollers out behind her. He glances over at me. I reel back. It's just us. My blood stops pumping. My hands get cold; my feet turn to ice.

I see a small bright red stain on his white uniform. He said jelly donuts are his favorite. The scene from the other day replays in slow motion. An awful feeling descends over my whole body. I wrap my arms around the pillow tightly.

He says nothing. Saunters out.

I exhale the air I've been holding.

Katia. Oh, poor Katia. What she says is true. It's a medical board loophole, especially for psychological stuff. Also, why the recruiter told me to keep my mouth shut about the rubber allergy thing. Nothing about us should exist, prior to service.

CHAPTER 20

Amanda, Plot Twist

KATIA SPENT THE night in Isolation. Alone. I'm feeling awkward about that as we sit together. I keep my hands stuffed into my pockets, twirling the two smooth un-swallowed morning meds around each other.

"Hmpf," she says, trying to pry the cover off the yogurt cup that she took from my tray a few seconds ago. She rips the lid off, spraying yogurt across the table. I take a napkin and wipe it up. I look around the room for a second, then back at her. She's not looking at me, but I see her face is a mess. Puffy eyes. Red splotches on her neck. I want her to have a do-over. Turn back time for the both of us.

"Why you so weird today?" Tattoo asks me as we all sit together in silence. He looks from me to Katia and back to me again.

"I'm not weird," I say, hearing the defensiveness in my own voice.

"Hell you ain't."

I shrug. "You're the one won't let cereal touch milk."

He swallows. Says with a shrug, "I'm a little picky."

I shake my head. "My baby sister only ate white things for a year. That's *picky*. You're straight up Cuckoo's Nest."

He chuckles. "That's the pot calling the kettle black, Ashe."

I snort. Sip my coffee. Don't really want to engage this morning. I put my Styrofoam cup down. Katia reaches over, grabs the muffin off my tray and rips it open. Small crumbs fall over the table. I notice the packaging. Otis Spunkmight.

She sees me notice and I smile faintly. Feel my face flush. I shift from butt cheek to butt cheek, but she doesn't look away. Crams most of the muffin inside her mouth. Mascara flakes down to her cheeks with the effort.

"You both are bizarre today," Tattoo says, "More than normal, I mean."

I stare at the table, trying to push down the irritation bubbling up. I've been suppressing it all night. Who the fuck does Muscrat think he is, just kicking her out like this? Every single thing Katia did in her life she had figured out for herself. No one had fucking helped her, even when she asked for it. This chubby jerk, who probably can't even tie his own boots, says she's not fit for service...and why? She didn't ask to join in this fucking sexual assault and rape club we got going on.

I exhale, reach over and take a large muffin crumb from Katia's tray. Popping it into my mouth, I gag. Fake sugar. Sticky sweet. Nasty. I spit it into a napkin. They both watch and I squeeze the napkin as I stuff it into my pocket, suddenly self-conscious and wanting to change the subject.

"Is today your last day?" I ask, wanting to know and not. She shrugs. I catch Tattoo's eyes but he keeps silent.

Katia leans in close to Tattoo, says smugly, "I told her what you asked me."

Tattoo's face warms up and soon I see reddish hues in his cheeks. He stammers out a few syllables. I shake my head and say, "Don't worry about it."

He lets out a *pffft* sound. "I wasn't..."

"Lesson learned," I say. "Don't tell her nothing you don't want repeated."

"Shit," he says, shaking his head and rubbing his hands together.

"We both should've known," I say as I roll my eyes and give a half-smile to show him I'm not mad. Katia was right, in a way. I feel better now that we are both exposed. I know about him and he knows about me. It's exhausting to explain, anyway.

I glance over at her. She's staring at me in a strange way.

"What?" I ask, suddenly nervous. I run my fingers over my brows. Yeah, I had plucked a few more last night. Too many, but it felt good to focus on something other than problems.

"It was something to do," I say. "They'll grow back."

She doesn't answer, but tilts her head in thought.

A staffer informs all of us in a loud voice, "Five minutes. Finish up."

I glance up at the small clock above the doorway. Sigh out loud.

Tattoo mutters, "Same shit, different day."

"Not for me," I hear Katia whisper.

"What does that mean?" I ask her. "What did they tell you yesterday?"

No answer. Suddenly, Katia stands. I look up at her to see she's smiling.

"Where are you going?" I ask.

She pushes her chair back, turns toward the staff sitting at the back table and yells over the chatter, "Gotta take a piss!"

A skinny white male staffer, the oblivious one who hands out our morning meds but never checks to see if we swallow, is hunched over a patient's foot, helping tie the laces. Patient is a big guy with droopy pants and gray hair that came in yesterday.

Staffer looks over, still hunched. Barks at her, "You don't have to yell."

She whines as she holds her pants. "But I can't wait two seconds."

He waves her off. *Go.*

Katia bolts from the room, half tripping over her untied moccasins. She moves like a jumpy, stray barn cat on the prowl. Doesn't stop at the closest bathroom and moves towards the hall, with an obvious purpose, but I'm not sure what that is now.

Cautiously, I touch a red grape on my plate and bring it to my mouth. I bite off a small chunk and roll the skin around on my tongue, which feels like a foreign object. In truth, grapes were always my favorite but they were expensive and we never got them. I take another bite, suck the juice.

Tattoo sits fully upright, eyes on me. Says, "I shouldn't have said what I said. Sorry."

I swallow the grape. "I get it." I give him a small smile.

Because I do. Tattoo didn't ask it meanly, I know. He was concerned, not nosy. After Katia told me what he said, I thought about the question for the rest of the hour. I decided it's not a question about love. It's about forgiveness and moving on. Tears form in my eyes. I close them to stop it, but I'm jolted out of my misery with a scream.

A loud, high-pitched shriek cuts the air like a knife.

"Plot twist, *bitches*!" a shrill voice screams out. My mouth drops open.

"That's *Katia*," I say.

Tattoo and I jump to our feet. We race towards the next scream. With my new moccasins, I have traction but my wound slows me down as he pulls ahead. The source of the cries comes from the nurses' station, which is empty.

Katia's back is to us. Her arms are pin wheeling as she falls in slow motion to the ground. When she lands, she's facing us. I scream.

"Katia," I shriek, "Oh my GOD." I suck in air and choke as we rush to her side. Kneeling by her, I see my sharp tweezers stuck inside her right eye.

Jesus Christ, a *tweezers* sticks out of her eye. Oh GOD. Bile rushes up my throat.

Her mouth moves, but I can't make out the words. Blood dribbles down her nose and into her mouth. She touches it and makes a gargling noise. Her fingers are bloody.

"Fuck," I whisper as I stumble back onto the floor. Tattoo holds me up.

"Bitches can't discharge me now," she says looking right through me. "Got me a physical wound."

Someone pulls us back. Darrell takes our place, cradling her. We stand by, helpless.

"Call ER – ASAP," he orders. Staff at the desk are already dialing.

Katia screams—loud and angry. Darrell restrains her from touching her eye.

By this point, everyone who can walk gathers around in a semi-circle, not speaking. I sway, and find Tattoo is right next to me. He grabs my arm. Gently. Firm.

"Hey, it's alright, she'll be alright," he says softly. I let him lie to me.

"Fuck you all," she yells loudly, then giggles. Bursts of loud laughter come from the pale waif. Absurd eruptions of laughs echo up and down the hall. Each laugh must hurt like hell. Two more staffers rush to her side. They block our view.

A heaviness presses down on every part of me. I'm thinking of all the what-ifs. *What if I hid it better? What if I never took it in the first place?*

Darrell yells, "Don't touch anything. Let the ER handle it!"

Staff tries to force the crowd away. "Go back to the Dayroom," they order. It's complete chaos, but we don't move.

The doors buzz open, the medics arrive and take charge of the scene. There's a stretcher. For a second I think this is all fake and she's about to make a run for it through the open door. But, no. It's real. I catch a glimpse of her bloody face as medics carefully lift her to the stretcher. She screams, then laughs. Darrell stands by her side and walks alongside her, her blood on his hands.

The new guy who claims to be General Pershing stands next to us, eyes glued to the action. One of Jackson's former posse members stands next to him and says, "Oh shit. I knew her. She was in Alpha Company. But she doesn't represent me, no way."

General Pershing drums his hands rat-a-tat-tat on the side of his leg. "Nah, she don't represent nothing but crazy. World War I was better, no women allowed in service."

There's so much I could say to these idiots but don't. Instead, I roll the uneaten meds inside my pocket against each other. I stare at a drop of blood on the floor. Katia's got a physical wound now. To stay in an Army that don't want her.

My hands shake as I slip the meds into my mouth.

The bitter pill sits on my tongue for a few seconds, before I make a decision.

I swallow.

Things are gonna be different for me.

CHAPTER 21

Amanda in the Tigris

I'M STANDING ON the banks of a muddy river. I take a step and my foot sinks. The sky is a deep forest green, then turns black as night. Fireworks explode, but I hear screaming. I realize it's mortars. Quick as possible, I retreat. Try to take a step back, but the mud turns into cement. I'm stuck. I panic.

I realize I'm standing in the Tigris River, back in Baghdad.

"Amanda. Amanda." Someone shouts. I turn around. The cement turns to sand and my feet become free.

"Baby." It's Manolo with his macho tank crew. He motions for me to follow him into their M1 Abrams. He disappears through the hatch. As I watch, the sandy banks on which the tank stands give way and the tank rolls into the dirty water. In seconds, it's submerged.

I rush towards them, but stumble. I'm caught by someone before I fall. It's Weisengard. She hauls me up, holds me firm, and yells, *'No. You can't do anything. Let him go,*

I twist away, even with her nails digging into my wrist. I jump into the river and dive under the murky, brown water. I see nothing. Manolo's nowhere. Neither is the tank. I panic.

I propel my body through the water with an all-out burst. I kick harder and stretch my arms in front of me, pulling myself ahead. I rotate my body down, down, down. My lungs burn the deeper I go. I need air. I turn towards the surface, but I perceive hazy outlines of dozens of crocodiles above. Terror grips my stomach as one croc swims directly at me, his wide mouth displaying razor-sharp teeth. Jaws smash shut, and he morphs into a soldier.

It's Butler.

Smiling a wide, toothy-blue grin. I'm paralyzed in the dense water. I sink, fast.

"Amanda, Amanda, Amanda," he sings and reaches out, "Trust me…"

Nothing exists but us in the river and I kick as fast as possible away from him. Little by little, I gain distance between us. The second I'm about to break the surface, Butler grabs my hair and pulls me further down, underwater. My lungs fill with sludge. We're both trapped together.

"You deserve this," he whispers as he puts his mouth over mine and bites me on the lips. A sharp pain stabs my side.

"Traitor," he says as he pulls out long, thin tweezers from my stomach. Blood mixes with the water and spreads around us. I look down and see my guts spilling out.

I bolt upright in bed.

My heart slams my chest. My legs are wrapped up in stiff sheets and I kick myself free. My thin, sweaty blanket is soaked and my clothes cling to me. I jump out of bed and flip on the lights. I'm alone, *or am I?* I rush into the small bathroom and rip the shower curtain back. All clear. Back in the room, I duck my head under the bed and pull out the drawers in my desk. All Clear.

I stagger to the sink and grip the edge. My arms are trembling, but I manage to look into the mirror. *Steady, Amanda.* Staring back is the same face I've always had—except now dark half-moons sag under my blue eyes, which seem almost fluorescent against bloodshot-red rims.

I hold my head under the sink and turn on the faucet. Cool water flows over my mouth as I gulp. My chest stops pounding *lubs* and morphs into *thumps.* I step back and sink to the floor like a stone. The water continues to run, and the sound is that of the river. Is death like that tap on the sink? Turn it off, and all the pain goes away?

My door swooshes open. Ponytail. Her concerned eyes and a slender body stand in the entry. I wipe my face and slowly struggle to my feet. I feel the blood drain from my face.

"Nightmare? I heard you yelling."

I nod and close my eyes. Without wanting to, I think about Manolo and my body betrays me. My knees go weak. I double over and my breath catches in my throat.

"Easy does it." She's soft. Her arms reach towards me. In two strides she's next to me and turns off the tap. Hands a small, folded white towel. I wipe my hands as she looks me up and down. I bite my tongue hard to stop tears forming in the corner of my eyes.

"When's the last time you got a full night's rest?"

I shrug. With Katia, I had six. I have no idea when I had more, besides when I was drugged up and cut into. Nightmares make me scared to sleep. It's exhausting even when I do.

I hear words. I don't understand until the last few words, *what do you think?*

"Sorry, what?"

"You want to take a shower? To clean up a little. Whaddya think?"

I nod, yes. I cross my arms and shiver under my cold sweat. I nod again, *please.*

"I'll get your sharps bucket. I'll sit on this bed the whole time and be right here. I'm gonna get you new clothes, too."

"I'll need a new bandage." I hold up my pajama shirt and she nods.

She gives a friendly smile. "Give me one minute."

My body shivers uncontrollably as she walks out, her ponytail swinging behind her. She leaves the door open. I want to follow her down the hallway. *Take me with you, Nice Ponytail Lady* I yell inside my skull. But my feet are stuck in the mud of the Tigris and I stay put. Time passes, maybe hours or years or seconds or minutes. I forget time. I forget people. Why don't I forget the bad memories?

Ponytail's back with my sharps bucket, a large towel, and a stack of new clothes. She steps into the bathroom and turns on the shower.

"Found some good shampoo and conditioner. Smells like cotton candy."

"Thanks." I barely have a voice.

"Sure." She hands me the towel and clothes. "Will you need help taking off your stuff? I mean with the tube..."

No. I shake my head. "It's okay."

"I'll be right here, on guard. Take your time." She sits on the bed and pats it, as if to say she's happy to be here.

I step into the tiny bathroom. I stack the towel and pajamas on the closed toilet seat. Peeling off the sticky clothes, I throw them on the floor and step into the mildew-smelling shower. The water is a little too hot. It turns my white skin pink. I dump shampoo on my hands and scrub my body, using my fingernails as a loofah. I visualize the tiny scratches opening my skin so the dirty pain can ooze down the drain. I breath in the foggy steam and a terrible ache I didn't know I had releases as the hot water scorches me clean. I rub conditioner all over my hair, finger brushing out the knots. Gobs of dark hair slide into the open drain.

Like Katia's dyed hair.

The more I think about what she did, the harder it is to breathe. I'm thinking about her. About Manolo. Jackson. Vincent. And worst of all, Butler. I'm thinking about me and them and all of this. It's just too much.

The water turns cool and my teeth chatter, but I let it run down my back as my neck bends into almost a 90-degree angle. My feet turn clammy blue and my body trembles under the arctic water. Yet, I can't turn it off.

I hear a soft knock, "Want help? I won't look, promise."

I wipe my eyes with wet, wrinkled hands. "No, no, sorry, just a minute."

I turn off the water and reach for the towel. I dry off quickly and put the new pajamas on, careful with the tube. The bandage is wet and feels gluey against my skin. I leave the old clothes on the floor and open the door to my room. My feet are wet so when I walk, I leave prints behind me. Evidence to me that I exist here and now. I'm not near the Tigris or the Euphrates. I'm here, in Walter Reed with this Ponytail nurse. She sits on my bed, which is newly made with a thick, white blanket and a soft pillow. I wrap the towel around my wet head. I breathe out.

I give her a small smile. "I'm feeling alright now. Thanks."

She looks me over. Gives me a little look.

"It's only 3 a.m.," she says. "I can get you a sleeping aid. Yes?"

I shake my head. I watch her stand. I love this Ponytail lady so much right now. I want nothing more than to hug her. I want to say something like, *Bless You* or *That was the kindest thing anyone's done for me in a while.* I say nothing like that.

"You look like my sister. Same green eyes." The words barely make it out of my mucky throat but it's true. Hazel-green.

"I like your blue eyes," she says then squints a little. Hesitates. "You have… perfect eyebrows." The last two words are more of a question.

I stop breathing.

I touch my face and trace my finger over my eyebrows. Feel like I'm underwater again as panic rises in me. *Plot twist, bitches!* rings in my head. Tears form in my eyes but don't fall. She bites her lip for a minute, scans the room.

Silence.

"Ashe—," she starts to say but I cut her off.

"I shouldn't have had it. But I hid it and I didn't think...," I can't find the right words. Instead, I feel myself get more and more desperate. I don't know what would happen to me if staff realized it was *my* sharp. Accessory to an eye-stabbing? I beg her. "Please."

I wait a few long seconds.

She sighs. Rests her hands on her hips. "Between you and me, this wasn't the first time she self-harmed. Katia was determined to stay in this hospital. She's scared of what happens next. That's all there was to it."

"She wasn't taking her prescription medications." I don't know why I say it. As if it lets me off the hook, but really it makes me feel stupid. My words hang between us but she doesn't react in any observable way.

"Just make sure you take yours," she says.

I nod as I chew on my lip. I promise myself that I will do whatever they say.

Her voice is calm. Ponytail asks, "Where're you from?"

I swallow hard. "Wisconsin."

"Cheese head?"

"Guilty."

She gives me a little smile. "I grew up in Minnesota near the border. There wasn't no such thing as a Viking fan near me. Just people who hated the Packers."

Funny. I give her a smile, relieved.

"When's the last time you called home?"

I look down at my hands. "Before all this."

Ponytail grabs the new bandage and walks towards me. Suddenly, I'm too tired for anything else, even talking. Definitely not changing the bandage. I don't make eye contact.

"Can we do that when I wake up?"

Ponytail stands a couple of feet from me. Slowly nods but doesn't turn. I close my eyes and when I open them again, I feel I have to say something. The guilt is crushing me.

"I'm sorry." It's a whisper.

"It's not your fault." She studies the bandage. "I understand you probably feel awful, but Private Moon made the choice. Not you."

"She didn't think she had a choice."

"Fair enough. But you do. Don't put yourself in that position."

I look at her. Wonder how much she knows about Katia. Or me. Her pretty mouth twitches but she says nothing.

"I won't," I whisper as a promise to her, and to me.

"You need to sleep."

I nod at her because she's right.

"Let me help you."

She pulls back the new blanket and I crawl into the bed. She tucks me in. Suddenly, I'm so tired. Even with the threat of a nightmare, I'll risk it. I'm ready to nod off.

Ponytail walks to the door. "Come and find me if you can't sleep. I'm at the front desk. Really, you can talk to any of us. Staff like me aren't in the army, but we care about you guys."

She pauses. Looks at her white shoes and puffs up her chest, like she might say something deep and profound. I don't want her to. I just want to go to bed.

I interrupt her train of thought. "You got anything to read?"

"The Army Times?"

"No thanks." God, no. Army Lies newspaper, same shit week after week.

"I know this is late, but I'm sorry about everything."

"Yeah, me too."

"Lights on or off?"

"On."

She smiles and shuts the door behind her. The warm blanket is pleasant and cuddly. I stare at the ceiling. Relief washes over me, which is bad, I know. But it's a relief that nobody is looking for the owner of the tweezers.

I can't let myself turn out like Katia. There are good people around here that can help us figure out our problems. LT is alright. Cat Eyes—er, Nurse Taylor—has been great. Ponytail is nice. Then there's Tattoo. He's been a good dude from the get-go. He's dependable and respectable. Solid. I can trust these people.

I've had some bad luck over the past few years. Maybe that's all it was—luck. Some people are luckier than others—easier deployments, better leadership, nicer barracks, joined the Air Force—but now I can make my own luck. I can let down my guard, get some help. I *have* potential. I'll find a way for justice so I can move on.

Life will be different for me.

CHAPTER 22

Amanda and Dad

I HOLD THE one pill in my palm. It's perfectly circular and white. Not much bigger than a corn kernel. I pop my pill, hold it on my tongue and sip water from a little Dixie cup to wash it down. Nurse Taylor, as I should and will forever call her, meets me at the blood pressure machine. Most times, I get my vitals done by the squirrely looking intern with a mullet.

I ask Nurse Taylor, "Where's the weasel?"

"Day off." No hesitation. She knows who I mean. Taylor wraps the scratchy band around my arm and the air automatically pumps. "You take your pill?"

I nod.

"And how do you feel this morning?"

I exhale a thin stream of air. "I'm not gonna hurt myself."

"I just want to know how you are." She shifts her dark eyes to me.

I shrug. "Fine, thanks."

"Uh-huh." But I don't hear what else she says because in my mind I'm thinking about Katia's eye leaking blood all over the floor. She must have been out of her mind in pain, even when she laughed. I shudder just thinking about it...

"Ashe?" I blink and look at Nurse Taylor. "Did you hear me?"

I shake my head. "Can I visit Katia?"

She frowns. "No visitors, that's what came down the pipe."

Oh, come on. I tell her, "Army rules are suggestions, you know."

She hears me and half snorts, half frowns, "Not at Walter Reed."

Now it's my turn to frown. Operational readiness exists because of exceptions. And there are so many more exceptions being made than anyone admits.

I'm not taking no for an answer. "Every rule in the army is negotiable."

"Not this one." She points to my abdomen. "May I?"

I nod. She lifts the corner of my pajama top to check on the tube insertion. I don't look but feel her pull off the bandage, swab my skin with liquid, cover it with gauze and seal it with adhesive film. I'm so annoyed, but try to ignore it.

"Still red. Does it itch?"

I shake my head no. It doesn't, really. "Nobody's shown me how to use it."

"That's 'cause you're eating food, honey." She pauses. "You sure it feels alright?"

I shrug. "When is it coming *out*?"

"We'll see." Her face shows a lot of tenderness, and in this moment I'm thankful she's with me in here. Taylor's gentle as she puts my shirt down. "Staff has a little surprise today."

"What?"

"You know I can't tell you that. It's a *surprise.*"

"Trip to the White House? Or maybe to the Capitol building?"

"Not quite, but you're on the right track."

"The parking lot?" She shoots me a funny frown, but I wouldn't mind. I've been inside too much. After yesterday, we all need a break from this ward.

"Your heart rate is low," she says as pulls at the Velcro and removes the cuff. "But your blood pressure is good. Eat breakfast, got it?"

I fake salute her. She pushes the machine away.

I follow the others towards the sharps closet. We brush our teeth and comb our hair, well, the ones of us with hair. Then it's on to the dayroom. We find our seats. I'd love to go back to bed. This tough guy attitude of waking up early even when there's nothing to do is getting old. I sit next to Tattoo, and I put my head on the crook of my arm. Close my eyes.

❧

I HEAR TATTOO grunt at me, "Wake up, Ashe."

I open my eyes and sit up. I wipe the drool from my chin.

"Did I fall asleep?"

He nods and points to his watch. 06:30 on the dot. We both look at the empty chair where Katia sat yesterday. He frowns. I chew my lip. Katia is gone. Disappeared down the deep dark hole of Walter Reed. God, makes me feel sick. I look away.

An orderly brings us our trays. Tattoo hands over his coffee and seems like he might say something, but doesn't. He watches me take a sip then looks at his plate.

Eggs. Toast. Butter. Oatmeal. Cereal. Squishy banana. Juice. Coffee.

I can barely force myself to unwrap it. The plastic cover sticks to my thumb and part of the milky-white scrambled egg falls to the table. My groggy mind sees it, but does nothing.

My last morning with Manolo I cracked our remaining eggs in a bowl and stirred them with a splash of water. Manolo put bread in the toaster. We had a thumbs length of chorizo left and moldy goat cheese from a squash salad we'd made two weeks ago, so I cut off the questionable parts. I found a packet of plain oatmeal and added raisins, cinnamon and half a stick of butter. I didn't waste food, not then. I made the coffee too watery, because there wasn't much left, and he called it *bolillo juice.*

"What is it, Ashe?" Tattoo says.

I wake from my daze and see my hand holding the banana in front of my mouth. I take a bite and chew. "I think I'm hungry."

Relief on his face, Tattoo says, "Took you long enough." He shovels a sketchy looking sausage in his mouth.

It's true that I haven't eaten much. Or kept it down, I mean. But every time I swallow food I feel a glob of Vincent's cum in my stomach. I can't. Not yet.

I change the subject. "Nurse Taylor says we get a surprise today. So maybe we get to call home or something. That'd be nice."

"The nurse with those blue glasses?"

"Yeah, Taylor. That's her name." I look at him curiously. "What's yours?"

"Hunt."

"I mean your first name."

He shakes his head. "Call me Tattoo, alright?"

"My name is Amanda Anna Ashe. A tongue twister. Can't be worse than that."

"It can." I think I see his cheeks turn pink.

I press it, mostly because I feel awful I haven't asked before. I was too wrapped up in myself. "My initials are AAA. Triple A. Auto insurance."

He says nothing. He shoves another sausage in his mouth.

"Harold? Hank?"

"Just drop it," he snaps.

I shrug. "Okay, okay."

Tattoo gulps his water. "You got family you want to call?"

"Yeah. It's been awhile. They don't even know I'm here."

His mouth hangs open. "You kidding me? You *gotta* tell them where you are. What if they return your mail to sender?"

I never thought of that. I can see Jo worrying herself sick if that happened. Dad. Connor. Maybe, Mom. I'd feel awful if I couldn't reach them and know they'd be the same. They'd feel powerless, the shittiest feeling there is.

I tap my plate with my thumb. "One problem, Tattoo. No calling card."

He looks surprised. "Why didn't you say so?"

He fishes a card from his pocket, then slides it across the table. An unopened calling card worth 200 minutes.

I stare at him, surprised.

"You don't need it?" I ask.

He shrugs. "I got plenty. You just need to ask if you need something, you know."

No, I didn't know. My mouth turns dry and my thanks is a mumble. I'm so grateful. Grateful he sits at this table and didn't give up on me. A true battle buddy.

❧

BREAKFAST IS OVER. I'm nervous, but I'm first at the phones. I sit down, dial the number as most of the patients shuffle out of the room. We get our surprise in an hour, so I don't need to rush. I punch in the numbers and it rings. Dad answers but the line crackles. He's using the phone in the entry of the barn. That's how it sounds.

"Yello?" he says hello with a y.

"It's me," I say. My lip quivers. I chomp down on it.

"Baby Girl!"

"Hi, Dad."

I haven't spoken to Dad for months, just before we left for Kuwait when I promised him I'd be safe and fine. Before that, we rarely spoke after Manolo's death. I clammed up, I guess. Sad and lonely. Embarrassed about what happened between me and Butler. Unwilling to explain, hoping they could read my mind and know I needed them.

"Yer moms with your Aunt at Wally World. How's the desert?"

I take in a deep breath. "I'm in a hospital in D.C."

The line's silent and I imagine Dad's face scanning the work he has to do at the same time trying to imagine why I'm in D.C.

He speaks low. "What happened?"

I take a big breath. "I'm okay. Physically. Gotta work on…well, mentally I got some things going on."

I close my eyes and wait for the new line of inquiry.

Instead, he says, "You get yourself a plane ticket home as soon as you can. You just need time back here, where you belong."

I lean forward, my elbows on my knees, phone pressed tight. I brace myself. "What about Mom?"

He whistles, low and slow. "Hell. She's had your bed made for years."

Words won't come. I don't know what to say. I thought Mom hated me.

Tears form in my eyes. "Dad," I say, holding in the sob, "I'm sorry I didn't call much. I was kinda lost after Manolo died..." My voice catches in my throat.

"Ain't easy, Baby Girl. Wasn't for me. Never is for anyone."

For a second, I don't understand. Then a framed photo of Uncle Jack flashes through my mind. Of course, Dad can understand. He's lost someone, too. I've been so wrapped up with me, I forgot how well Dad knows death. His dad died when he was 16. My Uncle died in Vietnam when he was only 18 and Dad was 20. We never talked about it much. But maybe Dad, out of everyone, knows how I feel.

"We got time to talk about this when you're home," he says firmly. "Today ya caught me when the vet's coming. Call back later. Jo's off work at 5. Yer mom'll be here."

I'm so relieved, I feel like crying. I promise, "I'll try, Dad."

"Smile, baby girl. We'll be here waiting for you."

He hangs up. 'Smile' is his way of saying 'I love you." A crushing weight lifts from my chest. Dad feels like my place is still in Wisconsin. No matter what, I have somewhere to go. I have people in my family who love me. I am not Katia in that way. I bet my family would take her in, help her get straightened out. Especially Jo. She always feeds the barn cats.

I hang up the phone and stare at the dirty floor. Nobody else is in line.

I think back to when Manolo died. True, they never met him. Maybe they were sorry when I told them. It was over the phone and I couldn't see their faces. Death is hard, like Dad said. I realize now that they just didn't know what to do or say. But I got options. Choices. Today Dad wanted to remind me I've got a home and that's more than just something. That's everything.

CHAPTER 23

Amanda Catches the Elevator

OUR SURPRISE IS fresh air. It's DC-pollution-smoggy-air, not garden-fresh, but I'm not an air snob. Manolo and I both liked the outdoors. I told Manolo about the skies of northeast Wisconsin where it's possible to see millions of stars at night. He would've liked it, but it sounds better than it is. The problem is the smell after manure's been sprayed on the fields. It drifts rotten egg-poop stank air for miles.

Most of us patients are allowed to go outside for Arts and Crafts. They led us through an underground maze and we popped out between two buildings, then walked to a small field. I can see the fence that surrounds the base and still hear the D.C. traffic. We stop near a group of trees that ditched their green leaves for rusty red and yellow. Smells earthy and looks pretty. An assortment of maples and oaks put on a multi-color show for us.

"Go ahead and sit on the grass," Sally says.

"I got a grass allergy," one of Jackson's boys says as he props himself up on a tree. By his nervous twitch and swiveling head, it's more likely he's got a mental reaction to being exposed out here in the open.

I sit down, away from the others. The ground is dry but spongy. I pluck the short grass with my fingers. Tattoo crosses his legs next to me and leans back. LT stays standing next to Sally who's brushing a rainbow of multi-colored ribbons in her left hand. Lots of staff nearby.

Sally waves her arms above her head to get our attention.

"Each person gets five pieces of ribbon," Sally says as she holds up a pink one. "On each one, you'll write something different. Two can be regrets, two should be your hopes, and one big wish for the future. Can be anything. I have black markers to write with and then we will hang them on the tree."

Patients look at each other, eyes narrowed. It feels super surreal to be outside, and now we're writing on ribbons? Therapy is weird.

"Does an honorable discharge count?" Someone shouts.

And then—oh Lord above—nobody can shut up. Soldiers talk all at once and shout out to each other. *Hot wife! New car! Win the lottery! Become Sergeant Major! Big house!*

"How do you spell Bacardi?" that General Pershing patient says to the group. Guys around him laugh, even the one by the tree.

Sally rolls her eyes with a smile. She's holding her arms up to calm them down. "Remember, this is a way for you to let go of any bad feelings, as well as think about the future. Leave them out here on the tree; let the tree regret for you and hope for you."

I shake my head. A tree of regrets—well, that's a new one. I stroke the blades of grass and look up into the blue sky as she hands out the ribbons and markers. A light breeze shakes some of the rust-colored leaves down to earth. I hear the snap of the American flag on and off in the distance.

Tattoo gets ribbons, then hands me some.

"I'd like to make E-7, even with what happened," he tells me as he writes.

"Uh-huh," is all I can say. E-7 was Manolo's rank. Senior NCO. Rank of the responsible and dedicated, respected leaders. "Think you can do it?"

"Maybe."

I don't know what to think—Tattoo sure did make a bad choice before I met him. Could've hurt someone and he's just damn lucky he didn't. I say nothing because anything I have to say about what *could've* happened, he already thought about 100 times. I'm sure of it.

"I don't plan to drink again," he says. "If I do, I'll walk a hundred miles before I even think about getting in a car. I was a freaking numbnuts. Thank God I didn't kill nobody."

He's shaking his head as he speaks in remorse.

"I stopped," I say and look away. I study the ribbons. "Sobering up wasn't a choice—I had to. Ever since the night I got drugged up, I haven't looked at liquor. Even thinking about it makes me feel like puking."

He peers at me. "We both had shitty years, huh?"

I swallow hard. "That best friend of yours that didn't make it. Was he—?"

Maybe we both lost the loves of our lives. It's not a club I *want* to be in, but am.

He shakes his head. "I lost a *friend*. Awesome dude, actually. He knew about me but didn't say nothing. Wasn't closed minded about it. He met my ex-husband."

Tattoo looks at me, searching. I'm stunned and my eyes go wide. I shift on my butt, lean in towards him even though we're far from everyone. "Husband?"

There are some states that allow for it. Wisconsin—no, but someday.

He lets go a big sigh. "Shit, it's complicated. Not technically married. We had this blessing ceremony. He wanted to get married in Boston before deployment but I kept pushing it off. I was so worried that somehow somebody would find out."

Jesus. That's tough. "He's in the Army?"

"No, but he knew the rules. Used that against me, too."

"Where's he live now?" I don't know why I ask, except I'd like to wring his neck.

Tattoo rubs his hand over his scalp. "Vegas," he says all quiet then clears his throat, "He broke it off right as I'm getting ready to get out of here."

While he speaks, I understand the timeline. "Right before you landed in Ward 54."

He nods. "Over the phone, not even face to face. It was a bad time."

I make a sympathetic sigh. "I'm picking that up."

I don't know what else to say. I can't imagine the shit he had to put up with and he couldn't say a word. Homophobia is rampant due to so many ignorant testosterone-crazed dudes thinking life in the Army is one long pissing contest. Tattoo would've had a tough time in a lot of units, I bet, if anyone knew.

He clears his throat. "Yeah, well, it's okay now."

I say in a mumble, "I hope you're feeling like you can talk to me. Sorry I didn't..."

I pause. Didn't what? Know his ex? I stop talking so I don't sound like an idiot. I try to catch his eye to give him a concerned look, but he isn't looking at me. He runs his hands over the ribbons with such intensity I stare at them, too.

"Don't be sorry about nothing. He blew over 14K of my savings when I was downrange. Knew I couldn't do shit about it since I gave him power of attorney before we deployed. Can't exactly tell my chain of command, you know."

I wince. "God, what a freaking mess. 14K is a ton of money."

He shrugs, "It happens."

I stretch my legs in front of me and slouch as I blow the air from my lips. There are no words I can think of that could help.

Wind blows a gentle breeze. Today is too nice. I don't want to ruin it with regrets. The breeze reminds me of a hope, not despair over him. Or Katia. It reminds me we have futures. The guys are still yelling their dreams back and forth. I catch some as I inhale and exhale. *Brand new F150! Brand new brain! Hot girlfriend and wife!*

I listen for a second then say, "Hopes are easy. I want to go to the beach in Mexico."

"Pacific or Atlantic Ocean?" Tattoo says as he writes.

"Pacific. I mean, Atlantic. Which side has Cancun?"

"Atlantic," he says, "I went to Puerto Vallarta a few years ago. Fun place, but it's on the Pacific side.

I feel dumb. I should know this. Manolo talked about us visiting together someday. I could have looked at a map. Dummy Amanda. I write down my hope to go there someday soon.

"I bet you regret you got a feeding tube," he says as he looks me in the eye.

"I don't really notice it too much." I'm embarrassed. I put my hand over it. It's been completely useless and physically painless. I think of Muscrat and my throat tenses up. I stop thumbing the grass and instead rip a handful and sit up, clutching the blades. I let the grass fall from my fingers and pick dirt out of my nails.

"Fall is so pretty," I say, trying to change the subject.

"Change can be a beautiful thing," he says.

Then with my next inhale: smoke.

We both get a whiff of cigarette smoke at the same time; it's coming from behind us. We turn around to see a skinny, older white lady about twenty meters away smoking right outside the hospital, in the No Smoking Zone. Her blonde, thin hair hits the collar of her acid-washed jean jacket. Black sunglasses cover half her face, but the half I see is full or wrinkles.

Nurse Taylor is on it. Beelines to her. I watch her talk to the lady. She argues a minute, then takes a long drag before she stomps it out. Spins around and heads towards the building she came out of.

"You ever smoke?" I ask.

"Not anymore," he says with a quick snort. Eyes me then writes more on his ribbons.

I watch him. He's a nice guy; there are some nice guys out there. Like Manolo. Good dudes. Maybe the Army has more good men than I figured. It was my bad luck that I ran into the wrong ones. Something that even I could never have controlled.

❧

THE TREE LOOKS like the outside of something you'd see at a circus with so many colorful ribbons attached. Since we didn't cause any issues, we walk outside towards the hospital, leaving behind the tree. Soon we're back inside, with its stuffy-stale air.

Nurse Taylor tells me to hold up. I don't ask why, but I wait as the others walk down the hall. Tattoo gives me a small wave.

Taylor turns to me when they're around the corner. "Didn't want to scare you, honey, but you had puss near that tube. Nothing major, but I didn't like the look of it."

I'm surprised. I thought it was just annoying. "Puss?"

"It's a sign of an infection. I'd like to swing by and see a friend of mine who works in the ER, see if we need to get you some antibiotics."

I fidget with my hands. "I'm kind of allergic to it."

"What?" she looks in disbelief.

"Rubber. Probably why it's not healing," I say, relieved and nervous that I said it.

She turns sharply. "Let's go."

I hope to God the nurse at the ER says it's bad enough to take out. I haven't even used it. Muscrat never spoke to me after it was inserted or attached or whatever they call it, and I've got more questions than answers at this point.

We walk. The hallways are narrow. Seems everyone knows her. It's all "Hey there" and "How you doing today" as we make our way to a new wing. Passing through the halls, I notice every single water fountain is covered up with plastic wrap and tape; not even a work order taped onto it.

"Why's it so broken in here?"

"Walter Reed's closing," she says like I should know this.

"It's like a hundred years old," I say in shock. Army likes to preserve its traditions, usually.

"Exactly," she says. "Some traditions need to be broken."

She keeps up the "Hellos" and "How are you's" as we walk. Left, left, left, right, left. I keep in step, head up. Walking through, people see me with her and they know that I'm One of Them. I get double takes. It was that way my whole time in service. Although I was immersed in the Army, and maxed every PT test I ever took, I was never really gonna be a part of it as a female. I'm immersed in Walter Reed, but with a different type of wound. A Nurse Taylor, Ward 54 type of wound.

We wait on the elevator to go up a level. She meets my eyes but doesn't say a word. Pushes the up button again. The elevator beeps. Doors slowly open and she sticks her hand along the side of the door to keep it open for me.

"After you," she says.

I step past her into the narrow area, slink all the way to the back. I keep my eyes on the floor but glance at a heavy-duty wheelchair, which takes up most of the limited space. Patient's right leg is up in a front rigging, covered with a light sheet. A male Oompah-Loompah-looking staff member in scrubs grips the handlebars. He's so tan, he's orange. Not even a glance over, and I learn quickly it's because he's in the middle of telling a story.

Whistling loudly, he says, "She was so dirty, man, I came home and took a shower. I didn't say no, though, you know what I'm sayin'?"

I grimace. Yuck. Nurse Taylor still holds the door, waiting for another staff member who I imagine is rushing towards the elevator from the outside. I hear someone shout, *coming!*

Oompha Loompah snorts. Says to the entire elevator, "That's what she said."

My eyes throw darts at the Oompah-Loompah. With his crooked buzz cut, he'd be lucky anyone touches him. He smirks at me and I don't look away until I see his patient shifting around in the wheelchair. I look at him to check on his reaction to this bullshit.

Time. Stops.

I'd know that shaved blond head anywhere. Patient sits in his chair, not looking at me, but I'm sure as hell looking at him. What are the chances?

Butler.

CHAPTER 24

Amanda and Butler

OH GOD, OH God, oh God. How. *HOW?*

I take in a sharp breath. He looks up.

The elevator goes dark; it's only us. For a split second, I imagine close quarters combat playing out with me eye-gouging the Oompah Loompah followed by an elbow strike to the back of Butler's fat head. My heart beats so fast it might explode, but I can't move. I'm stuck.

The cocky asshole looks me over. Slight grin, tilts his head. Says, "Hey, *Jelly*."

Jelly.

I feel shot in the chest. Point blank.

I explode.

"Fuck YOU!" I scream as I rush out of the goddamn elevator.

I trip on the floor and fall into Nurse Taylor's cushiony boobs. Surprised, she grabs for my wrists to hold me up, but I break free from her grasp and continue to run away.

"Hey! *Hey!* What'd you say to him? What's your name, soldier?" hisses the Oompah Loompah as he steps out of the elevator after me.

"Fuck OFF!" I shout as I turn to them, then back away.

Nurse Taylor yells for me, "Ashe! What's wrong?"

I rush away from her, and the terror in the elevator, as fast as I can. My unlaced moccasins flop against the floor, slowing me down. My throat squeezes shut, and no more words come up, but my mind says *get the fuck outta there, outta the elevator, outta the hospital.*

"Ashe." I hear Nurse Taylor call after me. I hear the elevator ping shut as I bolt towards the double doors that lead outside, the doors we came through just minutes ago. Minutes before I knew I shared a hospital with Butler.

I hear shoes squeak behind me, but I pump my arms to move. I hold the bandage over my tube as I go, not looking back. It hurts so bad but I don't stop.

She sounds far away as she calls out, *"Ashe. Ashe."*

I need the outdoors, the air. My vision narrows to the doors, to freedom.

I run smack into the exit handle bars and shove open the doors with one giant heave. I take a few steps before I stop. My legs protest each step. My lungs and legs burn while tears sting my eyes. I collapse to my knees, panting, holding the tube. My side throbs. I lift up the pajama top, look down and see red blood staining the bandage.

I dry heave to the ground, but nothing comes up, just sticky saliva that coats my throat and my tongue. I cough hard to get it out of me, the sticky goo hangs on and I have to pull it off of my lips with my fingers. I wipe my hands on my bottoms. Nothing makes me feel more of a loser than to see my spit on the concrete. It looks like cum.

"You alright?" a raspy voice asks and I look up. It's the smoking lady. She takes a deep drag and keeps a steady expression fixed on me, but not in a nosy way.

I shake my head. "Not really," I breathe.

She eyes me, frowns. "Want a cigarette?"

"I don't—" I say as I shake my head. My breathing and my heartbeat slow in unison. The fire on the corners of my lungs subsides and I finish my sentence, "—smoke."

Smoker clears her throat and takes a step in my direction, pulling one out of her pack. "Kind of looks like now's a good time to start." She holds out a cigarette. It's the Swisher Sweet type that was popular in high school. Smoke tastes of woody fruit, and not dirt.

I take it from her with a nod, but don't put it in my mouth. Holding it gives me a quick calm. Reminds me of the pit. And home.

"It *was* a good day," I say. My voice shakes as hot tears well up in my eyes.

"Life changes fast," she says, "Lord knows I understand that."

"Or not fast enough," I say as we meet eyes. She has hazel eyes and is Katia-skinny. A blue scrunchie holds back thin, blondish-grayish hair. No make-up to cover her deep frown lines, but she wears fake-pink diamond earrings that glitter in the sun. If this were another place, or another time, she could be one of my aunts.

I spit. Then wipe my mouth with the back of my hand.

"You sick?"

"No, no. I…saw a jerk. He makes me want to puke."

She shakes her head. "Men. Don't you go blaming yourself for something a man done to you. Don't be wasting your time."

"It's not that easy." I stand, clutching my side.

She squints her eyes at me. "Where you from?"

"Northeast Wisconsin."

She breaks out into a wide smile. "Well, no shit, it's a small world. That's what I thought," she says with a familiar twang that I notice for the first time. We sound the same.

I nod at her, forcing a polite smile. "You from there, too?"

"You betcha," she says the familiar line that all of my friends, family, enemies, teachers, grocery-store baggers, TV personalities, farmers, and any other cheese-head that hails from the Badger State will know and say at least once per day, and all the way up to a hundred. It's as deep in the DNA as Thursday morning cheese curds.

It looks like she wants to say more, but at that exact second Nurse Taylor bursts through the doors. I turn and pocket the swisher sweet in my bra. Turning back, her eyes zero-in on me.

She rushes me. "There you are! What's this about!?"

My eyes water and I'm afraid I'll dry heave again. Life changes fast, but it also doesn't change at all. Out of the corner of my eye, I see Smoker Lady smash her cigarette and head back inside. I shake my head.

"Who was in the elevator?" she asks.

I suck back in a dripping snot and my shoulders tense up again.

I look away. "The reason I'm here. He's the one I, well…I shot at."

I look back at her to see her staring at me in open-mouthed horror for a second. She embraces me and squeezes me so tight I think my eyes bulge. Her voice is soft. "You're okay, you're okay, you're gonna be okay. You're gonna be okay. He won't hurt you."

I feel a new wave of tears, but these are different. These are hot and brutal, not cold and sloppy. *Come on, Amanda. Enough with the tears and bawling.* I'm ashamed. I let HIM see me weak and running away. I was the hysterical one while he kept it cool. *Hey Jelly.*

Taylor hugs me close, then releases me, but still holds my hands in hers. Looking into my eyes, she says, "Ashe, you are a poster child for Flight or Fight."

"Fight or flight is for combat situations," I say, repeating what the commander told us a thousand times. We were service support, not as important as the warfighters.

"Isn't this combat?" Her question brings me back to the present, "You're fighting inside."

"I'm fighting and losing," Tears roll.

"You have to keep fighting," she says.

I say nothing because at this exact minute, I have no idea what I'm fighting for. I have no idea how this is going to end.

"At least I don't freeze," I say with a snort. Snot is flowing down my face.

"That you don't do," she agrees with a sad look on her face. "I'm sorry. That's some bad luck, really bad luck to run into him today, here at this hospital right after such a good afternoon. I am here to protect you, and I'm sorry that I didn't."

My gaze turns back to the doors I ran through. I shake my head. "It's not your fault. He's everywhere."

She nods for a second in silence. Smiles, then speaks. "And as much as you run, you're never gonna escape him. You already know this."

I nod. I do know this, and it sucks.

"We're going back and getting you taken care of," Taylor says. "We'll use the stairs." She holds my arm as she leads me inside. As we walk down the hallway, I'm thinking of the tree of regrets. I regret so much more than I can write on those little ribbons. I regret I don't know what to do. I either shut my trap, keep quiet, and take the heat for shooting at him or be brave and tell the whole truth. I regret more than anything that those are my choices.

Unless, they aren't.

PART 3

CHAPTER 25

Butler, Ten Days Earlier

THE SUNNI NEIGHBORHOOD was a mixture of charred and wet buildings, cement rubble and concrete dust, stray animals and garbage, kill-or-capture raid remnants and ruins, and of bullet-riddled buildings from open street fighting. Even still, the most prominent feature was the pervasive smell of burned carbon.

Despite the destruction and death all around, the community had magnificent birds. Pigeons, magpies, grouse and dozens of bird species filled the air. How they survived wasn't a mystery. Not many predators beyond the humans, simply birds.

Captain Mark Butler couldn't identify those that flew above the mess, but he liked to watch them as they glided serenely through the air. Waiting out the ground war. *Their guess is as good as mine for when this ends,* he thought.

One of the birds caught Mark's attention. It was a green parakeet just like one from a pet shop back home. *Are there pet shops in Iraq*, Mark wondered? He hadn't seen any. Most shops closed. His eyes followed it high into the sky, until out of sight.

As the parakeet disappeared, a spectacular explosion ripped through the earth. A giant clap of thunder roared under his feet and swiped away the sturdy ground; his body hurled through the air like a tossed sandbag. Heat shot from every direction. He landed with a heavy thud on a pile of debris a few feet away.

Mark felt a sharp object through his body armor digging into his back and tried to roll away. He was stuck on the heap. He smelled iron. He shook his head slightly and pain gripped his skull.

Stillness. Silence. Followed immediately by showering glass and a high-pitched ringing. Bullets cracked through the chaos and Mark squeezed his eyes shut to pinpoint the direction and distance, but he couldn't make sense of it. The metallic taste of blood coated his tongue. He couldn't catch his breath; the smoke was too intense.

For a split second, Mark floated above himself and looked down. His body lay splayed out on the filthy ground. On all sides of him were plastic bags of rotted rubble. With the smoke, his face looked eroded, as if it weren't his. Another blast shook him back to earth and turned his focus to his men. *Where was his team? Was anyone hurt?*

Dust and smoke filled the air like a thick fog. He twitched and tried to stand up, but his right arm didn't move like he wanted. He made a fist with his left hand; at least that worked, even though the rest of him wouldn't respond. Lifting his knee was impossible, the pain vibrated through him.

Man up, he told himself. Mark turned his head to the right and puked. Water spewed out of him and onto the dusty ground where it soaked up quickly. The parched earth would take anything. Seconds felt like hours. But it had to be only seconds before McHenry and the medic found him.

"Butler. You okay?" The medic scanned Mark's body.

The bird returned and soared. Mark was sure it was the bird. Nothing else was that shade of green. Not even a Russian grenade. It seemed to almost float above him and he lifted his arm to reach out and grab it.

"Mark! Stay with us, Mark!" The medic spoon fed the familiar line. Mark snorted. Of course, he'd stay with them, these were *his* men.

The medic tore Mark's clothes and part of his uniform was cut off. The deafening roar of a firefight ripped through the air. A whistle filled the sky. The blast had served as a warning.

"I'll get you out of here," McHenry hollered. Mark tried to disagree, tried to shake his head. Tried to speak, but his words were gone. McHenry grabbed Mark's right hand with his left and in one swoop draped Mark over his shoulders, then switched hands to keep him secure. Stood and ran. He moved as they had trained–right hand free to shoot at any would-be assailants.

Mark was fireman-carried away from the disaster. He kept his eyes open and through the steel-dusty air he could finally focus as he bumped up and down. He saw his lower extremities. Oddly enough, his sand-colored uniform was stained a bright red. He squinted. Sure enough, he had his limbs; what he was missing was his foot.

❧

MARK'S FEVER WAXED and waned. His nightmares and dreams mixed, twisted between reality and hallucinations. At the center of it all was that traitor-bitch Ashe. The only one who ever said she didn't like it, accused him of forcing her. What a whore.

The beginning of his deployment should have warned him that this time, things would be different. It was one of those hot early fall days in the Middle East, close to 120 degrees and brutal. The safety of Kuwait lulled him into complacency; if he was alert, he would have seen Amanda Ashe guarding the gate to the base way before she saw him. How many times did he repeat—stay alert, stay alive—and then he himself didn't even do it.

SF didn't need to go to that regular Army base, but they needed one lousy part. One part for one vehicle. In Camp Buehring. That's when he saw Ashe. She looked street-brawl terrible; dark, haggard circles under her once pretty blue eyes. After that, things moved quickly from him calling out her nickname to when she lifted her pathetic old M16. Worthless weapon for worthless soldiers.

Naturally he was a skeptic of omens; they were always just a product of imagination and circumstance; hocus-pocus. But not this time. This time it was *real.*

A tray fell in the hallway. Utensils crashed to the ground.

Mark opened his eyes.

He knew where he was—a hospital. He licked his dry lips and looked at the ceiling. It was white. He turned his head. The walls were white, too. The door was ajar and beyond it came voices and sounds; the squeak of nurses' shoes; the beep of medical equipment; the laugh of an orderly; the wheels of machines moving up and down hallways.

Landstuhl. What a shock to wake up here, in a hospital bed a few days ago from a medically induced coma, only to find himself missing his right leg right below the knee, it was amputated immediately upon arrival at

Landstuhl. His left foot was there but missing its battle buddy. The other injuries were secondary—punctured lung, possible TBI, cochlear damage, deep lacerations, fractured disk, fractured arm, fractured mind—injuries that would allow him to go back to war. Without a foot or part of his leg, Butler's military career was over.

His mom's thin Bowling League coat hung on one of the two sparse chairs situated in the corner. She was outside smoking, her lungs another bit of collateral damage from the blast.

Mark didn't say it out loud, didn't want to worry mom, but he said it to himself repeatedly when he was alone, "I wish I died."

All that work, all that training, all that experience was now for nothing he moaned to himself. Even without the cost of West Point, the Army had pumped $250,000 into him. Now his future hopes of becoming a General were destroyed. Chance to be Chief of Staff was over. He never thought it would be gone in a literal flash, an actual explosion.

On his nightstand was the remote control to the brand-new flat screen that hung on the wall. A large pink hospital cup filled with water and ice cubes sat on the moveable table. He kept the television turned off and even his parched lips and cracked skin weren't enough for him to take a sip. *Why bother?* With that thought, he heard a knock on the door. It opened. His fashionable, tie-wearing cocky-as-they-come doctor and a stocky blonde nurse walked in. Butler initially pegged the doctor as just-off-the-boat Chinese, but when he spoke, he sounded like Captain America. He stood in his usual cool dude stance. Mark knew the look well; he'd worn the same expression on many previous days. The nurse smiled and went to his IV bag, checked the fluid levels, and wrote notes on her clipboard. Through his perfectly straight teeth, the doctor spoke with enthusiasm.

"Captain, buddy, how are you doing? Nice to see you awake."

Mark nodded but didn't answer.

"Anymore nightmares?"

Mark slightly shook his head, unwilling to share. Ambien squeezed all dreams from his mind on most days, except today.

Doctor continued. "I have some good news for you, Captain. The team thinks you're stable enough and ready to move to Walter Reed."

The nurse piped up, "We were so worried about infection, Captain. But like everything else, you seem to be beating it."

Mark didn't find this to be particularly good news, unless they were growing legs in jars and attaching them to lame-dicks like himself at Walter Reed.

The doctor was candid, "Mark, you're strong and making terrific progress. Your residual wounds are healing well and of course; we will continue to monitor them closely. You were seriously injured, Captain, that's for sure. But they're doing amazing things with prosthetics at Walter Reed; it's cutting-edge. Your wound starts below the knee, which makes you an excellent candidate for a prosthesis. You could regain normal movement; be able to walk on your own two feet again."

Mark forced himself to stay in neutral, even with those crummy words. As if losing a limb wasn't a big deal. It was pathetic to pretend life would go back to normal.

The blonde nurse added, "D.C. is well within driving distance to Fort Bragg. I'm certain that when your team redeploys, they'd love to visit."

It was the only thing he hoped for. He couldn't help but feel he'd left them in the lurch. He should be out there, not here.

The nurse's words sent his eyes back to the doctor, he opened his mouth to speak and agree to the move, the quicker the better. He needed to figure out his future.

"When?" Butler's mom said. She'd slipped in unnoticed. The faint sweet cigarette smell was her only giveaway.

"Good morning, Ms. Butler," the doctor said as he braced for her inquisition. Every surgery and each tablet of medication had to have five reasons, which she considered good enough, to use on her son. Most spouses or parents let the doctors do whatever they wanted without even a single question.

Not Ms. Butler.

"What number did you graduate in your medical school?" Was her first question when they met. She grimaced when he told her it didn't matter; that he received the same level of training as number one. She didn't let it go. Fine, 109 out of 350. Not bad, but not great, she had told him, you should have studied harder.

Since Mark became more conscious, it was easier but not easy.

"I was just explaining to the Captain that we are ready to move him to Walter Reed."

"Does he want to go?" She placed hands on her bony hips.

"It isn't much of a choice," he told her, "It's the best option for treatment."

"What makes it the best—"

But before she commenced her interrogation, Mark raised his unbroken hand.

"I"ll go," he said in a mumble, "I want to go."

They looked at each other, surprised for a quick second. Words had been scarce. His mom reached and gently touched his uninjured shoulder, like she'd done since she arrived at the hospital on the Red-Eye out of Milwaukee.

"When do we leave?" she said.

"By the end of the week," the nurse said.

Butler's mom nodded in agreement then opened her mouth for a few follow-ons.

Mark's mind checked out of their logistical conversations. He heard their chatter but didn't follow. His mom stepped into the role of caregiver quite well; it would all be sorted for him; that's one thing about being a patient. The doctors and nurses treated him like he had regressed to third grade and was no longer capable of holding an adult conversation. Butler didn't protest. Instead of enduring the sing-song questions of the staff and orderlies, he let his mom deal with it. She cut through bullshit real quick.

CHAPTER 26

Amanda and General Order #1

WE'RE IN THE therapy room, waiting. LT is supposed to be here any minute but I don't know how she can help. There are no solutions in sight. So much is going absolutely freaking wrong in the worst ways possible. Butler's here. Jackson's here. What if Vincent is here, too? That thought makes me feel frantic. Stuck in here with no way out, and worse, helpless. Like a little pig waiting for the butcher shop to open.

Nurse Taylor sits with me, quiet. She takes my hand, and I let her. "You know that you got a lot of people who care about you."

She looks into my eyes, but I look away. She squeezes my hand, which is warm and comforting. Cozy is the word for how she makes the room feel, even though it's plain and white and harsh. Part of me wants to throw my arms around her and go in for a hug, especially since she's been so kind. Part of me wants to tell her: hey, there are a lot of people who don't care about me, too.

Taylor says, "You've had a hell of a time the past few days, honey, and I'm sorry."

I nod to let her know I'm listening, but keep quiet. Each time I open my mouth, I feel like barfing. I can't stop the image of Butler's sneer and the sound of him calling me Jelly from assaulting me. Being here is more of a mess than I thought possible. I'm mentally drained, physically shattered.

Taylor squeezes my hand again. Says, "You're safe, Amanda."

I look her directly in the eye, to see what she'll do as I say out loud what I think.

"No, I'm not," I say. "I won't be, ever."

"Is that really true?"

I jerk my hand away. "Yes, that's fucking true."

I look at the white wall and review the past few years. I let my boyfriend die, then I'm drinking like an idiot and get myself drugged and raped, and my whole chain of command turns on me. I shoot at a guy that everyone in the Army worships. I screw myself over all the time. Man, I just…I just cannot think of any type of solution to this mess.

I add, "I should give up. Join Manolo."

There, I said it. Fine, I'm feeling sorry for myself. So what? Tears form in my eyes. I lay my chin down on my forearms and wipe them away. I feel like such a loser.

"Hold on there, honey." Her expression is serious. "Now listen to me. And I want to see your bright blue eyes so you turn your head, please."

She puts her arm back on my shoulder. I catch her eyes.

"Listen to me. You can have a good life in spite of what happened, or a bad one because of it. That's your choice, honey. Not mine and not the Army's. And don't you go blaming yourself for things you can't control. You didn't plant that IED. You didn't put a roofie in a cup, okay? You did not make those things happen, but they did. You ain't even twenty-five yet, got a big life ahead of you. And the fact is, that not even thirty minutes ago you were face-to-face with that man that got you all mixed up. It's okay to feel bad, but a feeling comes and goes. You won't always feel like this. Me and the LT and everyone else here, we're not going to let you give up on yourself. You got that?"

I blink over and over again, feeling her words: *you can have a good life in spite of what happened or a bad one because of it.* First, I'm mad, then resentful, then relieved, and finally, thankful she said this.

"People here care about you, honey."

I swallow hard, nod into my arms. She's right, I know I have people in my life who are good to me. In my head, the past few years are a jumbled mess that makes no sense, so I avoid thinking. Memories can be too painful. That's when I binge and barf. I feel in control of something then. And forget about everything, and everyone, else.

I keep my head on my forearms but give her a thumps-up.

I whisper, "Thank you."

We both hear the door swing open.

LT stands in the door frame. I sit up in my chair. Nurse Taylor sits up straighter.

LT says, "Ashe."

"LT, what's—" I start to say then notice she's not alone. She leads the way to the table and another officer walks in.

This officer is a highlighted-blonde preppy female with the type of high cheekbones every man in uniform would try to touch. She wears dress greens instead of battle dress. On her perfectly small Cinderella feet are tall heels—way too high for regulation. I like her instantly. These shoes set the tone that she respects the regulations but does her own thinking. They both enter the small room, sit down opposite me.

Nurse Taylor stands and squeezes my shoulder. Moves slow and deliberate to the door, making eye contact with all of us.

"I should be getting back," she says, then looks at me. "Talk to you later, honey." She opens the door.

My voice is still cramped up but I manage to croak out a 'bye.'

"Thank you so much," LT says. Nurse Taylor waves before closing the door.

LT clears her throat, "Private Ashe, I want to introduce you to Captain Lynch."

"Nice to meet you," she says. "I'm a JAG officer here on base."

What? My helplessness melts away, leaving only confusion.

Captain Lynch reaches across and holds out her hand, I take it and we shake. Her hands are soft. I nod and she returns it with a smile, which shows her straight, white teeth.

Judge Advocate General...but why...As the words and situation sink in, I watch as she takes out some tinted watermelon-smelling lip-gloss and slides it all over her pout. Malibu Barbie in uniform.

"Wait," I say, a horrible realization hitting me. My stomach knots and I feel nauseous. "Am I getting arrested for that... for what happened in Kuwait?"

They exchange a look in front of me and LT shakes her head.

"Ashe, I invited Captain Lynch here today to hear part of your story. You mentioned that when you previously tried to report the incident in Iraq, you were told to keep quiet. I think that's flat-out wrong and is part of the reason that healing is difficult. Victims need justice, even if their perpetrator is considered someone of importance."

I look at her in amazement. LT really is on my side. She brought a lawyer in for me. Nurse Taylor is 100% correct when she said I have people to help me. I don't want to start sobbing, but I feel like it. Because the LT seems to know exactly what to do.

"The main perpetrator is here," I add, I stifle the sniffle that is bubbling up.

She looks into my eyes. "Yes, I heard. I'm so sorry you ran into him. Once I found out, I contacted Captain Lynch. I thought it would be okay with you. I want to ensure you get a fair chance to seek whatever justice you need."

Her words give me a jolt. Katia said it—*I need justice*—before hurting herself. I'm sure that if back in the day there had been some type of legal proceedings, I never would have set my own punishment via an M16. I *do* need justice.

Captain Lynch flips open a notebook. "Unfortunately, we don't have a lot of time today. We'll have to jump right in. Could you start by explaining who you reported these incidents to?"

I take a deep breath. "Yes, Ma'am. My First Sergeant, PSG, and Commander."

She writes as she speaks. "I understand there was a situation at the SF compound."

Her words hang in the air.

"I just—" I chew my lip. Give a pleading look to LT.

"Which we aren't going to ask you about right now," LT jumps in. "I don't think it would be a good idea to talk about that after seeing…"

Captain Lynch gives a tight smile. "Right. For today, we should know how this affected you afterwards. What were you like following the event? What happened on base?"

"It's kind of a long story," I say, glancing between the two of them.

"We have time," CPT Lynch says as she settles into her chair.

I take a deep breath and press my hands together. It looks like I'm praying. I'm not.

❧

I WAS TOO sick to think clearly that night. Vincent and Jackson dumped me on the outskirts of Tent City. I low crawled over the gravel into my tent.

The knees of my uniform ripped, so small stones stuck in my skin as I slid back to our tent.

Weisengard, my best friend, was waiting.

"And where have you been?" she asked like a middle-aged mom, then took one look at me and freaked. Took pictures with her digital camera. She scrubbed my face with a clean sock and bottled water. As soon as she got me clean, I vomited. That's how it went all night. I blacked out until I puked, then blacked out again. I felt poisoned.

Sometime before sunrise, she went and got the PSG. My PSG was known by everyone as a dickhead; but that night, he was decent. Asked who hit me, I gave names. He fetched First Sergeant, who asked me a bunch of medical stuff. Weisengard showed him the digital pictures.

First Sergeant was old and hardened, like he'd been leading soldiers since the Civil War. Even still, he looked sad when he saw me. Stared hard; his voice tight. "I should've known this would happen on deployment. Let's think about this for a minute before we talk to the CO."

First Sergeant knew as well as me that the Commander played the role of judge and jury in the system, making all the decisions downrange. The discipline system was owned and operated by commanding officers. He wasn't exactly fair or objective, but that's how it was.

I was authorized to miss morning formation. Sometime in late morning, First Sergeant came to my tent and told me to get dressed, said we would talk to the Commander together.

Day was dry, but I was sweating bullets on the walk over. As we walked, First Sergeant was giving me tips on what to say. Honestly, I didn't listen. Instead, I daydreamed about what could happen if the CO gave a fuck. Maybe he'd be enraged and charge ahead to speak to that small JAG office downrange. I saw myself in a courtroom and all those guys—Jackson, Vincent, and Butler—begging me for forgiveness.

CO's office was inside a former airline hangar. We knocked and the CO sent First Sergeant away; it was just him and me. Tall and wiry, he towered over me. I stood at attention, as if a bayonet was pressed against my back. Jerk never said, "Parade rest." He saw my busted nose, black and blue face. When he asked me to explain myself, I said their names. The look on his face frightened me, so I shut up.

CO laughed out loud, then got right in my face. Breathing down on me, he said he'd conduct his own investigation. Told me to wait as he interviewed witnesses. I tried to give more information, but he told me to get lost.

In a daze, I stepped outside into the hot sun. I was upset and confused.

"Go see the Medic about your nose," First Sergeant said, who was waiting for me.

My PSG met me outside the medic's tent. He asked me to sit on a pile of sandbags as he gave it to me straight.

"I'm not saying that officers cover for each other, but the CO's got the power in this situation." He pronounced it like sit-chway-chon. "Heard that our CO has some friends in SF."

I nodded and he went on, not making eye contact. This was very bad news for me. He kept talking, but I barely made out what he was saying. I knew I was at the mercy of officers, who continued to show me a downward trend in brains for years. Officers acted like wolf packs, having more power than the police and less restrictions. If anyone else dissolved roofies in drinks like Pepto-Bismal packets, they'd be g-o-n-e.

The CO waited just over an hour before he asked for me. First Sergeant found me as the medic finished bandaging my nose. It wasn't broken, just swollen and bruised.

I had to go by myself. I stood in his office, alone and nervous. His back was to me. A picture of his dull wife and annoying three-year-old boy, the one that kept hitting everyone's butts at the Going-Away party, grinned from a small dust-covered picture frame on the corner of his desk.

He turned to me, took a long swig of a cola. Belched, crushed the can, threw it into the waste basket, and looked at me square in the eye, "Prior to deploying, you read General Order Number One, correct, Sergeant Ashe?"

I nodded. We all read it; basically, everything was Prohibited besides eating and breathing and killing people that didn't wear a similar uniform.

He said, "The consumption of alcohol is strictly prohibited in theater."

I nodded again, the woozy feeling was pulsating from my stomach outwards, but I swallowed hard before I said, "Yes, sir."

He paced the room. "I have eyewitness reports of you directly disobeying General Order Number One last night. Specialist Jackson, Staff Sergeant Vincent, and a dozen more Special Forces soldiers wrote statements and submitted them to me."

His words were pure bullshit. No way in hell any type of investigation was done in one hour. We barely had phone service and relied on faulty DSN lines—the most he could have done was make a call.

My throat constricted, but I managed to say, "They're lying, Sir."

That pissed him off. He yelled at me. "Witnesses say you were drunk and disorderly on the outside of tent-city. After a successful dangerous mission, the SF team tried to help you as they re-entered base."

I protested, "Sir, no! That's not how it went at all!"

He got really quiet. "Who are *your* witnesses? Can you give me a list of people who might have seen your version of the story?"

He knew he had me trapped. Nobody was allowed to go. Hell, they weren't allowed to even happen. If I said one word, all those other females would get into deep trouble. I was not throwing anyone under the bus; they couldn't use my honesty against me.

I shook my head. He gave me a *I thought so* smirk. Sat down, picked up a stapled packet of papers that laid on his desk and began to read.

"Section Q: Cohabitating, residing, or spending the night with members of the opposite sex is also strictly prohibited." He looked up at me. It slowly dawned on me: *he was pinning it all on me.*

"You know that dating officers is forbidden, right? So why were you attempting to seduce Captain Butler last night by taking off your clothes?" He worked himself into a frenzy, throwing his hands up and gesturing around his office as he spoke.

I felt as if I'd vomit again. "No, Sir."

"As far as I'm concerned, you broke several codes. Luckily, Captain Butler was too smart to get fooled by a lowly Sergeant looking to get ahead. It's the oldest play in the book. Low ranking female soldiers ruined many men."

I was shocked. "He attacked me!"

"I'll not allow you to falsely accuse a classmate of mine, one who did nothing wrong except be in the wrong place at the wrong time."

Hot tears formed in my eyes, but I didn't know what to do.

He kept talking. "I'm glad I didn't authorize your emergency leave. Less than two months after this supposed boyfriend died and you're naked and trying to fuck a classmate of mine. The only thing I can think of is that you are attempting to become pregnant to leave theater. Is that what it is, Ashe? Trying to ditch your responsibilities?"

I held my hands to my ears and screamed, "Sir! Stop!"

I gagged bile. Jesus Fucking Christ, I shook my head, but got dizzy and stumbled.

"Sit down," he ordered. I sat in a folding chair.

"Ashe, this is your last chance. I should strip your rank. Don't know why I don't. What I *do* know is that I happen to personally know Butler and he's one of the finest officers in the Special Forces, no question asked."

My mouth watered and the familiar tug pulled on my lips.

He continued, "As for this Sergeant Vincent and Specialist Jackson you mentioned, Butler promised to conduct his own investigation. I am letting SF take care of SF."

"Sir—" I had no words to change his mind. My fate was sealed.

"Ashe, you deserve the book thrown at you. But I'm not going to do that yet, mostly because First Sergeant is defending you. I'll give you one more chance. Another word, another false move, I'm taking your rank, conducting my own investigation, and finding out exactly which one of your buddies was with you over there. I will burn you to the ground."

"I—I—," I never finished my defense.

I puked.

❧

PICTURES CAME OUT, both in print and online. If any soldiers logged in to the internet, they saw emails of me spread eagle. All Manolo's buddies saw these pictures, and never spoke to me again. Rodriguez told everyone I cheated on Manolo the whole time, called me a lying *pinche puta*.

First Sergeant and my PSG told the guys to delete the pics and leave me alone, which added fuel to the flame. Next rumor was I did them favors in the porta potties. Leadership kept their distance after that. I'm no loser but that shattered my self-worth. Guys in my unit humiliated me by calling me Jelly. Ignored it until I couldn't. Then either I busted into tears or tried to choke the offender. There's only so much shit one can take.

Unlucky for me, I still saw those SF assholes ALL.THE.TIME. Like heat seeking missiles, I felt followed around BIAP. *"Jelly, you need a cock to suck tonight?" "Jelly, your ass is stretching the seams of those pants." "I'll punch you tonight, if that gets you off."*

I think it was meant to get me to never, ever consider ruining their party set-up by talking to higher-ups. They made sure my reputation was trash so their parties could continue.

❧

I KEPT TO myself—woke up, did PT, worked, back to the tent. Going to the DFAC was dangerous, venturing out to the good porta potties was out of the question. I used the ones with the human poop up to the rim. Even seeing a man who looked like one of them sent me into full-panic mode, which was unfortunate since 90% of the Army is men and a lot of the white ones look the same.

I lived on crystal light mixed in warm water bottles and whatever Weisengard's mom sent her in the mail. Sometimes she brought food out of the DFAC for me, but we lived almost a mile away and I didn't want her to go through the trouble.

One morning I was starving. We just ran five miles in formation, and I used a bucket in the tent to clean up so I could rush in to get some chow quicker than the rest. I rushed through the line and took French toast, slathered peanut butter all over it and doused it in maple syrup. Tasted just like a peanut butter cup. I stuffed two bananas in my cargo pockets and just as I was dumping out my trash to get the fuck out of there, Vincent entered. *Vincent.*

My anxiety shot through the Bob Hope Dining Hall roof. A crease on his face deepened when he saw me and made it look like he wanted to say something shitty. I barely made it to the trash can again. I stuffed the Styrofoam plates down before puke rushed out of my body. Involuntarily, it just all came up. Nose was plugged with soggy bread.

As I stood gazing at my own glossy maple syrup barf, I felt peace. It was purifying, in a way, but only for a second. Vincent walked up to me and clapped me on the ass. I reared up my leg and kicked that motherfucker as hard as I could. He bent over in pain and screamed that he was gonna kill me. I wish I could've knocked his teeth out.

So that's how it was.

I stopped eating. Or, I puked when I ate. Puking took years off my life, but it was a good outlet. I didn't have any bullets to exit the planet since First Sergeant took away my clip. Scarfing and barfing actually helped me survive. It's just not a long-term solution, is all.

❧

THERE'S A LONG silence, and LT looks worried. Her lips are forced into a thin line.

Captain Lynch sighs and puts down her pen. She pushes an imaginary blonde strand behind her ear and rubs her temple. She gives me a sad smile.

"Seeing them every day must've been tough," she says. "Did the other SF team members ever touch you?"

I nod. "Some. A few of them slapped my ass or pinched my tit. Most called me names or made threats. My friend Weisengard called it Friendly Fire."

"Good term for it."

I actually feel the insides of my stomach tighten into a ball as the memories of the slaps, squeezes, and pinches rush back. Captain goddam Butler and his little wolf pack.

LT says softly, "They knew what they were doing to keep you quiet."

My shoulders are tense, up to my ears. I swallow hard as I scan their eyes. "Do you think, maybe, that we can do something about it?"

Captain Lynch drums her perfect French manicured hand on the table between us.

I'm suffocating as I wait for a response. After what feels like a million years, she plasters a smile on her pretty face and gives me a big smile. *Almost* convincing, but not quite.

She speaks, "I know as well as anyone that the prosecution rates are low for any type of sexual assault in the military." My heart sinks at her words. The shred of hope I have is slipping from my grasp.

She continues, "However, that doesn't mean we shouldn't get a case together. Try to find some type of justice for you. If we don't do something, we're part of the problem."

What? OH MY GOD! Her words are beyond awesome. I look at her and can breathe again. I stammer out a thank you as my stomach unclenches. Oh GOD. Wouldn't that be something…my mind leaps ahead…what would be a suitable punishment for Butler? Firing squad? Manure pit?

Captain Lynch twists in her chair as she writes down more notes. I'm so glad she's here. Now it's not a stupid idea to get justice for me. For Katia.

She looks up and meets my eyes. "Tell me if this is too much, but I'd like to hear what happened at the gate in Kuwait."

Jesus. My jaw tightens, but I manage a nod. With one hand, I feel for my tube and rub the small bandage covering. After a minute—which feels like an hour, maybe two—I respond.

"I don't know," I say, honestly. "One second I'm guarding this crappy Kuwaiti outpost and the next second my heart's beating so fast I think I'm having a heart attack. Seeing his face, and his voice…then he called me *Jelly* as if we were old buddies. I guess I snapped, if that's what you mean. I really don't remember those few seconds. I do remember the kicking and holding me down. Most of those bruises are fading, but it was pretty bad. You can ask the ER nurse that checked on me when I arrived."

She's silent for a second, tapping her pen to the table. LT speaks.

Speaking about me to Captain Lynch she says, "She had a series of severe traumas that were never resolved. There *may* be a possibility that PTSD led to this type of behavior—"

Captain Lynch puts a hand on LT's arm. She tilts her head towards me. "One step at a time, okay? Private Ashe, thank you for sharing your story with me. I can understand it's not easy. You should know that the LT and I are really proud of you for speaking about what happened between you and your chain of command. Most officers want to do what's right. Personally, I'm mortified your CO treated you like this."

LT nods as she speaks but doesn't say anything. I'm surprised she doesn't associate those words with Muscrat. I have the audience, so I sit up a little straighter.

I lean forward. "Um, Captain Lynch. Consent is important right?"

She nods, "Of course."

I lean back and point down. "I didn't give consent to have this feeding tube put in me."

Captain Lynch glances over at LT whose big brown eyes widen. Speaking slowly, as though she's picking her words from exploded glass, she says, "I am trying to resolve this situation, Ashe. I really, truly am. Can you let me work on that for you?"

I believe her, somewhat. I nod.

Captain Lynch continues, "I'm going to go back now and talk to my boss. We've got some research to do and a lot of work. Eventually you need to speak about that night. Could you do that?"

Slowly, I nod. My stomach is in knots thinking about it, but I won't let those bastards win without a fight. I know they'll do it again and again.

"Yeah," I say quietly as I meet her eyes. "I'll do whatever I can."

"I hoped you'd say that."

She gives me another smile and stands up. Puts on her dress green jacket again.

I say quietly, "Captain Lynch?"

She turns towards me. Her shaped eyebrows are raised in an arch. Captains are not my favorite rank, but she listened, took notes, and let me talk. Didn't try to shut me up.

The words have trouble leaving my mouth, but I force them out. "Um. I'm so grateful you believe what I said…thanks for coming and listening."

It's all I can get out before I start crying. I wipe tears from my face as quickly as they come, but it's not fast enough.

I take a tissue that LT offers me.

"You are welcome, *Sergeant* Ashe." She emphasizes my rank with a nod.

Captain Lynch makes her exit. Cool-ish air wafts in from the hallway before LT closes the door again. My eyes tear up as LT opens up a folder I didn't see before. She places a sheet of paper in front of me.

The document is titled: *What is a Stuck Point?*

I look up at LT. She opens her big eyes and says, "Keep reading."

The document goes on to answer its own question. *They are thoughts that you have that keep you from recovering! These thoughts may not be 100% accurate. Instead, they may be your understanding of your trauma, but is it the truth? Stuck points often use extreme language, such as "never" and "always!" Do you have ideas like this: Because I did not tell anyone, I am to blame for any abuse. I should have known he would have hurt me. Other people should not be trusted. I am damaged forever because of the rape.*

I look up at LT. Push the paper slightly towards her. "What's this?"

She clicks her pen open. "We have an extended session today. Let's get to work."

CHAPTER 27

Amanda and the Wolf

I'M BAREFOOT AND I feel the marble under my feet. It's sticky. I sense that I'm in the compound again, but I'm all alone in a dark, narrow hallway. Eerily, unusually quiet hallway. No music. No laughter. No*body*. Radio silence.

I stand in the dark: cold, alone, and with mixed feelings of fear and curiosity. I stare straight ahead, trying to see *anything*, but no, it's too dark. Luckily, I know this place—this hallway leads to both the dining room and the kitchen, which is suddenly aglow. A large shadow lurches about on the hallway wall, like a raging ghost. I sense I must avoid that shadow. Its shape pitches to the side. I know that I have to move. NOW.

Creeping slowly down the hall, my bare feet sweat with each step and I leave tip-toe marks behind me. I slip once, catch myself. Finally, I make it to the dining room entrance. Look in. A big plastic bowl of almost-gone rosy punch and dozens of empty wine boxes lie scattered on the large cherry-oak table.

No... It can't be... But yes, it is. I *know* that red, fruity punch.

I feel sick and my knees tremble. I'm distracted by a terrible memory. Then—

I hear a low, menacing *growl.*

It's coming from the kitchen. Without reason, I'm drawn to it and move towards the snarling noises, very slowly and with extreme caution. I'm right outside the door frame.

I crane my neck to see what's inside. I freeze. An enormous, tawny-brown wolf is directly to my front, standing on his haunches behind the kitchen island. Looks angry, even more than wolves usually look. Bared sharp canines stick out from his broad muzzle. In his paw, he holds a large plastic solo cup and he's stirring the liquid inside with his long claw. I know him, I do. But I can't remember how.

"Little bitch," the wolf sneers. I somehow understand he's talking about me.

"Fuck you," I say, but only in my head. Words stay frozen in my throat.

He goes about mixing. Faster and faster. Next to his other large paw, I see a small paper bag, like the type Mom used for our school lunches. Green tablets are scattered all over the island. He sniffs the drink with his massive snout. Leaves the kitchen from the other entrance. It leads to my hallway, but now his back is to me. Stalks down the narrow hallway, opposite my direction. The floor vibrates with his every step.

I'm relieved. For one second.

I see him reach for the door of another room. *Shit.* I have to stop him. I see it already: he's about to drug me, rape me, flip me over and do it again. Put himself in every crevice. I'll gag, but he'll laugh. Take photos. For hours. I'll be trapped in my body, unconscious and then conscious. I'll see and feel things that I can't stop. Only once, I'll have enough strength to fight back. Then he'll hit me to knock me out again. It's hell on earth.

"Stop!" I scream. "Butler, stop!"

This time, the words are loud and clear. He turns, eyes shining. Hysterical eyes. I'm shaky, but find my voice. "Don't hurt me!"

He pauses. Squares his broad chest in front of me. His piercing blue eyes stab me with their intensity. He lets out a spine-tingling howl. I'm terrified.

I try to move, but my feet had turned into marble flooring. I squirm desperately and grab the wall to the side of me. I plead again, "Don't hurt me."

As soon as the words leave my mouth, he charges. The drink he holds flies into the air and splashes against the white walls. Soon, his powerful jaws are locked around my middle. I feel his sharp teeth sink into me and he shakes my body over and over in his great mouth, shredding me from the inside out. Pain shoots through my body. I scream. He clamps down harder. Soon, my stomach and bloody intestines pour out from my body and onto the white marble floor. Chunks of my flesh hit the wall. Everything is being ripped out. I manage to bite his chest. I taste his blood. Suddenly, he howls in pain and releases me. My carcass falls to the floor and I'm alive, barely. The Wolf stands back, bares his teeth, howls, and....

Shit.

I roll out of my bed, land hard on my ass. Head hits the floor. My sheets are shrink wrapped around me, making me immobile. My blanket covers my body and part of my head. I think I feel something furry on my face. Wolf fur...or...?

"Help!" I yell, sick with fear.

Door opens a crack, then fully flings open. Lights flip on. I hear the squeak of Ponytail's pink rubber shoes as she rushes towards me and pulls the top blanket off. I struggle to free myself. Finally, she manages to sort everything, then carefully holds me in her arms.

"It's okay," she says, "it was a dream."

My throat is dry as dust. My heart is beating a million miles a minute. I shake my head, I can't talk.

"You got yourself wrapped up tight tonight," she says as helps me sit up straight. My middle feels as if all my vital organs were chewed up and spit out. I let out a groan.

Ponytail says, "You're soaked through, poor thing. You've got to change."

I shake my head again. That means she will go and find me new pajamas. I can't be left alone. Won't.

"Don't go," I whisper, scared stiff. She helps me stand up, slowly.

She sighs and says, "Your therapist told us that tonight might be difficult. I should've stayed in here with you." She pulls the sheets from the floor and throws them on to the bed.

"You want to take a quick shower?"

I shake my head again. My throat hardens and I choke out, "He's a wolf. I mean...he's a..a...man but a wolf. He charged—I..." I can't go on.

"It was a nightmare," she says and squeezes my shoulder.

I'm fully aware it's a nightmare. But it doesn't feel like that. It feels real. Butler is only a few floors away. Him and the rest of his wolf pack.

She attempts a smile. "Go into the bathroom, lock the door, undress, and I'll be back in less than two shakes of a lamb's tail. I'll knock when I come back so there's no surprises."

I don't move. "Don't leave me..." I start and stop. I feel so helpless.

"Go," she says and walks towards the door. "You're a big girl, hon. Come on."

I want to retreat under the bed, but instead I force myself to walk into the bathroom and lock the door. Strip off the sweaty pajamas, throw them to the floor, and take a seat on the closed toilet lid. Sitting in only my panties, I fiddle with the bandage over my tube. I hate this thing. I slide my finger over it again and again until I see a thin layer of blood seep into the adhesive tape. I think of my insides being ripped out by that damned wolf and press on the tube until more blood blots the white gauze.

I hear the knock on the door, open it, and take the clean clothes. Mumble a thanks. Pulling on everything quickly, I am out into the room and next to Pony tail in ten seconds flat.

"Your face is white as a sheet." she says in her sweet voice. "Looks like you've seen a ghost. What's wrong?"

Everything, but I can't tell her that—it's too complicated and too hard for me to understand. I say nothing and look at the floor. Shrug.

She clears her throat, "What was that dream about?"

I look at her. "Nightmare."

"Right. What was the nightmare about?" She looks at me for a few seconds, as if she really wants to know.

This I can explain. "He wants to kill me."

"Who does?" She sits on Katia's old bed but I stay standing.

"Butler. He's gonna rip me to shreds." I don't look at her, my eyes twinkling with tears. "He wants me dead, I know it. He wants me gone—and...quiet..."

She interrupts me. "He said that?"

"Not in the dream, but I know it. I mean, he was a wolf in the nightmare. He ate me."

"And then you woke up?"

"Yeah," I say, keeping my eyes downcast.

"Has he ever threatened you?"

Yes. Asshole and his friends did, many times to keep me from trying *again* for some justice. I nod and the tears start to fall. I wipe my eyes with my sleeve.

"Ashe. You're safe." She's calm. Soft. How is that possible?

I stiffen. Look away. Whisper. "He's here, do you know that? I can't be safe with him so close to me."

I watch her study my face. She says, "Dreams can be really disturbing. They tell us what's bothering us. But I guess you already know, don't you?"

"Yeah, I do."

My only small victory was that one bite I managed. Which was real—I did that. Even when I was drugged and unable to move, I somehow had the fight to bite the bastard.

I close my eyes tightly, falter, and start to cry. "What's gonna happen to me?"

"I'm not sure."

I can't stop the sobs. I wipe away tears, but they continue.

"Come to the sink, Ashe." She turns on the faucet, lets the water run cold then dampens a washcloth. I stand next to her. Grasp the sides of the sink. I can't shake the dream. I ramble, as if in a trance. "I know Butler got those roofies from BST. They sold them out of their trailers. BST guys were trash to the females. Treated us like second-class citizens, or worse."

"Here, honey," she places the cool washcloth behind my neck. "Take a deep breath."

I do. My heart rate slows.

"Who's BST?" She wets the cloth again.

I narrow my eyes. "You *really* don't know?" She shakes her head.

My heart pounds with anxiety. "Brewster, Smith and Thompson. BST for short. Civilian contractors who took the jobs that the Army doesn't have enough trained bodies to fill. Got paid bank—tax-free—for doing same jobs as soldiers."

She holds the washcloth on me, letting me relax.

I shake my head as the memories come back. BST. If you were American and willing to give up the comforts of 24-hour living and the quiet of home, then the money was hard to beat. Men didn't even have to be fit. Being a hundred pounds' overweight was no problemo. Bigotry was tolerated, along with drunks and not-technically-convicted former defendants. Management simply ignored these minor issues. The top eliminating factor was BST employees had to carry their own luggage. Bastards who could drive trucks but couldn't carry their own bags were shit out of luck. "Those fucks left theater every few months on R and R—Rest and Relaxation. Lots of them went to Thailand, came back with all sorts of illegal crap."

She removes the washcloth from my neck. We stand a few inches apart.

"I'm sorry that happened," She looks genuinely sympathetic. "Was that Butler guy you mentioned from BST?"

Words rush out of my mouth. I tell her, "I met Butler at a party on their SF compound. The BST and SF guys had these massive parties together. SF guys rounded up some girls now and then, got drinks from local vendors, and made a bonfire. Totally against regs, but they had a different set of rules."

"Butler is one of the SF soldiers?"

"He's an officer."

"I see."

I nod, starting to perspire again. "I barely knew him, but he thought he'd fallen in love after just a few conversations. Got totally pissed when I rejected the idea. I mean, you know what had just happened with my boyfriend. I went to the party to get some beer. To forget about everything for a while. I told him to leave me alone, but he wouldn't."

"Ego," she says with a sad smile.

I nod. "He said since we're both from Wisconsin, it was a natural fit. Never asked for my opinion. Couldn't accept that he wasn't God's gift to me."

"Oh, God. You poor thing."

It was my own fault. I close my eyes and start to shake. "I should never have drunk what he handed me."

"Ashe," she says sharply, meaning *stop talking like that*. I ignore it.

I admit out loud, "I had it coming. I should never have trusted him."

"Okay. Stop. It's not your fault he put a roofie in your drink. You rejected him, and that should've been it."

"I let my guard down."

She holds up a hand. "I go to parties all the time with my friends and none of us go in thinking that we will get drugged if we aren't careful. It's reasonable to trust people, you know, especially downrange. You wore the same uniform as him; it's natural to have trust amongst soldiers. It's on him, not you."

I say nothing for a few seconds, absorbing her words. She makes a good point, one that I'd thought about before, but didn't know if I was reasonable or not. When everyone doubted me, I started to doubt myself.

I feel exhausted, but I nod at her. "I feel pretty shitty tonight. Can you stay?"

"I'll make the rounds then stay in here while you sleep. Sound good?"

I nod again. I finally feel something like safe.

❧

I KNOW IT's time to get up. I can feel it. At home, I had this whole morning routine. Coffee machine was set to brew at 04:30, so it was ready when I got up. Drank a cup, then it was face wash, toner, moisturizer, SPF, toothbrush, mouth wash, and iridescent lip balm with sparkles that Jo sent me. Got on the sports bra and PT gear before Manolo was out of bed. After years of hating the morning, I finally liked it. Sometimes I'd drape myself on top of him to get him up, as heavy as a cement brick. Morning breath was lime-y sour when he kissed me.

God.

I flip off the sheets. Shoot out of bed. Turn on the lights, and look in the mirror. I see me. But—a shadow of me. The good life I lost, forever, is set in the bags under my eyes and the red rack lines on my face.

I splash water on my face and put on my moccasins. I turn off the lights and go into the hall. Find a place in the medication line, inch forward, swallow the medicine, and get vitals. All normal, routine stuff. Tattoo waits for me at the table, his face creased with a look I don't know yet. I sit down.

"Hey," I say and he gives me a nod.

He glances around the room. Stealthily slides a clipped newspaper article across the table. I unfold it and smooth it over my lap, hidden under the table. I'm scared to look, worried by the way he's acting. *Please don't let this be about Katia.*

He whispers low to me, "The Washington Post has a full expose on soldier's barracks at Walter Reed. Journalists interviewed a bunch of soldiers and Marines, got the full story on how it is to live here after being inpatient. Basically blasted the whole leadership."

I push my seat away from the table so I can scan the article in my lap; my mouth falls open at the details. Lots of reporting about the never-ending bureaucracy, stalled paperwork, ratty barracks, broken equipment, false promises and upset families. Lack of accountability on many fronts outside of the hospital walls. I'm not exactly surprised, but really hoped things were different than at Fort Shithole. Soldiers blinded by IEDs shouldn't have lost paperwork, in my opinion. I fold the paper. "How'd you get this?"

"That old guy on night crew was reading it. Came out yesterday, he said."

"What's gonna happen?" I'm glancing around, but not many staffers are in the Dayroom yet. And I don't know if they'd care we had this information, but I prefer not to have it ripped from my hands, just in case.

"Someone's gonna be held accountable. Old guy said it's all over the news. Reporters are outside the base, trying to interview soldiers. People are pissed."

"Was it like this at the Mologne House?"

He shakes his head. "It's a decent hotel. Even have maid service."

I peer at him. Tattoo is unshaven and his eyes are bloodshot. Under the surface, he seems uneasy. His pajamas are dirty, like he was low-crawling through the far-reaches of the Ward all night. He's usually neat and squared-away.

"What's bothering you?"

He looks at me, unblinking. Frowns. "I heard soldiers complaining about this. Thought they were whining just to pass the time. I should've listened. I should've gone to see a room."

"Yeah, well." Guilt. I feel for him.

I'm embarrassed to say I was judgmental many times. I judged Katia at first. I really judged Skittles. So what if she wears purple contacts? It's sick to think I was as bad as one of the men who expected—even wanted—women to fail. I didn't try to make many girlfriends besides Weisengard and Marge—we were too busy competing with each other. I devoted years and years to the Army, always trying to be the perfect soldier. And for what? Most guys were never gonna accept us, anyway. I fooled myself into thinking I was a part of the Big Army Club. In reality, I was always on the outside—whether I knew it or not.

I think about all the women I assumed weren't high speed: the finance females, the ones in human resources, mail clerks, the cooks. I saw them every day. Not once asked them about themselves. What would I have learned from the other female soldiers if I had? Looking back, a lot. Because women united is a powerful threat to their damned patriarchy.

I feel my cheeks flush. Suddenly, I'm deeply ashamed of myself.

I cup my face in my hands to hide it.

He looks at me intently, still unblinking. Whispers loudly, "Amputees living in buildings without elevators is total horseshit. Regular Americans—not just the media—aren't gonna stand for that, either. Lots of people support the troops and they don't want us treated like that. Guaranteed millions will be thrown at the problem until it's fixed."

I sit up straighter. "You really think that?"

"Sure. They got the money."

"I mean the part that if people *knew*, they'd pressure the Army to change."

He wipes his finger over Katia's smoking donut drawing. I can almost see his mind switch gears. His eyes look up, catch mine and hold them. "I get what you're saying."

Of course he does. A few days ago, he made fun of this idea. I bet Americans would care that females in uniform are constantly harassed. Would it be easy to find out? I know the answer: yes and no. *Yes,* because I feel ready to talk about it and bet some other women are, too. *No* because getting the information out—chatting to a journalist—would not be simple. First, there's actually finding a number of a human being that would listen. Getting a decent reporter can't be easy. Then, the actual discussion. Telling on others is also telling on ourselves—female and male soldiers and officers know this happens.

I need a number. I ask, "Would he give you the rest of the paper?"

"Probably." He looks at me and must see the hope I'm trying to hide because he changes his answer quickly to, "I'll get it."

Newspapers always have a list of numbers. Our *Post Circular News* always did. As a ninth grader, I had to call one for English class, so I know how this could work.

This might be the best way to get justice. While I trust LT and Captain, they don't control things. Stuck in the same patriarchy as me. Whatever higher power there is has to either decide to help or be forced. Screams and cries can be blocked out—from the inside. But from the outside—you can't. I need to be able to get this story out. The sooner, the better.

CHAPTER 28

Captain Butler

PAST LUNCHTIME, JACKSON found himself in front of Butler's door. His teeth chattered with nerves; his shirt was sweat soaked. What seemed so important just a few seconds ago—actually since he saw Ashe—was reduced to almost nothing; the panic he had felt turned out like a light. All that time begging the nurses to tell him where Butler was... well, it didn't matter anymore. He'd let it go. He took a step away from the door.

Except he *couldn't* just let it go. He knew he had to talk to Butler, even though Butler made him edgy. Scared shitless, actually. Jackson feared him, but so did every mechanic he worked with. Jackson took in a deep breath and softly knocked on the door. He thought he heard a voice call from inside, so he turned the handle and stepped in.

The room was dark. Every curtain closed and blind turned, totally sealed from the outside. Jackson scanned the room and saw Butler lying in his bed, sound asleep. A table nearby toppled over with presents and gadgets. A new laptop, still in its box, glowed on a folding chair.

Jackson walked closer to the bed then stopped, taken aback. He remembered Butler strong as a bull, but at this moment he looked shrunken and weak. Normally clean shaven, stubble grew in patches on his gaunt face. Jackson felt drawn to him and took a few steps forward until he was so close that they could touch. He stood over him, undecided if he should stay or come back later.

Butler's breathing came out staggered. For a moment, Jackson waited, unsure of what to do or if he should wake him—

A hand shot up and grabbed him by the throat. Even on sleeping medication, Butler's instincts told him to wake up and hold on. He clutched the front of the intruder's shirt with his one good hand and yanked him close. Soon, he stared into the eyes of his invader.

Jackson froze, unable to escape the grip. A wave of panic shot through them both.

Jackson shouted, "Captain! It's me, Specialist Jackson!"

"Who the hell!" Butler growled.

Butler stared into the pug eyes, caught by surprise. He released him with a small shove. Jackson stumbled back, his hands up. It took a few seconds for their pulses to return to normal.

"Turn on the light," Butler said. It was a command. Jackson stumbled over his feet to get to the switch.

As he returned to the bed, he said, "I was your mechanic in Iraq, remember?"

Butler stared straight into his eyes, an expression of cold determination. Remembering. Finally, he spoke. "Hey buddy…yeah, I know you…of course…" he nodded, but his eyes seemed far away.

Jackson opened his mouth but shut it again. He scanned Butler's body, registering his wounds and the gravity of his situation. Cast on his arm, the missing leg. The stump. The thought of it… he nearly choked as he tried to swallow. Captain Butler? Seriously injured? From everything he knew about him, this seemed impossible.

"I didn't know…" He sputtered.

With his one good arm, Butler pulled down his sheet to show off the wounds on his muscular frame. Under the bruising, Jackson could see the captain's well-conditioned body. He was relieved to see Butler was still the same guy, just bandaged up and battered.

"Got me good, huh?"

Jackson nodded, his mouth too dry to speak.

"Don't worry about me," Butler said. "I'll be back doing my job soon enough."

"Back to killing Haj." Jackson glanced at the stump.

Butler eyed him, trying to get a fix on the guy his team had nicknamed Doughboy. They departed on decent terms, so it was unusual for Jackson to be so nervous. This gave him the feeling, honed from years of training, that Jackson had something important to say. Maybe the most important thing he'd ever said in his life. But about what—and why here? His eyes looked everywhere, except at Butler lying in the bed. Nervous, nervous.

"What's going on, buddy?"

Jackson flexed his hands over and over. He was flushed. "The…the… Thing is… Captain, we got a problem. Ashe from that party at the compound, remember her? She's here."

Butler grimaced. "Yeah, I know."

Jackson couldn't hide his surprise. He licked his lips. "Well, Sir, she's been talking. And I mean *talking.*"

Butler cursed under his breath. No matter how many times he told himself to not let that dumb bitch get him mad, he got mad. He felt his anger rising.

"She's in the psych ward, though."

"Psych ward?" Butler thought, if she accused him, who would listen? Nobody, that's who. Perhaps the people she's 'talking to' are in the psych ward, too. Letting her vent while knowing she's nuts. "Don't worry about her, buddy. If she's locked up in there, she's harmless."

Jackson wanted to trust Butler, but wasn't convinced. "Sir, a JAG officer came in to talk to her. In the psych ward."

This was troubling. Butler frowned. "You sure?"

"Hundred percent," Jackson nodded.

Butler sighed. It seemed as if Ashe would make trouble forever. No matter that she was the one who shot at him, or that she was in a psych ward. He'd have to get her to *really* shut up this time.

"Anyone ask you to make a statement?"

"No, Sir."

With more force Butler said, "You'd have nothing to say anyway, isn't that right?"

Jackson shook his head in agreement, "Nothing whatsoever, Captain."

"Because we're on the same team, right?"

"Yeah, absolutely."

Butler nodded, forced a smile. "Good, that's right." He knew he had to keep Jackson calm. Knew that the soldier was scared to death of getting into trouble, or worse, of a dishonorable discharge if JAG became involved.

Together they heard a rough voice demanding, "Who's this?"

Their heads snapped to see Butler's mom in the doorway, hands on hips. A paper was curled up tight in her right hand. Neither had heard her come in.

Butler's expression didn't change, but Jackson shrunk under her gaze. Short and stick-thin, the woman had the intensity of a sniper. It was a quality that he was too worried to admire.

Butler said quietly, "Mom, this is Specialist Jackson. We served in Iraq together."

Her small eyes scanned his body and nodded a hello. She walked closer, rolling the paper between her hands. Asked them both again, "What were you two talking about?"

Butler glanced at Jackson. "Not much."

She snapped at him, "Don't give me that."

His mom sat down on the bed and crossed her bony arms. Butler looked up at Jackson. When his mom started up, he didn't need guests. Forcing another smile, he said, "Thanks for stopping by, buddy. Come again."

Jackson got the hint. Stepped back from the bed and turned towards the door.

"Nice meeting you," he said to Mrs. Butler. Looking at Butler, he said, "I'll stop by again soon. Especially if I hear something."

"Do that."

Jackson exited.

Butler tried to shift back into bed, to avoid her questions but she wouldn't allow it.

"What's that boy telling you about?"

Maybe he could avoid too much of an inquisition. He was feeling tired, run down. He needed time to think up a plan, maybe make a few phone calls. Hop on his new laptop and write some emails. First, he had to deal with mom and get her out of the room.

He answered her, "It's nothing."

She let out a warning: "Tell me now, Michael John."

Butler knew it was useless. He answered her, "Just some stupid girl."

She frowned. "What about her? You've never been worried about no girl before."

"Nothing about her."

His mom's voice came out as an order: "Speak. *Michael John.*"

More silence. He squirmed under her penetrating look. He shook his head unhappily.

"She's making accusations against me. Some type of vendetta. I barely know her."

Her face remained worried. "Is any of it true?"

His body bucked in anger. "*Mom.*" They locked eyes and she frowned at his outburst. Gentler, he stated, "A few weeks ago, I saw this girl named Ashe in Kuwait. She must've mistook me for someone else and shot at my vehicle. Nobody was hurt, and I didn't tell you because I didn't want you to get worried. Now I found out she's here and looking to stir up trouble. For no reason."

She said as evenly as possible, "Someone shot at you and you didn't tell me?"

"Mom, I can't tell you every time someone's shooting in my direction. I'm SF."

"She's a soldier! On your own side!" His mom was shaking in anger.

"Yeah, I know."

"Well, she should be in jail."

He nodded. "She's in the psych ward now. I don't know what's gonna happen next."

"Locked up. That's what should happen next." She let out a huffy breath. "What's that girl got to do with that kid who was just in here?"

"You know how the guys are. He heard some rumors. Came to make sure I was alright."

She nodded. "Mr. Popular. Well, you certainly don't need this right now. You just need to focus on healing and getting better."

"So I can get back in."

Instantly, his mom's eyes darkened. "I mean so you can go *home*."

Butler knew better than to argue. He'd already emailed the Battalion Commander to see if he could stay in, even with a prosthetic leg. His mom did not agree—she was adamant he go for the medical retirement and go home. He had to sneak around behind her back, which was difficult with her always around.

He returned to a safer subject. "The girl's name is Amanda Ashe. Believe it or not, she's from Wisconsin. Dairy farmer."

Her face darkened. "You seem to know a lot about her."

He answered scornfully. "*Mom.* That's all I know. She's making up these stories against me to deflect blame. Like I said, she mistook me for someone else. Now she's covering her tracks so she won't get into trouble for shooting at an unarmed officer."

His mom searched his face. "She won't bother you," she replied, "I'll make sure of it."

Butler laid back in his bed, eyes up at the ceiling. He didn't respond right away.

"Girls in the military are always accusing guys, looking for cash or fame. There's no way to prove anything, so they think they can just get away with dragging guys' names through the mud."

His mom frowned. "And you *want* to stay in this type of military? I'd rather just take you home where you belong. The VA is twenty minutes away."

He didn't respond, knew better.

Mrs. Butler continued to look down at her son, sad and defeated. She had an idea. She stood up. She walked to the table, set the new laptop on to the pile of gifts and took a seat. Flipped open the paper to the front page and held it up.

"Washington Post printed a whole paper dedicated to showing how bad conditions are here at Walter Reed for the soldiers who get discharged from the hospital but can't go back to their units yet. Said they face neglect and lots are frustrated, the article says."

Butler said nothing but looked curiously over at the paper.

"Got the leadership around here fired up. Today the halls are full of top brass, big generals going room to room conducting inspections, trying to see what's true and what not."

Butler shrugged. "Nobody's been here."

"Nobody's been in here 'cause I didn't want nobody in here."

They sat in silence for a second. His mom shook the paper shut.

"This girl shot at you?"

He nodded, but kept his eyes from hers.

She went on. "Well, then. With all that bad publicity for the hospital, sure would be time for some good news. I'm sure the Public Affairs office would be more than happy to get a few interviews together for an honest to goodness all-American hero. How many people did you save, Mark? Ten? Twenty?" She smiled down at him. "I'm sick of telling them 'no' all the time, anyway. Put you in the spotlight, show them what you've done for the country. What do you think about that?"

Butler nodded. He thought it was exactly what he needed to do. Deflect blame.

When people accused Captain USA of anything, they'd be the ones looking pathetic.

Not him.

CHAPTER 29

Amanda and the News

YESTERDAY, IT TOOK me all day and all night to finally get some numbers to call. Day two of my search was paused because I had to complete my daily chores—breakfast, group, and filling out more Stuck Point sheet with LT. I'm running on fumes.

Of course, the Washington Post wouldn't put me in touch with any of their writers, but I bothered their customer service agents enough until they gave me other papers to call that weren't a 1-800-number. Smaller papers in D.C. and one from Baltimore. Good news is that they are *real*—actual papers with genuine, unbiased reporters. Not published by the Army.

With my journal in one hand and the phone in the other, I settle down to call the fourth number out of five. So far, no luck talking to anyone willing to report and write. One woman from Baltimore asked me about the barracks, but I told her that's already been covered and she hung up. It's late afternoon, but I still have some time before our free time is over. With the television on, I'm alone by the phone.

I take a breath and dial. *Comeoncomeon….* Two rings. Then, a gruff male voice.

"Washington Regular. Richards here."

Yes! My whole body sighs. There's a pause as I realize I'm supposed to talk.

I clear my throat, "Um, hi. I want to get in touch with a reporter. I have a story that would be beyond interesting. I'm a soldier. In the Army."

Richards pauses on the other end. "I'm sorry, but who is this?"

Come on, I scold myself. I've *got* to get him interested.

I start over. "Good afternoon. My name is Amanda Ashe. Sergeant Ashe. I mean, I was a Sergeant but now I'm a Private. Anyway, I got your number from the Washington Post. I'm hoping the speak with someone about a story I have."

He sighs. I suppose he gets this a lot. "You at Walter Reed?"

I get excited. "Yes, yes, I am."

"And you're calling about that upcoming press conference?"

"No." Huh? What press conference?

He rushes, cuts me off before I can ask a question, like he wants to get rid of me as quickly as possible.

"We'll be there. It's the 9th. Right? I got all the details here, okay? So don't worry, we'll have a reporter on hand. Two, if I can swing it."

I have to stop him from hanging up. "Wait. No."

Brief pause, then that rough voice again. Harsher now. "What'd you mean, *no*? Is the press conference off?"

I feel like I've got less than three seconds to get him to really hear me. I clear my throat.

Brightly, I say, "Listen, Mr. Richards. I don't know anything about a press conference. But I've got a story. One the public needs to know about." He doesn't say a word, so I take this as a sign to keep going. "Sexual assault, rape, all sorts of stuff against women in the Army. Seems to me that a female soldier in Iraq is more likely to get assaulted by a guy wearing the same uniform than hit by enemy fire. We got to worry about guys trying to get us, inside and outside the wire."

Takes him a second to respond. "I'm a reporter. Not the police."

I nod, as if he can see me. "Exactly. I don't think many Americans know about what happens to their daughters once they join up. I mean, there are laws and regulations and rules. But the law doesn't apply *equally* to everyone in the Army. Military Police can let things slide if they want. It happened to me. I tried to report something and got blown off."

"Well…I…" he stammers and I jump in.

"My commander covered up a lot. Commanders can block all these reports and they do, more often than anyone would believe. Chain of commands get infiltrated by good old boy clubs, which makes life really hard for women."

He clears his throat. Answers, "I do features. Not investigative journalism."

I challenge him. "This story would be a great feature. If someone from your paper doesn't report it, then who will? This is good information for the public to have. Richards, the country needs someone from your paper to talk to me and see if they can use my story."

He says nothing but I hear him breathe on the other line. I frown into the phone and shift restlessly in my chair.

"Richards, do you have kids?"

He grunts. "A niece."

"Think about her. Suppose she wants to join the military someday. She signs up, thinking she's about to serve her country. Instead, she faces misogynistic jerks who hurt her, and it's all kept on the down low. I mean—I got drugged in Iraq, raped twice—both in one night. You know how gross that is? There wasn't even water to clean up right, and I was sick for days with no medicine, no IV. I think people would be shocked to learn that their daughters aren't allowed to serve honorably like their sons. Imagine that happening to your niece."

I try to stay calm, but my throat hardens as I speak, and small tears form in my eyes. I wipe them away, feeling more and more desperate by the second.

He says softly, "Listen, soldier, I know there are lots of problems in the Army beyond Abu Ghraib. The whole country's talking about the Walter Reed article in the Washington Post. It's a shame, really. But there's—"

My stomach knots up. I feel as if he's about to hang up. But he's my only chance. The last number I have is for something only online. Who would read that?

My heart pounds. I almost beg. "You *can* help. One little paragraph is all I'm asking. *Please,* Mr. Richards."

He goes quiet for a second. I hold my breath.

He asks, "You said you're at Walter Reed?"

I nod at the phone. "Yes, I'm here."

"Listen," he says slowly, "could you make it down to the press conference? Says here from the info I got, it's in the Physical Therapy area on the 9th. Starts at10:30. Haven't read the entire brief yet, but I planned on going myself.

We could meet up for a few afterwards. Let me speak to you in person. See what you're all about."

This is exactly what I want, yet...completely impossible.

"I'd really love to," I say, "but is there any way to just talk over the phone? I could write things down, hand you over pages and pages about everything that happened to me. A good story is a good story, even if it's just over the phone, right?"

"What's your last name again?"

"Ashe. My name is Amanda Ashe."

Sounds like he's typing. "Where's home?"

"Wisconsin."

"Your family living around Milwaukee?"

"No, my family is a bunch of dairy farmers. German and Irish immigrants who settled in the northern part. My great-grandpa built our farm."

I can sense him relax over the phone. "Well... Amanda from Wisconsin. I'd like to meet you. See what you're about, take a look at you. Figure out a platform. I only do stories that I feel are bulletproof. We're small and don't have the resources like the big papers do. Since you're there, it should be easy to meet up."

I feel dizzy. He's right—*it should be*. I can't tell him where I'm at—he'd call our future meeting off in a heartbeat. I have no way out of here to see Richards. My illusion that this could work is disappearing fast.

I ask softly, "You really need to see me?"

"It won't be hard to find me. I'm a fat, short, bald guy with green glasses. I'll have my blue laptop case with me. Can't miss me. Who should I be looking for?"

I tug at a loose strand of hair. I'll figure out a way for this to work. *I have to.*

"I have dark brown hair."

"Long? Short?"

"Long, I guess." I stop. Could he be asking this to find me *or* to decide if he wants to find me? I know he's my last hope, but I suddenly feel like I'm betraying myself and the rest of the women by describing my looks. I ask, "Does it matter what I look like? I can find you from that description, you won't have to search for me."

He speaks quickly, "Listen, everyone cares what people look like. Helps to form our opinions, especially in news. Especially about an all-American sweetheart, which I assume you think you are. Think Jessica Lynch."

"I guess." I pause. This isn't *exactly* how I thought this conversation would go. I envisioned a reporter being so upset they'd jump right on the story. Now the only reporter I found cares about my image. Gritting my teeth, I add: "I'm 5'5, blue eyes. I'll wear pink to stand out." *Pink?* What the hell did I just say? I bite my lip to stop from saying anything else.

I hear him typing again. "Write down some notes on what you want to say. We might not have much more than a few minutes. Not sure what the Public Affairs office has planned, but I assume there will be a reception afterwards."

A reception means this will be something special, and we will have minimal time.

"I can do that, yes, absolutely." I have plenty to say and an entire journal to fill. That part will be easy.

"Okay, then." I know he's about to hang up, but he has some information that I'd like.

"Hey—Mr. Richards. Do you happen to know what the press conference is about?"

He grunts into the phone. "Uh, yeah. One second."

I breathe out the air I've been holding. This is a long-shot; a 400-meter with a jammed M-16 rifle shot. A 100 mile with a short-range howitzer shot. A nailed-a-target-from-5,000-meters-away-shot. But it seems like my only chance for the outside world to find out about this type of abuse.

"I got it right here." I sense he's putting on glasses, then he reads to me: "Meet an officer who saved both Iraqi and American lives…blah blah blah...a hero who is valorous and furthered the mission…Captain Michael Butler…"

WHAT THE ACTUAL FUCK. I gasp so loud, that he stops reading.

"You okay?"

I resist the impulse to scream and shout. Instead, I answer quickly.

Heart pounding, I force the words out. "Perfect. Thanks for talking. Pink. I'll be wearing pink and I'll make sure to find you," I slam down the phone.

I'm in shock. That bastard is trying to be the good guy. It's about goddam time I make things equal.

CHAPTER 30

Amanda, Stuck

I'M IN THE Dayroom, trying to process the past few hours. TV is on. I sit as far away from it as I can. My back is pressed against the folding chair with my journal in front of me. Writing makes the memories real again, but I have to get over it and write. God, I have to make Richards understand how important this is. I lean over the table again, start a new paragraph.

I hear footsteps, very close. Look up.

"Haven't seen you all day," Tattoo says as he plops into the chair next to me. He's wearing his BDU's. My stomach twists and my mouth goes dry. Soldiers leave the ward in uniform, not jammies.

I know the answer but ask anyway. "You're leaving?"

He nods and tries to hide his smile. "Yup. They told me after lunch. I went searching for you as soon as I heard, but LT snagged me for Addictions."

"S-s-shit," I stammer out. "First Katia, now you."

He slides a piece of paper across the table. It reads: SSG M. Hunt. With a phone number and his Army email address. I slide it into my journal and close it.

"M?" I ask. Still would like to know his name.

Shakes his head. "*Tattoo* to you."

"A girl can try." I wink and he smiles.

"I'll have my cell phone as soon I get discharged. Call me anytime."

"Oh," I can't even pretend to be happy for him.

I feel him watch me. He clears his throat and motions towards my journal.

"What're you working on?"

I look down at my words. "I found a reporter who might be interested. His name is Richards and he works for the Washington Regular, which is a paper not too far from here."

He stares at me. "Really? That's great news."

I nod. "He's coming to Walter Reed on the 9th, so I've got two days to get out of here and make my way down to a press conference they're having that morning. I didn't want to tell him I'm in a psych ward so he told me to meet him there." I open my mouth to say more but close it again. I don't want to talk about Butler or deal with the idea of being near him again right now. I can't. Just can't.

"Can I help?"

I frown and shake my head. "Not unless we can trade places." I let out a fake laugh to cover my frustrations.

He shrugs. "Ask Nurse Taylor to bring you down to meet the reporter. Or the LT could. I mean, she brought in JAG to meet you. Or ask that nurse with the ponytail on night shift. She'd come in during the day to help. Or the old guy. Maybe even Darrell."

I cut him off. "You crazy? They won't take me. No way."

He sweeps his finger across the table and flicks at imaginary dust. "*Of course* they will. They want to help and I'm sure they would take you to see the reporter. They all know the deal."

I nod, but I'm not buying into his idea. I don't want to ask for help.

"I just need to get out of here," I blurt out, "do it on my own."

He leans back and gives me a side eye. "Listen, Ashe, I'm on your side, alright—so don't get pissed."

My stomach drops. Those words rarely end without someone going ballistic.

Okay, let's hear it. "What?"

He's silent for a second. Breathes out. I regret immediately that I asked him.

"It's good that guy Richards could write a story for you and JAG might help, and I think it's cool that you want to get these guys to admit their guilt. But you won't even make it halfway out the door if you don't eat."

I laugh out loud in shock. "Seriously?"

"You're starving yourself."

What the hell? "It's too hard to explain, Tattoo."

"I'm a good listener."

Oh, God. I'm so close to reaching over and shaking him. Instead, my jaw tightens as I answer him. "I eat."

He replies, "One banana and five corn flakes ain't enough to live on and you know it. Coffee and water don't count. You've lost weight since you got here. Maybe you should ask to get fed through that tube. Couldn't hurt. I mean, you need nutrients and minerals. You need calories. What if you faint on your way to talk to this reporter?"

His expression is grim, but I don't care—why'd he chose *today* to tell me this? Finally, I'm feeling good and now I get a lecture. One that I don't need right now.

My voice cracks in two as I attempt to stay strong. "I can't just eat, okay? You're not a shrink, so don't act like you know what's best."

His voice stays steady, "You've barely eaten anything. You're killing yourself."

I run my hands through my dark, knotty hair. Sure, my pajamas are looser now. Yeah, I haven't eaten much. But so what? My whole body constricts in anger. "I'm fine, Tattoo, okay? It's not like anyone here wants to help me anyway."

He looks at me, bug eyed. "Ashe, are you crazy? You have *everyone's* attention in here. All the staff is helping you out. You got JAG and LT bending over backwards. Nurse Taylor lets you order food, and nobody else gets to do that. Soldiers aren't bent out of shape about it, either. Nobody complains. Most of the guys in here are good dudes, and the only dud is gone. You know as well as me that soldiers help soldiers. Always have and always will. Tell your story to the guys in here, they'd be pissed off for you. Probably give you some good advice."

He's so wrong, I can't stand it. I'm about to flip my lid. I pound the table.

I hiss out my words, "Muscrat put a food tube in me! I was *violated!*"

"Ashe, I saw you puke. You fainted right after. I'm pretty sure you needed that thing."

"*You* know what I need." I can't stand him right now. Seems as if he feels that same way about me. His face is colder than I ever seen it.

"Ashe, I know what I see. Ward 54 is just like the Army. What you get out of it is directly proportional to what you put in. What's gonna become of your life if you just avoid everything? You avoid talking to people, you avoided taking meds. You avoided dealing with your boyfriend's death. Now you want to get even with this SF guy who screwed you over. Getting even means you never get ahead. You won't know what to do when you actually do get some justice. By that point, you could've died of starvation."

I'm so mad my whole body is boiling over. "The Army is *not* what you put into it. The Army is people. People who decide who's important and who's not. *You* of all people should know that. You put your heart into it, and they don't even want to know who your partner is."

His eyes look hurt. "I'm talking about you, not me."

"You should mind your own business." I stand up. Clutch the journal in my hand. "Good luck out there."

He runs his hands over his stubby hair. "I'm on your side, it's just *fuck*. Get help." He pushes back his chair and stands up. I look away. "I can go to this press conference," he half whispers, looking down to meet my eyes.

I look him straight in the eyes. "Don't fuckin' bother."

His look of pure pity irritates the shit out of me. I can't stand being around another Army dude who tells me what to do, like he knows best. I about-face, rush out, scurry as fast as I can down the hall, and find my room. I fling open the door and lock myself into my tiny little bathroom. I turn on the shower to drown out everything.

I hear a knock, over and over. It eventually stops.

Sitting on the toilet, I twirl my hair as I think about what Tattoo said: soldiers help soldiers. I think about Katia and how I can still help her. I think about Manolo, and know I can't. I wonder what Weisengard is doing in Kuwait. I wonder what my family is up to. God, I hate this half-life I'm living, not knowing what tomorrow will bring.

I rub my hand over my stomach. Pick at my bandage.

I hate this thing. I want to be normal and eat like regular people, but I don't know how anymore. It's not like bulimics and anorexics can turn their issues on and off. I know I need to go to a special facility for people like me, to learn how to digest again. To look at food not as a numbing device, or a way for us to kill ourselves, but rather as a way to stay alive. I also know they cost more than a car. Who's got that kind of money?

Soldiers help soldiers. I can't shake off those words. Of course, he's right, and I don't hate him for pointing it out. I hate that it ticked me off and I yelled like a spoiled brat. I hate that I may have lost my only remaining ally. GOD, I really hate myself.

CHAPTER 31

Amanda and Bad News

CAN'T SLEEP, SO I stare at the dark ceiling. Got no idea how much time is passing. I try to judge the hour by how empty my stomach is, but it's been hollow for days. I rub my fingers over my ribs, then stop. My hand aches from the hours I spent writing. My mind is worked up from remembering everything. And from HIM telling me what to do.

I'm in no mood to sleep. I know I'll have a nightmare if I go to bed, so I'd rather stay awake. I kick off the sheets, roll over, and get up.

I open the door and peer into the dim hall. Lights are on in the hallway, but it's dead out here. Clock on the wall tells me it's a little past two in the morning. I need to walk around a bit. Visit the night crew. Ponytail. Talk to her and see what she thinks about my story going to Richards. Ask if she could take me, like Tattoo said. He's right. I need help.

I'm alone in the halls. I hear voices coming from the nurse's station.

"Okay, Amanda," I tell myself, "see what she says."

I'm about to turn the corner when I hear my name. *Amanda Ashe.* I freeze.

"Did they figure out what's gonna go on with her?" I hear a staffer ask another. By the voice, I'm pretty sure it's Darrell. Haven't seen him on dayshift for a while. Now I know why.

I'm uncomfortable with this subject, knowing it's me.

"It's awful," I hear Ponytail say. "I overheard LT and the Major arguing about it. He got a phone call from SF Headquarters. They're pressing charges. God, it breaks my heart."

My stomach sinks immediately and I feel as if the ground is shifting. I'm shocked, but try to keep listening. *Assault. Deadly weapon.* I know I hear the word *jail.*

Darrell asks, "How long?"

"Major said a minimum of *four years.*"

Four YEARS. I let out a small gasp, cover my mouth quickly. My knees go weak and I grab the wall for support. They don't hear me and keep talking.

"Military prison," Darrell says. "What a waste. She's a real smart girl."

Me. Prison. Deep down, I've been expecting these charges. Even though LT is trying to get me help, she's only a LT. The JAG officer is only a Captain. Suddenly I feel very sick.

Someone else chimes in. A soft, low male voice I don't recognize. "She could say it was an accidental discharge."

Ponytail answers. "She can't. LT suggested the same thing, but they got surveillance of everything from the gate. The Major said they've got witnesses and sworn statements. Worst of all, the guy she shot at is *here.* At Walter Reed. He's some war hero who got his leg blown off a few weeks ago and now they're having a big press conference and celebration for him on the 9th. Interviewing him live on television."

There's some murmmers from the group, but I don't catch all of what they say. *Tragic. Sad. Not right. Unfair.* My throat tightens up so much, I almost choke.

Darrell speaks again. "Best thing Ashe could do would be to tell some of that story she's got. The worst thing for the Army would be for her to make this public. She's got to leverage that, help herself from too much trouble."

His words give me relief. Richards has to listen to me, he has to. The low-voiced staffer agrees. "I'll take her to that press conference. Imagine his face if she showed up, huh? We'd definitely get a reporter or two to talk to her."

I run my hand through my hair. Tattoo was absolutely right; the staff can help. More than that, they are willing. I take a step towards them, my sole hope right now.

Ponytail speaks in a sad voice, "That's what I thought. Muscrat gave a direct order to LT to keep her here. Said she doesn't leave the ward, under any circumstances. To be honest, I think he's worried about that. If you want to keep your job, don't even think about it."

There's a short silence. I slump back against the wall, my legs quaking. It's like I'm hearing them on a talk radio, except the show is about my life.

Darrell speaks again. "She could ask for a full trial. Go all in. You know that's what Makowski did three years ago."

The low-voiced staffer agrees. "Man, that sure did make a mess. But put that other bastard behind bars. Last I heard Makowski's in Cincinnati."

"Could she get a plea deal?" I hear Ponytail ask, "That's how it works on television."

They all start to talk at once, but I slowly walk backwards, away from them. I don't want to talk to anyone, see anyone. I shake my head, seeing myself in a court room as my mom, dad, and sister sit behind me. Imagine what would be said about me—all the dirty lies and rumors would be said over and over again. They'd butcher me. I can't do it to my family, or me.

No trial. Four years in a jail, though…no. There's got to be another option.

Think, think, think, Amanda. Oh my GOD. YES. I can make it down to see Richards. I CAN interrupt that interview. A new plan forms, and it's a good one.

I stand up straight, drag myself back down the hall, and head right towards the nurse's station. Turning the corner, I sense their collective surprise but zero in on the dirty-blonde hair.

"Ashe?" It's Ponytail sitting behind the wide desk. She stands up and I see her glance around, but the other staffers are silent.

"I need a liquid supplement drink," I say sharply.

"Sure," she says as she nods. Digs in a desk drawer and pulls out two bottles. Holds them up for me to choose. Chocolate or vanilla. I take the vanilla and crack it open.

"How're you feeling?" Ponytail says. A warm, but worried, smile spreads across her face.

"Okay, thanks. Hi, Darrell." I sip the drink. The thick liquid is warm, hard to swallow. I get down a mouthful.

"Hey there," he says with a nod. Dude looks conflicted.

I glance at Ponytail. "You don't need to watch me. I need it, I won't do anything stupid."

She nods and attempts to smile, "Okay. Need anything else?"

I shake my head. "No. I'm okay."

"Checks in twelve minutes," she says. "Get some sleep."

"I will."

Ponytail continues to look worried. I give a weak smile, then leave them at the nurse's desk. Her look stays with me. Really—what does she want? To know if I heard them talk about me? Well, I did. And I'll use that information. But only after I get a little nutrition. I'm going to need some energy.

❧

BEFORE I GET to my room, I peer into the Dayroom. Silent and dark. In the corner, there it is–the phone. I sit in the chair next to it and stare at the number written in ink on my hand. Something like half a day has passed, and I still feel terrible. I have to make things right. I grab the phone and punch in the number.

Three long, loud rings.

"Hello?"

"Hey. it's Ashe."

"It's like 3 a.m." He coughs.

I whisper. "Couldn't sleep. And…" A pause. My breath is caught in my throat as I can hear him shuffle around in bed.

"What's up?"

I breath out. "You're right about everything. And I was a jerk to you. I'm sorry." I don't say: was mad that you were leaving and that's why I was such a brat. I feel awful about our last conversation. I want him to know that.

He draws out his words. "So…you're sorry?"

"I'm a million times over sorry."

"I forgive you," he says. Simple. So why do I feel like I just ran a marathon?

"Good," I say, "That's settled. Thank-you, Tattoo. So where are you staying?"

"They put me in some type of barracks. It ain't bad. Share a bathroom with a dude but got my own room. Bed's comfortable."

I exhale. I'm SO glad he's not in one of those condemned places with rat shit.

"Have you seen Katia?"

"Nah. I asked around, but nothing."

I frown. Wonder where she is. I ask, "What are you doing tomorrow?"

"Morning formation, some meetings. Fill my prescription."

My gut churns in worry he's still mad. I make my voice soft and sweet. "Sounds boring…Would you be up for an adventure?"

I can hear him smile in the phone. "Depends."

Please, please, please. "Tattoo…I need some help."

I practically hear him grin through the mouthpiece. "Let me hear it."

CHAPTER 32

Amanda's Accident

MORNING. IN THE scalding shower my skin turns bright pink. I dress quickly and peel up the sides of the bandage from my damp skin. The former-sticky edges leave a glue print as I pull it off. I look in the mirror to see my eyes aren't dull today. I feel different. There's hope because THIS plan will work. I'll get the food tube SO red and agitated that it'll be a medical emergency. Just need to get my hands on some rubber craft supplies.

Half past six in the morning.

I'm not only hopeful, I'm more than that. Perhaps it's the anticipation over my plan. Perhaps it's my full stomach—I did drink the rest of the bottle. Whatever it is, I am ready for today. First, I'll get my meds, then breakfast, and take a look at the day's schedule. Then I'll find a perfect time to execute my mission. I grip my notebook and step into the hall.

I'm so focused, I don't see the football game being played in the hallway between the big guys that Tattoo called Doc, Hammer, Action, and Bloodstain. A moccasin sails through the air and I see it too late. Pummels me right on the head. Surprised, I fling my arms up to protect myself. My notebook falls to the floor. I'm dizzy and land right on my ass. Ouch.

Bloodstain jogs up to me, his face as surprised as mine.

He says as he picks up my stuff, "Sorry about that, we didn't mean to."

"It's okay," I say, still dizzy. He hands me my notebook as I stay seated. I grip it.

Eagerly he says, "Here. I'll help ya up."

I don't got time to say no. He grabs me around the waist. With both strong arms, he hoists me from directly below the uncovered wound. His forearm lands just right under the actual tube and as he lifts me, I feel part of it rip from my body. AAARRGGHHH. Pain shoots through my belly and up to my head and down to my feet. So. Much. PAIN.

"Stop," I beg, "STOP."

He pulls me to my feet, then let's go. "What's wrong?"

We both look down to see flecks of red on my pajama top. Bloodstain's arm is red on the inside of his forearm. I lean against the wall and slide down to the floor.

"Man down," one of the guys' yells. I pull up the edge of my shirt to inspect.

"Oh GOD." Bright red blood puddles around the top of the tube, which is half-way pulled out of my body. SO GROSS. I try to cover it and my hand is soon covered in warm, sticky blood. I dry heave into my chest.

"Don't touch it," Bloodstain orders as he bends over me. "It's okay, you'll be okay, it's not bad at all. Just need a little fixing."

"I'm getting a nurse," one of them hollers as I moan loudly.

I close my eyes as my body throbs. Okay, okay, okay...NEW plan. I have to do it NOW instead of later. Make it all look like a terrible accident, so the medics *can* take me away from this floor and into the hospital.

"I need my notebook," I whisper to Bloodstain and he nods. His face is blurry as he brings it to me. When it's tightly squeezed in my left hand, I take a deep breath.

NOW! My mind screams at my hand.

I grip the tube and I pull with all my strength. I yank hard until the tube makes a disgusting sucking noise. Soon it's in my hand, along with gallons of blood and a clump of some part of my body. OH MY GOD. Pain reverberates throughout my body. I'm absolutely dying of pain. I gag on the pain.

I hear a million panicked voices yelling. *Ashe! Help! It was an accident! Call the ER!*

I hold the plastic tube tightly in my right hand. Warm blood continues to flow out of me. Red starburst blots my vision but I keep my notebook held tightly to my side. I want to keep it with me, no matter what.

CHAPTER 33

Amanda's Plan

THE PAIN IS not gone when I wake up in a small, clean white room, but it IS tolerable. The excruciating level of agony has passed, I hope. Lord, I never want to experience that level of hell again.

I'm groggy, but I see that I'm hooked up to a drip and my body is tightly stuffed under a smooth white sheet, my legs outstretched underneath. My eyes follow the drip to see it go under the top of the sheet. I can see the clock on the wall. 11:00. Please God, let it not be the 9th.

My vision is spotty. *Was this a dream, too?* I pull my hands, but they can't move. Pure panic bursts through my body. I'm tied in restraints. I break out in a sweat. I try to pull free, but my hands don't budge.

Shit, shit, shit. No. No. NO.

My thoughts freak out. *Anyone can come in here and do anything they want—stick anything up my crotch, fondle these boobs, put something in my mouth and I can't do a thing.* I clamp my mouth shut. Tears well up and streak my cheeks. Can't wipe them off. I bite my big lip so hard that I tear a small piece of flesh off the inside of my mouth. I draw blood and suck it down. Tears stop. Forced pain makes it feel better. I rub my cheek on my pillow and clamp my thighs together. That'll have to do for now.

Come on Amanda. Be logical, logical and smart. Later, I can get my hands untied, slip out, find Richards, call Tattoo. I look around the bare room, but it's just me, the bed, the drip, and some beeping monitors. I need my notebook; I *need* it now. Where is it? My head flops around as I look in all corners of the empty room. I feel a sudden tidal wave of exhaustion—it knocks every intrusive thought from my head. Sleep, is all I care about now. My eyes close. What are they pumping in me? I wonder before my mind drifts. I'll find out, but now I need to sleep.

❧

SOME HOURS LATER, LT enters the room. I think I'm asleep, my eyes are shut but I hear her boots. She doesn't wear rubber shoes like the nurses. I open my eyes and see her pretty, light-pink nails against the cloud-white sheet. In her other hand she holds my notebook. Looks like someone wiped away my blood, leaving thin streaks.

"Good afternoon," she says as she smiles. Clock says 15:00.

"LT," I manage to say as I shake myself awake, "What day is it?"

"You've been here for just a few hours, not days."

Relieved, I breathe out. "Is this the ER?"

Shakes her head. "It's the recovery ward. Staff will keep you here overnight, maybe two nights, to keep an eye on you and access your vitals."

"Is the tube—"

"It's out."

A heavy, dead weight lifts off me. Thank you, God, I say to the ceiling.

She goes on, "They didn't re-insert the tube, but you're still undernourished. Has a nurse come in to explain?"

I pull on my restraints, rattling the bars. "LT, they *tied me up*."

She frowns her face in worry, pulls the bed sheet to see my hands tied to a silver side rail. I sense she understands how dangerous this is to me. Her eyes widen and she immediately unties my right hand then my left.

She apologizes as she works, "I came down as soon as I got the call about this. The specialist who ran into you is really sorry."

Good. My cover of innocence worked. As painful as it was, I'm glad I did it at that exact moment when I had the chance.

She shakes her head and mutters more to herself than me, "I specifically told the staff it was an accident, and not to do this to you. I'm sure they did it because they were afraid you'd touch the stitches in your sleep."

Stitches? I remember the sickening sucking noise. The reason I MUST speak to Richards. I throw the sheet off from me. Large granny panties cover my ass and stomach way past my belly button, up to my boobs. A large, clean bandage covers the area. I tuck the sheet under my arms. I tell myself: *Refocus,* Amanda. *Remember why you're here.*

I ask, "What room am I in?"

LT opens the door and steps into the hall to look at the number.

She comes back to my bedside. "R127. Far away from Butler, okay?"

LT coughs. Looks like she's got something to say. Overhearing the staff's conversation comes back. Why duck it? Let's hear it.

"LT, am I going to jail?"

She looks startled. "Who said that?"

I straighten up in bed. "I overheard some staff talking last night when I couldn't sleep."

"It's complicated," she says, not making eye contact for long. I bite my tongue to keep quiet. She sighs. "First off, Sergeant Vinny Vincent. He's out of the Army now and working for BST. He's overseas at the moment, working in Iraq. UCMJ won't be able to prosecute him."

Ugh, what awful news. I look away, stare at the ceiling. Vincent makes my skin crawl. Jerk was probably given an honorable discharge. Bastard.

I'm so agitated, my voice is on its highest pitch. "For how long are they trying to lock me up, LT? As that dumb-shit rakes in the cash, where will I be?"

I keep my eyes on her, but she doesn't look at me as she speaks. "I don't know all of the legal jargon, but they requested the maximum punishment. Called it assault upon a commissioned officer…that means dishonorable discharge, forfeiture of all pay and allowances and…. yes, there's a possibility of confinement. Captain Lynch is working it."

I admit, "I heard some nurse say maybe four years." Four fucking years.

LT looks away, her breath is deep and even. "That punishment is for soldiers who commit crimes with an *unloaded* firearm. Or if the Humvee only had one person in it."

My heart skips a beat. "Shit…don't tell me…multiply everything by four?"

Stony silence. For a moment, all I hear is the beep from the medical machines.

I beg her, "LT, please. Tell me, even if you don't know the details. It's better that I know than driving myself crazy thinking about the worst-case scenarios."

Her expression says she doesn't want to. I plead, "Please. *LT, please.*"

She nibbles her lips. "There were four Special Forces team members in the vehicle when you took a shot. They claim that should be called attempted murder. Four counts. Not only that, but the bullets hit government property."

Rage fills me. I fight to control my voice. "Lock me in jail and throw away the key?"

She shakes her head glumly. "No, of course not. You have memory loss, trauma and PTSD. Captain Lynch is willing to try a strategy of showing *why* you did it—we know that you didn't intend to hurt anyone."

I wince. "I don't even know why I did it."

"That's the point. I'll help you. Captain Lynch will help you. There are witnesses we can interview. We know that Butler and Jackson are close. We'll get this straightened out."

Or we *won't*, and my side will never matter to anyone. Commander won't talk. Vincent will stick to his story. Shorty Airman could also be interviewed, as well as Black Forest Cake. None of this will make me look good. I can't. I can't let it get that far. Shit, I have no choice. I have to get to Richards.

A long silence lasts between us. I ask, "Can I please have my notebook?"

"Sure." She sets it on the small table near my bed along with a pencil, "This was a lot of information to take in. Are you alright?"

I nod. "Would it be possible for me to make a call?"

LT opens her cargo pants and pulls out a flip phone. She hands it to me. Gives me a small smile. "Take your time." Steps outside the room.

I take my notebook, opening to the front. I pause for a second as a sharp pain slices through me. Damn, that hurts. I settle back in the bed. I dial quickly. One ring before he answers.

"Sergeant Hunt here." He sounds so strong I want to crawl into his bicep and *be* him.

"Tattoo," I say with relief. Tears sting my eyes, so I close them tight. "I made it out of the ward."

His voice sounds strained. "Already? You okay?" No, but no reason to go into it now. He tried to talk me out of it when we spoke, insisted there were other ways.

"Everything's fine. I'm in room R127 now, first floor. This is LT's phone."

He sounds concerned. "I'm serious. What happened?"

"Tattoo, I promise I will tell you. But I can't now. It's the 8th, right? So Richards comes tomorrow. It's 15:00. In less than 24 hours I need to square myself away and make sure to get to him near the PT clinic. I'll need your help. Please."

"I'm not sure if this is the best way, Ashe—your body needs to recover."

If only I HAD time. "They're charging me with attempted murder, four times over. It won't be four years—it could be life. At the minimum, I'm looking at years behind bars. LT just told me all of this, so I'm not making it up. If I don't get this story out now and get someone to care, then I never will. I'm not even sure where the military prison for women is located, but once I'm there it will be so hard to get help. The guards would control everything. Even if I do manage to talk to someone, who would listen to a prisoner?"

"Jesus," he says, "that's awful."

"I know that the LT wants to fight it, but you said before how powerful SF is."

He sounds worried through the phone. "Yeah."

I need his help. "Any chance you can swing by the PX? I said I'd wear pink."

"I got you," he says, "Women small, I'm guessing."

"I'll pay you back. I'm in room R127. Door is open."

"Don't worry about that. Be there by 17:00."

"You're awesome," I say with deep relief. "Thanks."

"See you soon."

He hangs up. The door, shut tight, seals me inside its safeness. It's quiet, which I know is only temporary, but I like it anyway.

CHAPTER 34

Amanda on the Move

MY FEET ARE in white sand. I am on a tropical beach near an aquamarine ocean that is as clear as glass. Air is balmy. Warm with a gentle, tickling breeze that floats my skirt up and around my legs. An incredible orange sunset is to my front. I feel a hand in mine.

"It's a beautiful day," Manolo says as he squeezes my fingers. I see his beautiful smile. In a second, he's gone.

I open my eyes.

I'm on my back, staring at the ceiling. I know that Manolo is dead and not on a nice beach with me, but it felt like he was truly with me. Maybe he is watching me from above. I don't know; this is the first time I've had a pleasant dream like this since he passed. I squeeze my hands into fists then let go, a feeling of peace all over.

I look to see the clock. 07:00. The 9th. Today is the day. I roll my head from side to side, trying to get out the stiffness, warm myself up.

Door creaks open. A small, short white nurse comes in and flips on the sink light. She's about my age, heavily perfumed in vanilla and wears little gold balls attached to her tiny earlobes. She grabs my chart from the end of my bed and flips through the papers.

"Hello, Sergeant Ashe and good morning."

"Hi," I say then add, "I'm a Private, though."

A short silence. She flips the papers on my chart. "Your paperwork says Sergeant."

Hm. Perhaps I can tell Richards that I'm a Sergeant.

"Did you sleep okay?"

"Actually, yeah." But never mind that. Moving on.

She nods and writes it down. "On a scale of one to ten, what's your pain today?"

"Um, a three?" I don't feel pain with the meds pumping into me. "Can I have breakfast?" Let's get the show on the road.

She seems surprised. "First let's check your vitals. After that, I'll go fetch it."

I try to sit up straight but can't quite mange. She helps me with surprising ease. She's farm-girl strong and holds me up to put a pillow behind my back. Swinging the portable tray, she whistles as she sets a glass of water in front of me. Then puts a thermometer in my mouth. Seconds later, she takes it out, checks it, and rips open the blood pressure sleeve. I sip the water.

I rest my hands on the tray and look at the back of my hands as she slips the sleeve around my arm and tightens the Velcro. A black bruise in the shape of Kuwait covers most of the right one where the needle is stuck in.

"Can you take this out? It hurts."

She leans over and looks. "When you get ready to be discharged, we will."

I frown. "When's that?"

She checks her watch as she listens to my pulse. Stops. Takes off the cuff. "Doctor said one more night."

Okay, good. Nobody is moving me this morning. She gives me a quick smile, which I try to return but can't. I'm too nervous.

As she pushes back the vitals machine she says, "I'll check on breakfast."

She exits and I'm left with my thoughts and the nerves eating me from the inside out. No matter what happens to me today, I want my story out there for the country to read. Let them demand changes for the females in uniform, so it's coming from the voters and not just the few of us.

Nurse returns with a plastic covered tray. She sets it down and removes the covering. Fruit cup, orange juice, and a box of cereal. In the middle, two large buttermilk pancakes stacked on top of each other. Butter sits stiffly on top. She sees me gawking. The pain in my chest expands.

She guesses. "Don't like pancakes?"

I shake my head.

She smiles. Shrugs. "No biggie. Let me go look. There's always options."

Options. The word hangs in the air as she exits. I breathe out, but I can't relax.

❧

OKAY, OKAY. I give the clock a death stare. Says 9:30. Surely, I should go? Or maybe I should wait a few minutes. I'm cutting it close if I make a mistake with directions, but what if I'm early and Butler sees me? No time to be nervous or second guess myself; I have to move forward. Advance, advance, advance, never retreat.

I wince from pain as I slowly slide the needle out of my hand and push a Kleenex on it to stop the bleeding. The machine does not betray me; it stays silent. I slip out of bed, but I still get dizzy. My head and belly throb in unison as my toes hit the ground. From under my sheets, I pull out a plastic bag that Tattoo dropped off.

Last night Tattoo said, "Don't do it, Ashe. Let me get Richards and bring him to you. He won't care that you're in a hospital bed. That's where patients *are.*" He'd been almost angry. In vain, he argued against my idea, but my mind's made up. I have to go to Richards, just like I said I would. Act normal, so he takes me seriously. If he sees me weak, that will change the image he has of me. "That's a bad choice," Tattoo told me. But he still let me have the bag of pink clothes. He promised to be there, to help if he could. Before he left, he told me his first name. "Mike," he said. "See why I use my nickname? My parents…well, English isn't their first language." It took me a minute to get it. Mike Hunt. HA…I didn't laugh, I swear.

Now, I smile a bit as I slowly pull a pair of pink sweats over each foot and stand. Even slower, I slide off the hospital gown. Each one of my arms goes in an armhole and glacially slow I pull it over my head. Wearing all pink makes me feel like a walking lipstick, but it's too late now. I slip on my moccasins.

My veins in my head pulse so hard it almost drowns out the squeaky shoes from the hallway. *The noise is coming this way.* Damn. Panic sweeps over me. With what I think is lightning speed, I jump into the bed and pull the sheet up. Barricade myself. The squeaky shoes keep walking down the hall. I breathe out in relief.

The clock says 9:45. Time is flying. I pull on my one last item—a bubble-gum pink baseball cap and pull it down as far as possible on my forehead. My attempt to disguise myself has made me quite noticeable, but it's all I got. I look in the small mirror above the sink. Jeez, I'm a unicorn burglar. I grab my notebook and glance around the bare room. It's empty.

Coast is clear, so I slip out. I know the way. Tattoo did a reconnaissance before he brought the bag of clothes and a wad of cash. I'll pay him back some day, he knows it. I'm not letting him lose another dime to a man or woman, even if it's me.

I head in the direction opposite the nurse's station. I'm in too much pain to do anything more than put one foot in front of the other. I call my own slow cadence—left, left, left-right-left. I reach a door that leads to a hallway outside of the recovery ward.

I push open an exit and turn right, making sure to keep my head down. I quicken my pace and hold my hand over the bandage, it hurts like hell without the medicine drip covering my pain. I turn again and this turn leads me to a noisy lobby with stairs leading up a level. I see medical staff in scrubs going every which way. A contingent of patients, civilians, and visitors are coming and going on the level above, making noise. Here we GO.

Tattoo told me to head towards the dining facility, so I check a way-finder and turn left towards the DFAC. As I move along the corridor, I keep close to the wall and slide my fingers along the rough painted wall. My nerves are eating me alive. Don't think, just *move.*

Minutes later, I see a crowd gathered–civilians, soldiers and staffers. I stop in my tracks, look around. Most of the soldiers are missing limbs, some standing without arms and some in wheelchairs, lost legs. A group of male officers stand tall in dress greens, watching and talking. Civilians are huddled near the double doors of a large clinic that's under a sign that announces, "Physical Therapy." I clutch myself through my pink sweatshirt. Don't panic. *Relax, Amanda*, I remind myself.

I hover way outside of the group, aware of the possibility of being seen by anyone I know. I pull the hat down over my eyes and partly cover my face as I watch out for the blue laptop case. My hands are shaking so I cross my arms over my chest, high above the stitches.

"Hey, Ashe," it's Tattoo calling to me. I know his voice anywhere and turn to it.

I shoot him a smile and he returns it with a wave. He stands in the hallway opening to the right of the clinic, next to someone who I can only guess is Richards. Not the journalist type by any stretch of the imagination. Looks more like a mousy desk clerk, with his balding head and pocketed blouse. He carries a notebook and the blue computer case, looking at the crowd.

They are on the edge of the group, a distance away from the star attraction. I appreciate Tattoo being so discreet. Only problem? The distance between us. I take a few slow steps towards them.

As I inch towards them, a good-looking, brunette woman with a ton of thick make-up steps out of the Physical Therapy room. A cameraman flanks her. People make way. She must be a reporter or a star, but I realize she's asking someone a question who is rolling up behind her. Camera is pointed at a wheelchair.

It's fucking Butler. I freeze in my tracks. He stops rolling his wheelchair on a taped X on the floor. Behind him, a large American flag hangs. A nifty illusion to trick the media.

I stare at him. A terrible feeling in the pit of my stomach…I gag…Stop. *Just stop, Amanda.* I've come too far to panic.

Anyways, I knew he was the star of this little get together. He won't even see me. Go, Amada. *Walk to Tattoo.* Let Richards stay for the press conference and I'll give him my story later. First, the world meets Butler. Then they find out how awful he is. I take a step, but WHAT. My elbow is grabbed from behind. I'm sharply pulled.

"Ashe?" My name is whispered into my ear, then a question: "What are you up to?"

That voice. Panic seizes my body. I turn to see Jackson on my left. His doughy hand grasps my wrist. He makes a motion with his arms to get someone's attention. I know who.

Butler locks eyes with me. His mouth hangs open, mid-sentence.

"Let go of my," I growl and rip my arm away. He falters and I'm free. Tattoo sees us and hustles over, but not fast enough. Life starts to move in double-time. The Oompah Loompah staffer from the elevator stands behind Butler's wheelchair and Smoker Lady is to his side. My mind pieces it together. She's his…mom? Butler clutches his mother's arm. They speak. She glances over at me. I can't hear, but I can imagine what he says.

New plan.

Get to the lady with the microphone. I grip my notebook. Give it to *her.*

I focus on my target. My moccasins skid on the linoleum floor as I rush as fast as I can, veering around others standing between us. I'm gaining ground—*don't stop, Amanda.* Thirty more steps, twenty-nine, twenty-eight….

"Security!" I hear a raspy voice scream. "The one in the pink hat. She's not allowed nowhere near my son!"

Anyone with a half a brain knows she's talking about ME. I pivot away from Smoker Lady's voice. Just keep walking, just keep walking. Be normal. Out of the corner of my eyes, I see a security guard take a step towards me, his hand on a holster. I freeze. A HOLSTER. Tattoo steps in between us, he looks as if he wants to protect me as much as possible.

"She's got an appointment with a journalist," I hear Tattoo say, Richards next to him.

"Hell she does," the Smoker Lady says louder, "I want her gone. Hear me, Security?"

I see the cameraman swing the camera over as the pretty reporter holds the microphone to her mouth. I move again. Another step. Another. I weave around people, avoiding the Security. Sweat slides down my spine, my body shakes, but I move to *the reporter*, ignore the rest of it.

She shouts at my back, "Oh no, you don't!"

The security guard yells over the crowd, "Stop!"

I flick a glance at the voice in time to see beady eyes on me. I'm grabbed around the waist by another guard. FUCK. I didn't him see coming. My notebook flies in the air. I scream in pain as the arms press into me.

Tattoo shouts. "Stomach injury!"

The security guard doesn't listen, as he tightens his grip around me and I howl in pain. I feel his holster press on my hip bone. He keeps pressure on my middle as he drags me off to the side of the crowd.

"Move it, let's go," he orders me as I go limp in pain.

Tattoo rushes towards me, real concern on his face. Rest of the crowd watches. No, no, no, no. This cannot be real. *Please* don't let this be real. I NEED to talk to the reporter.

"Tattoo, notebook," I say as loud as I can, which comes out in a strangled scream.

With all the commotion, the only person who hears me is *her*. Smoker Lady-slash-Butler's mom. She stops in her tracks and looks at where my notebook landed. I watch in horror as she picks it up.

Butler's mom keeps her eyes on me as she stuffs my notebook with all of my notes and stories for Richards in her large tote. Smiles a fake smile at me.

NO.

THIS CANNOT BE REAL. NO. No. My last opportunity—gone. My lungs feel as if they deflate. I do not want to believe this happened.

The crowd swarms past her, and soon the soldiers ignore us. My little distraction is over so they go back to their scheduled press conference. Richards fades into the crowd. The lady with a microphone starts the interview. I hear Butler's voice, calm and strong.

FUCK. I squeeze my eyes shut in utter, total defeat.

Tattoo reaches us. Demands to know where I'm going. I open my eyes to see him arguing with three guards. All upset-looking, but none touching their holsters.

He pleads with them, "She's got a stomach injury. Take her back to the recovery ward."

They argue and it's like I hear their words from a million miles away. A guard strengthens his hold on me. An explosion in the side of my stomach. I fall limp. Don't hear the response.

All I see is Butler giving a Press Conference. And everyone listening.

CHAPTER 35

Amanda at the End

I'M RESTING MY face on the same table, in the same room where I was interviewed by LT and Muscrat a few days ago. A solid pain grips my entire middle. I think about this morning for the millionth time, how it all went wrong. Butler's mom did that. Without her, I'd have made it to Richards. I'd be in an interview room right now.

Door unlocks. I un-suction my face from the surface and lift my head. Gasp to breathe normal. Door opens. Nurse Taylor's look is grim as she shuffles in and sits across from me.

"Hey honey," she says.

"Hi," I say in a flat monotone. I have no energy left to say more.

She clears her throat. She's not looking me in the eye, seems nervous but speaks slowly, as if choosing her words. "I wanted to talk to you before…"

"Before what?" I cut her off. We don't have time to waste if there's a "before."

We make eye contact. "To be very honest, Amanda"—she hasn't called me by my first name ever, so I sit up straight. "Looks like you'll be moving on. Even with the stitches on your stomach and our unfinished business in this ward."

I nod, breathe out. Fine. Whatever. I expected this. I tug at a strand of my hair as I ask her, "San Diego?" My face is hot and my stomach is sick.

She shrugs, which I take for a yes. Found out the prison for women in San Diego is near the Pacific, but it may as well be on the moon or Mars or in Antarctica as far as I'm concerned. I know little about all of them. The military prison system wasn't part of soldier knowledge.

She tries to reassure me, "You'll be alright." She sets down my meds on the table as well two Motrin. She unscrews a tiny water bottle. "Eat up, honey."

I'll be alright? Yeah, sure I will. I take the little pill and put it into my mouth. Swallow.

"Don't you forget what I said—you can have a good life in spite of all this. I understand what you were aiming to do and that took a lot of guts. You're a warrior. I know you got it in you to do many good things in your life. After you get where you're going, write yourself a book. Tell your story, get it out there."

No way in hell anyone cares. I speak to be nice. "Think so?"

Nurse Taylor reaches across the table and takes my hands in hers. "I know so, honey."

We hear a loud rap and the door opens. It's Dr. Muscrat, flanked by LT and Captain Lynch. Nurse Taylor squeezes my hand, stands up to allow them space, walks out into the dark hallway and I watch her until she's out of sight. I wonder if I'll see her again.

I sit up to face them all. Muscrat's directly across from me, shuffling papers. LT pulls up a chair next to him. Captain Lynch remains standing and leans against the wall. They all have Daily Donut coffees with them. LT places the one in her hand in front of me. Her big brown eyes glitter. Coffee? You know what? I'll take it.

"My treat."

"Thanks," I say in surprise. It has the feeling like it's the last meal of a death row inmate. Even scalding hot, I take a sip. Burn my tongue, but sip again. Tongue discomfort is worth it. Muscrat shuffles some papers, looking smug. GREAT. Can't WAIT to hear this.

"Sergeant Ashe," Muscrat says in that I-know-more-than-you-tone, "You've gotten yourself into quite a difficult situation. It seems like you enjoy getting yourself into trouble."

I cross my arms, sick of his voice. "No, Sir, I don't."

"I understand that you spoke with LT about possible charges against you."

I nod as LT and I make eye contact.

He proceeds, "I've spoken with Captain Butler and his chain of command. They are adamant that we begin the process immediately. Captain Lynch is here to present you with the paperwork."

She places the charges in front of me. I scan it quickly but all I see is a line on the form that allows me to invoke my right to a full trial at which I could call witnesses and defend myself—a court martial. I stop looking. A court martial.

I must have read the words out loud, as Muscrat shakes his head violently, "Private Ashe, have some common sense for once. This isn't some Hollywood movie! What could you possibly want to get out of a trial?"

What do *I* want from a trial, besides time and justice? Fair enough question, although he should know the answer to this by now.

Captain Lynch crosses her arms uncomfortably, "The leadership would like to keep what happened quiet, for the sake of you and him. An agreement of four years' jail time on the condition you sign a nondisclosure was settled on, if that's the path you agree to."

"Do they know about the party?" I ask Captain Lynch directly.

She glances at LT, then back at me. "They are aware of your statement."

"So…yes? They know what he did to me?"

She nods. So his chain of command knows. And they won't do anything about it. I think of these old men talking about me, sizing up the situation, and coming to the conclusion that no matter what, Butler is more important than me. I feel less than a zero right now. I feel as if I am nothing.

"And Vincent got out with an honorable discharge? Is that right?"

"Unfortunately, yes," she admits with a frown.

I shake my head in anger. "Those guys are monsters," I say, not looking at her.

Captain Lynch responds, "We don't have many options right now. It's not about them being bad or good. It's about a jury holding a person accountable for their actions. And in your case, their side has all of the documented proof."

So that's it. They have proof and I don't. And the power. Proof and power. Power being the more important consideration.

I open my mouth but close it again. Damn it all. A nondisclosure means my story stays with me. No writing a book, like Nurse Taylor said. Average Americans won't know what happens to the females once they join up. I lower my head and stare at my hands. A decision made. Cold and calculating and sharp, hurting as bad as a stab wound to the stomach.

In a gentler tone she advises me, “Why don’t we let you think it over tonight?”

Muscrat starts to object, but she talks over him. She takes the power.

She says, “Nobody says you have to sign it right now. Sleep on it, call your family, do whatever you have to do to make the right decision for your future. I’ll return before noon. Just think of it this way, you made a mistake. But it won’t keep you in prison forever. You’re young, and you could be done with everything before you turn thirty.”

Muscrat puts the paper back into his green folder, keeping his big, fat mouth shut for once. LT puts her hand on my shoulder. This shit isn’t new or surprising – support the troops everyone says, but when it comes right down to it, they mean support *some* of the troops.

And I’m not one of them.

CHAPTER 36

Mrs. Butler and Her Son

MRS. BUTLER WAS as tired as Mark after the live TV interview by that local celebrity host. The reception lasted for hours afterwards. Everyone wanted to shake her son's hand.

The entire event was exceeding their expectations until the "incident." After that, an annoying, bald journalist showed up. Asked Mark if he threw parties downrange. If he knew about illegal, unauthorized behaviors from his men that put our own female soldiers at risk. He asked Mark about *sexual harassment in the Army.* Acted as if Mark was guilty of something.

It made the hair on the back of Mrs. Butler's neck stand up. She stood proudly by as Butler stoically stated that Special Forces members were professionals. The journalist had ulterior motives and tried to ask follow-on questions. The other reporters recoiled at his questions. Tainted the whole morning.

Even though he was drained, those questions irritated both Mark and his mom. Kept gnawing at them, even when the bald guy left.

Back in the room, Mark ordered his mom to retrieve his new laptop. He was agitated and snappy. He opened up his computer and wrote email after email to his SF buddies. He could only hen-peck with one hand, so it took him over an hour. He got cranky tired. When he asked for sleeping medicine, his mom fetched it from his nurse, along with a chocolate milk that he requested. He'd liked chocolate milk since he was a toddler.

When she was certain he was asleep, she pulled the girl's notebook from her tote. It was thick with notes, letters, and stories. Mrs. Butler re-read them all a few times.

The accusations were disgusting. Worse—they *seemed* true. Full of names, dates, and times. A reporter would have loved these notes. The extreme details wrote about were filthy. In the wrong hands, like that bald journalist, these allegations could be life-ending.

When finished, she carefully tiptoed to her son. She shushed him, just like he was a baby, as she lifted up his grey PT shirt and searched for the biting scar. Sure enough, it was right where the notebook said it was. Impossible to be coincidental.

Butler's mom stood back. She cast a dark look on to him as his breath rose up and down. Suddenly, he seemed like a stranger. With silent steps, she walked around the bed and opened up the laptop. She punched in his password—BROTHER6—and the computer hummed to life.

She went into his email and read the last few letters Mark wrote.

Mark had typed, *"Ashe Bitch in the hallway. Caused a scene—throwing shade. You should've let the cops haul her ass away at Buehring instead of to the medics. I should've fired right back. We both fucked up that day, but doctors think she's a psycho, and are ready to lock her up. I called HQ and they are straightening things out for us. Colonel said it was the last time he'd stick his next out, but let's see how the Army does without SF."*

Butler's mom clicked the email shut.

The website MySpace was open, and she scrolled through his page. A picture of him looking like Captain America in uniform stared back at her. She scrolled down. More pictures of macho Mark filled the screen. All his buddies with their weapons. His men with Afghanis. Butler with Iraqis. Some with full battle rattle, some in full battle rattle over underwear. That made her laugh to herself. They were categorized with military precision. Afghanistan 2001, Afghanistan 2002, Iraq 2003, Iraq 2004, and the list continued.

She scrolled, stopped. Her breath caught in her throat. Within each grouping, there were pictures from the wars mixed in with loads of pictures of women. She spotted one that she thought was Ashe. Zoomed in. It *was* that Ashe girl. She was a few pounds heavier, but it was her. In the first photo, she was awake and holding a plastic Solo cup in one hand. She was gripping a necklace chain in the other. Necklace's charm looked very familiar—too damned familiar. Mrs. Butler felt her own. The one that Mark brought back from Iraq for her. Said he bought it at a bazaar. Fact it was Wisconsin's state flower seemed like an odd coincidence, but she bought the story.

Not anymore.

Mrs. Butler scrolled. Too many photos of the Ashe girl. In the worst one, Ashe girl's eyes were pressed shut, lifeless. Corpse-like. Buck naked. This made her feel sick inside.

The girl was posed, although she wasn't awake for any of them. The necklace was off her at that point. Afraid, Mrs. Butler forced herself to scroll down more. The more she saw, the more her fear turned to anger. She saw all sorts of topless women, crotch shots, and tongues licking skin. Butler's mom cringed at a nude woman crouched on a table with 550-cord wrapped around her neck, eyes unfocused. She clicked off the website and slammed the computer down.

Butler's mom looked at her baby boy, who was now an injured man. He had a grown-up male's strong body with his own mind, that she had little access to. She felt she had less and less influence on each day, and he shared the bare minimum. Her own son. A stranger.

Before the injury, she thought she knew everything about him—raising him as a single mom did that. No matter how she looked at it, though, during the last few years of his life, Mark changed. In some ways it could be explained with his experience in the wars, but his mom wouldn't accept this new version of her son. She'd raised him better than that, and needed to get him back to the way he was before the Army.

Once discharged, she would take him straight home to Wisconsin. He could forget about that fantasy to stay in and keep fighting. For what? It was hogwash, plain and simple. He didn't belong to the Army now any more than a barn cat belonged in the White House.

As angry as she was, she needed some time to think before waking Mark. She took the notebook in her hands and read it, again and again. It was hours later when she shook him awake.

After a long minute, he groggily spoke. "Let me sleep." He tried to swat her away but she shook him again. He kept his eyes closed.

She lost her patience. "Mark, you get your ass up."

Her words startled him and he opened his eyes. Saw her face screwed up in a snarl.

"You got some explaining to do," she said, "let's talk about that scar on your chest."

He looked at her and sat up in bed, alarmed. He answered, "An old injury."

"And this necklace," she spat out, "where'd you get this from?"

"Mom..."

"I know you took it from that girl."

His eyes fully opened. "It wasn't like that."

"Don't be lying to me, Mark Butler. I just read your MySpace posts. Saw the emails you sent out. I didn't raise you to be like this."

"Mom, relax," he ordered. Softer, "What time is it?"

Ignoring his question, she let out a grunt. "Seems like you got more in common with your dad than you know."

Mark turned to her, intrigued at her mention of his dad. He died before Mark was born, or so he'd been told.

"What are you talking about?"

She didn't look at him as she spoke. "I know that Ashe girl wasn't lying. What you don't know is that I met her once, a few days ago. She ran outside when I was smoking. Told me that a man had made her life hell. I'm guessing that was you she was talking about."

Her doubt irked him. He pleaded, "Mom, *come on.*"

After a moment, she spoke again. "Like that girl, I know about violent men. Kills me that she thinks of you like that. I hid things from you, Mark, but now's the time to talk and to get it out. Might help you understand why I'm getting you out of the Army. I know how it changes people, it happened to your dad."

Mark decided not to argue against her insistence to get him out. He was too interested in what she was saying. "Tell me more," he said, leaning towards her so he could face her if she looked down.

His mom nodded, a bit of dread rising in her that she swallowed down. She knew she hid the truth for too long.

"Your dad didn't die in no field training accident before your birth, Mark."

He raised his eyebrows. His mouth hung open. He choked out, "What?"

She continued, "He caused the accident. Six dead. He got into a bar fight over it a week later. Got stabbed to death, but nobody knows by who. As for us, I didn't know for weeks, 'cause I had already taken you back home. I was sick of getting beat on, blamed for his problems. Last straw was the day he left you home alone for hours while I worked my shift. You were only nine months. Lucky for us, the neighbor heard you wailing and called me. Your dad was good for fucking nothing. We split the next day."

Mark shook his head, unable to absorb the news so quickly. He felt groggy and strange. Clock over the door said two in the morning.

"Can we talk in the morning?" he asked.

She shook her head. "We need to get this sorted now. We both got some explaining."

"Jeez," he said, "I told you most—"

"You told me what you thought I wanted to hear," she said. "I can't have that girl on my conscience, understand? I want to stand by you and be proud, but I just can't when there's a girl in this hospital about to be put away 'cause she reacted to something you did. Found out that she's on her way to prison."

"She deserves it," he said.

"I'm not saying what she did was right, understand?" She sighed, paused. "I wanted to kill your dad when he beat me up, Mark. I was a pregnant young wife with a baby on the way, and here he was slapping and stomping me. After a couple of years of his bullshit, I was the one who changed. Couldn't sleep, couldn't eat, got all jumpy. Violence changes people, no matter if it's in a war or in the home. I almost snapped so many times."

They both paused. Mark struggled with the news, but it didn't jolt him into an understanding like it did to his mother.

"Doesn't excuse anything," he said.

"No, it doesn't. But it's a reason. I probably would've shot your dad, if given the chance. I'm glad someone else did it."

The room was silent. From the wall, they can hear the tick of the wall clock. It's 2:10.

She continued, "Your days in the military are done, Mark. Time we got you back home and back to your old self. Fight me on this and your other leg is gone."

His angry face turned to face her. She stood up.

She was going to learn everything, and so was he.

❧

THE NEXT MORNING came soon enough. By first light, Mrs. Butler had drunk over a pot of coffee and smoked a pack of cigarettes. Mark was back to sleep, knocked out on pills. Mrs. Butler watched him from the door, breaths formed steadily up and down, then she left to find the JAG office. A beautiful blond officer was very interested to meet her, and they she spoke for over an hour. From there, Mrs. Butler called her son's chain of command and gave them orders, not the other way around. Using the MySpace pictures of Mark and his colleagues as leverage, they agreed to her demands.

Following that, Mrs. Butler convinced the blonde officer to take her to Ward 54. Once there, she waited for an hour, until she couldn't take it anymore. She stood up, and marched over to the first set of doors to find what she was looking for. In seconds, she was stopped by a large man. They argued until he gave up and agreed to take her to the room.

Outside the door, Mrs. Butler leaned over Darrell and rapped on the door. She could make out a group of officers, in addition to the blond one, across the table from that Ashe girl. As she knocked, they looked over in unison. Darrell reached across her and opened the door.

"Excuse me, Sir, but the visitor is now here."

Dr. Muscrat pushed the chair back and stood up. He eyed the woman behind Darrel and stated as loudly as possible, "I said *do not interrupt* until I tell you."

Darrel apologized, "Sorry Sir, but she won't exactly take no for an answer."

Behind him, Mrs. Butler pushed past the big man and stood in the doorway, hands on boney hips. Pointed at Ashe, who sat across from the officers. Said loudly, "I need to speak to this young lady right now."

The female officer jumped in her seat, "I'm sorry, Ma'am, but we are in the middle of a discussion here."

The blonde said nothing. So Mrs. Butler pushed past Darrell and stood in front of the small table.

"I think she'd want to hear what I have to say."

"Of course she would," the blond one stated, "but we'd like to make sure things are certain. Well, you know."

Mrs. Butler cut her off. "It's a done deal. I'd like to talk to her alone."

She held out her clutched fist in front of Ashe's face. Slowly she opened her hand to reveal a beautiful necklace. Ashe reached for it but Mrs. Butler closed her fist again.

"What's going on?" LT asked, sitting up and leaning forward. "Ashe? You okay?"

Everyone watched the girl. Her eyes grew round and moist. She had almost a pained look on her face.

"Please," Ashe said to the room, her eyes on the jewelry, "let me talk to her."

"You sure?" LT cast a glance to Ashe, who didn't look back. She couldn't tear her eyes from the necklace. Almost in a trance, she nodded.

CHAPTER 37

Amanda and Mrs. Butler

WE SIT IN silence while the others stand outside the door; their combined breath steams up the glass window. They gaze in, but I don't look back. My eyes are focused on the woman and the jewelry in front of me. I don't care about anything else other than having it in my hands.

"That's my necklace," I say. "It's been missing." Silver glints beautifully between us, as perfect as the day Manolo gave it to me. Violet flower looks the same.

"I know," she says, which baffles me. I squint at her, wondering what is going on. A day ago this lady was screaming at me. What in the HELL does Butler's mom want?

Butler's mom sighs. Only the table separates us. Her face is saggy, and eyes are bloodshot. Her hair is washed and wet. She's got wrinkles and creases spread all over her face, but she looks like Butler. Or rather, he looks like her—same nose, same mouth, even eyebrows.

"Well, put it on," she says.

I take it in my hands and immediately my vision blurs with tears. The whole room is a shadow and nothing exists except me and this. Dear God, my feelings are churning together. Happiness, sadness, relief, terror.

"Need help?"

I shake my head. Slowly, I unlatch the clasp and manage to put it around my neck. Back where it belongs. I continue to clutch the flower pendant in my hand, a warm sensation filling me. Tears of relief this time. I wipe them away.

"Weird weather they have out here," Butler's mom says and glances at me. I nod. It's mild then warm. Opposite the Midwest in this time of year.

"You talk to your folks lately?" she says.

I shake my head. "Not lately."

"You should. Parents worry about their kids, especially the mothers."

"Not my mother." I immediately regret it. This woman prevented me from speaking to a reporter, why am I telling her anything? I bite the inside of my cheeks.

She grunts. "You know who I am?"

I nod my head yes. You're the *mother.*

She looks down at her hands as she speaks. "The day that they came to the door, I knew he was dead. It was no shock. Everyone knew he was a drunk and a wife beater. Once my head went through dry wall. I escaped but it wasn't easy. Mark was only a baby then."

It takes a second to understand she's talking about Butler's dad.

"I hoped I'd never hear another word about the Army again," she pauses to take a breath. "But you know, that's not how it worked out. I was against him joining from the start. Now look at this mess he's in. More than one mess, I mean."

She shifts uncomfortably. We look at each other for a moment.

I find my voice. "My mom didn't want me to join neither."

Her thin lips tighten into a straight line like Mom's did when she got upset. I keep quiet.

"I raised Mark differently. He's a good man. But he made some mistakes. I won't deny that one bit. But I think the man you know, well that isn't really him."

Huh? I sit confused for a sec. Oh, wait. It dawns on me—bright and clear. Unbelievable. I ask, "You read my journal?"

I thought she had thrown it away without another thought or action. I get excited, hoping to get it back.

She nods, talks on, "I wondered what would make someone shoot at my Mark, because he's all I got in the world. I read it to see if I could find the answers."

I swallow hard and look around the room. "Do you have it?"

She blinks and shakes her head. Says a firm, "No."

I cringe inside. What a loss. I spent so much time on something and then *poof!* Gone. I recognize that feeling—it's how I feel about the Army now. All that work for zilch.

She goes on, "He's eligible to be medically retired, so he could go home with me. There's a good VA not too far from us, but he won't do it as long as there's a chance to stay in. I've been fighting him on it, tooth and nail."

Her voice trails off, leaving me to wonder: What does this woman want from me?

She says, "I saw the scar. I checked MySpace. You're on there."

I state what is not obvious to me. "You believe me."

She acts like she didn't hear. "They interviewed Mark, but afterwards a journalist asked some different type of questions. I cut him off, but his questions made the other reporters act differently. I can tell he was waiting there for you, hoping to get a story from you. I could see it was not an accident that we were all there at the same time. I think you planned it."

I stay as steady as I can. "I was supposed to talk to the reporter. Name is Richards."

She purses her lips. "Everything that Mark and SF did in the war would be tarnished and ruined, after all they've done for this country. After all of his sacrifices, if some reporter wanted to find an angle. Look what they did to Walter Reed about those barracks."

"The barracks were dirty," I respond, "Isn't it good that people know, so they're forced to fix the problem?"

She shakes her head. "The whole world doesn't need to know the Army's dirty laundry. The people on the inside could've fixed the problem."

"But they didn't."

We stare at each other, clearly on opposite sides here.

"He's not more important than me," I say as the blood rushes to my face.

She holds up a hand and lets out a slow, deep breath. "All that happened between you two is in the past. I don't want him agitated and upset, so I don't want this UCMJ to get in the way of his recovery or anything else like this in the press. If your family doesn't know by now what happened to you, why not just keep it to yourself for their sake and yours?"

"You want me to keep quiet." It's a statement, not a question. It's the same thing that Butler's chain of command wants. So why is she telling me?

She continues, "I called Fort Bragg directly and I told them it's over. No charges against you, no nothing. Honorable discharge for the both of you to keep things even. Mark agrees to that, too. You both can act as if the past couple of years never happened. Now, I mean, as long as we all stay far away from the radio, papers and news stations. We have to protect each other."

"But..." I stammer out, incredulously, "That means he just gets away with it."

She shrugs and her fingers strum the table. "So do you."

I sit with that, for a minute. The humiliation, the shame, the wanting to kill myself over and over again—all that pain was horrible. But prison would be worse. I can live with this deal. I know I can get better as long as I'm free to find help. It's not a bad deal that she's offering me. And I'll take it. Well. Except for one thing.

"You got to promise me that he won't...do this again, to any other female..."

"He's got shrapnel in every part of his body and is missing a leg. Not to mention my foot up his ass," she says but doesn't smile., "So is it a deal, then?"

He tried to ruin my life. He tried to shut me up. He tried to finish me, but I'm alive.

I sigh. "If your deal is that I get out of the Army without UCMJ problems, then yes. I guess so. But women should know what could happen to them if they enlist, shouldn't they?"

She puckers her lips. "You're not a bad writer. Little wordy for my taste. Could be okay as a future job. But nothing about my boy, ever. Long as I'm alive, I've got to protect him. Understand? So that's part of the deal. So is it—a deal?"

My mind is so *done*. The past two weeks have been an absolute dumpster fire of a clusterfuck. The past few years have been a waste of a life. There are about a million things I could say to her, but in the end there's only one thing that will do. I look her directly into her worn-out, blue eyes and say the only words I can.

"You betcha."

CHAPTER 38

Amanda Martinez

I LEARNED SOMETHING at Walter Reed. I learned that women in uniform could work together. I thought Weisengard was an exception in the Army, but she's not. I got Skittles, LaTonya, Katia, Ponytail, LT, Captain Lynch, Art Teacher, and Nurse Taylor. We can work together really well. And I learned that I can't do it alone. Tattoo's a friend for life.

If Butler's mom can work with me, then it's all a matter of motivation. I lifted my weapon and pointed it at her son. I said I wanted justice repeatedly, but I mistook justice for revenge. Like Tattoo said, if I keep trying to get even, I'll never get ahead.

I don't have time to sit and ponder the past few days.

Within hours, Nurse Taylor leads me out of Ward 54 to out-process. Out-processing the Army is basically making sure soldiers meet with every single official office unit on base to make sure we don't have no army equipment to sell off to the surplus stores. Out-processing means we go to Finance to make sure we don't owe money or have payments we shouldn't. It's all paperwork.

Nurse Taylor leads me into the next Ward and says, "First stop is your case manager."

I am not aware I had one of those. "Huh?"

She smiles. "Case managers are in Ward 53. Under normal circumstances, she would have been part of the group to determine your care in outpatient and afterwards."

We knock on a wooden door, and we hear someone call out from inside, "Come in."

Nurse Taylor opens the door and we step inside. My assigned case manager is a big-boned, tall Black lady; even sitting I can see she's over six feet. Her face is broad, her lips have that loop-de-loop shape, and she has sparkly gold eyeshadow on her wide-set eyes. I like how she sits up straight. Dignified royalty in her cramped, narrow office. By the looks of it, her office used to be a supply closet.

Against the wall is a wooden cane with a pink, crocheted top.

"Please sit," she says with a smile. "I'm Linda."

"Thanks," I say and sit in a comfortable, cushion topped chair.

"Would you like one?" she holds out a blue bowl of lifesaver peppermints.

I take one and slowly unwrap it, throw the wrapper away. Nurse Taylor watches me as I stick it in my mouth. Drool accumulates immediately. I swallow the minty spit as she smiles.

Linda speaks. "I understand you're about ready to leave us. I can give you all of the information that I have for what could be your next steps. Your Lieutenant researched a great deal and found Eating Disorder clinics with solid treatment approaches."

She hands over shiny brochures for four eating disorder clinics. I take them from her, although I already know that I won't have enough money to go.

She says optimistically, "If you are headed back to your home state of Wisconsin, there is one famous clinic near Chicago with a good track record."

I open the brochure from near Wisconsin.

"It's expensive," I say as I glance at the prices. My eyes settle on a rubric of costs.

Oh, God. More like completely impossible. No one I know has got thousands of dollars for this. It's out of my league. Why look at the Lamborghinis if you only got money for a bike?

She watches me. "Those prices are for people without insurance. Although you won't be eligible for Tricare, there are other ways. Good health is priceless."

"I'll figure it out." I say this to make them feel better. In truth, I'd like to go somewhere to help me learn how to eat again. It's not like my problems go away the second I leave the Army. It stays with you. I'll have to find my own cheaper ways.

"Since you're still young, you might be able to go back on your parent's insurance."

I shake my head. "I haven't been on their insurance since age eighteen."

"Mm. Well, keep that in mind." She smiles at me and winks. "Would you like to call home before you leave my office?"

I stir in my seat, pondering. Yes, I should call them. I'll need a ride from the airport. I'll need their support. I nod.

She picks up the phone and hands it to me then dials the 9. I stand up, take the receiver from her then sit down again in a chair closer to the phone. A flutter of excitement hits me. Yes, I'd like to talk to Dad.

Linda lifts herself up and Nurse Taylor hands her the pink crotchet cane.

Nurse Taylor says, "You can now dial the number. We'll be right outside."

As they shuffle out of the room, I punch in the numbers and it rings. Another ring. And another. I let out a deep sigh. My family could be doing chores. I'll call back—

"Hello?"

Mom. Short, clipped hello. I hadn't expected this. She rarely answers.

"It's me, Mom," I say.

Mom shrieks into the phone, "Amanda. Where are you? Your father didn't know any details and I didn't have any numbers to call…and so we were trying to call your friend but…"

I smile into the phone. This is *mom*? She's babbling, so unlike her.

"Mom," I practically shout over her. "Mom, I'm *okay*."

She pauses for a second, then responds. "Thanks to God. Amanda, I was so worried. Jo was about to call the White House. Your dad and Connor were planning to drive down."

I'm surprised at her reaction, but it's exactly what I need—support. Love.

My heart pounds happily in my chest. Her reaction is a blessing. I say, "I'm getting out. I'll be flying home in a couple of days. Is that okay?"

I hear a sniffle in the phone. Mom *crying?* "Yes, Amanda. Can't wait to get you back home."

Another sniffle, a sob. Coming from *mom*.

"Mom, I have a friend who needs a place," I start to explain Katia, "do you think—"

"It's fine," she cuts me off, "Just come home."

A pause.

Mom says, "Love you, honey." It sounds like a foreign phrase from her mouth. I'm shocked. I can count on one hand how many times I've heard that.

"Love you, too," I say. Relief and happiness wash over me, giving me peace.

We hang up. Mom shocked me. Maybe she was sorry when I told them about Manolo. Maybe she's trying to change. She said yes to bringing Katia. Mom says I've got a home and that's more than just something. That's everything.

❧

AFTER THE CASE manager's office, I feel better. Mom wants me to be home. What a load off. The moms have really come through. Maybe mom can help me figure out this eating disorder thing. I don't want to eat and puke at home, but one thing at a time today. For now, I got more out-processing to do.

Next stop: Finance Out-processing. Finance's waiting room is tiny, and the four chairs are taken by fully uniformed, knee-bobbing soldiers, each clutching their paperwork and staring at the floor. Nurse Taylor and I stand.

I can see out of the glass window on the door and back into the hospital from which we just came. Everything in the hallway is buzzing with activity. Doctors rush down the hall, nurses wheel patients in beds, and I can even see a lady with two kids below her knees trying to get snacks from the vending machines. One of the little ones reaches in, but his arm is stuck trying to dislodge the dangling chips. She reaches in to rescue him, all the while yelling at him to be careful. That's love talking. Care.

Door to the other side of the office flings open. All of our heads swivel to see her. Hopeful, it's our turn. A short, white female soldier calls out, "Ashe."

I stand up straight and bounce myself off the wall. She motions for me to follow her. Nurse Taylor stands up straighter, too. Says, "You want me to go in with you, honey?"

"No. I got it. But thanks."

I walk slowly towards the clerk. She holds the door for me until I grab it and I follow the Finance soldier down the short, dank hallway. Area is stuffy with no windows and a bunch of chipped desks crammed together. She wiggles into her chair and clicks on the computer. Indicates for me to sit on the chair next to her desk, so I do. A sign taped to her computer warns, FAILURE TO PLAN ON YOUR PART DOES NOT CONSTITUTE

AN EMERGENCY ON MINE. I shake my head to myself. I can't wait to leave Walter Reed so I don't have to read these signs.

Clerk holds up her pale hand and I give her my packet of paperwork without saying a word. On the top is the checklist—FINANCE is in all caps. My stomach flip-flops. With the genuine confusion over my rank, I have no idea if I am owed money or need to pay some back.

"Medical board?" she asks.

"Kind of," I answer as I avert my eyes. Pick the skin around my thumbnail.

"You're supposed to be in uniform," she says. I look up at her to see a slight frown, which gets me thinking *wow, our military experiences are strikingly different.*

I shrug. "This is the only uniform I have. I'm in Ward 54."

The clerk snaps her gum; her face turns pale. It would be senseless for me to tell her there will be lots more of us coming her way. Maybe thousands more, until the wars are over.

"Okay," she says but avoids making eye contact. As the computer program loads up, she grabs the plastic soda cup on her desk. I see the wet ring it leaves behind as she slurps. I think of Marge. Marge always had that kind of pop. Making that annoying slurp. Still. She was a good roommate. Hope she's doing alright. I'll check on her. Someday.

I sit and watch as she types in my information. She sets the soda cup down, looks over at my paperwork and punches in some letters. Her glasses slip a bit down her nose, and she pushes them back up, as she studies the screen. Seems like there's a problem. I can sense it.

"There might be some confusion about my rank," I admit so she doesn't have to make things awkward. I've been dreading and expecting this moment when it's official and calls me a Private to my face. Worse will be to see it in print. All that hard work, down the drain in a moment. I'll have to suck it up.

The soldier peers at the screen and then at me, "No, you're definitely a Sergeant in the system, you're not even flagged. Sometimes the paperwork doesn't go through, and it won't before you're getting out, I mean your ETS date is Friday. There's nothing to pay back," she pauses for too long before saying, "but there's something else."

"Oh," I say, relieved. "What?"

"What's your social again?" A look of increasing alarm spreads on her face

I say it and she slowly punches it in. Her eyes squint, then she removes her glasses.

She stands up. Blurts out, "Wait one minute, I have to get my Sergeant, okay?"

"No problem," I say but my stomach feels hot, sick. As she disappears, I try to lean over and read what the screen says, but it's useless. I don't know the computer program and it's not in plain English. I sit back and wait, worried. What NOW?

She returns quickly with her wiry NCO. He sits at her computer, not looking at me at first. They both stare at the screen and a small sense of panic rises in me. What do they see?

Finally, he speaks, "Do you know anyone with the last name Martinez?"

I nod slowly. Wet tears form in my eyes.

I manage to say, "That was my boyfriend's last name. He...umm...didn't make it."

His eyes soften. "I see. I have to make a phone call to Personnel Services. One sec."

I feel shaky with fear at his words. What *situation*? *Am I back in trouble?* I have minimal time to fret. Not long after he said, "one sec," the sergeant and an officer are booking it towards my chair. Quickest sec in my career.

"Hi Sergeant Ashe, I'm Captain Yang," the slim Asian man says as he sticks out his palm for me to shake. I reach up and take his cool, clean hand in mine. He sits down in the soldier's chair and clicks the mouse.

He asks without looking, "You know about SGLI, right? How it works?"

"Yes, sir," I say. We all know. When we die, the beneficiary gets the sum. Our death pays out more money than any of us can earn alive. I had mine divided between my brother and sister, but I'm alive, no matter how hard I tried to starve myself.

He clears his throat, "So it appears there was an issue that wasn't resolved. A soldier by the name of Sergeant First Class Martinez had split his SGLI between his mother and his wife, 50-50. Just to verify what my Sergeant said—how did you know him?"

His wife? Holy shit. I nod and choke out, "My boyfr—I mean, my fiancée."

My head feels like it's floating above us. I'm in reality, but also a fantasy. I wanted to be his wife, really. To talk about him now...it breaks my heart.

Captain says, "He wrote that you're his wife on the form. Personnel Services confirmed that you *aren't* listed as his wife in DEERS–their system. But your Social Security number matches. He listed Amanda Ashe-Martinez as a beneficiary, so it should have been paid out."

With a soft smile, he pushes the SGLI document at me, faxed over from his old unit. I lean over the papers to see. The ink is light, but it's *his* handwriting—Manolo's. He listed me as his wife. I remember the night he said we'd get a ring, after deployment. I think of the scene: the drive, his advice, my exasperation, parking, the necklace, our plans.

I close my eyes, press the lids shut. When I'm out, I'll find a way to honor him—us—*and* figure out a way to grieve. Move on. Someday, but not now. I open my eyes.

I grip my necklace. "What does this mean?" I ask.

Captain pulls back the paper. Says, "It means you'll get paid. Won't impact your out-processing. I'm just glad that we caught this error. I don't know why the Finance near your unit didn't dig a bit deeper and solve this, especially since the Social Security number is correct."

OH MY GOD. He doesn't know *WHY?* It's the Army. It's paperwork. Takes one second to screw up and two years to straighten out. I shrug, knowing that it happens. I look down at my hands.

He continues, "I know this isn't good news, since it's from a loved one. The SGLI payment is 200K and we can do a direct deposit in a matter of hours. Of course, there are taxes, but you can think of this as a fresh start. We've seen surviving family members who, along with the GI Bill, go back to school and have a new career. In your case, *Some beauty for ashes.*"

Christ. I know that verse. It's somewhere in the book of Isaiah and the other kids made fun of my last name for it. *Console the mourners and give them beauty for ashes.*

"You're a Christian," I say as I wipe my eyes. "Ashes for ash. Book of Isaiah."

He nods, hands up. "Every Sunday from 0900 until 1500. The church was more like a sports arena than a place of worship. My mom wanted me to be a Chaplain."

Moms. I give him a weak smile. Our moment passes quick then he reaches for my paperwork. The checklist is still on the clerk's desk. He signs his name as he says, "We'll get this straightened out today."

Feelings are swirling around inside of me. My eyes blur and I blink back the tears.

He returns the papers to my hands. Says, "Best of luck for the return home."

"Thanks," I say. I take the papers and stand up. *Almost.* I can *almost* return home. I have a few loose ends to tie up first.

CHAPTER 39

Amanda's Rights

GOOD-BYES ARE HARD, so I say, "see you later." I say see you later to Nurse Taylor and LT. Darrell pats me on the shoulder. Muscrat was mysteriously in some emergency meeting. Good. Only person I don't get to say "see you later" to is Katia. LT managed to get her moved to Bethesda. New hospital, new team, new chance.

I'm outside the Ward, in the hallway. In my hands are my Physical Evaluation Board (PEB) Proceedings. LT handed it over to me before I left the ward. Name, rank and SSN are correct but the words were confusing.

"...Bulimia nervosa manifested by dangerous behaviors that has required inpatient psychiatric treatment...these behaviors began prior to service and there is no evidence of permanent service aggravation..."

"Do I really have to sign this shit?" I asked LT, my hand hovered over the pages. The medical board doctors listed all my problems as existed prior to service. All except the rubber allergy. For that, it was listed as a service-related condition.

LT said, "You *do* have to sign, but look at 13—election of soldier. It's up to you which box you check."

There were seven choices:

-Concur

-I do not concur
-I concur and waive a formal hearing
-I do not concur but waive a formal hearing
-I do not concur and demand a formal hearing
-I request counsel
or -I will have counsel of my choice.

I checked the box: I do not concur but waive a formal hearing.

I am getting out, but I'm not admitting this all existed before. I made my initials and signed the bottom of the page. She made me a copy.

Before I left, I asked her: LT, do you like jelly donuts? She looked at me like a deer in headlights. I gave her the answer, "Well you should. They have fillings, too."

"I don't think I'll ever eat a jelly donut again," she said with a weak smile. "Keep the paperwork, someday you might need it."

The narrative summary was attached. I put it away, decided to read it later.

"That's it?" I asked. After the past few weeks, this can't be it. As if nothing happened. But new patients filtered in the halls. New problems to fix. One out, more in. The war machine just moves on, spending trillions on war but cents to the dollar on those who were in it.

She nodded. "As far as the Army is concerned. Have your plane ticket yet?"

"Yeah, I do."

LT gave me a hug. After we let go, she opened up her purse. "I almost forgot. One more thing. Open it when you're away from here. Consider it light travel reading."

She handed me an envelope and I stuffed it in my pants pocket. Nurse Taylor buzzed the doors open. I stepped out of Ward 54 for the last time.

Now I'm here, headed to a visit I need to make.

CHAPTER 40

Butler's Bird

MARK DOESN'T DREAM. The sleeping pills knocked the nightmares from happening again.

So, it wasn't a nightmare that woke him up. It was a bird pecking at his good toe, his only good toe. The one that he got to keep. He tried to shake it away. It persisted. He kicked and then he tried to scream but couldn't. It was gigantic for a bird but he could kill it, if only… the bird spoke.

"Hey, don't freak out," it squawked.

The bird's voice wasn't hummingbird light; it was bloody vulture. As best as he could, he pulled his body towards the head of his bed, away from it. He opened his eyes.

It was Ashe.

He sank as low into his bed as he could and pulled the thin sheet over his body. Butler shook his head, trying to calm his pounding heart. "What the fuck you want?" he said as she came into focus.

She ignored the question. "I like your mom." Mark looked at her. Amanda Ashe still had red lips and black hair. Once upon a time, he wanted those lips forever but now he wanted her to go away and to never come back. The End.

He said nothing.

"I'm not good at small talk, so here goes," she said and took a deep breath, "I don't want to re-open wounds, Butler, I'm here to say I forgive you, even if you don't think you need it. You trashed my reputation and turned everyone against me. But I forgive you."

She stood there, which might have been seconds. Maybe minutes. He said nothing.

"This whole time, I wanted justice from the Army but it can't and won't ever give it to me. I tried to get it myself. It's not worth it."

He didn't know what to say to that, so he said, "You're a lousy shot."

"I have the expert badge; 39 out of 40 targets. Not all targets need to be engaged."

She turned and slowly moved towards the door. She was graceful in her movements when she wasn't drunk. He never, ever thought he'd want to see her again, but he became incredibly lonely the instant she opened the door and walked out. It was as if the love and hate of his life in one and now it was all gone. He felt the urge to call her back, but Amanda flitted away from him. She could fly and he's stuck on the ground.

He really hated birds.

CHAPTER 41

Amanda and the Rest of Her Life

IT'S MY LAST few minutes on post. Once I walk off, I'm forever a veteran and never allowed back on base. The gate guards and razor wire ensure that. Post is for active duty, the retired, and those not discharged for being nuts. Fine by me.

Outside, the sun shines above me. After all the darkness inside, the stark blue sky seems like a fresh start. I head over to the Mologne house, a brick hotel for recovering soldiers, and where Tattoo moved to last night. He's back in his old room. Halfway there, I see him coming towards me like he knew I was on my way. He's in civvies, shorts and a polo shirt.

My heart beats incredibly fast as he gets closer. I keep myself from running.

He smiles and says, "They finally got rid of you, huh?"

I open my arms and he bear hugs me. He's taller than I remember. He holds me for a few seconds then releases me carefully.

Frowning he says, "Sorry, I forgot about the stitches."

"It's okay, I'm fine," I say, though it throbs a bit.

He says, "looks like you're on your way home."

"Yep, you're my last stop," I pause before I ask, "Do you have any leave saved up?"

He nods. "About a month's worth. Why?"

"I'm thinking about taking a road trip to Texas. Visit a grave. Then on to Mexico, hit up a beach or two. Need a battle buddy."

He grins wide. Relief floods my entire body because I already know the answer will be yes. Going to Texas was a decision I made quickly, but I made a new journal. One that has my hopes and dreams. Plans. Nothing about revenge or hate. All about forgiveness and love. Going through the process to recovery.

Tattoo says carefully, "I don't got much money, unfortunately."

I smile wide. "I do."

He smiles. Adds, "Texas. My home state. We can see my ma, if you want."

I hesitate. News to me. "I thought you were from Nevada. Or Vegas?"

He gives me a crooked smile, "I guess we got a lot to discuss during the ride."

Don't we ever.

❧

I ALMOST FORGOT about the paper that LT handed me. I feel it in my pocket as I search for watermelon flavored lip balm. I glide it over my lips then pull out the paper on the flight home. It's a small news clipping from the Chicago Tribune.

Jesse "Vinny" Vincent, a native of Humboldt Park and contractor for BST, was driving a fuel truck in the southern region of Iraq when insurgents attacked his vehicle with rocket-propelled grenades. Mr. Vincent was rushed to a local hospital where he was pronounced dead. He is survived by his mother and sister.

I shudder. Oh. My. God. I take a deep, astonished breath. I let it out slowly. Vincent the bastard. I'm not angry or irritated or upset. I'm tired and relieved, a feeling I haven't felt in a while. Ever since that night, I knew he could hurt others. Knew he could abandon them in the night all screwed up and barfing. He was a shit-bag capable of trampling newborns to save his own ass. Now he's doomed, damned, and done with. He won't hurt anyone else, which is its own sort of justice. I think of that damn sign. You are Responsible for Your Actions.

I smile to myself then close my eyes and fall into a deep, unbothered sleep.

CHAPTER 42

Months Later

TATTOO'S A FUN road trip partner. Met me in Green Bay and we took off for Texas. Tattoo somehow charmed Manolo's mom and we all went to the cemetery together. Manolo's mom looks like him, or he looks like her. His dad is buried near him, just a few plots over.

I make the sign of the cross and wipe away tears.

"Ready?" Tattoo asks me softly and I nod.

I take a step back from the grave and blow a kiss.

I'm on a new path, in a world that keeps on spinning. It will go on forever, with me in it.

EPILOGUE

THE WAY I wrote this story, sometimes I sound like the victim. I hate that word. I was, don't get me wrong. I was drugged, abused, hushed, judged, rejected, and ignored. In my case, though, I was a victim with a second chance to change the rest of the story, which a lot of females don't get. I got that chance not from the Army, but from everyone else.

I bought Manolo's Mustang from his mom for too much money. She didn't want to be paid, but what is fair is fair and I'd pay even more for the memories of those nights we drove around. Me and Tattoo caravanned all the way home to Wisconsin with it. He flew home after a few lessons on milking cows from Dad. Seems like dad wants another son besides Connor.

I did go to the Eating Disorder clinic, and I got better even before I hit the this-is-too-much-money mark. I was inpatient and then I was outpatient. My parents came to visit me. Mandatory family therapy turned into regular non-mandatory visits. I lived with them for a couple of months. I see them all the time now, like old days. We are in our own Family Therapy. I still do weekly support meetings with other women. We help each other.

Weisengard and I share an apartment in Milwaukee. I go to UW and she's already fast-tracked into the Urban Planning department. She took classes while she was deployed, so she's almost got her Bachelor's and then on to her Master's. I'm Pre-Law. I might go to UW-Madison for Law school; that's something I don't know yet and I'm okay with that. Not knowing everything is okay for me. I don't always need control.

I never did see Katia again, even though I tried to call her and email her. I thought about hiring a detective, but Tattoo advised against it. He said that some people don't want to be found. Tattoo did some digging instead. Found out she got out with compensation from a thyroid problem she developed in

AIT; she was one of the few that received a Medical Board in her situation. I'm sad for others, but happy for her.

Tattoo is still in, but he's got a desk job since he's not supposed to deploy after being so blown-up. He says he was flagged for going to Walter Reed. Luckily, or unluckily, chain of command knew he had a DUI and so that's a forgivable offense to most soldiers and officers. Nobody knows about his former boyfriend, or his new one. When he needs to vent, he gives me a call – he's letting me help him. Only has four years left, he says he'll retire at twenty years. Says he may go back to Texas. Wherever it is, I'll visit.

Captain Lynch stayed in. LT got out of the Army and has a private practice in Virginia. I think that's a waste for the Army. In fact, I think I need to look her up.

I even found my Landstuhl friend, Skittles. She's a single mom working as a cashier at a home building store but she's making her way, she says. I can't call her Grape Skittles; she wears green now. Cortez is doing alright in the Green to Gold program. Will be an officer someday. LaTonya I can't track down. I don't want to know, but I hope Black Forest Cake choked on a schnitzel.

Butler succumbed to his wounds a few years later, while living back home. Infection after infection made his conditions worse. Funeral was a private ceremony, but I sent Butler's mom a card. She helped me. I'll never forget it.

No idea about Jackson. I don't really want to know.

I can't find everyone, but that's okay. We're all humans, just trying to find our way.

Americans forget that soldiers are people, you know. Not machines or robots. Most are good, some are bad. The problems come when the bad silence the good and the good let it happen, out of fear. Fear shouldn't be what runs the army. That's why I'm Pre-Law. I can't let the bad—even in a warzone—keep the good from being all that they can be.

I still miss Manolo, and I will always miss him. I'm not ready for anyone else, still working things out. I'm getting better. That's what I'm striving to be each day. One day at a time. One second, sometimes. I strive to be a good person, a good friend. Friends and family. They're all we have in this world. We only have each other.

Acknowledgements

THIS BOOK WOULD not exist without the vision, guidance, patience, and hours of help from Onward Press' Timothy Wurtz. He saw the potential in my lump of a manuscript many years ago and guided me until this became a finished, readable book. Along with editor Lindsey Anthony Baccione, they worked closely with me every step of the way. Thank you. Special thanks to: USVAA/Onward Press Writers Workshop members and mentors, especially the wonderful Keith Jeffreys. Teddi Black who designed the cover and laid out the pages and gave me advice, College of DuPage's Writers Workshop, the Heroes to Heroes foundation, Wounded Warriors, friends, and family who spent time reading and suggesting improvements. Without help, this book is nothing.

Much love to my mom/cheerleader—who is an excellent mom and always was—not like the mom in this book! So much love to my sister, Heidi, who wrote me a letter each day I was in Iraq and later read this book, giving it a 'meh' rating, which motivated me to make it better. Thank you to my brothers, Jere and Grady, who kept me motivated while deployed and give me comic relief now. So much love to my daughters: Liliana and Zinnia, you are both truly the light of my world and will not be allowed to join the military. Ever. And of course, thank you so much to my husband, Nick. He made sure I had the time and space to dedicate the hours I needed to create this. He's a former Ranger who made sure I used the correct terms since I was 'only' in service support. Ha. One more: Dad. Miss you every day. So glad I gave you something to be proud of. Love, Baby Girl.

USVAA/Onward Press would like to thank the following organizations for their support in publishing this book and their support of the USVAA/ Onward Press Veteran Writers Workshop, held monthly since 2013, free of charge to military veterans and personnel.

The Nathan Cummings Foundation

Sony Pictures Entertainment

Warner Bros. Discovery

The Golden Globes Foundation

The Los Angeles County Department of Arts and Culture

Thanks to Timothy Wurtz on behalf of USVAA/Onward Press for his tireless work getting all of our books to publication.

www.ingramcontent.com/pod-product-compliance
Lightning Source LLC
Chambersburg PA
CBHW020302030826
48979CB00027B/1930/J
* 9 7 8 1 9 5 4 9 8 8 1 5 6 *